Dedalus Europe

General Editor: M

M000188260

*The Angel of the
West Window*

Gustav Meyrink

The Angel of the West Window

translated and with an introduction
by Mike Mitchell

Dedalus

Published in the UK by Dedalus Limited,
24-26, St Judith's Lane, Sawtry, Cambs, PE28 5XE
email: info@dedalusbooks.com
www.dedalusbooks.com

ISBN 978 1 903517 81 9

Dedalus is distributed in the USA by SCB Distributors,
15608 South New Century Drive, Gardena, CA 90248
email: info@scbdistributors.com   web: www.scbdistributors.com

Dedalus is distributed in Australia by Peribo Pty Ltd.
58, Beaumont Road, Mount Kuring-gai, N.S.W. 2080
email: info@peribo.com.au

Dedalus is distributed in Canada by Disticor Direct-Book Division
695, Westney Road South, Suite 14, Ajax, Ontario, LI6 6M9
email: ndalton@disticor.com web: www.disticordirect.com

Publishing History
First published in Germany in 1927
First published by Dedalus in 1991, reprinted in 1999
New edition with minor corrections in 2010

Translation & Introduction copyright © Dedalus and Mike Mitchell 1991/2010

The right of Mike Mitchell to be identified as the translator of this work has been asserted by him in
accordance with the Copyright, Designs and Patents Act, 1988

Printed in Finland by W.S. Bookwell
Typeset by RefineCatch Limited, Bungay, Suffolk

A C.I.P. listing for this book is available on request.

THE TRANSLATOR

For many years an academic with a special interest in Austrian literature and culture, Mike Mitchell has been a freelance literary translator since 1995.

He is one of Dedalus's editorial directors and is responsible for the Dedalus translation programme.

He has published over fifty translations from German and French, including Gustav Meyrink's five novels and *The Dedalus Book of Austrian Fantasy*.

His translation of Rosendorfer's *Letters Back to Ancient China* won the 1998 Schlegel-Tieck Translation Prize after he had been shortlisted in previous years for his translations of *Stephanie* by Herbert Rosendorfer and *The Golem* by Gustav Meyrink.

His translations have been shortlisted three times for The Oxford Weidenfeld Translation Prize: *Simplicissimus* by Johann Grimmelshausen in 1999, *The Other Side* by Alfred Kubin in 2000 and *The Bells of Bruges* by Georges Rodenbach in 2008.

His biography of Gustav Meyrink: *Vivo: The Life of Gustav Meyrink* was published by Dedalus in November 2008.

His website can be visited at homepages.phonecoop.coop/mjmitchell

Books by Gustav Meyrink published by Dedalus

The Golem
Walpurgisnacht
The Green Face
The White Dominican
The Angel of the West Window
The Opal (and other stories)
The Dedalus Meyrink Reader

Dedalus has also published the first English language biography of Gustav Meyrink:

Vivo: The Life of Gustav Meyrink by Mike Mitchell

INTRODUCTION

Gustav Meyrink (1868-1932) came relatively late to
literature. He began his first story in a sanatorium, where
he was convalescing from tuberculosis, in 1901. It was
published that year in the famous satirical magazine,
Simplicissimus, and was the first of many short stories in
which he combined fantasy and humour with biting
satire of the complacency of the pre-war bourgeoisie.
His first – and best-known – novel, *Der Golem*, appeared
in a magazine in 1913; in its book form published in 1915
it was an immediate success. Three more novels followed in the next few years: *Das grüne Gesicht* (The
Green Face) 1916, *Walpurgisnacht* 1917 and *Der Weiße
Dominikaner* (The White Dominican) 1921. In the 1920s
he largely abandoned his own creative work to edit
mystical and occult writings, an activity which was the
product of his profound personal interest in the
occult. Like his hero, John Dee, Meyrink in his own life
experienced the suspicions and rumours which preoccupation with the occult engenders; indeed, he may well
have encouraged them in his early years. During the war
he was attacked both by the pen and by stones thrown at
his house, though these attacks were probably directed
more at his satire than at his occult tendencies. *Der Engel*

11

vom westlichen Fenster was his last novel and appeared in 1927 when he was already beginning to be plagued by both health and financial problems. It, too, derives from his studies of the occult and is his longest and most complex work.

It is said that Meyrink's first story was thrown into the waste paper basket at the *Simplicissimus* offices, whence it was retrieved by the editor, Ludwig Thoma. This is probably a legend, but so many of the real facts of Meyrink's own life were fantastic that he is the type of person around whom legends gather. He was born in Vienna, the illegitimate son of an actress, Maria Meyer, and an aristocrat in the service of the King of Württemberg, Karl Freiherr von Varnbüler. Later rumours that he had royal blood in his veins were not discouraged by Meyrink. (Meyrink was originally a pseudonym; in 1917 he adopted it as his real name.)

Although the difference in status made a marriage out of the question, his father paid for his education. Most of his schooling took place in Munich but was completed in Prague, where his mother had moved in 1883. In the twenty-three years he lived there, until he moved to Bavaria in 1906, he became a well-known figure, above all as a dandy and man-about-town capable of outrageous behaviour. He followed the principle of *épater le bourgeois* in practice long before it became the dominant tone of his writing. Although he only settled in Prague as an adult, the city and, above all, the atmosphere of mystery about its old streets was a determining factor behind his writing, even after he had moved away. Meyrink was probably the author who more than any other created the romantic image of Prague which played an important role in the German literature and cinema of the first decades of this century. (Others were the young Rilke and Kafka, with whom this image of Prague is now mostly associated.)

In 1889 he founded a bank (was it mere chance that his partner was the nephew of the German poet, Christian Morgenstern, who mingled nonsense humour with mysticism?). He married in 1892 but later had an affair with Philomena Bernt, whom he eventually married (in Dover, a kind of continental Gretna) after he had finally managed to get a divorce in 1905. This affair caused one of the many scandals he was involved in. Meyrink challenged two officers to a duel but they, afraid of his reputation as an outstanding swordsman, refused on the grounds that he was illegitimate and therefore not *satisfaktionsfähig*, whereupon Meyrink challenged the whole officers' corps. In the same year, 1902, came the events that led to the ruin of his business. Meyrink was accused, by an official he had attacked in the press, of using spiritualism to influence his clients, especially female ones. He spent almost three months in goal before his name was cleared, by which time the bank had collapsed. His blossoming career as a writer was an important source of income, though he did find other work at times, most congenially, perhaps, as a representative for a champagne producer.

Meyrink's interest in the occult was aroused by another of those incidents which are almost too good to be true and in which his life was so rich. In 1891 he suffered a nervous breakdown; his decision to commit suicide was overturned by an occultist leaflet which was pushed under his door. Whether this is fact or part of the self-created legend, what is certainly true is that from that time onward he showed an active interest in all aspects of the occult. Some of that interest was scientific and scholarly: he exposed tricksters and false mediums, carried out alchemical experiments and published critical editions of mystical texts. But he was also interested in mysticism as a practical art and as a counter to the prevailing materialism and positivism. He took hallucinatory drugs, practised yoga and studied Eastern philosophy. In the same year as the publication of his final novel he became a Buddhist.

*

The Angel of the West Window is a fictional summation of

13

Meyrink's preoccupation with the occult, but not in any simple, direct way. The reader should not look to it for a message, for, say, Meyrink's final distillation of the wisdom of the mystics. Many of the theories and ideas he would have come across in his researches are there, it is true. But none is presented as the sole key to knowledge. They all contribute to his portrayal of the search which is all we can know of the ultimate goal. Through the fictional world he has created, Meyrink is trying to convey to the reader the sense of a reality where, as one commentator puts it, "everything is different from outward appearances, but only the outward appearances are accessible" (Marianne Wünsch). It is a comment that is also frequently made about the world of Meyrink's contemporary, Franz Kafka.

The two main characters of *The Angel of the West Window*, the historical figure from the age of Queen Elizabeth, John Dee, and his fictional modern descendant, the narrator, both pursue a tightrope course between normally distinct categories which merge and separate in varying constellations. Male and female, for example, are on one level distinct: the symbol of the male blood line of the Dees is the suitably phallic spear of Hywel Dda, whilst at the end Jane "takes the woman's road of sacrifice"; and in the transcendental sphere where the novel ends there are separate male and female realms. On another level, however, they intermingle: the narrator's mystical marriage with "Elisabeth" is a union with the female element dormant within himself which produces the self-enclosed whole which has echoes of both incest and hermaphroditism; "the Queen is within me, I am within the Queen: child, husband and father from the very beginning. ... Woman no more! Man no more!" This ambiguity − in which opposites can be distinct and at the same time merge, can be external to the hero and at the same time are situated within him − appears in the theme of sex which is an undercurrent running through much of the novel. The woman who is the eternal temptress of man appears in different guises with different names which are all variants of the same basic form: Isaïs, Sissy, Assja. Jane/Johanna appears to be a counter-figure embodying self-sacrificing love. But it is the erotic that attracts Kelley to Johanna, and when the narrator calls on Jane his cry is intercepted by Assja because, Lipotin tells him, 'Jane' represents his "vital erotic energy". The distinctions are further blurred by the fact that 'love' and 'hate' are also closely related; the succubus, Assja, feeds on the hatred that the narrator thinks will protect him from her. He succumbs to the succubus and yet is saved. In another reversal of expectation, what looks like the road to destruction turns out to be a detour that leads to his goal.

The conclusion is not explicable in neatly rational terms, in terms of good v. evil and the ultimate triumph of the former confirming a one-dimensional moral universe. Rather, Meyrink's universe is multi-layered and different 'worlds' exist alongside, interlinked with, each other. The hero's triumph is not that he overcomes evil, but that he recognises himself and fulfils his destiny within his own allotted sphere. Instead of being "erased from the Book of Life", which was the threat posed by Isaïs, the entelechy that is both the narrator and John Dee becomes a link in the great chain of being.

*

If Meyrink's own life was full of fantastic episodes, then this was even more the case with the person he chose as the central figure of his last novel: the life of John Dee was so remarkable that Meyrink had to invent little. John Dee was one of the outstanding scholars of the Elizabethan age, especially in the field of mathematics and related disciplines. Meyrink even makes him *less* of a prodigy than he was: born in 1527, he went up to Cambridge in 1542 and in 1550 was lecturing to the assembled scholars of the Sorbonne on geometry and was offered a permanent post there. At that time the occult and the natural sciences were not as rigidly separated as today. Dee was an astrologer and hermeticist and gradually became more and more involved in alchemy and crystallomancy. He fell under the influence of an obviously very plausible rogue called Kelley, travelled the continent looking for noble and regal patrons – they included Count Lasky, the Emperor Rudolf, the King of Poland and Count Rosenberg – and finally returned to England where he died in poverty in 1608.

Beside his scientific works, Dee published a self-justificatory pamphlet which included a biography; he also kept minutes of the séances (which he called "actions") in which he called up various spirits. Meyrink has used a wealth of this material, from the main events of Dee's life down to minute details. Thus the historical Dee was imprisoned by Bishop Bonner (on suspicion of using magic to assassinate Queen Mary – in the novel Dee is imprisoned under King Edward); in prison he shared a cell with a certain "Barthlett Grene" whom Meyrink builds up into an important character. The first protestant martyr under Mary was John Rogers – is that where Meyrink took the name for the narrator's cousin?. Dee briefly mentions a "Moschovite" he encountered – whom Meyrink turns into the figure of Mascee. The biography also briefly mentions someone called Gardner who "declared to me a certayn great philosophicall secret of a spirituall creature"; in the séance minutes one of the many mysterious statements from the spirits is "The Tree is sprung of a graft" and another, "He that is before is a Gardener". From this kind of material Meyrink builds up the mysterious figure of Gärtner/Gardner, the imagery of the rose-trees and grafting and the whole mystic brotherhood into which the hero is taken up after his death. The real Kelley had had his ears cut off (for counterfeiting) before he met Dee, he was knighted by the Emperor Rudolf and he did die when he fell while attempting to escape from prison. He did also lust after Dee's young (second) wife, but the details of that episode are stranger than Meyrink's version: Kelley

16

transmitted (invented?) orders from the Angel that they were to have all things in common, including their wives (Kelley was also married). When Dee demurred, he refused to take part in any more séances and left. After a while he returned and Dee had become so desperate for Kelley's clairvoyant skills that he agreed to the wife-swapping arrangement; they even drew up a contract for a *mariage à quatre* which Meric Casaubon included in his edition of Dee's records of his séances, *A True and Faithful Relation of What passed for many Yeers Between Dr John Dee ... and Some Spirits* published in 1659.

*

In *The Angel of the West Window* there is a great difference between those parts of Dee's life that take place in England and those that are set in Prague. The Castle of Mortlake could be a castle anywhere, it is merely the indistinct background to Dee's experiments in alchemy and spirit-raising. Prague, on the other hand, is so vivid – both visually and in atmosphere – that is it almost a protagonist in the story. The castles of Hradčany and Karlštejn have a physical presence lacking in any of the English settings, a presence as powerful and as brooding as anything in *Der Golem*. The same is true of the two monarchs: both have an incalculable capriciousness, both rule in an atmosphere of suspicion, but whilst we see this in Elizabeth merely through Dee's complaints about the way he is treated, in Rudolf it is there in the detailed physical description (including the famous Habsburg lip) and the repeated image of the bird of prey. Even today one can follow Dee and Kelley round those of the streets of old Prague that still survive, along the Street of the Alchemists, say, or through the Old Town Square. The Ghetto, where he goes to visit Rabbi Löw (who is also one of the main figures in *Der Golem*) has disappeared, but lives on in the imagination through its recreation by writers such as Meyrink. In spite of the figure of John Dee, *The Angel of the West Window* belongs to Prague, not to Prague the Czech capital. but to that Prague of the mind where the "other" world seems to make its presence tangible and in the creation of which Meyrink's stories and novels played the most important role.

My New Novel

Sir John Dee of Gladhill! A name that few people will ever have heard of! It was about 25 years ago that I first read the story of his life – a life so adventurous, so fantastic, so moving and terrible that I have never found anything to compare with it. The account so etched itself on my soul that as a romantic young man I used to wander up to the Street of the Alchemists on the castle hill in Prague and daydream of John Dee coming out of one of the dilapidated doors of the crooked little houses and speaking to me of the mysteries of alchemy; not of the alchemy by which man seeks to solve the riddle of how to make gold from base metals, but of the occult art by which he strives to transform himself from mortal clay into a being that will never lose its self-awareness. There were months on end when the figure of John Dee seemed to have been purged from my memory, but then, often in dreams, it would reappear, distinct, clear and ineradicable. These dreams were rare but regular, not unlike the 29 February in a leap year that you have to imagine composed of four separate quarters before you can call it a whole day. We are all the slaves of our ideas, not their creators, and later, when I became a writer, I knew for certain that John Dee would not leave me in peace until I had resolved to record his life-story in a novel. It is now two years since I made the "resolve" to start the novel. But whenever I sat down at my desk I would hear an inner voice mocking me, "You're going to write a historical novel?! Don't you realise that all historical material gives off the stench of the grave, a sickening smell of mouldy feathers with nothing of the freshness of the living present?!"

But as often as I decided to give up the plan, "John Dee" would call me back to the work, however much I tried to resist. Finally I solved the problem by hitting on the idea of interweaving the story of a living, contemporary figure with that of the "dead" John Dee, of making the work a double novel, so to speak. – – Am I that living, contemporary figure? The answer could be yes or no. They say an artist painting a portrait always involuntarily puts something of his own face into the picture. It is probably the same with writers.

Who was John Dee? That is what the book is about. Suffice it to say he was a favourite of Queen Elizabeth of England. He advised her to make Greenland – and North America – subject to the English crown. The plan had been approved, the military were waiting for orders, but at the last minute the capricious Queen changed her mind. The map of the world would look different today if she had followed Dee's advice! At the failure of the plan on which he had set his whole life, Dee decided to conquer a different country from the terrestrial "Greenland", a country beyond the imagination of most people today, a "country" whose existence is mocked today just as much as "America" was at the time of Columbus. John Dee set off for this country, as unwavering in his determination as Columbus. But his journey took him farther, much farther than Columbus, and was more wearisome, more gruesome, more gruelling. The bare recorded facts of Dee's life are harrowing enough, how much more harrowing must the experiences have been of which we know nothing? Leibnitz mentions him, but history has decided to ignore him: it prefers to categorise anything it cannot understand as "mad". But I take the liberty of believing that John Dee was quite the opposite of "mad".

One thing is certain: John Dee was one of the greatest scholars of his age; there was no monarch in Europe who would not have welcomed him at his court. Emperor Rudolph brought him to Prague where, according to legend, he made gold from lead. But, as I have already indicated, his most fervent endeavours were not directed towards the transmutation of metals but towards another kind of transmutation. What that is I have tried to demonstrate in my novel.

(Gustav Meyrink, printed in *Der Bücherwurm*, Leipzig, 1927, no. 8, p. 236-238.)

THE ANGEL OF THE WEST WINDOW

A strange feeling: this packet I am holding in my hand was all neatly tied up and sealed by a dead man! It is as if fine, invisible threads, delicate as a spider's web, lead out from it into a dark realm.

The complex pattern of the string, the care with which the blue wrapping paper has been folded – it all bears silent witness to the purposeful designs of a living man sensing the approach of death: he gathers together letters, notes, caskets filled with once vital matters that already belong to the past, suffused with memories that have long since faded, and he arranges them and wraps them up with half a thought for his future heir, for that distant, almost unknown person – me – who will know of his death and who will hear of it at the moment when this sealed packet, left to find its way in the realm of the living, reaches the hand it is destined for.

It is sealed with the massive red seals of my cousin, John Roger, bearing the arms of my mother's family. For years this son of my mother's brother had always been referred to by aged kinswomen as 'the last of his line'. To my ears this description sounded like a solemn title, especially when added to his foreign-sounding name with the strange, somewhat ridiculous pride of those thin, wrinkled lips which coughed out the last breath of a dying line.

This family tree – in my brooding imagination the heraldic image grows to monstrous proportions – has stretched its grotesquely gnarled branches over distant lands. Its roots were in Scotland and it sprouted all over England; it is said to be blood-kin to one of the oldest houses in Wales. Vigorous shoots established themselves in Sweden, in America and, finally, in Germany and Styria. Everywhere the branches have withered; in Britain the trunk rotted. Here alone, in southern Austria, one last shoot sprouted – my cousin John Roger. And this last shoot was strangled by England.

How my grandfather on my mother's side – 'His Lordship', as he liked to be called – had clung to the name and tradition of his ancestors! He, who was nothing but a dairy farmer in Styria! My cousin, John Roger, had followed other paths, had studied science, become a doctor and dabbled in psychopathology, travelling far and wide, to Vienna and Zurich, to Aleppo and Madras, to Alexandria and Turin, to learn from the foremost authorities about the depths of the human psyche. He visited them all, the licensed and the licentious, caring not whether their shirts were stiff with western starch or oriental grime.

He had moved to England a few years before the outbreak of the war. There he is said to have pursued his researches into the origin and fate of our line. The reason is unknown to me, but a persistent rumour had it that he was on the trail of some strange, deep secret. He was surprised there by the war. As an Austrian reserve lieutentant he was interned. When he came out of the camps five years later he was a broken man; he never crossed the Channel again and died somewhere in London, leaving a few meagre possessions which are now scattered amongst various members of the family.

My portion, besides a few mementos, is the parcel which arrived today; it bears, in angular handwriting, my name.

The family tree is withered, the escutcheon shattered.

That was just an idle thought. There was no King of Arms to perform this sombre ceremony over the family vault.

The escutcheon is shattered – the words I said softly to myself as I broke the red wax. No more will anyone use that seal.

It is a magnificent coat of arms that I am breaking. Breaking? Strange, I suddenly feel as if that word is a lie.

It is true that I am breaking up the coat of arms, but, who knows: perhaps I am just waking it from a long sleep! The shield is split at the foot; in the right-hand, azure field is a silver sword thrust vertically into a green hill, representing the ancestral manor of Gladhill in Worcestershire; on the left in a field of argent is a tree in leaf with a silver spring gushing forth from between its roots, representing Mortlake in Middlesex; and on the forked field – vert – above the foot there is a light in the shape of an early Christian lamp. The last is an unusual heraldic device, which has always puzzled the experts.

I hesitate before breaking off the last, beautifully clear seal; it is such a pleasure to look at! But what is this?! That is not the burning lamp above the foot of the escutcheon! It's a crystal! A regular dodecahedron surrounded by a sunburst of rays? No dull oil-lamp, then, but a radiant jewel!

And again I am gripped by a strange sensation: I feel as if some memory is trying to force its way up into consciousness, a memory that has been sleeping for … centuries, yes, for centuries.

How did this precious stone come to be in the coat of arms? And look, a tiny inscription around it? I take my magnifying glass and read, *"Lapis sacer sanctificatus et praecipuus manifestationis."*

With a shake of the head I examine this incomprehensible modification of the familiar coat of arms. That is a stamp that I have certainly never seen! Either my cousin, John Roger, had a second signet in his possession or – – now it's clear: the sharp cut is unmistakably modern.

John Roger must have had a new ring made in London. But, why? The oil-lamp! It suddenly seems so obvious it's almost ridiculous. The oil-lamp was never anything other than a late, baroque corruption, the escutcheon was always meant to bear a shining rock crystal! But what can the inscription around mean? Curious how the crystal seems so well-known to me, inwardly familiar, so to speak. Rock crystal! I know there is an old tale of a lustrous jewel shining from above, but I have forgotten the tale.

Hesitantly I break the last seal and untie the parcel. Out tumble ancient letters, documents, deeds, excerpts, yellowing parchments covered with Rosicrucian cyphers, pictures with hermetic pandects, some half-decayed, a few volumes bound in pigskin with old copper engravings, all kinds of notebooks tied up together; then there are some ivory caskets full of marvellous antiques: coins, pieces of wood mounted like relics in silver and gold leaf, pieces of bone and specimens of the best Devon coal, iridescent and cut into facets like a gem-stone, and more of the like. On top, a note in the stiff, angular handwriting of John Roger:

> Read or read not! Burn or preserve! Ashes to ashes and dust to dust! We of the line of Hywel Dda, Princes of Wales, are dead. – – Mascee.

Are these words intended for me? They must be! They make no sense to me, but neither do I feel the urge to brood over them. Like a child, I think: why should I bother with that now, it'll all become clear in time! What does the word "Mascee" mean? That does intrigue me. I look it up in the dictionary: "Mascee = an Anglo-Chinese expression meaning something like 'What does it matter!'" It is the equivalent of the Russian "Nitchevo".

I spent many hours yesterday musing on the fate of my cousin John Roger and on the transience of human hopes and of things material. It was well on into the night when I rose from my desk; I decided to leave a detailed inventory of the legacy until the next day. I went to bed and was soon asleep.

The thought of the crystal must have pursued me into my sleep; I cannot recall ever having had such a strange dream as visited me that night.

The crystal was hovering somewhere in the darkness above me. A dull ray emanating from it struck my forehead and I had a clear sensation that this established some significant relationship between my head and the stone. I felt afraid, and tried to withdraw by turning my head from side to side, but I could not escape the ray of light. And as I twisted and turned my head I had a disconcerting sensation: it seemed to me that the ray from the crystal was playing on my forehead even when I buried my face in the pillows. And I clearly felt the back of my head take on the form of the front – a second face was growing out of the crown of my head. – I felt no terror; it was merely a nuisance because it meant I could not avoid the ray of light any more.

The head of Janus, I thought. Even in my dream I knew that was merely a half-remembered scrap of knowledge from the Latin classes at school, yet I hoped that would be the end of it. But it would not leave me in peace. Janus? Nonsense, it wasn't Janus. But what was it, then? With irritating obstinacy that "What then?" kept running through my dream, even though I could not seem to remember who I was. Instead, something else happened: slowly, slowly the crystal floated down from the heights above me and came close to the top of my head. And I had the feeling that the stone was something alien to me, so utterly alien that I could not put it into words. Some object from a distant galaxy could not have been more alien. – I don't know why, when I think of the dream now, I think of the dove that descended from heaven when Jesus was baptised by John.

– – The nearer the crystal came, the more it shone directly down onto my head; that is: onto the line where my two heads met. And gradually I started to feel an icy burning there. And this feeling – which was not even unpleasant – woke me up. – – –

I spent the whole of the following morning pondering over the dream.

Hesitantly and with great difficulty I prised a fragment of memory loose from the rock face of the past: a recollection of a conversation, of a story, of something I had thought up or read – or whatever – in which a crystal occurred and a face – but it was not called "Janus". A half faded vision rose before my mind's eye:

When I was still a child my grandfather – the noble Lord who was, in fact, only a Styrian farmer – used to take me on his knee to play ride-a-cock-horse, and at the same time he would tell me all sorts of stories in a hushed voice.

All my childhood memories of fairy-tales are set on my Grandfather's knee – he was almost a fairy-tale figure himself. And Grandfather told me of a dream. "Dreams", he said, "are a stronger legal title than any parchment or fee simple. Always remember that. If you are to be a real heir, then, one day perhaps, I will bequeath our dream to you: the dream of the son of Hywel Dda." And then, in a low, mysterious voice, as if he were afraid the very air in the room might be listening, close to my ear and yet still jogging me up and down on his knee, he told me of a jewel in a land where no living man could go, unless he were accompanied by one who had overcome death; and of a crown of gold and crystal on the double head of, of – – –? I think I remember him talking of this double-headed dream creature as of an ancestor or a family spirit, but then my memory fails entirely. Everything is blurred in a misty light.

I never had a dream of that kind until – until last night! – Was that the dream of the sons of Hywel Dda?

There was no point in going on brooding about it. Anyway, I was interrupted by a visit from my friend Sergei Lipotin, the old art dealer from the Werrengasse.

Lipotin – in the city he is known by his nickname of "Nitchevo" – was formerly Antiquary to the Czar, and is still an impressive old gentleman, in spite of the dismal fate that has befallen him. Once a millionaire, a connoisseur, an expert in Asiatic art with a world-wide reputation – now a back-street dealer in junk *chinoiserie*, marked by death and hardly able to make ends meet, he is still a czarist to the core. I owe a number of rare pieces in my possession to his infallible judgement. And, strange to say, whenever I am gripped by the desire for some special *objet* which seems inaccessible, Lipotin appears and brings me something in that line.

Today, as I had nothing more remarkable to hand, I showed him my cousin's consignment from London. He was full of praise for some of the old prints; *"Rarissima"* he called them, using a favourite phrase of his. There were also a few objects in the manner of medallions which aroused his interest: "Solid German Renaissance work, above average quality." Finally he examined John Roger's coat of arms, gave a gasp of surprise and gazed at it abstractedly. I asked him what it was that had excited him. He shrugged his shoulders, lit a cigarette and said nothing.

We chatted about unimportant matters. Just before he left he casually remarked, "Did you know that our old friend, Michael Arangelovitch Stroganoff, is unlikely to survive the last packet of cigarettes he bought. It is for the best. What has he left to pawn? No matter. It is an end we shall all come to. We Russians are like the sun – we rise in the East and go down in the West. Farewell!"

Lipotin went. I mused on what he had told me. Michael Stroganoff, the old Baron I had first met in the coffee house, was about to cross over into the green realm of the dead, into the green land of Persephone. Since I have known him he has lived on tea and cigarettes. He arrived here after his flight from Russia with nothing but what he could carry on his person, half a dozen diamond rings and about the same number of gold pocket watches – all that he had been able to stuff into his pockets when he broke through the Bolshevik picket line. From the proceeds of these jewels he lived a carefree life in the grand manner. He smoked only the most expensive cigarettes, specially imported from the East; who knows what hands they passed through before reaching him. "To let the things of this earth go up in smoke," he used to say, "is perhaps the only favour we can do God." At the same time he was slowly starving to death; and whenever he was not sitting in Lipotin's little shop he was freezing in his tiny attic somewhere in the suburbs.

So Baron Stroganoff, former Imperial ambassador to Teheran, is on his deathbed. "No matter. It is all for the best," Lipotin had said. With a mindless sigh to the empty air, I turn to the books and manuscripts of John Roger.

I pick out this and that at random and start to read. — — —

I have spent the whole day rummaging through the documents John Roger has left me and the outcome is that it seems pointless to try to arrange these scraps of ancient records and antiquarian studies into any kind of ordered whole – it is rubble and no effort can reconstruct the building it came from! I seem to hear a voice whispering, "Read and burn. Ashes to ashes, dust to dust!"

Why should I care about this story of a certain John Dee, Lord of the Manor of Gladhill? Just because he was an old Englishman with an *idée fixe* who may have been one of my mother's ancestors?

But I cannot bring myself to throw the rubbish away. There are times when things have greater power over us than we over them; perhaps they are more alive than we and are just shamming lifelessness? I cannot even bring myself to stop reading. I do not know why, but the musty pages tighten their grip on me with every hour. The jumble of fragments begins to sort itself into a picture which emerges, sad yet splendid, from the mists of time: the portrait of a man, high-minded and fearfully betrayed; radiant in the morning of life, dimmed by the gathering clouds at midday, mocked and persecuted, nailed to the cross, refreshed with vinegar mingled with gall, cast down into hell and yet one of the elect, called to delight in the mysteries of heaven with all noble souls, a steadfast witness to his faith, a loving spirit.

No! The story of John Dee, a late descendant of one of the oldest houses of these Islands, of the old Welsh Princes, an ancestor of my mother's line – that story shall not be lost for ever!

But I realise that I cannot write it as I would wish. I lack almost all the necessary background, especially the great knowledge my cousin enjoyed in those sciences which some call the occult and others think they can brush aside with the word "parapsychology". In such matters I lack experience and judgement. The best I can do is to sort these scattered fragments and order them according to some clear plan: in the words of my cousin, John Roger, "to preserve and pass them on".

The result will surely be a mosaic with pieces missing. But does not the fragment often exert a stronger attraction than the complete picture? The way the curve of a smile breaks off to continue in the crease of a tormented brow – an enigma; the eye still staring out when the forehead is missing – an enigma; the sudden blaze of crimson from the crumbling wall – enigmas, enigmas ...

It will take weeks, if not months, of meticulous work to bring some order to this tangle of already half-decaying documents. I hesitate: should I undertake it? If I felt certain that some inner spirit was compelling me to it, I would refuse out of pure contrariness and send up the whole bundle in smoke to ... "to do the good Lord a favour".

I keep on thinking of poor Baron Michael Arangelovich Stroganoff, who will not even finish his packet of cigarettes – perhaps because God has scruples about allowing one man to do him too many favours.

Today the dream with the jewel returned. ░
followed the same pattern except that the i░
the crystal came down over my double hea░
no pain, so that I did not wake up this time. Q
whether it had anything to do with the fact ░
touched the top of my head, but, at the very mom...
when the beam of light illuminated both faces equally, I
saw that I was the double-headed man and yet, at the
same time, was another person: I saw myself – that is, the
"Janus" – move both lips of the face on one side of the
head whilst those on the other side remained motionless.
It was the silent one that was the "real" me. For a long
time the "other" made great efforts to produce a sound.
It was as if he was struggling to find some word from the
depths of sleep.

Finally a breath came from the lips, wafting the words
through the air towards me:

"Order not! Do not presume! Where reason imposes
its order it dams up the fountainhead and opens the way
to ruin. Let me guide your hand as you read so you bring
not destruction. – Let – me – guide – –"

I could feel the torment that the effort of speaking
caused my "other" head ; it was probably that that woke
me up.

I don't know what to think. What is going on? Is there
a ghost somewhere inside me? Does some phantom
from a dream want to come into my life? Is my
consciousness about to split, am I becoming ... "ill"? For
the moment I am sure I am perfectly healthy and whilst
awake I do not feel the least temptation to grow a second
face; even less do I feel under some "compulsion" to act
or think in a certain way. I am completely master of my
emotions and of my will: I am free!

Another fragment of memory from the ride-a-cock-
horse conversations with my grandfather surfaces: he
told me that the family spirit in the dream was mute but
that one day it would speak. That would mean the end of
time for our bloodline; the crown would no longer
hover above the head but shine forth from the double
brow.

"Janus" about to speak? Has the end of time for our line? Am I the last heir of Hywel Dda? No matter; the words that are lodged in my memory are clear:

"Let me guide as you read!" And: "Reason dams up the fountainhead." – – – So be it; I shall obey. But no, no, it cannot be an order, otherwise I would refuse; I will not submit to orders. It must be advice, yes, yes, advice – merely advice! And why should I not follow the advice? I will not order the material. I will record whatever comes to hand.

So at random I picked up a sheet bearing the angular handwriting of my cousin, John Roger, and read:

> It is all long past. All the figures whose desires and passions mark these fateful records and in whose dust and decay I, John Roger, now venture to delve are long since dead. They too disturbed the ashes of others who were then long dead.
>
> What is dead? What is past? All that once was thought or moved is still thought and motion – might and power live on! Not one of us, though, has found what he sought – the true key to the treasure-house of life, the secret key, the search for which makes all life meaningful and worthwhile. Who has seen the crown with the crystal above it? What have we found, we that sought – only misfortune and the sight of death: yet we were promised death should be overcome! The key must lie deep beneath the waters. Who dares not dive down will never recover it. Was not the end of time prophesied to our bloodline? None of us has seen the last day. Was that our joy? It was also our guilt.
>
> Often as I tried to conjure them up, I have never seen the twin faces. My eyes have never beheld the crystal. So be it: as we make our inexorable journey to the land of the dead we will never more see the light as it rises – unless the Devil himself twist our heads round on our necks. Whoever would rise,

must first descend, for only then can the bottom-most rise to the top. But to which of us of John Dee's blood came the voice of the Baphomet?

John Roger.

The name "Baphomet" hit me like a hammer blow.

By all the saints – the *Baphomet!* – Yes, that was the name I could not remember! That is the head with the crown and twin faces, that is my grandfather's family dream god! That was the name he had whispered in my ear, with rhythmic emphasis, as if he wanted to hammer something into my soul whilst the child I had been was riding a cock horse on his knee:

Baphomet? Baphomet!

But who is Baphomet?

He is the arcane symbol of the ancient and secret Order of the Knights Templar. He is the essence of that otherness which is closer to the Templars than the immediate physical world; he is and remains an unknown deity.

Were the Lords of the Manor of Gladhill Templars? That could well be. One or other of them might have been, why not? What can be gleaned from encyclopaedias, rumours and traditions is the abstruse description of the Baphomet as the "lower demiurge". What a pedantic obsession with hierarchies! And why then should Baphomet be double-headed? And why should it be I who sprouts these two heads in my dreams? There is one thing that is true in all this: I, the last heir of the English house of the Dees of Gladhill, I stand at "the end of the days of the bloodline".

And I have a vague feeling that I shall be ready to obey if the Baphomet should ever deign to speak.

– – – Here I was interrupted by Lipotin who brought me news of Stroganoff. As he coolly rolled himself a cigarette he told me the Baron had coughed up blood until he was exhausted. Perhaps one should not rule out a doctor, even if only to make the end easier. "But... " with a languid shrug of the shoulders Lipotin made the gesture of counting money.

I understood at once and opened the drawer in my desk where I keep my cash.

Lipotin put his hand on my arm, and, clenching his cigarette between his teeth, raised his thick eyebrows in his inimitable way as if to say, "No charity, please".

"A moment, my dear sir". He went to his fur coat, took out a small box and said gruffly:

"The last possession of Michael Arangelovitch Stroganoff. If you will be so kind as to accept it, it is yours."

Gingerly I took the object in my hand: a plain box in heavy silver, secured with bands and trick locks patterned after the manner of old silverware from Tula in Russia, at once solid and decorative. All in all, it was a not uninteresting *objet d'art*.

I gave Lipotin what seemed to me a decent sum. He crumpled up the notes without counting them and shoved them into his waistcoat pocket. "Michael Arangelovitch can die in decency" was all he said about the matter.

Soon after that he left.

I am still holding the heavy silver box in my hand and I still can't find how to open the locks. I have been trying for hours – it will not open. It would take a saw or shears to cut through the heavy bands, but that would ruin the beautiful box. Better leave it as it is.

Obedient to the command from my dream, I have just taken out the first fascicle of papers and started to make excerpts from it to record the history of my ancestor, John Dee. The excerpts follow the order in which the papers happen to fall into my hands.

Baphomet only knows what the result will be. But I have suddenly become curious to see a life unfold before me – even if it is only the fate of someone long departed

– without the interference of my ordering hand, without my mind trying to cheat destiny.

The very first "catch" brought up by my obedient hand should have made me suspicious. It is a fragment of a document, a letter, which on the surface seems to have nothing to do with John Dee and his story. It deals with the exploits of a troop of the "Ravenheads", who seem to have played some role in the religious conflicts of 1549 in England.

Confidential report to his Grace, Bishop Bonner, in London; from his agent under the sign

In the year of our Lord, 1550.
" – – – and as Yr. Lordship can well testify, it is no mean feat, as you have commanded me, to keep under observation a gentleman such as Sir John Dee, one so justly suspected of most satanical heresy, a strumpet apostate – Yr. Lordship knows well that even the Governor daily exposes himself to that same infamous suspicion; notwithstanding I venture to send this secret report to Yr. Lordship from my make-shift headquarters by a trusty messenger so that Yr. Lordship may see how keen is my ardour to serve him and that Heaven may look graciously on my labours. I well know that failure to discover the ringleaders of the most recent outrages of the mob against our holy Church will be rewarded with Yr. Lordship's anger, torture and excommunication. I do beseech Yr. Lordship to hold back your terrible judgement on your faithfull servant a little while yet, in consideration that I have today matter to report that does most clearly prove the guilt of two evil-doers.

Yr. Lordship is well acquainted with the scandalous conduct of the present council under the Lord Protector who in his sloth – to call it nothing worse – has allowed the poisonous hydra of disobedience, rebellion and the desecration of the holy Sacrament, of the churches and monasteries to raise its dark head in England. Now at the end of the month of December in this year of grace, 1549, there have appeared in Wales bands of seditious rabble, as if spewed up from the bowels of the earth. They are vagabonds and men escaped from the galleys, but there are also some peasants amongst them and ranting artisans, a motley undisciplined crew who have made themselves a banner whereon is the form of a hideous black raven's head, like unto an alchymical sign, for which they give themselves the name of the "Ravenheads".

Foremost among them is a cruel ruffian, a master butcher from Welshpool by trade, Bartlett Greene by name, having made himself the captain of the band. He curses and rails against God and the Saviour but chiefly he utters the most vile blasphemies against the Blessed Virgin; item, he says the holy Queen of Heaven is nought but the creature of their highest deity or, rather, demon and arch-fiend, that he calls "Black Isaïs".

This same Bartlett Greene does also maintain with bold effrontery that his Princess of Darkness, that devil's whore Isaïs, has made him wholly invulnerable and that as a token of this she has made him a gift of a silver shoe that he may march from victory to victory wherever he will. And truth to tell, this Bartlett Greene and his band do seem everywhere to enjoy the protection of Beelzebub and his Captains, for to this day no bullet nor poison, no ambush nor direct assault has done the least harm to his power.

A second matter there is to report, though until now precise details have eluded me: namely that the guiding hand behind the raids and pillage of the Ravenheads, and even behind treaties with the blackest scoundrels in the land, is not that of the cruel and monstrous Bartlett Greene but of some secret commander who does provide them with all manner of goods, gold, letters and secret counsels; such a one must surely be an emissary of Satan.

Such a one that does pull the strings and direct the mob where he will must be a gentleman of rank: indeed, we must seek him among the rich and powerful. And is not Sir John Dee such a one?

Most recently, that they might bring the common people over to the devil's side, they have carried out an attack on that holy place of miracles, the grave of Saint Dunstan at Brederock, the which they have plundered and utterly destroyed, casting the sacred relics to the four winds, that to report it makes my heart bleed. This they did because it was said among the people that Saint Dunstan's grave was inviolable and that a thunderbolt from heaven would instantly strike any wretch who dared to desecrate it. Now that the said Greene has exposed the holy shrine to his scorn and mockery, many of the simple folk are deceived and flock to his standard.

Further to report, it has just come to my ears that Bartlett Greene has several times been in secret conference with a Muscovite, who is travelling through the land, a curious fellow about whom the strangest rumours run.

The name of this same Muscovite is Mascee, a nickname, though what it might mean, I cannot tell. People call him the Tutor to the Czar of Muscovy; he is gaunt and grey, well over fifty years of age and has the look, almost, of one of Tartary. He is said to have entered the country as a merchant with many kinds of strange and curious articles from Russia and China, and that he still peddles these same wares. A dubious cur, there is none that knows whence he comes.

Until now all my attempts to lay hold of Master Mascee have met with failure, he vanishes into the air like smoke.

There is one more thing concerning this Mascee, and one that may serve to trap him: there are children at Bangor who say they saw how, after the worst of the tumult was over, this Muscovite went to the desecrated grave of St. Dunstan, reached in between the broken stones with his hand and took out two fair, smooth globes, the one red and the other white, of the size of a ball such as they might play with and made, so it seemed, of precious ivory. The children report that this Mascee did look mightily pleased with his work, hid the globes in his pocket and hurried away. It seems to me a reasonable thing to suppose that this Muscovite coveted the globes for their rarity and that, as a dealer in suchlike trifles, he will try to sell them for a good price as soon as he may. I have therefore sent out word to report to me any such ivory globes, the more since there has been no trace of the Muscovite himself since then.

On one matter I have some scruples which I will not conceal from your Lordship, being appointed by God my Father Confessor. Namely there has fallen into my hands a package of documents from my secular master, the Lord Protector. It seemed a sign from heaven and so I secretly concealed it about my body. In it I found a report from a learned Doctor, at present tutor to her Royal Highness, the Princess Elizabeth, and right strange was that report. Enclosed within was a strip of parchment which I am sure I can extract from the package without fear of suspicion and I therefore enclose it *in originali* with my report. In brief summary, the tutor's report to the Lord Protector is as follows:

"The Lady Elizabeth having just completed her fourteenth year, so her tutor writes, all things seem to be turning out for the best. Marvellous to relate, the Princess had abandoned her former excess and turned to occupations more fitting for a lady. Suchlike habits as boxing, climbing, pinching and otherwise maltreating her maids and companions, as well as tormenting and cutting up mice and frogs, seem to have lost most of their attraction for the Princess, who has turned her mind to prayer and the study of holy books ..." – to which the Devil and his followers must have seduced her.

That notwithstanding, I have heard rumours that there have been complaints from Lady Ellinor, the daughter of Lord Huntingdon who is scarce sixteen, that in their play the Princess does sometimes take hold of her with such a hot hand that her private parts are bruised green and blue. On St. Gertrude's Day past the Lady Elizabeth commanded a pleasure ride in the Forest of Uxbridge and the company streamed without escort over the hills in a wild gallop like a pack of demons, forgetting womanly modestly as if they were accursed heathenish Amazons.

This Lady Ellinor did one day secretly report that the Lady Elizabeth had visited a witch in the said Forest of Uxbridge and had sworn by the blood of Our Lord she would ask the old hag to show her the future, as her ancestor, King Macbeth, had done.

The witch mumbled prophecies and adages to Lady Elizabeth, but she also gave her some foul drink, such as one would imagine a fiendish love potion, which, not regarding the peril to her immortal soul, tis said she drank it. Afterwards the witch gave her the prophecy written down on a parchment; the corpus delicti enclosed will be the witch's scrawl – of which I can understand not a word, the whole seems to me mere devilish prattle. The parchment is affixed hereto.

All this I have undertaken most humbly in Yr. Lordship's service and I remain etc"

Signed:) + (Secret Agent.

The precise wording of the strip of parchment which the secret agent had attached to his letter to the infamous "Bloody Bishop Bonner" in 1550 was as follows – my cousin, John Roger, added in explanation that it clearly must be a prophecy by the witch of Uxbridge to Elizabeth, Princess, later Queen, of England –:

Parchment Strip

To Gaia, the Black Mother, I put my question;

Into the chasm I plunge: full fifty fathoms I fall.
Thus saith the Mother: "Thou hast drunk of Thy
salvation!"
"Be of good cheer, Elizabeth, Queen," I hear the
Guardian call.

"My potion has the power to loose and to bind:
It sets woman from man apart again.
The body alone is sick, sound is the mind:
The whole will see, if the half be blind;
I shield – I command – I ordain.

The groom I lead to Thy bridal couch:
Become one in the night! Be one to the end of days!
No more divided by the lie of I and Thou!
One body, one blood united in praise!

My draught is a sacrament, making of two the One
That looketh before and behind in the night,
That never shall sleep, eye eternally bright,
In which aeons are but as a day alone.

Be comforted Elizabeth, Queen, be of good cheer:
The Black Crystal is freed from the Mother!
Take this as a token for England's broken crown,
saith the seer:
Soon shall its sundered halves conjoin with one
another.

For Thee, and for the Lord of the silver spring
Gushing from the roots of the blossoming tree,
The furnace awaits, and wedlock's ring:
'When ancient worth's renewed, and gold to gold
doth cling,
Then shall the riven crown again united be.' "

The following postscript from the secret agent was
attached to the witch's parchment strip. It briefly reports
the capture and imprisonment of the ringleader of the

Ravenheads, the "Bartlett Greene" mentioned in the letter to Bishop Bonner. Its text runs as follows:

Postscriptum: the Monday following the Feast of the Resurrection of Our Lord, 1550.

"Bartlett Greene's band of outlaws has been cut down and he himself captured; he was unwounded, which seemed a sheer miracle, the skirmish was fought with such ferocity. Now lies this rogue, brigand and arch-heretic in strong chains, tied over and over, guarded day and night that none of the demons that do look on him, not even his Mistress, Black Isaïs, may free him from them. Thrice the *Apage Satanas* has been said over the locks that bind him and most liberally has holy water been sprinkled on them. – –

I do now most fervently pray to the Lord that the prophecy of Saint Dunstan may be fulfilled and that he that instigated the desecration – perchance the said John Dee? – shall be pursued with torments until he meets his deserved end. Amen!"

Signed) + (Secret Agent

Once more I take a bundle of papers at random from the legacy of my cousin, John Roger, and I can see immediately that it is a diary of our common ancestor, Sir John Dee. It is related to the letter of the secret agent, that is obvious, and comes from almost the same year. The text runs as follows:

Fragments from the diary of Sir John Dee of Gladhill, beginning with the day of the celebration following the award of the degree of Master of Arts.

The Feast of St. Anthony, 1549.
... of Arts we shall sup mightily like good Christian gentlemen. The brightest spirits of Old England will shine – at least their foreheads and noses will! But I will show them all who is the master!

41

... o cursed day! O accursed night! – – – No! – o blessed night, I trust. – The quill does scratch most miserably, my hand is still drunk, yes, drunk! – But my mind? As clear as clear! Yet again: take thee to thy bed, thou cur, and do not presume! – One thing is clearer than the light of day: I am the Lord of posterity. I see them one after the other in an endless line: Kings! Kings sitting on the throne of England.

My head is clear again, but I feel it is about to burst whenever I think of last night and of what happened! It needs cool reflection and a precise account. A servant led me home from the carousal with which Guilford Talbot had celebrated my elevation to the degree of Master of Arts, though God knows how he managed to bring me here. If that was not the noblest quaffing since England began ... Enough, it is enough that I was drunk as never before in my life. Noah himself cannot have been worse drunk.

The night was mild and damp. That added spice to the wine. I must have crawled home on all fours, my filthy garments bear eloquent witness to that.

When I was back in my chamber I sent my servant about his business, for I do not care to be coddled like a child when I wrestle with the wine demon, nor do I suffer another to cover my nakedness as did Father Noah.

I tried to undress myself and succeeded. It was with pride that I stood before my mirror.

There, grinning out at me was the most vile, most wretched, most filthy face I have ever encountered: a fellow with a high forehead but with his hair straggling down in greasy locks, as if to make manifest the base desires that proceed from a degenerate mind. Blue eyes that were not regal and commanding, but glazed over with alcohol, narrow and insolent; a loose, drunkard's mouth hanging open over the grimy goatee beard instead of the thin, imperious lips of a descendant of Rhodri the Great; a fat neck, sagging shoulders – in brief, the very travesty of a Dee, Lord of Gladhill.

I threw my shoulders back and screamed in fury at the fellow in the looking-glass:

"Thou filthy cur, soiled from head to toe from the midden, art thou not ashamed to show thy face to me?! Hast thou never heard it said: Ye shall be as gods? Look at me; dost thou in the least resemble me? Me, the scion of the line of Hywel Dda? No! thou misbegotten, misshapen apology for a noble knight, thou blown-up scarecrow that would be a *Magister liberarum artium*, no, I will stand thy insolent gaze no more. I will smash thee and thy mirror in a thousand fragments before me!"

I raised my arm to deliver the blow. And the figure in the mirror raised his. To my heated mind it seemed like an appeal for mercy, and I was seized with sudden pity for this Jack i' the glass so that I said:

"John – if thou still deservest that name of honour, thou cur – John, I beseech thee by St Patrick's Purgatory, examine thy soul. Thou must repent thy ways, thou must be reborn in the spirit if thou value my companionship! Pull thyself together, thou wretch – – –!"

And at that instant the figure in the mirror stood erect with a proud toss of the head, just as any sober man would have expected. But in my drunken state I took my Jack i' the glass's abrupt straightening up for a sign of his desire for improvement and, much moved, I addressed him thus:

"Ah, my Lord of the Midden, at least thou dost acknowledge that things cannot go on in this manner. And right pleased I am, Sir, that thou seekest spiritual rebirth, for" – tears of heartfelt pity were coursing down my cheeks – "what would otherwise become of thee?"

And now the one I thus addressed was also shedding tears, which only served to strengthen my foolish belief that I had said something of the utmost significance. And so I called to the repentant sinner:

"Truly, Heaven has favoured thee, my fallen friend, that it hath caused thee to reveal thyself to me this day in all thy wretchedness. Awake now and do what thy innermost soul desireth; for – this I tell thee now – I will – from this day forth – no more – – no more – – – "

– I gasped and choked as a retching fit brought on by the over-indulgence in wine smothered my voice.

But then – Oh! the icy terror of it – I heard, as if through a long tube, my Jack i' the glass speaking in soft tones:

"… shall know neither rest nor repose till the coasts of Greenland, where the Northern Lights glow, shall be conquered, – till I have set my foot on Greenland and Greenland is subject to my power. He who holds the Green Land in fief, to him shall the Empire beyond the sea be given, to him shall be given the crown of England!" –

With that the voice fell silent.

I no longer know how, in my drunken state, I managed to get to my bed. Thoughts poured over me in a wild frenzy; there was no resisting them, but they poured over me and rushed on, without entering my mind, it seemed. I could feel them above me and yet I could not direct them.

From the mirror on the wall a ray shot down – that was what all these milling thoughts were at heart, shooting stars! – the ray struck me and continued along the track of the future, shining on all my descendants. A fountainhead is created for centuries to come! – – – My mind grasped a fragment of the message and my trembling hand committed it to my diary. Then I carried off the long line of kings – all of my blood and in some mysterious way hidden within me – to my sleep.

Today I know: should I become King of England – and what can hinder me from turning this miraculous revelation, incorporeal and yet plain to my senses, into reality? – should I become King of

44

England, then shall my sons and grandsons for generations to come sit upon the throne that I shall mount. Behold, I have my salvation! By the flag of Saint George, I see the way! I, John Dee.

The Feast of St. Paul 1549.
Thought long and hard about the way to the crown.

Grey and Boleyn are names on my family tree. There is kingly blood in me. Edward, the King, is wasting away. He will soon have coughed his last. Two women stand in line for the throne. Surely a sign from God! Mary? – in the hands of the Papists. The priests are no friends of mine. Moreover, Mary has the same maggot in her chest as her brother Edward – she coughs. Her hands are cold and damp. God forbid.

So, then, a bargain with God and fate: Elizabeth! Her star is in the ascendant, in spite of the machinations of the Antichrist.

What has been achieved thus far? We have met. Twice in Richmond. Once in London. In Richmond I picked a water-lily for her and ruined my shoes in the marsh.

In London ... I did fasten a ribbon for her that was hanging loose from her bodice and for thanks she slapped me across the face. That, I think, will suffice me for the moment.

Have sent a reliable messenger to Richmond. I must find a suitable opportunity to ...

Good news has come of Lady Elizabeth's disposition. She tires of being schoolmastered and seeks excitement. If only I knew where to find the Muscovite, Mascee!

Today was sent to me from Holland a map of Greenland, engraved by my friend and master cartographer, Gerardus Mercator.

The Feast of St. Dorothy.
Today Mascee suddenly appeared at my door. Asked me if there was anything I needed. Said he had

wondrous objects from Asia. – – Was mightily surprised to see him as it was not long since I had enquired after his whereabouts in vain. He swore his arrival had gone unnoticed. It is no light thing to have him in my house. I am risking my neck. The eyes of Bishop Bonner are everywhere.

He showed me two small ivory spheres, the one red and the other white, each formed of two halves screwed tight together. They are nothing special. I bought them off him, in part out of impatience, in part to keep him well-disposed towards me. And he promised to serve me well. I asked him for a powerful potion, such as would bring forth love – and good fortune for him that blessed the potion. He said he knew not how to prepare such a potion, but would procure one. – That is all one to me. He that would make haste toward his goal, needs take the shortest route. – As for the ivory spheres, a mood did suddenly take me to scratch strange signs upon them and then, of a sudden, I was taken with fear of them and threw them out of the window!!

For the love potion Mascee, the Tutor to him that doth call himself "Czar", asked me for hair, blood, spittle and – – it doth offend me, but he has that which he requires. Loathesome; but wholesome if it bring me nearer my goal.

The Feast of St. Gertrude 1549.
It is remarkable: today my mind is filled with amorous thoughts of Lady Elizabeth. That is something new. Until now I have been completely indifferent to her charms. – I only obey the prophecy from the mirror. I am sure I have not been deceived. The reality of those moments is still branded on my soul as if it were yesterday.

But today all my thoughts flutter around one flame, around – – by St. George, I will write it down – – around my bride! My Elizabeth!

What does she know of me? Nothing, most likely. Perhaps that I got my feet wet when I went fishing for water lilies; perhaps that she slapped my face.

Certainly nothing more.

And what do I know of the Lady Elizabeth?

She is a strange child. Both hard and soft. Upright and plain-spoken, but reserved and withdrawn. I mind how she used to treat her maids and the girls she played with – sometimes my hand itched to thrash her, as if she were a boy in woman's clothing.

But I like the bold, vigorous look in her eye. She is, I think, no respecter of persons, and will tread on the priests' corns whenever she can.

But she can wheedle like a cat when she has a mind to. Why else did I go crawling through the marsh?

And that slap on my face was more than a gentle pat, but the hand that delivered it was as velvety as a cat's paw.

In summa, as the logicians say: regal!

My quarry is a noble beast; even now, my blood runs hot at the very thought.

Mascee has disappeared once more.

Today I heard from one who is beholden to me how the Princess rode out on the Feast of St. Gertrude. It was the day on which I was visited by such strange thoughts. The Princess lost her way riding in the Forest of Uxbridge and Master Mascee directed the company to Mother Bridget's hut on the moor.

Elizabeth has drunk the love potion! The Lord's blessing be upon the potion.

Lady Ellinor Huntingdon would thwart the marriage, I guess; in her overweening pride she tried to dash the potion from the Princess' hand, but the attempt failed.

I hate this arrogant, cold-hearted Ellinor.

I am burning with desire to go straight to Richmond. As soon as a certain piece of business is completed, as soon as I am free of certain obligations, I will find an excuse for my presence at Richmond.

Then shall we meet again, Elizabeth!

The Feast of the Sorrows of the Virgin.
I am plagued with anxieties. I am much concerned at
the most recent affairs of the Ravenheads.

The Feast of St. Quirinus.

I cannot understand why the Lord Governor of
Wales is so half-hearted. Why is nothing done to
protect the Ravenheads, to remove them from
danger, if necessary?

Is it the end of the Protestant movement? Is the
Lord Protector betraying his faithful followers?

It may be I have done a foolish thing. It is never
wise to make common cause with the mob.
However you try to extricate yourself, some mud
always will stick.

And yet on reflection I find I should not blame
myself. My information from the camp of the
Reformers is reliable: there is no going back for
them either. The Lord Protector ... (here the page is
torn) ... for the conquest of Greenland. If this bold
venture to the northern lands should become necessary, what other men could I gather together in haste
than desperate mariners and soldiers of fortune?!

I shall obey my star! There is no point in idle
thoughts.

Maundy Thursday.
A curse on my fears! They trouble me more and
more every day. Truly, if a man could be completely
freed from his fears, even from those that lie hidden
within him, I think he might work miracles. I think
even the Powers of Darkness would be compelled to
obey him. – – – Still no news of Mascee. No news
from London.

My last contributions to Bartlett Greene's war-
chest – oh, that I had never heard that name! – were
too great a drain on my resources. I can do nothing
unless gold arrives from London.

Today I read a report of the most insolent attack on
a Papist lair that the said Greene ever carried out. The

Devil may have made him proof against blade or bullet, but his followers are not! A most ill-considered enterprise.

Should Greene be victorious the consumptive Mary will never reign. Elizabeth! Then shall my star rise!

Good Friday.
Has that cur in the glass awoken once more? Doth thou stare at me again, thou drunken wretch? What has made thee drunk, hell-hound?

Burgundy wine?

No, confess it, thou craven heart, thou art drunk with fear.

Lord! Lord! My premonitions! The Ravenheads are doomed. They are surrounded.

The Governor, his Lordship ... I spit in his face ––
–

Pull thyself together, John. I will lead the Ravenheads myself! The Ravenheads, my children. For England and St. George!

Be fearless, John, fearless!

Fearless!

Easter Sunday 1549.
What is to be done? – – –

This evening, as I sat over Mercator's maps, the door to my chamber opened as if of its own accord and an unknown man entered. He bore no device, no seal, no weapon. He came up to me and said:

"John Dee, it is time to leave this place. Things go badly for thee. Thy way is beset with enemies, thy goal is ever more distant. There is only one course open to thee – cross the sea."

Without a farewell the man left as I sat there paralysed.

At last I leapt up, rushed along passageways, down stairs: there was no sign of my visitor. I asked the gate-keeper, "Fellow, who didst thou let in at such a late hour?"

"No-one that I know of," was the gate-keeper's reply.

Wordlessly I returned to my room, and since then I have been sitting here, thinking, thinking ...

The Monday after the Feast of the Resurrection of Our Lord.

I cannot make up my mind to flee. – Across the sea? That would mean to leave England behind, to abandon my hopes, my plans and – I must say it aloud – my Elizabeth!

The warning was true. I hear the Ravenheads have been defeated. The Catholics will say that the desecration of St. Dunstan's grave has brought his curse down upon them! Will it strike me, too?

What of it? Courage, John! Who will dare to accuse me of conspiring with outlaws? Me, Doctor John Dee, Lord of the Manor of Gladhill?

I confess it was rash, foolish even. But be fearless, John! I have never left my study where I devote myself to the ancients, I am a respected nobleman and scholar.

I cannot rid myself of my doubts. The Angel of Fear has many weapons at his disposal. Would it not be better to leave the country for a while? But – curses on Bartlett Greene – these latest subsidies have left me completely without means. And yet, I could ask Guilford, he would lend me money.

Agreed! Tomorrow morning I will – – –

By the Lord and all the Saints, what is that outside? Who is – what is that clash of weapons outside the door? Is that not the voice of Captain Perkins giving orders, Captain Perkins of the Bloody Bishop's police?

I breathe deeply and force myself to continue writing until the last moment. Hammers are beating against the oaken door. Calm, my friend, it will not give way that easily and I must finish my writing.

There follows a note in the hand of my cousin, John Roger, to the effect that our ancestor, John Dee, was arrested by Captain Perkins, as can be seen from the letter appended below:

Original of a letter from John Dee's papers, a report from Captain Perkins to His Lordship Bishop Bonner in London.

Date illegible.

"Report to Yr. Lordship that we have taken John Dee in his house at Deestone. We surprised him studying geographical maps. His quill was in the inkwell, but we could find no written matter. I ordered that the house should be searched most thoroughly.

He was taken to London that same night.

I locked the prisoner in no. 37 as that is the strongest, most secure cell in the Tower. That will, I believe, cut our captive off from his many influential connections, but if I am compelled to report his capture, I will give his cell number as 73 – the power of some of his friends is too great. Also the goalers cannot always be relied upon since some are greedy for gold, with which the heretics are well supplied.

John Dee's connection with the bloody Ravenheads is as good as proven; the rack will do the rest.

Yr. Lordship's obedient servant

Guy Perkins, Captain.

St. Patrick's Purgatory

The jangling of the doorbell interrupts my reading of John Dee's papers. I open the door. A street urchin hands me a letter from Lipotin.

I dislike being disturbed when I am working and that made me commit what is almost a capital crime in our country: in my irritation I forgot to give the lad a tip. How can I make good my omission? Lipotin only occasionally sends me letters by messenger, but each time it is a different youth. Lipotin must have a wide acquaintance among the waifs and strays of the city. But to his note. Lipotin writes:

1st May. The Feast of St. Socius.

Michael Arangelovich is grateful for the doctor. He feels some relief.

A propos, I forgot to mention that he says you must place the silver box as precisely as possible along the line of the meridian and in such a way that the stylised Chinese wave pattern engraved along the lid runs parallel to the meridian.

What the point of all that is, I really cannot say; as he gave me the message for you, Michael Arangelovich started to cough blood once again and I could ask him no further details.

Clearly the silver box needs to be parallel to the meridian and feels most comfortable in that position. Humour it, if you can! If that sounds mad, then you must excuse me. Someone like myself, who has spent his whole life looking after old – I'm even tempted to write: elderly – things, knows something of their habits, and gets a feeling for the hidden needs and little idiosyncrasies of these pernickety objects. I like to make allowances for them!

I think I can hear you object that you would never find such considerate behaviour in Russia, neither today nor in the past. It is true that of course one maltreats people of no spiritual worth; but beautiful old objects are sensitive.

By the way, as I'm sure you know, the Chinese wave pattern on the Tula-ware box is the old Taoist symbol of infinity, in certain cases of eternity, even. That was just an idle thought that crossed my mind.

Your devoted servant,

Lipotin.

I threw Lipotin's letter into the waste-paper basket. – –
Hmm. This "present" from the dying Baron Stroganoff is beginning to be a nuisance. I'll have to dig out my compass and go to the trouble of determining the line of the meridian. I knew it! My desk is at an angle to

the line. Respectable antique that it is, my desk has never been so presumptuous as to claim that it only feels comfortable standing along the line of the meridian.

How arrogant is everything that comes from the East. However, there it is, I have placed the Tula box along the meridian. So much for those who would claim that man is master of his fate! And what is the result of my compliance? Everything on my desk, the desk itself, indeed, the whole room with its familiar order – it all now feels lopsided. It seems that it is no longer I but this charming meridian that is in control – or the Tula-ware box. Everything is lopsided in relation to this blasted *objet d'art* from Asia! I sit lopsidedly at my lopsided desk and what do I see out of the window? The whole district has become "lopsided".

It can't go on like this; lack of order disturbs me. Either the box must disappear from my desk or – – – for goodness sake, I can't rearrange my whole room just to bring it into line with this thing and its meridian!

I sit here staring at the silver sprite from Tula, and I sigh. By St. Patrick's Purgatory, there is nothing for it; the box is "right", it has "orientation", whilst my desk, my room, my whole existence is haphazard, completely without any meaningful arrangement – and I had no idea until today! – – – But why do I torment myself like this?

I am becoming obsessed by the notion that I must immediately "reorientate" my whole flat around my desk. To escape it I quickly grasp the first of John Roger's papers that comes to hand.

It is a set of notes and excerpts in his angular handwriting, entitled:

"St. Patrick's Purgatory."

What on earth is going on inside me that I should have used that oath – which I have never heard before – only a few minutes ago? It appeared on my lips without my having the slightest idea where it came from! But wait! A thought has just struck me; it was ... it is ... I flick

53

furiously back through the manuscript on my desk: it's there in John Dee's diary, "John, I beseech thee by St. Patrick's Purgatory, examine thy soul. Thou must repent thy ways, thou must be reborn in the spirit if thou value my companionship" – that was what John Dee said to his mirror image, "by St. Patrick's Purgatory, examine thy soul!"

Strange. More than strange. Am I then John Dee's mirror image? Or my own, even, gazing back at myself, neglected, grimy, befuddled with drink? Is one inebriated if – if one's house is not – is not aligned to the meridian? I must be dreaming in broad daylight! The musty odour from John Roger's bundle of papers must have befuddled my senses.

What is this St. Patrick's Purgatory, then? I pick out a paper at random and – a shiver runs down my spine – in my hand I have the explanation. My cousin, John Roger, had copied out an old legend:

> Before he set out on a journey from Scotland to Ireland the holy Bishop Patrick climbed a mountain to fast and to pray. He saw the land around and he saw that it was full of snakes and like poisonous creatures. And he raised his staff and commanded the vipers and creeping things that they withdraw, and they did so. Then came some men to mock him, and he preached to them and his words fell upon deaf ears. So St. Patrick called upon God for a sign that the men might fear Him. And he struck the rock on which he stood with his staff and the rock split apart and there appeared a chasm from which issued smoke and flames. And the chasm reached even unto the depths of Hell and they could hear the cursing of the damned souls rising up from the chasm. And those who saw this were struck with terror and knew that St. Patrick had revealed to them the fires of Hell.
>
> And St. Patrick spake: whosoever shall descend into the chasm shall be freed from any other penance and he whose soul is of true gold shall come forth

purified the next morning. And many went down into the Chasm but few returned. For the fiery furnace consumes or purifies each according to the nature of his soul.

And that is St. Patrick's Purgatory in which any man may test the temper of his soul to see if he will pass through the Devil's Baptism in the life to come.

To this day it is said among the common people that the chasm is still open. But it is invisible except for one who is the son of a witch or a whore and born on the First of May. And if the black disc of the new moon should stand direct above the chasm, then the curses of the damned will rise up to it from the depths of the earth like the prayers of the Black Mass and fall upon the earth beneath in drops; and wherever it touches the soil there appear black cats that shall be witches' familiars.

Meridian – wave pattern – a Chinese symbol for eternity – my lopsided room – St. Patrick's Purgatory – a warning from my ancestor, John Dee, to his Jack i' the mirror if he valued his future friendship – "And many went down into the Chasm but few returned!" – black cats, witches' familiars: my mind is awash with a meaningless jumble of images. And yet: now and then I glimpse some design, some purpose in them, suddenly shooting out in an almost painful shaft of light, like a ray of sunshine through racing clouds. But when I try to hold on to it, my mind goes numb and I have to let it go. – –

All right, yes, yes, I give in. Tomorrow I will "align my room to the meridian" if that is what I must do to get some peace.

I'll have to waste the whole day shifting furniture – blast that Tula-ware box!

I have been rummaging around in the papers again. On the desk in front of me is a slim volume bound in bilious green morocco. The binding dates from the late seventeenth century at the earliest and the manuscript text must be by John Dee himself – the flow and shape of the letters corresponds to the diary. The tome shows signs of having been burnt, parts of the text have been destroyed.

There is an inscription in tiny letters on the fly leaf, and in a strange hand! It reads:

> "To be burned if the eye of Black Isaïs should appear in the waning moon. If thou ever hope to be saved: burn it!"

Some later, unknown (!) owner of the book must have taken the warning to heart. Perhaps he sensed "Black Isaïs" was observing him from the waning moon and threw the book into the fire to be rid of it. That would explain the burnt pages. But who was he who felt it come alive in his hands? And who can have recovered it from the fire before it dissolved into ashes?

There is nothing to tell me that.

What is certain is that the warning is not in John Dee's own hand. One of his descendants must have inserted it after some terrifying experience.

I append such portions of the morocco–bound volume as are still legible:

Notebook of John Dee, dated 1553, that is, 4 years after the "Diary".

The Silver Shoe of Bartlett Greene

These notes have been written down by me, Master John Dee – vain, bungling fool that I was – after many days of torment, to be a memorial and a glass wherein I may look on my soul. And may it serve as a warning to those of my blood who may come after me. They shall wear the promised crown, of that I am more certain today than ever before. But the crown will grind them into the dust – just as I have been cast down to the ground – if they let their folly and their pride blind them to the Enemy that every

56

hour lurks in wait, that he might encompass our destruction.

> The higher the Crown,
> The farther the Devil can pull us
> down.

The following is an account of what God allowed to happen to me on the day after Easter Monday, in the year 1549:

On the evening of the day when my uncertainty and torment about my future fate had reached its peak, Captain Perkins and the armed guards of the Bloody Bishop – as people justly call that monster in human form that sits in his lair in London under the name of Bishop Bonner – forced their way into my house and arrested me in the name of the King: in the name of that consumptive child, Edward! My mocking laughter only served further to enrage the guards and it was with difficulty that I escaped physical violence.

I had managed to gather up the papers to which I had just committed all my doubts before the soldiers came crashing through the door, and I concealed them in a safe place in the wall where, fortunately, anything that might betray me was already hidden. It was fortunate, too, that I had long ago thrown Mascee's ivory spheres out of the window, for I deduced from one of Captain Perkins' clumsy questions that they were particularly interested in those spheres. There must be something about those "wondrous objects from Asia"; the lesson to be drawn from that is not to trust the Muscovite at all.

The escort of brutish soldiers rode hard through the damp night and the early morning saw us in Warwick already. But there is no point describing the nights spent in the saddle and the days in guard-rooms and towers until we finally reached London and Captain Perkins thrust me into a cell below the ground. From all these and other measures that were taken I could tell that secrecy was paramount and that they went constantly in fear of an attempt to free me by force – though I cannot think who would have undertaken it.

It was the Captain himself who did me the honour of pushing me down the steps of my cell. When the last bolt had thundered shut I found myself in silent, pitch-black darkness; my senses were dazed and my cautious foot slipped on damp, decaying matter.

I would never have imagined how complete a sense of desolation can overtake one after only a few minutes in such a dungeon. The pounding of blood in my ears had previously gone unnoticed; now it overwhelmed me like the crashing of breakers on a deserted shore.

All at once I was startled to hear a fearless mocking voice reverberating round the cell; like a greeting from the depths of darkness, it seemed to come from an invisible wall opposite me:

"Welcome, Master Dee, welcome to the dark realm of the lower gods. That was a pretty trip you took down those steps, my Lord of Gladhill."

This scoffing welcome was followed by a peal of laughter; at the same time there was the rumble of an approaching storm outside, and straightway the eerie laughter was drowned by a deafening clap of thunder. Immediately the darkness of the cell was lit by a flash of lightning; the brief glimpse afforded by the sulphurous glare sent icy needles round my scalp and down my spine: I was not alone in the dungeon; a man was fastened to the massive blocks of the wall opposite the door through which I had been pushed; heavy shackles kept his arms and legs spread wide apart, like some human St. Andrew's cross.

Was he really there? I had seen him in the glare of the lightning – the length of a heartbeat and then he was swallowed up by the blackness again. Had I

58

imagined it? Behind my eyelid, burnt onto the retina, I could see the fearful image, as if it had no existence outside myself, as if it had been produced from within my brain, as if it emanated from the depths of my soul and had no corporeal reality. How could a sentient being be stretched out in the awful torture of that cross and still talk calmly, mockingly, and still let his scornful laughter ring out?

Again the lightning flickered; the flashes followed in such quick succession that the dungeon was lit by quivering waves of pallid light. By Our Saviour! there was a man hanging there, there was no doubt of it: a giant of a man, with flowing locks of ginger hair almost concealing his face; above the tangled beard the thin-lipped mouth hung half open, as if he were about to let out another roar of laughter. His features showed no sign of suffering in spite of the excruciating pain the heavy iron rings, into which his wrists and ankles had been forced, must have caused. At the sight of him I could only stammer a few words, "Who are you, hanging on the wall?" when a thunderclap drowned the rest. "You should have recognised me in the dark, my dear Doctor!" came the mocking reply. "It is said that one who has lent money can recognise his debtor from the smell alone." A dart of icy terror constricted my heart. "Does that mean you are ...?"

"Yes: Bartlett Greene, chief raven of the Ravenheads, Protector of the Faithless at Brederock, victor over St. Dunstan's empty boast and now mine host here at the Sign of the Iron Ring, ready to receive a benighted traveller such as your Honour, O mighty Patron of the Reformers."

The mocking speech ended with a wild burst of laughter which, miraculous though it seemed, made his whole, crucified body shake without appearing to feel the slightest pain.

"Then I am lost," I muttered, and collapsed onto the worm-eaten wooden stool that I now noticed.

The storm reached its thunderous peak. Even if I had wanted to converse with him, the raging elements would have made question and answer inaudible; as it was, I did not feel much like speaking. My death seemed inevitable and in my imagination I saw that it would not be an easy death. Clearly it was public knowledge that I was the wire-puller behind the Ravenheads. I was only too aware of the nature of the measures the Bloody Bishop thought essential "to bring the fallen sinner to a state of penitence, that he might glimpse paradise from afar."

Fear clawed at my throat. It was not fear of death, of a clean death befitting a gentleman; the fear that unmanned me and left my senses in turmoil was the fear of the slow approach of the inevitable torture, the fear of the fumbling fingers of the executioner as he drew out my lingering death. It is fear of the pain that precedes death that traps us in the net of earthly life; were it not for that pain, man would live free of fear.

The storm raged, but I heard it not. From time to time a shout or a rumble of laughter would reach me from the blackness of the wall opposite; I heeded neither. Terror and reckless plans for my impossible escape were all my mind had room for.

Not for one moment did it occur to me to pray.

After the storm had abated – when, I do not know, it may have been hours later – my thoughts, too, became calmer, more collected, more cunning. The first thing I recognised as certain, was that I was in Bartlett Greene's power, assuming he had not already confessed and betrayed me. My fate depended on his silence alone.

I had just come to the decision that I should cautiously try to work on Bartlett Greene to get him to see that he was doomed and therefore had nothing more to lose in keeping silent about my part in the affair, when I was startled by something so unbelievable and terrifying that I forgot all my plans and artifices, even all my hopes: Bartlett Greene had set his huge body swaying from the iron chains, as if he were dancing. As the first light of a May morning filtered into the cell, the crucified outlaw swung higher and higher, and with a lithe gracefulness, as if he were enjoying the motion of a hammock slung between two silver birches. And all the while his joints and sinews crunched and cracked as if he were stretched on the rack.

And then Bartlett Greene began to sing! At first his voice was almost melodious, but it soon took on the screech of the bagpipes as he ground out a hoarse hymn to earthy pleasures:

Heave ho! Heave ho!
The blossom hangs on the bough
After the moult of May.
Heave ho!
Miaow, Tom Kitten, miaow
Sing your roundelay.
Heave ho!

Heave ho! Heave ho!
Tom shall go seeking his Kitty
After the moult of May.
Heave ho!
Come follow me, my pretty,
On the green grass we will play.
Heave ho!

Heave ho! Heave ho!
All night Tom plays on his fiddle
After the moult of May.
Heave ho!
While Kitty sings hey diddle diddle
To the moon and Black Isaye.
Heave ho!

I cannot describe the fit of horror that shook me as I listened to the wild chanting of the leader of the

Ravenheads; I thought the torture had suddenly driven him mad. Even today, as I write it down, my blood runs cold.

Then there was a rattle of the bolts of the iron-clad door and a warder came in with two underlings. They released the crucified Greene from the wall and let him tumble to the ground like a toad caught by a harvester's scythe. "That's another six hours over Mister Greene," one of the turnkeys mocked. "I reckon you'll soon have outswung any other prisoner on that wall. If you're lucky you might be allowed another go at it; and if Satan turns the pain to pleasure, then there'll be a fiery chariot calling for you like Elijah; but it won't take you up to heaven, oh no, I reckon it'll head straight for St. Patrick's Purgatory and that'll be the last we'll see of you."

Bartlett Greene gave a satisfied grunt and dragged his stretched limbs to a heap of straw. Then he turned his blasphemous fury on the turnkey:

"Verily, I say unto thee, David, thou holy turd of a goaler, today thou wouldst be with me in paradise – if I had a mind to go there. But I would not raise thy hopes, thou'll end up in a different place than thou thinkst, papistical scum. Or shall I spit on thy forehead and baptise thee in the name of the Lord, my son?"

I saw the rough soldiers cross themselves in fear. The goaler drew back in superstitous awe and made with his hand the sign the Irish use to ward off the evil eye. He screamed at Greene:

"Look not at me with thy wall-eye, thou first-born of hell! St. David of Wales, that has watched over me ever since I sucked at my mother's breast, will shield me against thy curses."

Then he and his henchmen stamped out of the cell, followed by the mocking echo of Bartlett Greene's laughter. They left a loaf of bread and a pitcher of water.

For a while all was quiet.

As the light grew stronger I could see the features of my fellow prisoner more clearly. His right eye was a pale, milky-white disc which seemed to follow you with a fixed glare of infinite spite. It was the eye of a dead man who had seen some horrible sight as he died. The white eye was blind.

This is the first of a number of pages that have been damaged by fire. The text becomes more and more deficient, but the general sense is clear.

"Water? That's malmsey, that is," roared Greene, clamped the pitcher between his wrists – his hands hung down useless – and took such a great swig that I feared my portion, too, would run down his throat, for I was was parched. "To my twisted body it is like wine – glug – I never feel any pain – glug – nor fear! Fear and pain are twin weaknesses. I will tell you something, Master Dee, that none of your scholars know, for all their book-learning – glug – I will be truly free when I have cast off this mortal flesh – glug – I am proof against what they call death until I have completed my thirty-third year. – glug – On the first of May, when the witches dedicate their cats to the Black Mother, my time will be over. O that my mother had kept me one month longer in her belly, my stench would be none the worse for it and I would have time to show the Bloody Bishop, that novice, that bungler, how a real master carries out torture. You will find the Bishop – – –" (scorch marks)

– – – Greene tapped me with his finger below the neck – my jerkin had been torn by the guards and my chest was naked; he touched my collar bone and said, "That is the mystical bone I am talking about. It is called the *corvine appendix* – the Raven's tail. It contains the mystical salt of life that does not decay in the earth. From this comes the Jews' talk of the resurrection of the body at the last judgment – – – but they misunderstand; – – – we who are initiated into the secret of the new moon – glug – rose again long ago. And what is the sign by which I know this, Doctor Dee? In spite of your Latin and all your learning, you seem not to have made much progress in the Art. I will tell you, then: because the bone shines with a light that the others cannot see – – –" (scorch marks)

– – – understand." These words from the outlaw made my scalp crawl with fear and I had great difficulty in keeping my voice steady as I asked, "So for my whole life I have borne a sign which has not been revealed to me?" To which Bartlett Greene replied with great earnestness, "Yes, Master, you are marked with the sign of the Living Lord, the High One, the Invisible One, The Keeper of the Chain, which none ever enter because none ever leave it who are born to it; one from outside would never find the entrance before the end of the days of the blood. – Be of good cheer, Master Dee, even though you may be of the other stone and part of the contrary circle, yet I will never betray you to the vermin that is beneath us both. We are raised above the common herd, that sees but the outer show and will be lukewarm for ever and ever! – – –" (scorch marks)

– – – confess that I heard these words with an inner sigh of relief, even if secretly I began to feel ashamed of my fear of this simple giant, who bore his torture with such a light heart; a most fearful martyrdom awaited him as a reward for the silence he had promised me.

" – – – was a priest", continued Bartlett Greene, "and my mother a lady of rank. Lady Tenderloin she was called. I still do not know where she came from, nor where she went. A fine figure of a woman she must have been; she was called Mary – until my father made a whore of her." At this Greene let out his strange, unfeeling laugh, paused and then went on, "My father was the most fanatical, cruel, and at the same time most cowardly priest I ever met. He told me he had taken me in out of pity, so that I might do penance for the sins of my unknown father – he was unaware that I had secretly discovered that he was my father. – – –

"– – – ordered me to do penance and forced me to stand on the stone flags in the church in my nightshirt for hours on end, praying all the while that the sins of my "father" might be forgiven. And when I fainted with exhaustion and lack of sleep he took his whip and beat me till the blood ran. My heart was filled with black hatred of Him who hung there on the cross above the altar. And then, I know not how it came about, I found that the litany I was forced to repeat had turned itself round in my brain and came out of my mouth the wrong way round – I was saying the prayers backwards and it was balm to my soul. It was a long time before my father noticed, since I murmured the words to myself, but when he did he roared out in fury and terror, cursed my mother's name, crossed himself and ran to fetch the axe to strike me down. But I was quicker and I split his skull from scalp to chin; one eye fell out and stared up at me from the stone slabs. And I knew that my widdershins prayers had gone down to the centre of Mother Earth, instead of rising to heaven, as the Jews claim the singsong whinings of their holy men do. – – –

"I have forgotten to tell you, Brother Dee, that one night my right eye was blinded by a great light that suddenly appeared to me – it could also be that it was struck from behind by a whip lash from my father, I cannot tell. Perhaps when I split his skull it was the fulfilment of the law that says "An eye for an eye and a tooth for a tooth". – Yes, my friend, I can truly say that this wall-eye, that fills the rabble with fear, is the fruit of long nights of prayer.

"– – – fourteenth year when I left my father lying on the altar with a double head and fled by devious routes to Scotland. There I was bound apprentice to a butcher, for I thought I would find it easy to strike the bulls and calves with the cleaver, I who had hit my father clean through his tonsure; but it was not to be, for, whenever I raised the cleaver, the scene in the darkened church rose before my inner eye and I was loath to desecrate the fair memory with the murder of an innocent animal. So I left and for many months wandered around the Highland where I played wailing pibrochs to the crofters and villagers on a set of bagpipes I had stolen. Whenever they heard my music, it made their blood run cold, though they could not say why. But I knew full well that the tunes followed the text of the litany which I had been compelled to repeat before the altar; they still sounded within me, still the wrong way round, still back to front. And I played the goatskin pipes at night when I strode over the darkened moors alone. Especially when the moon was full I felt a longing to hear the music of the backwards prayers, and it was as if each note ran down my spine to my feet as they walked, and from there into the womb of the earth. And once, at midnight – the first of May, the night of the Druids' feast, and the moon was on the wane – an invisible hand rose from the ground and held me fast by the foot, that I could not move forward nor back. Straightway I stopped my piping and stood as if rooted to the spot. An icy blast – from a chasm in the earth before me, so it seemed – blew over me and froze me from head to toe; and as I also felt it on my neck I turned round and saw standing behind me One in the garb of a shepherd, with a crook in his hand that was forked at the top like the letter Y. He was followed by a herd of black sheep. But on my way there I had seen neither sheep nor shepherd, so that I thought I must have walked past him with my eyes closed and half asleep, for he was not like an apparition, as one might think, but of flesh and blood; so too were his sheep, as I could tell from the smell of damp wool their coats gave off – – – (scorch marks) – – – He pointed to my wall-eye and said, 'Because thou art called'. – – –" (scorch marks).

This must be a description of some deep esoteric mystery, for written in red ink by another hand at the top of the half-burnt page was:

If Thy Heart be faint, read not on! If Thou trust not in Thy Soul's strength, choose now: ignorance and peace, or Lust for knowledge and damnation!

There follow pages that are utterly ruined. The fragments of script that are still legible suggest that the shepherd revealed to Greene mysteries that seem to be connected with the cult of a dark goddess of antiquity and the magical influences of the moon; there appears to be reference to that terrible rite that is still known in Scotland today as the *Taghairm*. It further appears that at the time of his imprisonment in the Tower Bartlett Greene was still a virgin, which is all the more remarkable as chastity is not a quality one normally associates with brigands. The text is too fragmentary to tell whether this was from deliberate choice or from an inborn aversion to women. From then on the text is relatively undamaged:

" – – – only understood the half – but at that time I was only a 'halfling' in such matters – of what the shepherd told me of the gift that Black Isaïs would give me, for how could it be that a tangible object should come from the incorporeal realm. When I asked him how I would recognise that the time had come, he said, 'Thou shalt hear the cock crow.' That made no sense to me – the cocks crow every morning in the village. Nor could I see that it should be a special boon not to know fear or pain on earth; it seemed of little account to me, that thought myself bold and fearless enough. But the fruit ripens on the bough, and when its season came I heard the cock-crow the shepherd talked of, but within me. Until that time I had not known that everything must first come to pass in the blood before it can take on corporeal shape. Then I received the gift from Isaïs – the 'Silver Shoe'. In the long years of waiting I was subject to strange visions and visitations: damp, invisible fingers touched me; I felt a bitter taste on my tongue, a burning sensation on my head – as if a hot iron was branding me with a tonsure – and stabbing, shooting pains on the palms of my hands and soles of my feet; I could hear a sound as of a cat crying in my ear. Strange characters, which I could not read, but which looked like those in Jewish manuscripts, appeared like a rash on my skin, but vanished as soon as the sun shone on them. Sometimes I was hot with desire for a woman, which then did seem strange to me, since I had ever felt disgust at the daughters of Eve and their lewd dealings with men. – – –

"Then, when I felt the cock-crow rise up my spine and, as had been foretold, a cool shower sprinkled my head in baptism, although there was no cloud to be seen in the sky, I went on the first of May, the night of the druid's ceremonies, to and fro across the moor; I sought not, but I found, of a sudden, a chasm opened up in the ground before me. – – – (scorch mark) – – – drawing the cart with the fifty cats, as the shepherd had ordained. I made a fire and carried out the rite of the cursing of the full moon – the horror of it sat deep in my heart and my blood was like icy needles coursing through my veins. Then I took out the first cat, impaled it on the spit and began the 'Taghairm' by slowly roasting it over the fire. Its dreadful screaming pierced my ears for many minutes – they seemed like days to me and time itself seemed to stretch until it was nigh unbearable. How could I bear the same horror repeated fifty-fold? For I knew that I must not stop until the last cat was roasted and I knew that I must not let the screaming be interrupted. Soon those still in the cage lent their voices to the chorus and I felt the spirits of madness, that slumber in every man, begin to stir and tear my soul to shreds. However, they did not stay inside me, but poured out of my mouth like breath in the cold air and flew up to the moon and wreathed it in swirling mist. The shepherd had told me that the goal of the 'Taghairm' was to transfer, by the torment of the ceremony, the deep roots of fear and pain that were within me to the black cats that had been dedicated to the Goddess; of such roots of fear and pain there were fifty. And when the 'Taghairm' had drawn all fear and pain out of my blood and they had been absorbed in the moon-world whence they came, then would my true being appear and death and his minions would be overcome for ever. And when this came to pass, I would forget who I had been and lose all consciousness of myself. 'When its time is come', he had also said, 'then shall your body be devoured by flames, as the cats were, for the law of the earth must be satisfied, but what is that to you!' – – Two nights and one day the 'Taghairm' lasted, and I lost all feeling for time and all around, as far as my eye could see, the heather was black with the dreadful suffering. But during the first night my inner senses were made manifest. The first thing I noticed was that I could distinguish each individual voice in the cats' screeching chorus of terror. The voices plucked at my heart-strings till each one snapped. Then my ear awoke to the music of the abyss and since then I know the real meaning of 'hearing' – you can take your fists out of your ears, Brother Dee, I have finished with the cats. They are beyond pain now, perhaps they're in heaven playing cat and mouse with the souls of fat priests.

"The full moon was high in the sky and the fire was extinguished. My legs trembled so that I swayed like a reed in the wind. For a while it seemed as if the earth itself were staggering through the sky, for I saw the moon flutter hither and thither until it was drowned in blackness. Then I knew that I was blind in my other eye, since I could no longer see the woods or hills around me, only darkness and silence. I know not how, but of a sudden I could see with the wall-eye that had been blind before; and I saw a strange world where blue birds with bearded faces like men hovered in the air, stars with long spider's legs ran across the sky, stone trees walked about and fishes signalled to each other with their hands in dumb show. There were many other curious things, and all seemed strange to me and yet also familiar, as if I had been there from the very start of memory but had just forgotten it. And 'before' and 'after' had a different sense for me, as if time had slipped sideways – – – (scorch marks) – – – the distance a black pall of smoke rose from the earth and spread out as flat as a board, widening at one end until it stretched like a dark triangle pointing down out of the sky; then it burst and a fiery red gap split it from top to bottom and within was an enormous spindle whirling round – – – (scorch marks) – – – saw the dreadful figure of the Black Mother, Isaïs, plucking human flesh from the distaff to spin it with her thousand hands – – – blood dribbling down from the gap – – – some drops splashed up from the ground, sprinkling my body, like one that has the red plague, which must have been the mysterious baptism of the blood – – – (scorch mark) – – – the Great Mother called and woke her daughter, that had slept within me like a seed-grain, by which I came to Life Eternal, ever conjoined with her in dual being. – Even before that time I had never been subject to the lusts of the flesh, but since then I was proof against them for all time, for how could a man be gripped by the Curse who had found his own womanly nature within himself? – Then, when I could once more see with my human eye, a hand appeared from the chasm in the moor bearing something that gleamed dully like silver. I could not grasp it with my mortal fingers, but Isaïs' daughter within me stretched out a cat's paw and gave me the shoe – the 'Silver Shoe' which takes away all fear from him that wears – – – (scorch marks) – – – joined a troupe of strolling players as a tightrope walker and animal tamer; the tigers, leopards and panthers hissed and spat and drew back from me in terror when I turnd my wall-eye on them, and I found I could walk on the high wire, although I had never been taught to. Since I had been wearing the Silver Shoe, all fear had left me and my 'bride' within me drew all the heaviness from my body so that giddiness and falling were impossible. – I see by your face, Brother Dee, that you are asking yourself, 'With all these gifts, why did Bartlett Greene remain an outlaw and a mountebank?' I will tell you: the baptism of fire and the 'Taghairm' released my strength that I might become Captain of the Ravenheads that go unseen and that I might pipe a pibroch to the Papists from over the water that their ears would ring with it for centuries to come. Let them draw up their cannon and fire – boom! – they will not harm me. – Do you doubt that I wear the Silver Shoe, learned Master Dee? See here, o you of little faith" – and Bartlett Greene placed his right foot against the heel of his left shoe, in order to push it off then suddenly paused, drew his nostrils open like some beast of prey, sniffed the air and bared his sharp teeth. I heard his mocking voice say, "Can you smell it, Brother Dee? The panther comes!" – I held my breath and it seemed that there was indeed a stench of panther in the air. Straightway I heard a footstep outside the cell door and a moment later the heavy iron bolts creaked open.

Here the account of my ancestor, John Dee, broke off and I abandoned myself to brooding thoughts.

A stench of panther!

I have read somewhere that old things can be charged with a spell, a charm or a curse, which is passed on to anyone who brings such stuff into his house and occupies himself with it. You never know what you are letting yourself in for when you whistle to a stray poodle that happens to cross your path in the twilight. You feel sorry for it and bring it into the warm and before you know where you are, the devil is eyeing you from under the black, curly coat.

Is the same happening to me, the descendant of John Dee, as happened to Doctor Faust? Has John Roger's legacy brought me within the ambit of an old enchantment. Have I awakened nameless powers that are lodged in these musty papers like beetle larvae in wood?

I am going to interrupt my work on John Dee's morocco-bound notebook to examine what is happening to me. I must admit that I do so almost unwillingly. I am in the grip of a strange curiosity, a compulsion to continue reading my ancestor's account of his experiences in prison. It is as if I were reading a novel: I am eager to read on and find out what Bloody Bishop Bonner did to his heretics and what Bartlett Greene meant when he shouted, "The panther comes!"

And yet for days I have had the feeling that in everything that concerns my cousin's legacy I am – to put it bluntly – obeying a command. I am physically aware of my decision not to impose an order of my own on the strange life story of my English ancestor, right down to the tips of my fingers. As the Janus-head or, if you insist, "Baphomet" commanded me in my dream: I read and write whilst "he guides". I hardly dare ask myself whether what happened a few moments ago is part of the "guidance".

Since I started on the task of reconstructing John Dee's conversation with Bartlett Greene scarcely an hour has passed. And yet I cannot say for sure whether certain sense impressions registered real physical manifestations or whether they were hallucinations, like a shadow event passing through my semi-consciousness. Above all, I wonder at the fact that my room suddenly smelled of panther, or rather, my nostrils were filled with the stench of beasts of prey and with my mind's eye I saw the rows of cages behind the circus tent with the big cats pacing restlessly up and down.

I started as I heard a hurried knock at the study door.

My response was gruff and unwelcoming – I think I have already mentioned that I hate being disturbed whilst I am working – but the words were hardly out of my mouth before the door was thrust wide open. My housekeeper, whom I have trained in my little ways, stood there timidly, looking horrified, her face a silent plea for forgiveness; but immediately a figure swept imperiously past her, a tall, slender lady in a dark, shimmering dress.

How is it that I come to describe the 'entrance' of the lady in such an excessive way, even though she did give the impression of a certain imperious *insouciance*, of the assurance of one accustomed to giving orders. Written there on the paper, the phrases sound as if they come from the pen of a romantic lady novelist, but they are a fairly accurate description of the immediate impression this unknown lady made on me. A lady of the *haut monde*, indubitably. Her beautiful, pale face seemed to be straining forward on her neck, searching for something. She walked – she glided rather – past me, coming to a halt by the side of my desk. Her hand, like that of a blind person who has learnt to 'see' with his fingertips, groped along the edge of the desk-top, as if looking for support. Finally it came to a rest, and the woman's whole body seemed to relax, supporting itself on the firmly clenched fist.

It was right next to the silver Tula-ware box.

Her inimitable, natural ease overcame the awkwardness, I might even say strangeness, of the situation with a smile and a few words of excuse, in which the Slav accent was unmistakable. She chatted a while and then posed a question which forced me to gather my confused thoughts:

".... In brief, I have come to ask a favour. Will you grant it me?"

When an exceptionally beautiful woman deigns to put her pride and grace behind such a request, there is only one possible answer for a gentleman:

"If it lies within my power, then with the greatest pleasure, madam."

I must have given some such answer, for she shot me a swift glance that was indescribably gentle and that seemed briefly to nestle up against me in passing, like a cat. And her next words vibrated with a slow, gentle, remarkably pleasant laugh:

"I thank you. Do not worry, my request is nothing out of the way. It is very simple. Its fulfilment is merely – a matter – of your – – willingness – " she hesitated.

I hurried to reassure her, "In that case, if you would just tell me – – –". She immediately understood the meaning of my drawn–out pause and said, "But my card has been lying on your desk for – " again the agreeable, tripping laugh.

Puzzled, I followed the direction of her hand – a slim though not small hand, soft and yet firm – and saw that there was indeed a card lying near the edge of my desk alongside Stroganoff's silver casket. I had no idea how it had came to be there. I picked it up.

Assja Shotokalungin

it said, in copperplate. Above the name was an odd–shaped princely crown. I know that in the Caucasus, to the south–east of the Black Sea, there are still Circassian tribal chiefs who, under Russian or Turkish sovereignty, have kept the title of Prince.

The severe, eastern Aryan cut of her features, which recalled both the Greek and the Persian ideal, was unmistakable.

I gave another brief bow to my visitor, who was now sitting stretched out in an armchair by my desk; from time to time she ran her fingers idly over the Tula box. I watched them closely, for I was suddenly struck by the awful thought that they might move the box out of line with the meridian. They did not.

"Your wish is my command, Princess."

Without warning she sat up straight in the chair, and again I was electrified by her bewitching, lambent eyes as she started to speak:

"I should tell you that Sergey Lipotin is an old acquaintance of mine. He catalogued my father's collections in Yekaterinodar. It was he who awoke in me the love of finely-worked old objects. I collect old, how should I put it – old artifacts from the country of my birth: embroidery, wrought iron and ... and, especially, weapons; above all a certain type of weapon that is, I may say, very highly valued in my country. Amongst other things I have ..." her soft, rippling voice, with its alien accentuation which violated the cadences of German in a marvellously musical way, lapped over me like waves until my blood began to respond with a scarcely perceptible beat. For the moment what she said was a matter of complete indifference to me, but I found her accent intoxicating and that, I think, is why today it seems to me that I must have dreamed much of what was done and said – and possibly even thought – between us. Abruptly, the Princess broke off her description of her tastes as a collector, and came to the point:

"It was Lipotin who suggested I come to see you. He told me that you have in your possession a ... a very fine, a very precious, indeed, a venerable object: a spear, or rather a very finely-worked spearhead. It is inlaid with silver and gold. I know exactly what it looks like; Lipotin gave me a complete description. Perhaps he even acted for you when you acquired it. No matter" – she waved away my astonished protestations – "no matter; I wish to procure this spearhead. Will you let me have it? That is my request."

The last words tumbled over her lips. She was sitting bent forward – "poised to spring" went through my mind. I was surprised, and permitted myself a momentary inward smile at the incomprehensible craving which makes collectors, as soon as they see, or even only scent, a desirable piece, crouch like a panther ready to pounce.

A panther! There is that word again! – John Dee did well when he dreamt up Bartlett Greene. His words stick in one's mind.

But to return to my Circassian princess: she was rocking back and forward on the edge of her chair, her beautiful features a register of shifting emotions: expectation, gratitude, concern and overpowering flattery.

I could scarcely conceal my real sense of disappointment at the answer I was forced to give:

"Dear Princess, you see an unhappy man before you. Such a trifling request! Such a unique opportunity to be of service to a lady, to an enchanting lady who has so generously put her trust in me! I can hardly bring myself to tell you but I'm afraid I do not possess the aforesaid weapon, nor have I ever seen it."

To my surprise, the Princess gave me a radiant smile; she leant towards me with an expression of patient indulgence, like a proud mother whose darling boy has just uttered a mindless fib, and whispered:

"Lipotin knows. I know. You are the fortunate owner of the spearhead, which I wish to acquire. I am sure you will ... sell it to me. I will be extremely grateful."

"I feel awful to have to tell you this, my dear Princess, but Lipotin is wrong. Lipotin has made a mistake. Somehow Lipotin seems to have confused me with someone else. That is – – "

With one willowy movement the Princess stood up. She came towards me. Her walk – – yes, her walk! Suddenly it comes back to me. It was silent, with a rocking, springy gait and an incredible, flowing grace – – – where was I?

The Princess replied:

"It is possible. Of course. Lipotin must have made a mistake. He was not the one who purchased it for you.

But that is irrelevant. You have promised to make a present of it to me."

I felt my scalp crawl with desperation, but pulled myself together, determined with every fibre of my body not to arouse this beautiful woman to anger. She stood there before me, her wonderful, gold-flecked eyes wide with expectation, her smile exerting a force I had never felt before; I could hardly restrain myself from taking her hand to cover it with kisses or tears of frustration, frustration that I could not grant her wish. I pulled myself clumsily up to my full height, looked her straight in the eye and gave my voice as deep an expression of honest regret as I could:

"For the last time, Princess, I repeat that the spear, or rather spearhead, that you seek is not in my possession. It is true that at various times in my life my little enthusiasms have led me to collect various objects, but at no time, never, have I collected weapons, parts of weapons or, indeed, any kind of metalwork at all – – –" I broke off with a guilty start and could not prevent a blush from spreading across my face: this magnificent woman was standing before me with a charming smile and not the least bit angry – and her right hand was stroking back and forth across the beautiful silver of Lipotin's Tula box, a piece of metalwork, if ever there was, and one that gave the rather obvious lie to my declaration. What explanation could I give? I hunted for words. The Princess waved away my embarrassed stammering:

"My dear sir, I believe you, I believe you with all my heart; there is no need for further explanation. I have no wish to pry into the secret of your little enthusiasms. I am sure Lipotin has made a mistake. I can make a mistake. Such things happen. But I do ask you one last time, in all humility, but in hope – perhaps a vain hope – that you will think again; the spearhead which Lipotin – – –"

I fell down on my knees before her. Looking back, it was somewhat over-dramatic, but at the time it seemed to be the only way of emphasizing my fury that my fervent impatience to serve her should be thwarted. I tried to gather my thoughts. I had just about managed to concoct a convincing little speech when, with a quick, gentle and – yes, I must write it: bewitching – smile, she slipped past me to the door, turned round and said:

"I see what a struggle it is. Believe me, my dear sir, I do understand; I feel for you. Think it over. You will come to the right decision! I will return another time and you shall grant me my wish. You shall give me the spearhead."

And with that the Princess disappeared.

Her presence has left the room around me filled with a subtle fragrance. It is a perfume I have not encountered before: sweet, evanescent, like exotic blooms, and yet with a trace of something stronger, something strangely exhilarating, something, I can't help it – something *animal*. That visit: I confess it has left me excited – confused – happy – apprehensive – chasing a will-o'-the-wisp – full of disquiet and ... fear.

I feel incapable of doing any more work today. I think I'll pop over to Werrengasse to see Lipotin.

There are two quick notes I must make of things that have just come back to me: when Princess Shotokalungin came into the room, the door was in deep shadow from the heavy curtain behind my desk that was already half drawn. Why do I now have the impression that for a second the Princess' eyes glowed in the darkness with a phosphorescent light, like an animal's eyes? I know that it wasn't like that! And then: the Princess was wearing a dress of black silk. I felt it must have had a silver underskirt, there were matt, metallic waves constantly rippling through the weave. As I picture it in my mind, my eye is suddenly drawn towards the Tula box on the desk in front of me. Black inlaid with silver – I think that is what the dress must have been like.

It was already quite late in the evening when I left my flat to visit Lipotin in his shop in Werrengasse. It was a wasted walk: Lipotin's shop was shut. Stuck to the drawn blinds I found a tiny piece of card with "Closed" written on it.

I did not turn round and go back home. Nearby there was an entrance which led into a dark courtyard; from there one could see the one room at the back of the shop which served Lipotin as his living, sleeping and cooking quarters. I went into the close and found the curtains of Lipotin's grimy window drawn, but my repeated knocking did bring a woman to the neighbouring door who asked what I wanted. She told me the Russian had gone away that very morning; she did not know when he expected to be back; he had mentioned that someone had died, some half-starved Russian Baron, and Lipotin was going to settle his affairs. It was obvious what had happened: Baron Stroganoff had smoked his last cigarette and Lipotin had to go away to clear up his will. How annoying! It was only now, standing there outside the darkened window, that I realised how urgently I needed to see Lipotin and talk to him about the Princess. I also wanted an explanation about the matter of the mysterious spearhead – and advice as to where I might find it. The most likely explanation still seems to me to be that Lipotin has either confused me with another client, or that he still has it himself but, in his habitual absentmindedness, just imagined he sold it to me. In either case it should be possible to obtain the spearhead, and I must admit that I am prepared to part with a considerable sum to be able to present it to Princess Shotokalungin. The events of today keep going round and round in my mind; there is something afoot which involves me, but I cannot work out what it is. Why is it that I keep thinking that Lipotin has not gone away at all, that I spoke to him in his shop and asked him about the spearhead, and that he told me something about the spearhead which I have completely forgotten? Or did I really go into the shop and discuss the whole matter with him, but have no recollection of it? It suddenly seems to me like something that might have happened to me a hundred – yes, a hundred years ago, if I had been alive then.

My way back home took me along the old ramparts with their splendid view across the fields and hills to the mountains. It was a pleasant evening, and the landscape stretched out below me was clear and distinct in the moonlight. It was so brightly lit that my eyes instinctively sought the moon, which must have been hidden behind the tops of some mighty chestnut trees. Immediately, between the tree trunks above the ramparts, the moon began to appear, almost a full moon, with a strange greenish tinge and a red halo. As I looked at the coagulating light, strange images of wounds dripping blood forced themselves into my mind and once more I was unsure: is this real or just an ancient memory? The moon cleared the rampart wall, and at that moment the slim silhouette of a woman passed across the shining disc. It was obviously someone out for an evening stroll and she was coming along the wall in my direction, for a little later I caught a glimpse of the figure as it seemed almost to glide between the tree trunks – yes, glide, that was the right word – and I was struck with the thought that it was the Princess in her silver-black dress coming towards me from the waning moon ...

Suddenly the figure disappeared and with it all my self-control. I ran back and forth along the rampart wall like a madman until I regained my senses, slapped my forehead and told myself I was behaving like a lunatic.

Feeling uneasy, I continued on my way home. As I walked, I hummed to myself, and words suggested themselves which, I don't know how or why, I tried to fit to a tangled melody in the rhythm of my footsteps:

> From out of the waning moon,
> From the silver black of the night,
> Look down on me,
> Look down on me
> Lady, bless me with Thy dark light,
> Come to me, Lady, o come to me soon
> ...

This meaningless doggerel pursued me all the way to my room and it was only with a great effort that I managed to clear my mind of the monotonous singsong. But now I feel it has some strange significance.

From out of the waning moon ...?

The words are offering themselves to me, I can feel it, they come up and rub themselves against my skin like – like black cats.

Much of what has happened to me of late has this sense of strange significance. Or is it all in my mind? It all began, so it seems to me, with my work on the papers of my cousin, John Roger.

What on earth has the waning moon – a tremor runs through me as I realise what put those last three words into my mouth: they appear in the warning written in another hand on the fly leaf of John Dee's notebook, the little tome bound in green morocco!

And yet I repeat: What on earth has a mysterious warning from some superstitious inhabitant of the seventeenth century about Scottish satanic rites and the terrors of initiation to do with my evening stroll and a picturesque moonrise over the ramparts of our respectable old town? What concern is it of mine, what has it to do with me, a man of the twentieth century?

My body still aches with the events of yesterday. I slept badly, plagued by nightmares. My Lord Grandfather made me ride-a-cock-horse on his knee and kept whispering two words in my ear, two words which I have forgotten but which were in some way connected with "ring" and "spear". Also, I saw the "other face" behind me again; it had a wideawake, I am almost tempted to say warning, expression. But I cannot remember what it was warning me against. The Princess appeared in my dream vision, as well – naturally! – but, again, I cannot remember in what connection. Anyway, it's nonsense to talk of connections in such dream fantasies.

The end result is that I have a muzzy head and I am glad to have an undemanding occupation for today which means I will not have to exercise my brain. Rummaging around in old manuscripts is about all I am fit for today. And it is all to the good that from the point where I left off yesterday John Dee's notebook seems to be undamaged. I will carry on translating and copying out:

The Silver Shoe of Bartlett Greene

The first weak rays of the early morning sun had just penetrated to our cell when a man, scarcely of middle height and all in black, entered alone. In spite of his corpulence his gait, indeed, his whole body, betrayed a supple agility. I was immediately struck by the pungent smell given off by his cassock as it fluttered out behind him in a gust of air: the cell was filled with the stench of a beast of prey. This chubby-faced, red-cheeked man of the cloth – one would have taken him for a jovial wine-soak of a monk had it not been for the strangely fixed, half imperious, half furtive look in his yellow eyes – this man in the garb of a simple priest and without any bodyguards – if there were any, they kept well out of sight – was, I knew straightway, none other than Edmund Bonner, the Bloody Bishop of London, in person. Bartlett Greene remained squatting on the ground in silence opposite me; only his eyeballs swivelled slowly back and forth, attentively following our visitor's every move. Strange to relate, at the sight of my abused fellow prisoner all my fear left me and I followed the example of the Captain of the Ravenheads and sat quietly on my stool, as if completely indifferent to the presence of our visitor pacing up and down between us.

Without warning he whirled round on Bartlett Greene, gave him a light tap with his toe and, like a panther pouncing, suddenly bellowed at him in a parade-ground voice:

"Up!"

Greene scarce raised an eyebrow. With a smile in his eyes he squinted up at the man who had ordered

his body to be broken, drew a deep [...]
broad chest and roared back his mocki[...]

"Too soon, o trumpeter of Judgmen[...]
the resurrection of the dead has not yet [...]
I am still alive!"

"That I can see, thou abominati[...]
replied the Bishop in a remarkably gentle voice, full
of priestly concern and contrasting both with the
sense of his words and with his previous bellowing
assault. And my Lord Bishop continued in the same
mild tones:

"Hear me, Greene: the Lord in His wisdom and
His unfathomable compassion has provided that
should you repent – and confess – your descent to the
burning pitch of Hell may be postponed, perhaps
even for all eternity. We will not cut short the time
you have for repentance here on earth."

The only answer from Greene was a half-repres-
sed, rumbling kind of laugh. I saw a spasm of fury
cross Bonner's face, but he had himself well under
control. He stepped up to the miserable lump of
maltreated flesh that was still twitching with silent
laughter on the rotten straw and went on:

"I can see you have the constitution of an ox,
Greene. The search for the truth with the instruments of torture has merely twisted your body a
little, when others would already have rendered up
their stinking souls to Satan. I hope to God that our
barber, or even the physician if need be, can patch
you up again. You can trust in my mercy as you have
come to know my severity: This very hour you can
leave this sty together with – " the Bishop's voice
throbbed with a most cordial, persuasive purr –
"your fellow sufferer here, good Doctor Dee, your
intimate companion."

That was the first time the Bishop had taken the
least notice of me. Now that he suddenly spoke my
name I felt a shock run through me, as one who is
rudely woken from some dream. For until that point

d seemed to me as if I was observing from a stance some flight of fancy, some play performed by the comedians that had nothing at all to do with my own fate. Now that was all over as the Bishop, gently but ruthlessly dragged me from my daydreaming onto the stage of this most cruel tragedy. If Greene confessed he knew me, I was lost!

But scarce had the sudden horror at my precarious situation set my heart pounding and the blood throbbing in my veins than the imperturbable Greene turned his face towards me with incredible composure and growled:

"A doctor? Here with me on this straw? – I thank thee for the honour, Brother Bishop. I thought thou hadst given me a tailor for company, one thou wouldst teach how fear makes the soul fly out at the breeches?"

Greene's insults were so unexpected that they wounded me in my old pride and I leapt up in real anger – none of which escaped the cold, observant eye of Bishop Bonner. But straightway I perceived honest Greene's intent and was filled with a great calm, so that I played my part in the comedy with great aplomb and responded to my cues from Greene or the Bishop with an apt response.

Although inwardly fuming that his panther's leap had once more missed its prey, my Lord Bishop concealed his disappointment behind a snarling yawn that, indeed, recalled the baffled fury of a great cat.

"You are sure, then, you do not know this man, neither in person nor by reputation, my dear Bartlett?" the Bishop went on in cajoling tones. But Greene merely replied in a surly mumble:

"Would that I knew the chicked-livered poltroon, the milksop thou hast brought to my door, good Master Cuckoo. I would give much for my eyes to behold this whining cur precede me through thy flaming gate to Heaven – but that does not mean I will clutch any turd of a quacksalver to my bosom like thee, Cousin Bonner."

84

"Still thy blasphemous tongue, thou son of Belial!" – the Bishop finally lost control of his temper and screamed at Greene as a threatening clash of weapons came from outside the cell door. "Pitch and wood are too good for thee, thou first-born of Beelzebub! Thou shalt burn at the stake on lumps of sulphur so thou shalt have a foretaste of the pleasures that await thee in thy father's house!" the Bishop shouted, livid with fury and grinding his teeth so that the words could scarce come out. But Bartlett Greene gave a peal of laughter and started to swing wildly back and forth on his broken limbs; the mere sight of it made me flinch in horror. "Thou'rt mistaken, Brother Bonner," he brayed. "Sulphur is nothing to me. The French have a use for sulphur baths such as would not come amiss for thee, neither, coz – – but listen, my son: in the place where thou shalt come when thy time is up, mere sulphur is counted as musk oil, or as balm of Arabia!"

"Confess, thou swine, thou demon," Bishop Bonner flung back at him with a roar as of a lion; "confess that this John Dee is confederate in thy outlawry and murder or – – – "

" – or?" echoed the mocking voice of Bartlett Greene.

"The thumbscrews!" panted the Bishop, and warders and men-at-arms swarmed in. But Greene raised his racked body with a wild yell of laughter, proffered his right hand to the Bishop, then suddenly stuck the outstretched thumb between his teeth and bit it off at the root with one crunching snap of his mighty jaws and with a jeering cackle spat it into the horrified Bonner's face, so that blood and spittle ran down from his cheeks onto his cassock. "There!" with a fearful shriek of laughter he roared, "there, screw that up your – – – " and a host of the most obscene imprecations cascaded over the Bishop, such that, even if my memory could retain the smallest part, yet my hand would refuse to write them down.

In the main Greene was assuring the Lord Bishop, with the most loathsome promises, of the care and attention he would lavish on him from "the other side", when he, Greene, had flown from the flames of the bonfire to the land beyond, that he called the "Green Land". He would not tease or torment the Bishop with pitch or sulphur, oh no, he would repay evil with good and send to his "dearly beloved son" most sweet-smelling and irresistible she-devils, such as would make a Frenchman of any pope. And his every hour on earth should be spiced with the honey and gall of hell, for "on the other side" – – –

" – on the other side, my lad," – thus Greene finished his monstrous sermon – "shalt thou wail and gnash thy teeth in thy hell, and thy stench shall rise up to us from the mire, to us, the Princes of the Black Stone who are untouched by pain."

It would be impossible to describe the succession of dreadful thoughts, the stream of furious passions, or even the shadow of the horror that crossed Bishop Bonner's broad face during this flood of curses. The powerful figure stood there as if rooted to the ground; behind him the rabble of mercenaries and turnkeys shrank into the darkest corners, for each and every one had a superstitious fear of the wall-eye, as if it were an evil eye that might put a curse on them for life.

Finally Bishop Bonner roused himself and slowly wiped the sweat from his face with his silken sleeve. Then calmly, softly, but with a hot, hoarse voice, he said:

"Think not thou canst teach me any new tune of the Arch-Deceiver, thou witch's spawn. But thou remindst me to hasten, for such an evil demon should enjoy the light of Heaven's sun no longer than is needful."

"Go thou", was Greene's brusque reply. "Take thy stench from my nose, carrion crow, the very air thou hast breathed needs purifying!"

The Bishop gave an imperious wave and his henchmen rushed to grasp Greene. He, however, curled himself up into a ball, rolled over onto his broad back and stretched his bare foot towards them, at which they stumbled back. "See," he shouted, "see the Silver Shoe that the great Mother Isaïs gave me. As long as I wear it I shall know neither fear nor pain. I have outgrown such childish frailty!" – – – I winced to see the foot had no toes; the naked stump looked like a crude metal shoe – the silver leprosy with its glittering crust had eaten them away. Greene was like the leper in the Bible of whom it is written: he was white as shimmering snow. – – –

"Plague! Leprosy!" shrieked the men-at-arms, throwing down their spears and rushing out of the doorway of the cell in mindless flight. The Lord Bishop stood there, his face yellowish-green with horror and repugnance, wavering between pride and fear, for even those learned in the art do count the silver leprosy the most contagious evil. Slowly the Bishop, who had come to slake his lust for violence on his miserable prisoners, retreated step by step before the approaching Greene who, thrusting his leprous foot forward, continued to spit out his scorn and blasphemy at the prince of the church. Bishop Bonner put a stop to it, though in no way that testified to his bravery; as he hurried to the door he gasped:

"Even today this canker shall be consumed in seven-fold flames. And thou, thou accomplice of the lowest depths of hell" – the reference was to me – "thou shalt taste of the flames that free us from this beast, that thou mayest examine thy soul, perchance it can still be purified. It will be a merciful favour then if we hand thee over to the fire that burns for heretics."

That was the last blessing I received from the lips of the Bloody Bishop. I must admit that it gave rise to the most horrible fancies which sent me tumbling through chasms of fear and torment. It is said of the Lord Bishop that he has mastered the art of killing his victims three times: the first time with his smile, the second by his words and the third by the executioner; and truly, he subjected me to the most agonising martyrdom before the unbelievable miracle of my salvation saved me from the third death at the hand of that man. – – –

Scarce was I alone with Bartlett Greene again than he broke the silence with a rumble of laughter and turned to me with an almost benevolent air:

"Brother Dee, I can see your scalp crawling with fear, like a thousand fleas and ticks in your hair. But: as truly as I have done my utmost to free you from suspicion of association with me – good, I see that you do recognise it – just as truly can I say that you will escape from this trap alive; at most they will singe your beard a little when I am despatched to heaven. You must suffer it like a man."

Incredulous, I raised my weary head that was throbbing painfully with all the fear and anxiety I had been through. As so often happens when the soul is exhausted with an excess of excitement and calamity, I was suddenly indifferent to all around me, as if I was free of all care; I even laughed indulgently at the cowardly fear that had filled the Bishop and his henchmen at the sight of my cell-mate's "Silver Shoe" and, my defiant spirit aroused, I moved closer to the doomed giant.

Greene remarked my intent and gave a strange grunt by which – with the sharpened ear shared suffering gives – I understood that the savage was moved by something that was, considering his utterly different nature, akin to human emotion.

He cautiously felt inside his leather jerkin, which was all he had to cover his naked chest, and called to me:

"Fear not to approach, Brother Dee; the gift of my gentle mistress is such that each man must earn it himself. I could not bequeath it to you, even if I would."

Once more his half-muffled laughter sent a chill down my spine. Then he went on:

"So; I have played my part in denying the Romish priests the pleasure of discovering we make common cause. But I did it not for love of thee, my noble companion, but because that which I know and cannot change compelled me. For thou, Doctor Dee, art the royal youth of this age and to thee is promised the crown in the Green Land and the Mistress of the Three Kingdoms awaits thee."

These words from the mouth of a common outlaw struck me like a lightning bolt and I was hard put to it to keep my composure. Quickly my mind coupled the possible with the probable and at once it seemed to me I perceived the connection between Greene, a vagabond and necromancer, the witch of the moor of Uxbridge and Mascee.

As if he could read my thoughts, Greene went on:

"The weird sister of Uxbridge I know well, and the Tutor to the Czar of Muscovy, too. Beware him! He is a gambler; but thou, my Brother, shouldst rule of thy own design! The red and white globes, which thou threw out of thy window – – – "

I laughed defiantly:

"You are well informed, Greene; is Mascee, then, one of the Ravenheads?"

"If I say 'thou'rt wrong' or if I say 'it may be' thou art none the wiser for it. But what I will tell thee is – – – " and the brigand detailed, by hour and minute, everything I had done in the night when the Bishop's men had taken me and he described the very place where I had all my writings hidden, the place I dare not even confide to this diary. With a laugh, he told me things I had done which no man could know, as if he were me myself, or a spirit that had ever been about me.

I could no longer keep back my astonishment and my secret horror of the mutilated leader of the

brigands, the condemned man who laughingly commanded the most mysterious arts and powers; I
stared at him and stammered, "You know no pain;
you – so you say – enjoy the powerful aid of your
mistress and goddess, that is named Black Isaïs, who
can see the most secret doings of man, – how comes
it then that you lie here in chains your limbs all torn
and soon to be consumed by flames, and do not walk
out through these walls by thy magical power?"

Whilst I spoke Greene had taken from within his
jerkin a small leathern purse which he held loosely in
his hand so that it swung to and fro like a pendulum.
He said with a laugh:

"Did I not tell thee, Brother Dee, that my time is
up according to our Law? As I consecrated the cats to
the fire, so must I now consecrate myself to the fire,
since today my years number three and thirty. Today
I am still that Bartlett Greene whom they may
torture, tear apart and burn, and it is that son of a
priest and a whore that speaks to thee; but on the
morrow I shall put that off and the Son of Man shall
be the groom in the House of the Great Mother.
Then shall the time of my reign be come, and all of
you, Brother Dee, shall feel my rod as I rule in
Eternal Life! – – – That thou shalt alway be mindful
of these words and shalt follow my road, take this,
my earthly wealth for thine inheritance – – – "

The text of the diary has once more been deliberately
damaged. It looks as if it was destroyed by John Dee's
own hand. But the nature of Bartlett Greene's gift to
him is clear from the first lines of the next passage
preserved in the diary.

(Scorch mark) – – – so that towards the fourth hour
after noon all the torments that the Bloody Bishop
could think up for his revenge had been made ready.

When they had taken Bartlett Greene away and I,
John Dee, had been alone for an half hour, I took out

the gift yet again; it was nothing remarkable, a piece of black coal, about the size of my fist and polished in the form of a regular octahedron. I looked closely to see if there were not, according to the instructions of its former owner, images of present events in distant places to be seen on its gleaming faces, or even whether future happenings from my own life might appear as in a mirror. There was nothing of the like to be seen because, as I suppose, my soul was troubled, which Greene himself had said was detrimental to any such operation.

Finally I caught the sound of the bolts being drawn back and quickly hid the mysterious coal in the innermost lining of my jerkin.

Hardly had I done so than a troop of the Bishop's heavily armed guards entered and my first thought was that they had come to execute me on the spot and without trial. But their purpose was otherwise; in order to break my obdurate spirit, I was to be taken to the fire to see Greene burn at the stake and be brought so close that that it would singe my beard. Perhaps Satan himself whispered in Bonner's ear that Greene, in his mortal anguish, or I myself, confused by the terrible sight, might yet be brought to confess our complicity or some other deception. But he deceived only himself. I will not waste many words describing something that has been branded on my soul for life; I will briefly tell how the roasting of Bartlett Greene made a very different dish for the Bishop to swallow than the one he had pictured to himself in his desire to savour his victim's torment.

At the fifth hour Greene mounted the pyre with such a spring in his step as if it were his bridal couch. And as the words appear under my quill, I am reminded of what he said to me, namely that he hoped this day to be the bridegroom of his Great Mother, by which blasphemous speech he doubtless meant his return to the bosom of his black mother, Isaïs.

As they tied him to the stake he laughed aloud and called out to the Bishop, "Take care, priest, when I sing the Hymn of the Journey Home, that thou mind thy bald pate, for I am minded to sprinkle it with drops of pitch and fiery sulphur that thy brain shall burn until thou make thy own journey to Hell!"

The bonfire had been constructed with cruel and devilish cunning, such as has never been seen before, nor, God willing, will ever be again in this vale of sorrow. It was a pile of damp, ill-burning elm logs with above it a stake to which they fastened Greene with iron clamps. Around this martyr's pole hempen threads full of sulphur were twined from top to bottom and above the head of the victim hung a broad crown of pitch and sulphur.

When the executioner pushed his torch into the pyre the first things to flare up, as if they were touchwood, were the sulphured threads which took the oily flames to the garland over the malefactor's head so that drops of sulphur and pitch slowly began to rain down upon him.

However, although it was horrible to behold, for the singular man at the stake it seemed as if it were but a refreshing spring shower or manna from above. And all the while he kept up a stream of insolent remarks at Bonner so that it seemed more as if the Bishop on his velvet cushions were the accused, rather than his victim on the bonfire. His sins were trumpeted abroad in public; Greene knew of his most secret transgressions and did not withhold them, so that had he been able to with good grace, my Lord Bishop would gladly have sacrificed the pleasure of watching the execution. He seemed bound by some spell and must needs sit there silent, trembling with shame and fury; then, foaming at the mouth, he screamed order on order at his henchmen that they should hasten to put an end to the spectacle that he had thought before to draw out to the last terrible second. It was miraculous to see how none of the arrows that rained upon Greene could silence him; it was as if his whole body were invulnerable. Finally dry wood, with much kindling and tow mixed in, set the pyre blazing, and Greene disappeared in smoke and flames. But then he began to bellow out his song, more joyfully than in the cell, where he had swung from the wall, and the crackling of the wood was drowned in the spine-chilling rapture of his wild singing:

"Heave ho! All night Tom plays on his fiddle
After the moult of May.
Heave ho!
While Kitty sings hey diddle diddle
To the moon and Black Isaye.
Heave ho!"

It was deathly still around the place of execution; all the executioners and guards, the judges, priests and nobles felt their skin crawl with fear and loathing until every limb seemed paralysed; and the sight made me want to laugh out loud. Before all the rest, however, sat my Lord Bishop, Edward Bonner, like a grey ghost on his throne, his hands clamped on the arms, gazing fixedly into the flames. As the last note of the song died away on the lips of the blazing Greene I saw the Bishop stagger forward with a cry like a condemned man. Was it a gust of wind blowing through the fire or were there truly satanical powers at work there? – from the top of the pyre a wreath of flames, like yellow tongues of fire, suddenly flew up, fluttered, plunged and whirled upwards into the sky over the episcopal throne and the head of Bishop Bonner. Whether it really was singed by a drop of sulphur as Greene had prophesied only minutes before, I cannot say; from the grimace of terror on the face of the Bloody Bishop it would almost seem so – it was impossible to tell in the general tumult of men and weapons that filled the reeking courtyard.

One final detail I must record for accuracy's sake: when I regained my senses a lock of hair, singed off my own head, floated down to my feet as I brushed the confusion of the last hours from my forehead. The night that followed these terrible events was full of the most strange happenings, of which I can confide but a small part to these pages; but I shall never forget that night, nor anything that befell me in the Bloody Bishop's dungeon.

That evening and the first part of the night I spent in constant expectation of a renewed interrogation, if not torture, by the Bishop's men. I must confess that I did not put much trust in the words of Greene, yet I kept taking out the black coal to see if there were an image of my future on the polished surfaces of this common mineral. Soon, however, it was too dark in the cell: as on the previous night, the turnkeys did not think it necessary to give me a light; they may well have been following an express order.

I spent I know not how long sitting there pondering my fate and that of Bartlett Greene; at times I even sighed with envy of the outlaw, who was now beyond all chains and cares. Towards midnight I must have fallen exhausted into a leaden slumber.

Then it seemed to me that the heavy iron door to my cell swung open – by what agency I know not – and Bartlett Greene entered, hale and hearty, sound of limb, a very giant of a man, alive in every sinew, that I was sore amazed, since not for one moment did I forget that he had been burnt at the stake but a few hours ago. I said that to his face in a calm voice, and asked him in the name of the Holy Trinity if he did confess he was a ghost or whether he was Bartlett Greene in person, in some incomprehensible way returned from another realm.

At this Greene let out his usual rumbling laugh and replied that he was no ghost but Bartlett Greene made whole, and that he came not from another realm but from our present world, except that he lived on the other side: there was no "world above", only this one world, but that had many – countless – aspects and reticulations; the one where he now resided was, admittedly, somewhat different from mine.

These words are a mere blind groping after the great clarity with which all seemed plain before me in those half-sleeping moments of spiritual awareness; for the truth of what Greene told me was steeped in a sunlit radiance, so that the mysteries of space and time and the essence of all things lay open before me. In that night Greene revealed to me secret knowledge of my self and my future, all of which, down to the tiniest jot and tittle, is preserved for ever in my memory.

In that night I was still in doubt, thinking it was some phantasm come to mock me, but since then so many of his prophecies have come to pass in ways that defy all reason, that it would now be foolish of me not to believe that those that remain unfulfilled shall yet bear fruit. In all this there is one thing I do not understand: what can be the reason that Greene looks down on me with such favour and guides me in the paths of plenty, for to this day he has nothing required against the law or against my God – if that were so I would fling a thunderous *"apage Satanas"* in his face that would send him tumbling back down to the very jaws of Hell to which, in his pride, he thought to drag me down.

His way cannot be my way; the moment I perceive that he seeks my soul's damnation, I shall put him behind me for all eternity! –

To my pressing question Greene replied that I would be freed on the morning of the morrow. And when in my disbelief I pressed him more urgently, for all likelihood spoke against his assertion, and tried to show him that what he had promised was impossible, his eerie laugh tumbled out as loud as ever as he said:

"Brother Dee, thou'rt a fool! Seest the sun and wouldst deny the eye! As thou art a beginner in the Art, perhaps a stone wrenched from the earth will say more to thee than the living word. Take my Gift, when thou awakest, and see what thy spirit will not accept."

The main part of the instructions that followed concerned the conquest of Greenland and the inconceivable importance of this enterprise for my whole future existence. And I will not conceal that at later visits – his appearances have become frequent – he does most truthfully and solemnly aver that this is the way to achieve my highest, my longed for goal, for the Crown of Greenland is assured me; and I do begin to understand the signs! – – When I awoke from my vision the waning moon stood high in the sky so that a bluish-white shaft of light shone down through the tiny window. I stepped into the moonbeam, hastily drew out the polished coal and held one of its dark gleaming surfaces out in the ray from the heavenly body. It flickered with bluish, deep purple reflections and for a long time there was nothing more to be discerned. But at the same time a wondrous peace, such as I could feel in every fibre of my body, spread through me and the black crystal in my hand stopped flickering as my fingers, like every part of me, became strong and steady.

Then the light on the coal mirror became iridescent. The surfaces were veiled with milky, opalescent clouds which dispersed again. Finally the clear contour of a bright image became discernible; at first it was tiny, as if I were peering through a spyhole at dwarves playing in bright moonshine. But soon the picture began to grow in breadth and in depth until the vision overflowed – it was intangible, and yet it was, too, as if I were standing there myself. And I saw – – – (scorch mark)

For the second time there is a section of the diary – not a very long one, it is true – that has been carefully destroyed. As far as I can judge, it was the hand of my ancestor that rendered the passage illegible. It seems that soon after he had written it down he must have been struck by the thought that here was a secret he would not want revealed to unwelcome readers. After his experiences in the Tower he would be sensitive to such dangers. However, the fragment of a letter has been placed in the diary between these pages. Obviously my cousin, John Roger, must have come across it somewhere in his researches and inserted it here, as it is prefaced by a note in his hand:

Sole remaining fragment of a document relating to the secret of John Dee's liberation from the Tower.

In its present state, it is not clear whom the letter is addressed to, but that is irrelevant; what is important is the light the fragment throws on John Dee's life. It indicates that it was due to the intervention of Princess Elizabeth that John Dee was freed.

I reproduce what remains of the letter in full:

– – – that hereby I (John Dee) do reveal to you – and to no other person on earth – this secret that is the proudest and at the same time most dangerous in my life. And this, if nothing else, should justify me in all that I undertake, and shall in future undertake, to the Honour and Glory of our most gracious Lady and virginal Majesty, Elizabeth, my great Queen.

In briefest summary:

When the Royal Princess received news of my desperate position she secretly sent – with a courage and circumspection to be found in no other child of her age – for our mutual friend Leicester and asked him to pledge his word as a nobleman to prove his courage and his love and loyalty to me. As she found him resolved and ready to sacrifice his own safety if necessary, she boldly set about delivering me from the Tower. And I believe, though I have no evidence

97

to prove it, that it was through a childish excess of spirit that knew no danger, through a wildness that oftentimes seized her, that led her to do what was impossible, and yet the only possible means of rescuing me:

At night, using both true and copied keys – Heaven knows how she came by them! – she crept secretly into the royal chancellery, King Edward at that time being particularly close in both friendship and coop-eration to Bishop Bonner. She found the chest, wherein was kept the King's own paper with a royal watermark, opened it and wrote, imitating the King's own hand, an order for my immediate release which she sealed with Edward's own Seal – in what manner she obtained it I do not know, it being always kept locked away.

All this she did herself boldly and yet with care and caution since there was never the least doubt cast upon the document – indeed, King Edward himself, when it was later presented to him, was so con-founded to see a product of his own hand of which he knew nothing that it seemed to him as if it had been written by magic, and he silently accepted it as his own. It may be that he saw through the counter-feit but condoned it rather than admit to such sorcery or presumption in his own immediate vicinity, – however that may be, the next morning Robert Dudley, later Earl of Leicester, strode into Bonner's registry, handed over his urgent missive and insisted on receiving both reply and prisoner from the episcopal court himself. And he did!

Neither I nor any man ever learnt what was in the supposed letter from King Edward, devised and written by a sixteen-year-old child. What I do know is that, in the presence of Dudley, as the emissary of the King, the Bloody Bishop, ashen-faced and trembling, gave his bodyguard orders to hand me over. And that is all, dearest friend, that I may reveal to you. And from this, which I have only set down after much hesitation, you can see whence comes the "eternal obligation" to our gracious and sublime Queen, of which I have often spoken to you ...

That is the end of the fragment.

In John Dee's diary the illegible section is followed by this short passage:

That very morning the words of Bartlett Greene were fulfilled; without delay and without formality I was released from my grim situation and led from the Tower by the companion of my youth, Robert Dudley, and taken to a safe place where even the Bloody Bishop would scarce think me hid and where he would have found it difficult to take me if he should come to regret his compliance regarding the release of my person. I will make no further commentary on the matter, nor even presume to explain *secundam rationem* the mysterious ways in which God moves. I will only add that, besides the incredible boldness and skill of my saviours and God's visible assistance, Bishop Bonner's state of mind after the execution of Bartlett Greene also played some role in the matter. I heard from the Bishop's chaplain – through what intermediary need not trouble us – that Bonner spent a sleepless night: for hours he paced up and down in his chamber in a restless perturbation of the spirit and then fell into a strange delirium in which he seemed to suffer the most indescribable horrors. He spoke, as if with an invisible guest, in despairing, often incomprehensible tones and for hours fought a desperate battle with all kinds of imagined demons; finally he cried out, "I confess that I cannot command thee, and I confess that I am consumed by Fire – Fire – Fire!" At this the chaplain rushed in to find him unconscious on his bed. I will not record the many rumours that have come to me on this matter. What I heard is so terrible that I think my soul would faint with the torment if I should even try to set it down on paper.

Thus ends John Dee's report on "The Silver Shoe of Bartlett Greene".

A few days away in the country and rambling in the mountains have done me the world of good. On a sudden impulse I left my desk, the meridian line and old Uncle Dee's dusty relics behind me and broke free of the spell that had bound me to house and work.

Isn't it funny, I said to myself as I strode out over the heather-covered foothills, that I feel the same as John Dee must have felt when he walked over the Scottish moors after his release from prison? And I had to laugh at the idea that kept going through my mind: John Dee must have tramped over moorland just like this, just as happy, with his heart almost bursting with the new sense of freedom, just like mine as I trot over these Austrian hills almost three hundred and fifty years later. And it must have been in Scotland, in those same Sidlaw Hills that I used to hear my grandfather talk about. It is not surprising that I should make the connection– my Anglo-Styrian grandfather used to tell us often enough about the similarities in landscape and atmosphere between the Scottish moors and the uplands that form the foothills of the Alps.

And I continued to daydream –

I saw myself sitting at home; not as one usually sees oneself, looking back into the past, no: it was as if I were still there, seated at my desk in the city like an empty husk, the cast off cocoon in which an insect larva had spent the winter, dead and abandoned since I emerged as a butterfly a few days ago, spreading my wings in the new freedom of the purple heather. So strong was the hold this feeling took on my imagination that it came as a shock when mundane matters took over again and I had to think of returning home. I gave a shiver at the thought of the empty skin, like some pallid *Doppelgänger* still attached to my desk, into which I would have to crawl back to be reunited with my past.

But such fancies quickly dispersed when I entered the vestibule of the house where I lived, for there, coming

down the stairs from an unsuccessful attempt to see me, was Lipotin. In spite of the fact that my limbs were aching from the journey, I insisted on dragging him straight back up with me. I suddenly felt the need, stronger than ever, to talk to him about the Princess, about Stroganoff and about so many other things that –
– –

In short, Lipotin came back up and spent the rest of the evening with me.

A remarkable evening! Or, to be precise, an evening's conversation that took a remarkable turn: Lipotin was more talkative than usual, and a certain scurrilous tendency in him, which I had noticed before, was more marked than usual, so that many things about him seemed new, or at least different.

He described Baron Stroganoff's death – a philosopher's death, if ever there was! – and told me some uninteresting details of his own problems as executor of an estate consisting of a few articles of clothing hanging on the walls of the empty room like butterfly chrysalises. I was struck by the fact that Lipotin used an image similar to the one that I could not get out of my head during my walking holiday, and a host of fleeting thoughts swarmed over my mind like ants: was the sensation of death very different from the feeling of going out into the open air, leaving behind an empty cocoon – the cast-off garment – our skin, which even while we are alive – my recent experience had taught me this – we sometimes at eerie moments see from outside, like a dead man who is able to look back on the corpse he has left behind.

All the while Lipotin prattled on about this and that in his disjointed, half ironic manner; in vain I waited for him to bring the conversation round to Princess Shotokalungin of his own accord. For a long time a strange reserve kept me from giving our chatter the turn I so much desired, but eventually my impatience won and, as I made the tea, I asked him straight out what he thought he was doing, sending the Princess to see me, and what made him tell her he had sold me antique weapons.

"And why should I not have sold you such things?" Lipotin calmly replied. His tone irritated me; I became more worked up than I intended when I cried:

"But Lipotin, you must know whether you once sold me an ancient Persian or God knows what kind of spearhead or not?! Or rather, you know very well that you never ..."

He interrupted me, as impassive as ever:

"But, my dear friend, of course I sold you the spearhead."

His eyelids were half closed and his finger tamped a few tobacco threads back into a cigarette; his whole expression was one of blasé self-assurance. I flared up at him. "A strange kind of joke, my friend! I have never bought anything of the kind from you. I have never even seen anything like that in your shop. You are wrong, so wrong that I cannot understand it!"

"Really?" Lipotin answered languidly. "Well, then, it must have been some time ago that I sold you the weapon."

"Never! Not recently nor some time ago! Some time ago, what does that mean, some time ago?! How long have we known each other? Six months, and your memory really ought to be able to cope with that."

Lipotin cocked his head, looked up at me and replied, "When I say 'some time ago' then I mean in another life – in a former incarnation."

"What do you mean? In a –."

"In a former incarnation", Lipotin repeated pronouncing each syllable distinctly. I sensed an undertone of mockery and responded with an ironic, "Of course".

Lipotin said nothing.

However, as I was desperate to know why he had sent the Princess to me, I took up the thread:

"Anyway, I am grateful to you for allowing me to make the acquaintance of a lady who – – – "

He nodded.

I continued, "Unfortunately, the trick you felt you had to play to achieve that put me in an awkward spot. If at all possible, I would very much like to procure the desired weapon for the Princess – – – "

"But it is in your possession!" Butter wouldn't have melted in Lipotin's mouth.

"Lipotin, you're impossible today."

"Why ever so?"

"It's grotesque! You allow a poor lady to believe I possess a weapon – "

"– which you acquired from me."

"But, my dear chap, you have just admitted – "

"– that it was in a former incarnation. Maybe." Lipotin pretended he was deep in thought and mumbled, "It is possible, now and then, to get the century wrong."

I realised there was no chance of a serious conversation with the antiques dealer that evening. I was still rather irritated, but I concealed it. I fell in with his tone – I had no other choice – gave a dry laugh and said:

"Pity I can't tell Princess Shotokalungin in which particular former incarnation she might find the spearhead she so much desires."

"Why not?" asked Lipotin.

"Because the Princess is likely to find your philosophy merely a very convenient excuse."

"I wouldn't be so sure." Lipotin smiled, "The Princess is Russian."

"So what?"

"Russia is a young country; very young even, in the opinion of some of your compatriots, younger than everyone else. Russia is also old. Age-old. Nothing about us ever surprises. We can whine like children, we can watch the centuries pass, like the three ancient greybeards on their island in the sea and still – "

The same old arrogance. I could not conceal my scorn:

"I know. The Russians are God's own people on earth."

Lipotin gave an apologetic grin:

"Perhaps. It's a devil of a country. Anyway, it's all *one* world."

The urge to mock this tea-and-tobacco philosophy, the Russian national disease, became even stronger:

"Wisdom worthy indeed of an antiques dealer! When we touch an object from the past, from whatever period, we have a living demonstration that the categories of time and space are not absolute. We alone are bound to them – –" It had been my intention to produce a stream of such and similar banalities, chosen at random, to drown his philosophical rhetoric, but he interrupted me with a smile and a darting movement of his bird-like head:

"It could well be that I have learnt from antiques. Especially as the oldest of the antiques I have come across is ... myself. My real name is Mascee."

Words cannot describe the jolt of terror that shook me as Lipotin said this. For a moment my head seemed to have become a seething mass of cloud. My whole body was in turmoil, and it took the greatest effort to keep my expression one of mild surprise and curiosity as I asked:

"Where on earth did you come across that name, Lipotin? You can hardly imagine how fascinating it is! You see, the name is not unknown to me."

"Really?" replied Lipotin. His features remained inscrutable.

"Yes. I have been interested in that name and its bearer for – oh, for some time now."

"A fairly recent interest?" Lipotin's tone was mocking.

"Why, yes. Certainly!" I replied eagerly. "Since these – these – – – " Automatically I took a step towards my desk, piled high with the evidence of my endeavours. Lipotin must have noticed; it was not difficult to put two and two together. He interrupted me with a smug expression of self-satisfaction:

"You mean, since these documents on the life of John Dee, that dreamer and necromancer from the days of Queen Elizabeth, came into your possession? You are correct; Mascee did count both of them amongst his acquaintance."

I was growing impatient: "Now listen here, Lipotin", I expostulated, "that's enough pulling my leg for one evening. I don't mind putting up with your mystical clap-trap, but how on earth did you come across that name, Mascee?"

"Well now", said Lipotin, as languid as ever, "he was, as I think I may already have suggested – "

"A Russian, of course. 'Tutor to the Czar' the documents call him. But you. What have you to do with him?"

Lipotin stood up and lit another cigarette.

"A mere joke, my dear fellow! The Tutor to the Czar is well known in our – let us say in our circles. Is it an impossibility that a family of archaeologists and antiquaries such as mine might be descended from the said Mascee? Only a suggestion, my friend, only a suggestion!" – and he picked up his coat and hat.

"Very amusing, indeed", I cried. "You know this strange figure from the history of your country and, lo and behold, it appears in old English papers and walks into my life – so to speak – – " – the last phrase seemed to appear on my lips of its own accord.

But Lipotin was shaking my hand and at the same time his left hand was on the doorknob:

" – and walks into your life, so to speak. At the moment, of course, you are merely immortal, whilst he – ", Lipotin hesitated a moment, his eyes twinkled and he gave my hand another squeeze, – "for simplicity's sake, let's say 'I' – I, you must know, am eternal. All beings are immortal; they just don't know it, or forget when they enter the world or leave it. That is why it would be wrong to say they have eternal life. But more of this another time. We will continue to see a lot of each other, I hope. Goodbye for now!" And he hurried down the stairs.

I was confused and uneasy. I shook my head to try to clear my mind. Had Lipotin been slightly tipsy? At times there had been a gleam in his eye that suggested a few glasses of wine. But he had not seemed at all drunk. A little mad, rather, but he's been that since I've known him. To suffer exile at the age of seventy, as he did, can loosen a person's hold on reality.

Still, it's remarkable that he knows about the "Tutor to the Czar", – even claims to be related to him, if that was meant seriously.

It would be useful to find out from him precisely what he knows about Mascee. But, damn! I didn't get anywhere in the matter of the Princess. But when I catch Lipotin in broad daylight and stone-cold sober I'll get a straight answer out of him. I won't let myself be led up the garden path again.

And now, back to work!

A random dip, exactly as I had decided, into the depths of the drawer containing the rest of John Roger's package, brings up a notebook bound in ragpaper. When I open it I see immediately that it must be one of a series of such books; the entries begin straightaway, without fly-leaf or title page; there is an occasional date given. The hand is much altered from that of the diary, but still unmistakably that of John Dee. I begin to copy out:

Notes from the later years of John Dee, Esq.

Anno Domini 1578.

Today, the Feast of the Resurrection of Our Lord, I, John Dee, rose early from my bed and slipped silently out of the chamber so that I should not disturb Jane, my – second – wife, nor my beloved baby son Arthur, who was sleeping in his cradle.

I felt an inward urge to go out into the mild silver light of the awakening spring morning. I could not say what drove me out of house and farm, unless it were the thought of the evil that had befallen me on this same Easter morning twenty-eight years ago.

I have great cause to give up my heartfelt thanks to fate or, as it is more seemly to say, to Divine Providence and Mercy, that has allowed me life and health in this, my fifty-seventh year, to enjoy the glorious vision of the sun as it rises above the eastern horizon.

Most of those who had designs against me are long since dead, and all that remains of Edmund Bonner, the Bloody Bishop, is the loathing of the people wherever the old stories are told; when children misbehave, their nurses tell them that the Bloody Bishop will come to fetch them.

But what has become of me and of the prophecies and of all that I strove for in the vigour of my youth? – – – I would rather not reflect on the passing years and how my plans and projects – and my strength – have gone with them.

In such thoughts, which oppressed me more than they had for many a year, I wandered along the banks of the Surrey Dee, which, I presume, once gave its name to our family; and the comical haste of the Dee, a mere bustling brook, reminded me of the all too rapid flow of human endeavour. Eventually I came to the place where the stream, winding its many twisting curves around the hillock at Mortlake, spreads out in an old claypit forming a kind of reedy pool. The Dee seems to have come to a standstill and disappeared in a swamp.

I stopped beside the marshy pool and spent I know not how long gazing at the reeds stirring in the breeze over this haunt of frogs and toads. I was filled with feelings of dissatisfaction and my head began to throb with the notion that here in the fate of the Dee Brook was a reflection, a visible symbol of the fate of the John Dee who was standing there beside it: a rapid course to an early swamp, stagnant water, frogs, toads, weed and reeds – and above it in the gentle sun a shimmering dragon-fly on jewelled pinions: but when you catch the trumpery marvel, all you hold in your hands is a horrid grub with transparent wings.

As I became immersed ever deeper in such thoughts, my eye fell on a damselfly that was just emerging from its dull brown larva in the warmth of the spring morning. For a few brief seconds the insect clung trembling to the yellowing reed-stem close by the place where the larva, now an abandoned, ghost-like husk, had attached itself for its birth-in-death. The delicate wings were soon drying in the warm sunshine: after a series of upward jerks they unfolded daintily and smoothed themselves out with dreamy movements against the busy polishing of the back legs, gave a voluptuous shudder then – suddenly the tiny elf rose with a flash of colour and the next moment it was darting to and fro in ecstatic flight through the balmy air. The brittle husk of the larva hung on the dry reed-stem above the stagnant decay of the pond – dead.

"That is the secret of life", I cried out loud. "Once more the immortal part has sloughed its skin, once more the victorious will has broken out of its prison to seek its destiny."

And suddenly I saw myself many times in a long train of images disappearing into the mists of my past life; squatting in the Tower with Bartlett Greene; hunting rabbits or hunched over musty tomes in Robert Dudley's Scottish mountain hideout; in Greenwich, putting together horoscopes for the wild, untameable Lady Elizabeth; – – – bowing and scraping and holding forth before the Emperor Maximilian in Buda in Hungary; spending months of foolish mystery-mongering with Nikolaus Grudius, private secretary to the Emperor Charles, and even more privately an adept of the Rosicrucian order. I saw myself in the flesh, but as it were frozen in the various stages of my pilgrimage: exposed to ridicule, in fear and trembling, distraught and numb of soul: ill in the house of the Duke of Lorraine in Nancy; in Richmond, burning with ambition, love, hopes and plans for Her, a Lady hot and yet ice-cold, now blazing with determination, now smouldering with distrust, a Lady ...

And I saw myself at the bedside of my first wife, my enemy, the unfortunate Ellinor, as she wrestled with Death; and I saw myself quietly slip away from her death cell and out into the garden at Mortlake to – to her – to Elizabeth!

Puppet! – Phantom! – Ghost!! – And all myself; yet not myself, but a brownish grub desperately fixing its claws into the earth, now here, now there, to await the birth of the Other, the True John Dee, the winged Conqueror of Greenland, the Royal Youth with the world at his feet!

Again and again the wriggling grub and never the bridegroom! O youth! O fire! O my Queen!

Thus was the morning stroll of a fifty-seven-year-old man who had thought, when he was twenty-seven, to grasp the crown of England and to have the throne of the New World for his footstool.

And what had happened in the thirty long years since I lectured in the celebrated School of the Sorbonne with learned scholars for pupils and a King and a Duke eager to hear me? Which was the thorn bush that had caught the eagle's wings as it strove toward the sun? In what fowler's net had he become enmeshed so that an eagle shared with thrushes and finches the fate of a household pet, and still had to thank the Lord that he had not shared the pot with partridges?!

On that tranquil Easter morning I saw my whole life pass before me: not in the usual manner as one would speak of memories of the past; I saw my physical body, the larval form of each period of my life, and from my earliest awareness to the present day I have tasted again and again the torment of having to crawl back into each cast-off husk of the body. But this voyage through the hell of my vain endeavours was still not without its usefulness, for my astonishment threw a harsh, clear light on the confused route of my wanderings. And it seemed good to me to use this day and the experience it had brought me and to write down all that I had "seen". So I shall use these pages to record everything that has happened in the last twenty-eight years as a

Rhodri Mawr – Roderick the Great – of Wales was my ancestor and Hywel Dda – Hywel the Good –, who has been celebrated in folk songs down the centuries, is the pride or our line. Thus I come from a line of blood that is older than that of the "twin roses" of England and as royal as any that has ruled in the Kingdom.

My pride in our blood is no whit lessened by the fact that the lands and titles of the Earls of Dee have been blown away by the winds of time. My father, Rowland Dee, Lord of the Manor of Gladhill, a madcap and a rake-hell, preserved little of the family inheritance apart from the fortress of Deestone and tolerably extensive estates, the rent from which sufficed to gratify both his coarse passions and his inexplicable ambition to cultivate in me, his only son and the last of the ancient line, a blossom that would renew the old glory of our house.

As if he were determined to make good the omissions of generations of Dees, he restrained his wild nature wherever my future was concerned and although he only observed me from afar and we were as different in character as fire and water, yet it is him alone that I have to thank that my every inclination was allowed free rein and every wish, however contrary to his own, was granted. This man, who had a horror of all books and naught but mockery for all learning, most solicitously encouraged the development of my intellectual gifts and ensured, herein showing his old pride, that I enjoyed the most excellent schooling, as any rich and honourable gentleman in England. In London and Chelmsford he retained the first teachers of the day.

I completed my studies at St. John's College in Cambridge in the company of the noblest and keenest minds in the country. And when, at the age of twenty-one I received my Master of Arts from Cambridge, it was bought neither with money nor influence. On that occasion, my father gave a feast at Deestone which compelled him to mortgage one third of his possessions in order to pay the truly royal debts which he had incurred in celebrating my graduation as sumptuously as possible. It was soon after that that he died.

As my mother, a quiet and sensitive woman whose life had been embittered, had died many years ago, I found myself at twenty-two the sole heir to a not inconsiderable estate and an ancient name.

If at first I so strongly emphasised how contrary our two natures were, I did it on purpose to reveal the miracle of the soul of a man who, himself living only for the clash of arms, the roll of dice, the excitement of the hunt or the cup, yet held the seven free arts, which he surely despised, important enough to hope they might, through my love of them, bring new glory to what was a somewhat blotched and weatherbeaten family escutcheon. However, I did not want to suggest that I myself had not inherited a goodly part of my father's wild and unbridled nature. Drinking, brawling and other, even more questionable sides to my character had, in earlier years, led me into the most ticklish situations, at times even into mortal danger. The old affair with the leader of the Ravenheads – a youthful prank as much as a real revolt – was by no means the worst, though it was to have the most fateful consequences for my life.

So it was a devil-may-care love of adventure and a complete lack of concern about the future which led me, immediately upon my father's death, to leave my castle and estate in the hands of my steward and to travel the world like a lord with more than sufficient means at my disposal. I attended the great Schools at Louvain and Utrecht, at Leyden and Paris, attracted by the company of scions of the noblest houses in Europe and also, of course, by their blossoming reputation in the Natural and Occult Sciences.

I studied under Gemma Frisius, worthy successor to Euclid in the northern latitudes, and under the celebrated Gerardus Mercator, foremost among men skilled in measuring the earth and the heavens. I returned home with a reputation in Mathematics and Astronomy second to none in England. And all this before I had completed my twenty-fourth year! I felt no little pride in all this, which freely confirmed the excess of self-confidence I had inherited from my father.

The King discounted my youth and my madcap ways and, when he founded the College of the Holy Trinity at Cambridge, installed me there as Reader in the Greek language. What could have tasted sweeter to my pride than to return so soon as a master at the place where I had been a pupil?

Tutor to men of my own age, often older, my *Collegium Graeciae* was more often a *Collegium Bacchi et Veneris* than a *Collegium Officii*. And truly, even now a laugh comes to my lips when I think of the performance of *Pax* by the ancient author of comedies, the divine Aristophanes. It was acted out by my pupils and colleagues, with most magical effects. According to the poet's instruction I constructed a giant *Scarabeus* of fearsome appearance, which had, concealed within its body, a machine so that my dung beetle rose straight up in the air and flew with great din and stench over the heads of the terrified superstitious onlookers to bring the messenger to the Palace of Jupiter.

How the good Fellows and Professors, not to mention the honest burghers and magistrates, did wonder greatly and in fear and trembling did pray to all the Saints for protection against such wonders and the Black Arts of the insolent young magician, John Dee.

Had I harkened to the noise, laughter, hubbub and uproar of that day with a more attentive ear, I might have learned more of the way of this world in which I am condemned to live. For the mob, which governs this world, responds to high spirits and harmless pranks with bitter hatred and the deathly earnest of its vengeance.

That night they stormed my house to take me, whom they thought must be in league with the Devil, and drag me before their court of witless judges. And the Dean and Chapter led the mob, cawing like black carrion crows, all to punish the "blasphemy" of a lighthearted mechanick! And had it not been for Robert Dudley, Earl of Leicester, my friend and the worthy Master of the College, who knows, but the mob – both learned and profane – might have parted me from my life at that very hour and slaked their lust on streams of my blood.

But I escaped on a swift horse to my stronghold of Deestone and then once more over the sea to the great School of Louvain. Behind me I left an honourable office, a modest income and a name dragged through the mire by the foul suspicions and vicious calumnies of the justified and the pious. In those days I cared too little for the slanders hissed abroad by men beneath my station and whom I therefore thought of no account. I had but little knowledge of the world; it was only through bitter experience that I learnt that no-one is born too high nor any slanderer too low, but that the enmity of an even greater might not bind the two together and distil from the venom of the guttersnipe poison for the nobleman.

O my peers, how bitter was the lesson that taught me to know them!

Chemistry and alchymy were the objects of my study at Louvain and I learnt all that there was to be learnt about the nature of matter. And then I had constructed there for me – it cost me a pretty penny – a laboratory wherein I could study the natural and divine mysteries of the world in solitary peace. Therein I acquired much knowledge and understanding of the *elementa naturae*.

I was *magister liberarum artium*, and as the foolish, venomous rumours from England could scarcely pursue me this far, I was soon held in high honour by both the learned and unlearned; and when, in the autumn, I delivered lectures on astronomy at the College of Louvain, I counted amongst my auditory the Dukes of Mantua and Medina Celi who, especially to hear me, came every week from Brussels where the Emperor Charles V was keeping court. And several times His Majesty was Himself amongst the audience and would not permit the least change to be made to the normal order of the *collegii* for His sake. Also foremost amongst my hearers were Sir William Pickering, a learned and honourable gentleman from my own country, and Matthew Haco and John Capito from Denmark. And in those days it happened that I advised the Emperor to leave the Low Countries for a while, since I saw, by certain unmistakable signs such as I had studied before, that a plague would visit the land in the damp of the winter; and I faithfully reported this danger to the Emperor. Charles was astounded and laughed and refused to believe the prophecy. And many gentlemen of his entourage seized the chance to rob me, by mockery and slander, of the Emperor's good opinion, which had long caused the worm of jealousy to gnaw at their vitals. But it was the Duke of Medina Celi who, in his solicitude, urged the Emperor not to disregard my warning. For when I understood his good opinion of me, I showed the Duke certain signs on which I based my prophecy.

Soon after the turn of the year the signs of the plague increased so much that the Emperor left his camp in Brussels in great haste and soon departed the country, not without requesting my company and, when I was forced to refuse the honour because of other, urgent plans, rewarding me with a most flattering and princely gift of gold and a golden chain with a medallion bearing his own fair likeness.

Soon after that the coughing death arose in Holland and raged in town and country so that thirty thousand were dead within two months.

I had fled the plague myself and moved to Paris. There Turnebus, the philosophers Peter Ramus and Ranconetus, the great physician Fernet and the mathematician Peter Nonius were all my pupils in Euclidian geometry and astronomy. Soon King Henry XI too entered the hall and wanted to sit at my feet like the Emperor Charles in Louvain. The Duke of Monteluc brought me the offer of the Rectorship of an Academy that would be founded especially for me or of a Chair at the Sorbonne with many promises for the future.

But all this was like a game to me and in my pride I rejected the offers with a laugh. My dark star was drawing me back to England, for in Louvain Nicholas Grudius, Privy Chamberlain to the Emperor Charles, had found, I know not where, a weird Scottish piper – could it have been Bartlett Greene's mysterious shepherd? – who urged me that I was destined to rise to the highest honours in England. This prophecy etched itself upon my soul and seemed to have a magical meaning for me which I could not explain. Whatever the cause, I could hear it constantly in my ear and it aroused my ambitious lust. And so I returned and entered upon the dangerous and bloody trial of strength between the Papists and the Protestants which, from the Royal Palace down to to the least village, set brother against brother and man against wife. I threw in my lot with the Reformers and thought in a swift assault to win the love and the hand of Elizabeth, who sympathised with the Protestant party. I have already recorded on the pages of other notebooks how my venture failed and need not repeat it here.

In the days following my release – it would be better to say my escape – from the Tower where Bishop Bonner had had me in his grasp, Robert Dudley, Earl of Leicester, the best friend I ever had in my whole life, kept me company in his Peel Tower in the Sidlaw hills and shortened the long hours with repeated accounts of the plottings and actions that led to my rescue. And my greedy ears could not hear enough of the youthful audacity and bold resolution which Princess Elizabeth had displayed. For I knew much, much more than Dudley could even suspect. I knew, and I could hardly keep the jubilation from my voice, that Princess Elizabeth had done everything for me, had done as much and more than if it had been for herself – had she not drunk the love potion which Mascee and the witch of Uxbridge had prepared from my body fluids?!

I was uplifted by this thought, and by the assurance of the power of the potion which seemed confirmed by the Princess' incredibly audacious act. With magical power I had contrived, through my essence distilled in a potion, to penetrate Elizabeth's soul and will, and to lodge there so that I could never more be driven out and, truly, have not up to this very day been driven out, despite all the stumbling blocks an unfathomable fate has cast in my way.

"Do or die!" – that had been my father's lifelong motto and he had inherited it from his father who had it from my great grandfather; the device seems to be as old as the Dee family itself. And "Do or die!" had been my resolve from the days of my youth and the spur to all my deeds and my successes in chivalry as in scholarship. "Do or die!" – that device had made me when still young in years the teacher and adviser to Kings and Emperors and, I may justly add, one of the foremost masters of natural and occult sciences my country, indeed, the age has produced. "Do or die!" – prised me from the claws of the Inquisition ...

What foolish prattle! Can I name one important thing which I have done in thirty years?! In the years of my virile prime?! – Where is the crown of England? Where is the sovereignty over Greenland – and over the states in the West that today are named after a penniless sailor: The Lands of Amerigo Vespucci ?!

I will skip over the five miserable years during which a fickle fate allowed the consumptive Mary to give the Papists a brief respite to reestablish their false and intolerant rule and plunge England into a vain turmoil of strife.

As far as my own life was concerned, those years seemed like a gift from the wisdom of Providence to teach me to curb my passions, for I used the quiet, to which I was compelled, to pursue in depth the studies and preparations necessary to my Greenland scheme. I was assured of my triumph, assured that my – that our – time would come, the time of the glorious Queen and of me, her consort chosen by prophecy and fate.

When I think back, I feel that this prophecy must have been in my blood since birth. My childhood was full of the secret knowledge of my royal destiny, and perhaps it was because of this blind conviction, passed on to me through the blood, that it never occurred to me to test the claims on which it was grounded.

Yet even today, after so many defeats and disappointments, this knowledge and certainty in the innermost depths of my soul is no whit shaken, however much the *facta* seem to testify against me.

But do they?

Today I feel a compulsion to draw up an account of my fortune, like a merchant, wherein I may set out honestly all the claims of my mind and my will and the successes of my life on the debit and credit leaves of my ledger of fate. For I feel an inner voice urging me to take stock of my life.

There is no evidence I can adduce, no documents or memories, to support my opinion that even my earliest childhood was marked by my certainty that I was bound up with some throne; and that could only be the throne of England, I repeat to myself again and again, for there is something within me that quells all doubt. It may well be that my father, Rowland Dee, in the manner of noblemen who have come down in the world and foresee a miserable end to their line, often praised the rank and reputation of his forebears with high-sounding words and made much of our relationship to the Boleyns and the Greys. But he principally did so when the royal bailiffs had once more come to distrain another meadow or patch of woodland. It can hardly be the memory of these humiliations that fed the fires of my dreams of future glory.

And yet the first token and the first prophecy of my future came from within myself, namely from the glass in which I saw myself, filthy and befuddled with drink, after the celebration of my degree. The words that the ghostly image spoke to me on that occasion still ring in my ears; neither the image nor the words seemed to come from me, for I saw myself in the glass as a separate person from the one I was, and I heard the words coming not from my own lips, but from my companion in the glass. There is no delusion of the senses in this, nor of the memory, for I suddenly went stone cold sober from head to toe when the jack i'the glass addressed me.

Added to this is the strange prophecy the witch of Uxbridge spoke to Lady Elizabeth. Later the Princess herself sent me a secret copy through the mediation of my friend, Robert Dudley, to which she had added three words, which today as then I bear inscribed on my heart: *verificatur in aeternis*. And then there were the even clearer hints and promises of my destiny that Bartlett Greene revealed to me in the Tower and confirmed by unmistakable signs – Bartlett Greene who, as I well know today, was an initiate of the mysteries whose adepts are still to be found in the Scottish Highlands. He greeted me as the "Royal Youth"; often I am gripped by the notion that this expression can, nay must, be interpreted in terms of alchymical symbols, and that the "crown" that was promised me is other than a physical earthly crown. Greene, an ignorant butcher, opened my eyes to the significance of the Nordic Thule, Greenland, as a bridge to the immeasurable lands and treasures of the Indian Continent of which the adventurers, Columbus and Pizarro, had discovered but the smallest and most worthless part and subjected it to the Spanish throne. He showed me the riven crown of the Western Sea, of England and northern America, that is to be made whole, and the King and Queen, conjoined and united on the thrones of the Islands and the New Indies.

And again I am seized by the thought: is all this to be understood in an earthly sense?

And it was *he* – not only in the Tower but twice since when he appeared bodily before me and spoke to me face to face – who planted Rhodri's motto in my breast and fixed it there, as if with an iron clamp: "Do or die!"

And he it was who shook me out of my lethargy for one last endeavour, one supreme exertion, and it was he who, with all the silver-tongued power of an eloquence as clear as the fountainhead of all knowledge and as refreshing as an icy spring on a fevered brow, lured me on and tempted me to prevail upon my Queen whenever the irresolute side of her nature seemed to draw her back trembling from the brink of decision.

Yet again the thought seizes me: is all this to be understood in an earthly sense merely?

But as it is here my purpose to relate everything in its true time and place, I will return to my scrutiny of my past life to see if I can find the cause of the failure of these my most fervent endeavours.

After the death of Queen Mary, which fell in my thirty-third year, my time seemed to have come. At that time, too, I had drawn up in great detail all my plans for a military expedition to take Greenland and to station there a garrison which would serve as a bridgehead for the conquest of the northern regions of America. Not the least circumstance – geographical, navigational or military – that might serve to prosper or hinder such a great enterprise had been forgotten and all had been prepared for an immediate expansion of the power and sovereignty of England.

The beginning was most propitious. In November of the year of her accession, 1558, the young Queen commanded me through my friend Dudley, now Earl of Leicester, to prepare a horoscope for the day of her coronation in Westminster Abbey. I took it as a sign of her friendship for me and was fired with zeal to seek in the configurations of the stars and constellations testimony both of her ascent to power and glory, and of our joint royal destiny, vouchsafed me by the prophecies.

This horoscope, whose miraculous configurations did, indeed, presage a matchless blossoming and harvest for Elizabeth's reign and for England, brought me, beside the warmest praises and a considerable gift of money, hints of an even greater reward from my royal mistress. The purse I tossed aside to a servant, but I hoarded the many secret tokens of her favour which she repeatedly sent to me through Leicester and which confirmed in me the assurance of a speedy fulfilment of all my dreams.

But – nothing was fulfilled!

Queen Elizabeth began to play with me and to this day there is no end to the cat-and-mouse game in sight. At what cost to my energy, to my peace of mind and trust in God and the eternal powers, to my strength of purpose, to all my lower and higher faculties, this account can never reveal. A force strong enough to build a new world and destroy the old was wasted.

Above all, the fawning title of the "Virgin" Queen, which she soon heard from all sides caressing her ear, and which fashion quickly transformed into nothing less than a cypher for majesty itself, so enraptured her that she resolved to honour the name in all she did. Her untamed nature and her love of her own freedom nourished this fatal posture although, on the other side, it clashed with her strong fleshly desires; soon her body screamed for carnal satisfaction, and her lust often took the most perverted forms.

And once, shortly before our first violent falling-out, I was desired to come to Windsor Castle – I am sure I was not mistaken in this – to meet with her unchaperoned. On a sudden impulse I declined, for my ambition was not to spend the night with a virgin on heat, but to share in her royal dignity in the clear light of day.

It may well be, then, that the rumours are true and that my friend Robert Dudley was more accommodating and took the pleasures I denied to both myself and the object of my spiritual desire. God alone knows whether I chose well or not.

It was much later and at the urgent command of Bartlett Greene – the unborn, undead, who comes and goes at will – that I finally drew down upon my head the thunderbolt of her wrath, the threat of which had so long sucked at my strength and which would anyway have struck sooner or later; maybe it was foreordained if not foreseen. Although my vital force and peace of mind had been shattered beyond recall, I did survive the thunderbolt, and who can say whether at another hour or under another constellation her curse might not have totally destroyed me?

However that may be, today I am but the ruin of my former self. Only today I know against whom I must struggle.

Elizabeth continued to treat me in a cruel and capricious manner and when she once more broke her promise to command me to Windsor for conferences on weighty matters of state, instead of for tittle-tattle and teasing love-making, I decided in a fit of anger to leave England once again and go to the Emperor Maximilian in Hungary to offer that enterprising monarch my plans for the conquest and settlement of the northern parts of America.

During the journey, however, I was filled with contrition and I felt I had betrayed the innermost secret I shared with my Queen, and something warned me, and drew me back as if some magic umbilical cord still bound me to my Lady's womb.

So I merely explained to the Emperor some of my ideas on astrology and alchymy in order to secure a position for some months as Imperial mathematician and astrologer. But our signs could not be brought into conjunction, and the next year, the fortieth of my life, I returned to England and found forgiveness from Elizabeth, who was as sweetly alluring and as coldly, regally proud as ever. I spent days of deep satisfaction as her guest in Greenwich; for the first time she bent a willing ear to my propositions and accepted the fruits of my learning with earnest gratitude. She promised me her protection against all who secretly plotted to harm me and I was soon drawn into the intimate circle that was privy to all her plans, hopes and fears.

She confessed to me, by turns calm and tempestuous, that her heart disavowed none of the wild passions of her youth, insofar as they concerned me, and she freely acknowledged that she had not forgotten the potion that she had had from the witch.

To my astonishment I saw that she knew more than I had thought. At the same time, however, she declared with rare solemnity that she felt now and forever for me as a sister for a brother and no longer desired me as her paramour; our companionship must be based on the blood-bond of brother and sister so that it might one day be consummated in the communion of the blood. I understood but little of such fantastical speech – even at that time I felt that some otherworldly being were speaking through the Queen – unless it were intended to put a barrier between us which all my hopes and ambitions would find the greatest difficulty in acknowledging. Still it is strange that I cannot rid myself of the thought that some other being than she, some unknown force and voice, were speaking through her lips, some being whose message I may perhaps never unravel. What could that mean: Consummated in the communion of the blood? In those days in Greenwich I wrestled openly with Elizabeth for love and its requital, for a man's natural right to a woman. In vain. Elizabeth withdrew, more unapproachable than ever.

Yes, after those days of deepest spiritual communion she suddenly turned to me whilst we were taking the morning air in the empty park with a face completely transformed. Her eyes mocked me with an inscrutably equivocal expression, and she said:

"As thou dost plead man's natural right to a woman with me, my friend, I have this last night thought over the matter and resolved not only to grant thy virile urge relief, but to help thee to the satisfaction of thy desire. I would join the spear to the ring and add it to thy achievement as a sign of a happy marriage. I know that thy affairs in Mortlake stand not well and that Gladhill is mortgaged up to the last roof tile. I am sure a rich wife will not come amiss, especially if it is one whose ancestry would not offend the pride of a descendant of Rhodri Mawr. I have decided that thou shalt wed the charming and most gentle companion of my youth, Lady Ellinor Huntingdon. The wedding will take

123

place on the earliest seemly occasion. – Lady Ellinor was informed of Our desire this forenoon, and in her devotion to Us did not hesitate to accept Our wish. By this thou seest, John Dee, how tender is my concern, my sisterly concern, for thee."

The mockery – at least so it seemed to me – of this speech wounded me to the quick. Elizabeth must have known just what my feelings were for Ellinor Huntingdon, that arrogant, overbearing – and tale-bearing – bigot who had shattered our childish dreams and youthful affection. The Queen well knew the injury she would do to me and to herself if, in her absolute power, she ordered me to marry the born enemy of all my instincts, of all my hopes. Again I was consumed with hatred for that incomprehensible something in the character of my Royal beloved; full of bitterness and wounded pride I bowed my head before this disdainful earthly Majesty and, without saying a further word, rode away from Greenwich Park.

Why rehearse once more the battles, the humiliations and the "politic" reasoning that followed? Robert Dudley played the marriage broker and the Queen had her will. I married Lady Ellinor and spent four frigid summers at her side and five frustrated winters, warmed only by the heat of our dislike. Her dowry has made me rich and free from material care; her name has made me envied and honoured among my countrymen. Elizabeth enjoyed her malicious triumph, for she knew that I, her spiritual bride-groom, was in the cold arms of an unloved wife whose kisses were no cause for jealousy for the "Virgin" Queen. As I stood at the altar I swore two oaths: marital fidelity to my wife and, from the depths of my blighted eternal love, vengeance on the cruel mistress who toyed with me, Queen Elizabeth.

It was Bartlett Greene who pointed the way to my revenge.

In the meantime, however, Elizabeth sucked the last drop of malicious pleasure from my torment by involving me in the most intimate aspects of her political schemes. She confided to me that reasons of state made her own marriage advisable. As she asked my opinion as to what kind of qualities I thought her ideal consort should possess, her eye never left my face and her lips were parted in the smile of a torturer observing his victim's suffering. Finally she decided that I was the ideal person – to travel the courts in search of a husband. And this burden, too, I shouldered to complete my humiliation. Nothing came of the marriage projects, and my diplomatic career finished when Elizabeth changed her political alignment and I fell seriously ill in Nancy – and in the guest chamber of one of the candidates for the hand of my Royal Mistress. My pride and courage crushed, I made my way home to England.

On the very day of my dismal return to Mortlake – it was a warm early autumn day of the year 1571 – I learnt from my first wife, Ellinor, who had the nose of a beagle when it came to news, that Elizabeth had sent word that she was to return to Richmond, which was unusual so late in the year. Ellinor could scarce conceal her spiteful jealousy, even though she remained as cold as marble towards me, in spite of the fact that I had been away for so long.

And Elizabeth did, indeed, return to Richmond. She came with but a small retinue and took up residence as if she intended to stay for some considerable time. Now, it is scarcely a mile from Richmond to Mortlake; an early encounter with the Queen was inevitable and likely to be repeated, unless she had expressly desired not to see me. The opposite was the case and Elizabeth received me the next day with great honour and friendship, just as she had sent two of her own physicians to attend me in Nancy and ordered her most trusted courier, William Sidney, to see to my every need.

Even now she showed herself most concerned for my welfare and, through words casually dropped here or there, through the bewildering shower of favours she poured on me, made it daily clearer how relieved, how happy she was in her regained liberty and how grateful she was to have escaped the bonds of a marriage which could have inspired in her neither love nor fidelity. In brief, her hints often seemed to flutter round the flame of our secret union, and it often seemed to me as if my unfathomable Mistress were at the same time mocking Ellinor's quibbling and fruitless jealousy and justifying it. For more than a month my blind devotion kept me tied to my Lady's apron strings; and more than at any other time she bent an earnest and approving ear to my boldest plans to bring glory to her and her government. Once again she seemed fired with enthusiasm for the idea of a Greenland Expedition and set everything in train to examine the plans and make preparations.

In several reports drawn up by the Admiralty my meticulously prepared dispositions and projects were judged to be practicable and the military advisers were in enthusiastic agreement. Week by week the Queen became more impatient to start the Great Enterprise. I believed I was close to the goal of my life's ambition, and Elizabeth's lips – lips magically radiant with a most auspicious smile – had spoken the word that would have made me Viceroy of all new lands subject to the English crown – "King of the Throne beyond the Western Sea". But in one single night my life's glorious dream was shattered in the most cruel, most miserable, most bitter reversal any man's heart and soul have ever had to suffer. What the hidden event was that led to it, I do not know. Even today darkness surrounds the dreadful mystery of the collapse of my hopes.

This much I do know:

A final meeting of the Privy Council with all the Queen's closest advisers had been arranged for that evening; in particular, the Secretary of State, Sir

Francis Walsingham, had been commanded to appear. Late in the afternoon I had an audience with my Mistress to give counsel on a number of matters – or, rather, I conversed with her under the autumn splendour of the trees in the park as with my closest and most intimate friend. At one point, when we were in accord on all aspects of my project, she grasped my hand and said to me, her regal gaze fixed questioningly on mine:

"And wilt thou, John Dee, as Lord of the new provinces and subject to Our Crown, ever keep thine eye fixed on Our advantage?"

At this I threw myself to my knees before my Queen and swore, as God was my witness and my judge, that from that time forward my sole aim should be to expand her Power and influence on the new Indian continent.

A strange light flashed in her eyes. With her strong hand she herself raised me from my knees and said slowly:

"Thou sayest well, John Dee. I see that thou art determined to devote thy self and thy life to the service of – – – England by subjugating the new continent to Our power. The country thanks thee for thy good will."

With these cool and impenetrable words she dismissed me.

That very night the envious and short-sighted Secretary of State, Walsingham, succeeded in persuading the Queen to put the enterprise off until some vague future date when it had been scrutinised once more.

Two days later Elizabeth removed the court to London without having taken leave of me.

I was prostrate with a despair that words cannot express.

It was then, in the night, that Bartlett Greene appeared to me once more with his thunderous laugh and mocked me in his coarse manner:

"Ho there, brother Dee; thou wouldst be a mighty warrior and conqueror to the wife of thy soul – thou dost but trample on her fondest dreams like the bull in the adage and stirrest up her maidenly jealousy. Thou art surprised the cat doth scratch when thou strokest it's fur widdershins!"

Greene's mocking speech suddenly opened my eyes and I could see into Elizabeth's soul and read it like an open book: she could not bear that I should devote my passion and zeal to anything other than to her person and to win any other prize than her commendation. And in my need and dire despair I raised myself up in my bed and beseeched Bartlett Greene to counsel me, what I might do to make good the hurt I had done my noble Mistress. And in that night Greene revealed to me many things from the marvellous power of his knowledge and instructed me how to see into the magic coal which he had given me on the night he had departed this side of the world and wherein I was shown proof that both Queen Elizabeth and Walsingham were my implacable enemies – he, because he was about to become her paramour, she because of the wound I had done her woman's pride. Thereupon I fell into a rage; my long curbed desire for vengeance for all the torments I had suffered was unchained and I surrendered to the counsel of Bartlett Greene, who told me what must be done to render the "woman" Elizabeth once more compliant to my will and my blood.

In that same night, therefore, with my lust for revenge boiling over, I prepared myself according to the instructions of the wraith-like Bartlett Greene.

I dare not here describe all the ceremonies I performed to gain power over Elizabeth's soul and over her body. Greene stood by me as the sweat dripped from my every pore and my heart and brain throbbed so violently that I thought every moment I would collapse in a faint. All I can say is: there are beings the very sight of which is so dreadful that it

128

freezes the blood – can one comprehend that even more dreadful is the awareness of their unseen presence! The fear is compounded by a terrible feeling of impotence and blindness.

I finally completed the conjurations, the last part of which had to be performed naked, out of doors and by the light of the waning moon. I raised the black coal scrying glass up in the moonlight and, for the time it takes to say three *Paternosters*, concentrated all my will-power on its gleaming facets. Greene disappeared and the figure of Queen Elizabeth, eyes closed and in mysterious haste, approached with a kind of floating gait over the lawn of the park. I could see that my Mistress was neither awake, nor sleeping a natural sleep. Rather she seemed like a ghost. I shall never forget the sensation that filled my breast. My heart was not beating – no, it was a wild, unarticulated scream that tore itself away from my throbbing blood and awoke, distant and yet deep within me, a ghastly echo, as of a chaos of voices that made my scalp prickle with horror. But I gathered all my courage, took Elizabeth by the hand and led her into my chamber, as Greene had commanded me. At first her hand was cold, but soon it and her whole body became warm, as if, the longer I touched her, the more my blood flowed into her. Finally my tender caresses opened her lips in a warm smile, which I took as a sign of her inner acceptance and a revelation of the true longing of her soul. I hesitated no longer; in joyous exultation of my victory, I consummated our marriage with all my senses afire with the fury of lust.

Thus I took by force my predestined wife.

In John Dee's diary this account is followed by several pages covered with strange and confused signs, which it would be impossible to reproduce, a jumble of symbols and calculations, letters and numbers, perhaps with some cabbalistic significance. It does not appear to be a meaningful secret code, but, on the other hand, nor does it look like haphazard doodling. I suspect that these cyphers are connected with the conjurations my ancestor performed to compel Elizabeth to appear. These pages exude a sense of horror, like a subtle odour, so that it is impossible to concentrate upon them for more than a few minutes at a time. I feel distinctly the presence of madness on these pages of John Dee's notebook, pressed flat like the crumbling petals of flowers between the leaves of an ancient diary, and the madness rises like some unmentionable aura and threatens to engulf my own brain. Madness has scrawled its unmistakable mark on these pages, and the next legible lines, scribbled down in haste, seem to confirm it. They rise, if I may put it like this, like the head of a drowning man spluttering up from the waves.

Before I continue copying out the book there are a few things I want to note down, for my own justification and to confirm my own memory:

First of all: I have always felt the need to be consciously aware of what is going on within me. Thanks to this characteristic I know that something is happening to me: the more I continue to work my way through John Dee's inheritance – the less I feel sure of myself. At times I lose my grip on myself; I suddenly find myself reading with another's eyes, my thoughts seem to come from an alien mind: it is not my brain which is thinking, the thoughts are produced somewhere physically outside the body sitting here. At such times I need the guiding hand of consciousness to jolt myself out of this state of uncontrolled vertigo – a "spiritual" vertigo.

Secondly: I note that John Dee did indeed flee to Scotland after his imprisonment in the Tower and did indeed find somewhere to stay in the area of the Sidlaw Hills. I note further that John Dee had the same experience with the chrysalis as I did, right down to the similarity of formulation. – Is it only the blood that one inherits? Can one inherit experiences? Of course, it could easily be explained if one assumes "coincidence". Of course, of course; but to me it feels different. To me it feels the opposite of coincidence; what I am experiencing is... I don't know what. And that is why I need my consciousness in control.

Continuation of the Notebooks of John Dee

Elizabeth returned another time, but after so many years do I really know that it was truly Elizabeth herself? Was it not rather a ghost? She sucked at me like a vampire. Was it not Elizabeth after all? Dreadful thought. Was it Black Isaïs? A succubus? No, Black Isaïs has nothing to do with my Elizabeth! But do I? – – – And yet Elizabeth partook of the experience; yes, Elizabeth herself! Whatever I did with the demon, if such it was, Elizabeth also experienced through some inexplicable manner of metamorphosis. And yet the Elizabeth who came to me through the park by the light of the waning moon was none other than my Elizabeth, and not Black Isaïs!!!

And in that night of dark temptation I lost my most valued heirloom: my talisman, the dagger – the spearhead of my ancestor Hywel Dda. I lost it on the lawn in the park where I performed the conjuration, and it seems to me that I was holding it in my hand, according to the instruction of Bartlett Greene, when the ghost approached me and I held out my hand. Then it was gone. – Did I pay to Black Isaïs what I later was to receive from Black Isaïs?

Today I seem to understand it thus: Isaïs is the woman within all women, and one word may transform all womankind into Isaïs!

After that it became impossible for me to see into Elizabeth's mind. She had become completely foreign to me and yet I felt her as close as never before. Very close: that is the worst thought that the lonely soul can torture itself with. Very close, without union: that is almost like death. Queen Elizabeth was

131

very gracious to me. Her cold gaze scorched my heart. Her Majesty was as far above me as Sirius. She exuded a great and ghostly coldness when I was in her presence. And she often commanded me to Windsor. But when I came she only had empty words for me. It was enough for her to kill me again with one glance. The silence between our souls was terrible.

Once she rode by Mortlake. With her riding crop she smote the linden tree by the gate where I stood to greet her. The tree sickened and the branches withered. – – –

Later I met the Queen in the marshes close by Windsor Castle where she was flying her hawks at a heron. At my side was my trusty bulldog. Elizabeth signalled me to approach. She received my greeting graciously and stroked my dog. It died the following night. – – –

The linden tree withered from the base upward. The splendid tree had become a pitiful sight and I ordered it to be felled. — -

I did not see my Queen again for the rest of the autumn and the whole of the winter. No invitation, no attention at all paid to me. Leicester kept his distance, too.

I was alone with Ellinor, who had hated me from the beginning.

I buried myself in the study of Euclid. But there is one thing that the Father of Geometry failed to understand: our world is not limited to his three dimensions, length, breadth and height. For many years I have been close to working out a theory of the fourth dimension. The world is not bounded by our five senses, not even our own nature is ….

The clear winter nights allowed me to make wonderful observations of the heavens. My soul settled and became once more a fixed point in my breast, like the Pole Star in the immeasurable vastnesses of the cosmos. I had begun a treatise entitled,

"*De stella admiranda in Cassiopeia*". Cassiopeia is a mysterious constellation; it changes in size and brightness, often within hours. So stars, too, may be soft and disappear like the light in a man's soul. Marvellous are the soothing powers that stream down upon us from the vault of heaven.

In the middle of March Queen Elizabeth, most unexpectedly, most perplexingly, sent Leicester to announce her intention to visit me in Mortlake. What can she want!? I asked myself at the time. Dudley had appeared on the Queen's errand. To my astonishment, to my horror even, he asked me abruptly and in forthright words about a certain "*glass*" or magic crystal that was said to be in my possession and which the Queen would like to see. I was so taken by surprise that I could not conceal the truth and deny the stone, which Bartlett Greene had given me and through which I had already achieved so much. In a few brief words Dudley revealed that Her Majesty was informed of the stone, having seen it in my possession in a dream one night the previous autumn. My heart stood still for a moment when Dudley repeated his message but I managed, with some difficulty, to keep my composure, and recommended myself through him to my Lady's favour, saying that, of course, everything in my possession was hers to command.

As Dudley left – oh, how long ago it all is! – he kissed the hand of my former wife, Ellinor, which she withdrew in unseemly haste. Afterwards she confessed to me, with a dark look, that as the lips of the noble Lord had touched her hand she had felt the breath of Death brush her skin. I rebuked Ellinor for such unbecoming words.

So the Mistress of Windsor came with Dudley and one squire. She knocked at my window with her riding crop. Ellinor was much startled, clutched at her heart and collapsed to the floor in a swoon. I bore her to a couch but ran out without examining her to

133

greet my Lady. But she asked me how my wife did and, when she heard of the incident, told me to see to Ellinor – in the meantime she would rest in the park. She would not enter my house, however much I did entreat her. Then I went to the room where my wife lay and found her dying. With my heart full of dread, I crept away to my Mistress and took the "*glass*" to her; but no word was spoken between us of Ellinor. I could see from Elizabeth's face that she knew my wife was at Death's door. After an hour the Queen rode off. And that evening Ellinor was dead. A stroke had put an end to her life. – – – That was on the twenty-first day of March in the year 1575.

In the time before and after these terrible events my life force was at its lowest ebb. There is no need to say more on this than: I thank Heaven that today I can look back on those times of distress sound of mind and soul.

Whenever demons enter upon our frailty we are always touched with a premonition of the death of the body or, what is worse, the death of the spirit, and it is only by grace if we escape it.

After that day Queen Elizabeth never came again to Mortlake. Nor was I again commanded to court, and right glad I was of it. I had taken an aversion to my Mistress which was worse than hate, for it meant we were as far apart as possible and yet cursed with inward closeness.

To conclude, I decided to do of my own free will what once my Mistress had compelled me to: after three years as a widower and in the fifty-fourth year of my life I took a wife after my own heart, a wife who had never known nor seen Elizabeth and London, the court and the great world, an innocent and healthy child of nature; Jane Fromond was the daughter of a yeoman farmer, a commoner and therefore unworthy ever to be presented to her Majesty. But what did that matter? She was a sweet young woman of twenty-three years and completely devoted to me. And soon I sensed, by some strange knowledge of the blood and the certainty within my heart, that I had deeply wounded my Mistress and that far from me the impotence of her anger embittered her days. It doubled the pleasure I felt in the arms of my young wife that I was knowingly and wittingly hurting the one who had caused me so much pain. Then one day I heard that Elizabeth was sick with the ague in Richmond and when I heard it I was pierced with the dagger of remorse and sped, uncalled, to Richmond, to my Mistress; and I was not turned away but presently commanded to her sick-bed where I found her in great danger.

When I approached her she ordered with a wave of her hand all those, nobles and servants, who were about her to leave the chamber, and I was alone with her for half an hour and will never forget our talk for the rest of my days.

"Thou hast wounded me sore, friend John", she began. "Twice thou hast put the witch between us, twice, with the potion and then with dreams, thou hast allowed another influence to step between us; little hast thou profited by it."

My immediate response was to reject the imputation, for through my Jane's simple and natural affection I had recovered my peace of mind and I did not intend once more to be caught up in equivocal games of lustful glances and cold rejection such as the capricious Queen loved. So my answer was duly respectful to her Majesty but, as I thought, both cunning and manly:

"Any potion that was drunk, if it were of free will and, perhaps, from an excess of high spirits, could not violate the laws of nature, nor those of the divine spirit. According to nature, anything harmful to the body is either the death of the body, or is killed by the body, which devours and discharges it. According to the law of the spirit, however, we are granted freedom over our will, so that our dreams, whether they feed the mind or are excretions from it, always come in fulfilment of our own will. Thus anything that was drunk without harm to the body is long since vanished; any dreams that were forced upon us will have been discharged by a healthy organism, so that we have every reason to hope that God will grant that Your Majesty will arise from any such afflictions strengthened in health and freedom."

My speech had turned out bolder and more of a rebuff than I had intended when I began; I was afraid at the pale and severe features which stared at me from the pillows. However it was not anger I saw, but an unapproachable and alien grandeur which chilled me to the marrow; it seemed as if I heard the "spiritual" Queen speaking:

"You have wandered far from your destined course, scion of the line of Rhodri. At night you observe the stars in the sky above your roof in the cool light of reason; but you have forgotten that the way to them passes through the image of them that lies within you, and you do not realise that there are Gods there that would see you rise to join them. You have dedicated a learned treatise to me, *De stella admiranda in Cassiopeia*. Oh, John Dee, you admire too many things and have neglected to become a wonder of the cosmos yourself! But you were right in your supposition that the admirable star in Cassiopeia was a double star which revolves blissfully around itself, forever blazing forth and then drawing in upon itself, like the nature of love itself. Go on making your observations of the double star in Cassiopeia; I may soon leave this tiny Kingdom of the Islands to seek the riven crown which is reserved for me when I cross over – – –"

At these words I collapsed at my Mistress' bedside and in my stupor was only half aware of what else was said between us.

But the Queen's illness proved to be much worse than had been at first thought and the doctors began

136

to despair of her life. Then I set out for Holland and Germany to seek the famous physicians who were known to me from Louvain and Paris, but none were to be found in the cities where they lived, so that I spent day and night galloping in search of them until news of Her Majesty's recovery reached me in Frankfort on the Oder.

And so I returned for the third time from a fruitless expedition in my Mistress' service and found my wife Jane had been delivered of a child, my dear son Arthur whom she bore me in the fifty-fifth year of my life.

Since that time my commerce with Queen Elizabeth and the court in London has been scanty and free of terrors as of joys, of sorrows as of the secret thrill of hope. My life in the last two years has flowed as smoothly as the little Dee outside my window – not without its pleasant aspects as it winds its way through the peaceful countryside, but without violent rapids or the majestic sweep of a mighty river in its destined course towards a distant ocean.

Last year Queen Elizabeth accepted one last *tractatus* from my pen: as a summation of my North American ambitions, which I had carefully planned in such rigorous detail, I dedicated to her the *Tabula geografica Americae*, in which I once more dwelt on the incalculable advantages of this enterprise, an opportunity to be seized which would never arise again. I have done all that lay in my power. If Her Majesty prefers the counsel of narrow-souled envy to that of friendship, then England will let this moment of destiny pass ungrasped. But I can wait, that I have learnt in my fifty years. Now it is Burleigh who has the ear of our Mistress – an ear that all too easily takes its cue from the eye and inclines itself to a handsome figure. There is no love lost between Burleigh and myself. I expect little from his judgment and less from his goodwill.

But there is another matter which serves to strengthen my composure, so that I no longer tremble at the decisions of the Privy Council. After the trials of all these years I have come to doubt whether it is the earthly Greenland that is the goal of my striving, the true object of the conquest prophesied me. Recently I have found cause to doubt whether I interpreted the words of my jack i'the glass aright; I have cause to distrust my satanic counsellor, Bartlett Greene, in spite of the accuracy of his supernatural foresight. His most devilish trick is to tell the truth, but in such manner that it is misunderstood. – – – This world is not the whole world, that was the message Greene gave me in the hour of his death. This world has a counterworld, a plurality of dimensions, which by no means exhaust themselves in the world of our bodies and our space; Greenland, too, has its mirror image, just as I do: on the other side. A Green Land! Are not my Greenland and my America over *there*? This thought has occupied reason and intuition since I sensed the *other side*. And Bartlett Greene's insistence that I should seek the fount of being here alone, here and nowhere else, has become rather a warning to my intuition than an argument to support my reasoning. For I have learnt to mistrust reason as if it were Bartlett Greene himself. Greene is not my friend, however much he may play the part of my saviour and counsellor. It may be he saved my body from the Tower to destroy my soul! I recognised him when he brought the demon to me that clothed herself in Elizabeth's astral body to take possession of me. I have received tidings from my inner self which make my whole former life seem foreign to me, as if seen in a green mirror, and which impel me to renounce that mirror whose prophecy once transformed my life.

I have become other than the one who was the chrysalis which now hangs dead from a branch of the tree of life.

This last twelvemonth I have no longer been the marionette, dancing on the strings that came out of the green glass; I am free!

Free for metamorphosis, ascension, empire! Free for the "Queen" and the "Crown"!

That is the end of the notebook in which John Dee recorded his life from his release from the Tower to the year 1581, that is a period of almost twenty-eight years, taking him up to the fifty-seventh year of his life, an age at which most ordinary men look forward to calm repose and the descent into old age.

A vibrancy, an inexplicable excitement, a more than usual involvement in the vicissitudes of this strange career all tell me, John Dee's descendant, that the real storms, the decisive struggles, the titanic upheavals are only about to begin, they will erupt, seethe, rage – – my God, how is it that I am suddenly filled with horror?! Is it I who am writing? Have I become John Dee? Is this my hand? Not his hand? – Not his? – And my G..., who is that standing there? Is it a ghost? There, there at my desk!

– – –

I am tired. I have not slept a wink all night. The shattering experience and the hours struggling to preserve my sanity are now behind me; the raging storm, which brings both devastation and refreshment, has passed over and the landscape is clear and calm once more.

At least now, in the first light of a new day, I am able to set down the external course of last night's events.

It was about seven o'clock in the evening when I finished translating the Dee notebook with the retrospective of his life. The last words I wrote down reveal how deeply moved I was by his life history, more deeply, perhaps than seems necessary for someone mechanically transcribing old family documents. Were I given to such fancies, I would say that the John Dee that I, as the heir to

139

his blood, bear within me, has risen from the dead. From the dead? Is someone dead who still lives on in the cells of his offspring's offspring? – – – But I will not attempt to explain this excessive sympathy. It is enough that it is there, that it has taken possession of me.

It went so far that, in a way that is difficult to describe but that was not merely a kind of memory, I shared in all those fluctuations of fortune, shared the life of the the disappointed scholar living in seclusion with his wife and young son at Mortlake; I could not only see the house with its park, rooms and furniture – which, of course, I had never visited – I could see them with John Dee's eyes and felt attached to them as he had been; but beyond that even, I could sense, with an uncanny, painful and oppressive force, fate looming up on my unfortunate ancestor, an explorer of the soul rather than of the globe; it was as if I could see in my mind's eye my own inevitable fate, gathering like a dark bank of cloud over a landscape that was the geography of my soul.

I must stop myself from saying more, for I can feel my thoughts beginning to become entangled again and words are starting to slip the leash. It fills me with fear.

I will say no more of the nameless dread of that moment, but record the events as objectively as I can:

As I wrote those last few lines I had a physical vision of John Dee's future from the point at which the notebook breaks off. It was a vision of such vivid intensity, as if I had lived through those later years with John Dee. What am I saying: with John Dee? I saw it as John Dee, I had become John Dee, of whom I knew, and still know, nothing other than what I have written down on these pages.

And at that moment of certainty when I knew I was John Dee, I felt a vague sensation at the back of my head, as if I were growing a second face there, a Janus head – – – the Baphomet! And as I sat there observing myself and my transformation with an icy, numb detachment, John Dee's destiny took physical shape and played itself out in the room around me.

Between the desk and the window Bartlett Greene materialised out of thin air, his leather jerkin open at the neck, red hair on the pale skin of his chest, his broad butcher's face on its thick neck fringed with a fiery beard and showing a wide, friendly grin not two paces from me.

Instinctively I rubbed my eyes and, when the first awful shock was over, examined what was happening in the clear light of reason. But the figure stayed there, standing in front of me, and I knew it was no other than Bartlett Greene.

And then the incomprehensible happened: I was – and was not – myself; I was here and over there at the same time, I was present and had long since passed over: everything at once. I was "I" and another, I was John Dee in memory and in immediate consciousness at the same time. It was a dislocation which words cannot put back into joint. Perhaps the best way to put it is to say that both time and space were dislocated, like something seen when you squeeze one eyeball: askew, real and unreal at the same time – which eye is seeing the "real" image? Hearing was as dislocated as vision. Greene's mocking voice seemed to come both from the immediate vicinity and from the distant centuries:

"Still trotting along, are we, brother Dee? By my troth, thou takest the long way round. And it could have been so straightforward!"

"I" wanted to speak. "I" wanted to find words to ward off the ghost. But my throat was blocked, my tongue tied. I was fully aware of the unpleasant physical sensation, but at the same time I heard a voice "thinking" within me and speaking over the centuries, producing sound waves which my physical ear received; and the words were not words of my choosing, and they said: "Once more you stand in my way, Bartlett Greene, and try to stop me reaching my goal. Desist, and leave the way free for me to join my image in the green glass!"

The red-bearded ghost – or, if you like, Bartlett Greene in person – stared me straight in the face with his milky-white wall–eye. His smile gaped like the yawn of a big cat: "Out of the green mirror, out of the black coal the face of the maiden in the waning moon looks down on you – you know, brother Dee, the good lady who is so concerned about the spearhead."

I stared at Greene, holding my breath in horror. A welter of thoughts, curses, regrets, incantations poured in on me from outside, but they were held back, turned aside, repulsed by one single recognition, which suddenly galvanised my benumbed consciouness out of its lethargy:

"Lipotin! – – The Princess' spearhead! – The spear is demanded of me! –"

With that it was all over. But I fell into a dreamlike musing in which my half-awake senses seemed to experience the conjuration of the succubus in the moonlit garden at Mortlake. What I had read about in the notebook now took on an immediate and sharp–contoured corporeality, and what had appeared to John Dee as the hovering figure of Queen Elizabeth was for me that of Princess Shotokalungin; and the Bartlett Greene before me faded before the dream I summoned up of John Dee's carnal delight in the demonic phantom of Queen Elizabeth. – – –

That is all that I can recall of the mysterious events of yesterday evening. The rest is all hazy with mist – a dream gone out of focus.

John Roger's legacy has taken on a life of its own. I can no longer play the role of uninvolved translator. I am involved, somehow involved with these – these things here, these papers, books, amulets – and with this Tulaware box. No, surely not that; the box is not part of the legacy. It came from the dead Baron – – from Lipotin! From the descendant of Mascee! From the man who comes here looking for the spearhead for Princes Shotokalungin! – – It all hangs together!! – But how? Can chains of mist, bonds of smoke waft down the centuries to bind me, to enslave me?

My life here, with all the objects that surround me, is already determined by the "meridian"! I need calm nerves and a cool head. Waves of confusion lap over me. At any moment my reason might go under. It is foolish, it is dangerous. If I lose control over these visions then – – –

When I think of Lipotin and his inscrutable, cynical features, or of the Princess, that magnificent woman – I come out in a cold sweat. I am completely alone, completely without outside help against – – let us say, against these monstrous products of my own imagination, against – – ghosts!

I must pull myself together.

Afternoon.

Today I cannot bring myself to reach into the drawer and pull out a new notebook. It is partly because my nerves are still tingling with the agitation; partly, it is the – pleasurable – impatience caused by the news, that came with midday post, of a surprise reunion.

It is always a tense occasion to meet a friend of your youth, with whom you were once very close but who vanished from view more than half a lifetime ago and who promises to bring back the past unscathed. Unscathed? An error, of course: surely he will have changed just as I have; none of us can preserve the past. That is an error which often causes disappointment. I must keep my expectation within bounds when I think of this evening when I will collect Theodor Gärtner from the station: Theodor Gärtner, the wild companion of my student days years ago, the young chemist whose love of adventure took him to Chile, where he found position, reputation and wealth. He'll have become americanised, a smooth operator who has decided to spend his booty in the peace and quiet of his native heath.

On thing that irritates me a little is that it happens to be today, when I am expecting this visit, that my housekeeper, who knows all my little ways, had finally gone on holiday to the village where she comes from. I could not legitimately keep her here any longer. When I think about it, she has been due this trip for three years now! Her conscientiousness – or my selfishness – kept making her put it off; in this case it would be the turn of my selfishness again – no, impossible! I will just have to grin and bear it and try to manage with the replacement she has arranged for me who is due to turn up tomorrow. I am curious to see how I shall get on with this doctor's cast-off who is supposed to replace my old housekeeper:

Divorced lady, – the innocent party, of course; *without means* – supposedly – *compelled to seek position*. – *Quiet household; honest and reliable* – Hm, we'll see –

More likely: "Lena comes to look
          With fishing rod and hook"

as the old poem has it. So beware! I have to laugh when I think of the dreadful dangers that might threaten an old bachelor like me! Anyway, she's not called "Lena" but Johanna Fromm. On the other hand, this ex-doctor's wife is only twenty-three years old. We'll have to be on our guard on all fronts and make sure that the safe stronghold of bachelordom is well-defended.

    Let's hope at least she's a good cook!

I don't think there will be any work done on John Roger's legacy today. First I must sort out the events and impressions of yesterday evening.

    It seems to me that keeping a diary must be another characteristic I have inherited along with the Dee blood and the Dee coat of arms. If things go on like this I will have to start keeping a similar record of my own adventures. At the same time I feel the urge more strongly than ever to penetrate the long forgotten mysteries of John Dee's life, for I feel the key must lie hidden somewhere amongst them – the key not only to the forces and fates that determined his life, but also, oddly enough, to the understanding of the labyrinth I plunged into when I started to investigate the life of my adventuresome ancestor. All other thoughts and desires

144

are pushed aside in my feverish impatience to open the next volume of his diaries or, even more, to force open the silver Tula-ware box sitting there on my desk. – – – My imagination is running riot after the overexcitement of the past night. The only way to calm it down and bring it under control is to set down what happened in a neat and orderly fashion. So:

Yesterday evening – on the dot of six – I was waiting for the arrival of the train by which, according to the telegram, my friend, Dr. Gärtner, was to arrive. I took up a perfect position at the barrier so that no-one could leave the platform without my seeing them.

The express arrived on time and I checked every passenger; my friend Gärtner was not among them. I waited until the last of the travellers had passed the ticket control; I waited until the train had been shunted to another line. Somewhat disappointed, I turned to leave the station.

Then I recalled that another train coming from the same direction, though not an international one, was due in a few minutes. I turned back, took up my position again and waited for that train.

In vain! His old punctuality and reliability must be one of the things, I thought irritably, that has changed with the years, and not for the better. Annoyed, I left the station to make my way home, expecting perhaps to find a telegram cancelling the visit already there.

I had hung around at the ticket barrier for almost an hour and it was getting on for seven and dusk already when, aimlessly wandering down a side alley that was not even on my route home, I ran into Lipotin. It was such a sudden surprise to meet the old antiques dealer that I stopped and responded to his greeting with the rather foolish question:

"What on earth are you doing here?"

Lipotin looked at me in astonishment – my bewilderment must have been obvious to him – and his sarcastic smile, that I found so irritating, immediately spread across his face. He gave the street a quizzical look and said:

145

"What I am doing here? May I respectfully enquire what is special about this street? Its one advantage is that it takes me in an almost straight north-to-south line from my coffee house to my flat. And, as I am sure you are aware, a straight line is the shortest distance between two points; – – but, if you will permit me to mention it, you seem to be taking a roundabout route; I can't imagine what would bring you to this alley, unless you are walking in your sleep!" And Lipotin gave a loud laugh which contrasted with the threat that seemed to lie behind his words. I must have given him a rather blank, disconcerted stare, as I replied:

"Sleepwalking – quite right. I – I was on my way home."

"Isn't it remarkable how easy it is for a dreamer to get lost in his native city! If you want to get home, my dear sir, you should go back and turn off left down that street there – – – but, if you permit, I will accompany you a few blocks."

In irritation I shook my head to clear it of the foolish trance I was in and said, a little shamefacedly, "Indeed, Lipotin, it does seem that I have been sleeping on my feet. Thank you for waking me up. But do allow *me* to accompany *you*." Lipotin seemed pleased and we walked to his quarters together. On the way he told me – without prompting! – that Princess Shotokalungin had been asking after me recently – I had obviously made a great impression on her; I could congratulate myself on a flattering conquest. I told Lipotin rather emphatically that I was no "conqueror" and had no intention of – but Lipotin raised his hands in mock horror and laughed; adding lightly, but not without a clear hint of mockery, "By the way, she didn't even mention the famous spearhead. That is the way she is. Obstinate one day, indifferent the next. The female prerogative, is it not, my dear sir."

I must say that I felt a certain amount of relief at this information. Only a caprice, after all!

When, therefore, Lipotin suggested he take me to visit the Princess some time in the next few days – he was sure the Princess would be pleased if I were to call, indeed, she was expecting it after she had, so to speak, forced her way in on me – it seemed to me a courtesy that was perfectly in order and the ideal opportunity to renew my acquaintance with the Princess – perhaps even to clear up the matter of the antique spearhead.

Meanwhile we had reached the house where Lipotin had his shop and his room. I was about to take my leave of him when he suddenly said, "Now that you're here I've just remembered that I had a delivery of some rather nice antiques from Bucharest yesterday – you know, the backdoor route by which I occasionally manage to get the odd thing out from under the noses of the Bolsheviks. Nothing sensational, I'm afraid, but there might be something you'd like to cast your eye over. Have you a minute to spare? Why don't you come up and have a look?"

I hesitated for a moment because I thought there might be a telegram from my friend Gärtner waiting for me at home; it did occur to me that if I stayed out I might miss a rearranged time. But then I remembered my irritation at Gärtner's lack of punctuality and made up my mind rather more quickly than I intended and without allowing myself the chance to think it over carefully:

"I've plenty of time. I'll come up."

Lipotin was already pulling an ancient key out of his pocket; the lock grated and I was stumbling through the shop door into the dark room.

I have often visited the Russian's poky little basement by daylight; it is as romantic in its seediness as one could wish. Had it not been that by normal European standards this damp cellar, ridden with dry rot, was regarded as uninhabitable, Lipotin would have been unlikely to have obtained even this hovel, given the shortage of housing in the years after the Great War.

Lipotin lit the tiny flame of his cigarette lighter and rummaged around in a corner. The gleam of dull light from the alley was not enough to enable me to get my bearings among the pile of fusty jumble. Lipotin's tiny flame flickered and spluttered like a jack o' lantern over a dark brown swamp from which lumps and knobs protruded, fragments of half-drowned objects. Finally the meagre light of a candle stump glowed in the corner, at first only illuminating the object in its immediate vicinity, a dreadful, obscene idol in matt polished soapstone; the candle was wedged into a hole in its fist. Lipotin was still bent over it, presumably to see whether the flame would survive on the dusty wick; – it looked as if he were performing some sketchy, secretive ritual before the idol. Then, in the cold flicker of the candle, his fingers finally fumbled their way to a paraffin lamp and soon a relatively cosy glow spread from its green glass. I had spent the whole time cramped motionless in a corner and now I heaved a sigh of relief.

"The mystery of 'Let there be light' unfolding step by step, just as in the days of creation!" I called to Lipotin. "After such a revelation of the three-fold intensification of the sacred flame, how mean and vulgar is our unpoetic electric switch."

From the corner where Lipotin was bustling about came his dry, almost croaking voice:

"Quite right, my dear sir. If you move too quickly out of the benign darkness into the brightness, you will ruin your eyes. That sums up your history, you Europeans."

I was forced to laugh. There we had it again, that asiatic arrogance which – hey presto! – turned a wretched back-street basement into a positive advantage. I was tempted to take up the pointless argument about the advantages or disadvantages of our beloved electricity industry, for I knew that such challenges usually drew a few witty, if caustic, remarks from Lipotin, but glancing around the room my eye was suddenly caught by the dull golden glow of a beautifully carved, antique Florentine frame around a spotted, clouded mirror. I gave it a close examination and could immediately see that it was excellent, very painstaking and yet sensitive workmanship from the seventeenth century. The frame appealed to me so much that I felt an immediate urge to have it in my possession.

"I see you have already found one of the pieces that arrived yesterday", said Lipotin and came over to me, "but the worst one. It's valueless."

"The mirror, you mean? That certainly."

"The frame as well", said Lipotin. His face, greenish in the rays of the lamp, was suffused with a reddish glow as he inhaled deeply on the cigar in his mouth.

"The frame?" I hesitated. Lipotin did not think it was genuine. That was his affair! But immediately I felt ashamed of my instinctive collector's reaction when dealing with someone as poor as Lipotin. He was watching me closely. Had he noticed that I felt ashamed? Strange – something akin to disappointment flitted across his face. I had an uncanny feeling in the pit of my stomach. I finished my sentence on a note of defiance: "The frame is, in my opinion, good."

"Good? Certainly! But a copy. Made in St. Petersburg. I sold the original years ago to Prince Yussupoff."

Hesitantly I turned the mirror this way and that in the light of the lamp. I am well acquainted with the quality of St. Petersburg forgeries. The Russians rival the Chinese in the art. And yet: this frame was genuine! – – – Then, quite by chance, concealed on the underside of a voluptuously curving piece of scrollwork, I discovered the mark of the Florentine studio, half hidden by the old varnish. The collector in me rebelled against the idea of revealing my discovery to Lipotin. Honour would be satisfied if I stuck by my original judgment. So, honestly and openly I said, "The frame is too good, even for the best of copies. In my opinion it's genuine."

Lipotin gave an irritated shrug of the shoulders:

"If this one here is the original then Prince Yussupoff must have been given the copy. – – Anyway, it doesn't matter, the price I received was for the original; and the Prince, his house and his collections have been swept away from the face of the earth. Any further argument is pointless; to each his own."

"And the old mirror, obviously English?" I asked.

"Is, if you insist, genuine. It is the mirror that was originally in the frame. Yussupoff had a new Venetian glass put in the frame as he was buying the mirror for his own use. He was superstitious. He said too many people had already looked into the mirror; that kind of thing could bring bad luck."

"And so –?"

"And so you can keep it, sir, if it has taken your fancy. It's not worth talking about a price."

"But if the frame is genuine after all?"

"It has been paid for. Genuine or fake – let me make you a present of this memento from my native land."

I know Russian obstinacy. It was as he said: genuine or fake, I had to accept the present. Otherwise he would have been offended. Better to let it stick at "fake" so that he wouldn't get annoyed at his mistake later on, if he should realise he had made a mistake.

And that's how I came by a little masterpiece of an early baroque frame.

I silently decided to find a way of compensating him for his generosity by giving him a good price for some other piece. But nothing else that he showed me was of any interest. That, I'm afraid, is the way things usually are: the opportunity of turning a good intention into action is much rarer than that of satisfying a selfish urge. So it was somewhat shamefacedly that I left, half an hour later, with Lipotin's gift under my arm, without leaving behind anything more than a promise to make up for it with several purchases on my next visit.

It was around eight o'clock that I arrived home and found nothing on my desk, apart from a note from my housekeeper saying that her replacement had come about six and asked if it was all right not to start until eight o'clock as there were some arrangements she still had to make. My housekeeper had then left at seven, so I had made good use of the brief interregnum with my visit to Lipotin. I could look forward to the arrival of my new chatelaine in a few minutes, always assuming Frau Fromm kept her word.

In something of a bad mood because my old friend, Gärtner, had not kept to his promise, I decided to cheer myself up by unpacking Lipotin's present, which I still had under my arm.

The harsh electric light could not disguise its perfection. Even the deep green glass with its opalescent spots seemed to have an antique charm; it glowed in the frame, more like a beautifully polished, smoky moss-agate – in places almost like a gigantic emerald – than the murky glass of an old mirror.

Strangely fascinated by the chance beauty of an ancient mirror-glass with its oxidised silver backing, I propped the thing up before me and immersed myself in its unfathomable depths shot with mysterious, iridescent reflections.

How did the change come over me? I began to feel as if I were no longer standing in my study, but was at the station in the middle of the throng of arriving passengers and people waiting at the barrier. And wasn't that Dr. Gärtner waving his hat at me from the crowd?! I pushed my way through the press and managed, with some difficulty, to reach my friend who was coming laughing towards me. For a moment I was struck by the fact that he had no luggage: strange, he must have sent it all on ahead, I thought, but then I forgot the matter completely.

We greeted each other warmly; we hardly even bothered to mention the fact that we had not seen each other for close on thirty years.

Outside we took a cab and soon reached my flat – the journey was strangely smooth and silent, almost as if the carriage were gliding along. We kept up a lively conversation all the way there and all the way up the stairs so that I did not really concentrate on other matters, such as how the cabby was paid, for example. Everything seemed to take care of itself and was forgotten in the instant. And it was just the same when we entered my flat: my astonishment at finding some things were not quite in their usual places was brief and, so to speak, absent-minded and peripheral. The first phenomenon of this kind that I noticed was when I glanced out of one of the windows and saw, instead of the expected row of houses and gardens, a huge meadow with the outlines of unknown trees and an unfamiliar horizon.

Strange! I thought – but that was all, for on the other hand the view also seemed familiar and expected. And my friend Gärtner kept my attention occupied with his lively questioning and appeals to my memory of this or that incident from our student days.

Then when we had settled ourselves comfortably in my study I felt like jumping up out of the chair I had sat down in: it was an old-fashioned armchair with high armrests and huge, padded wings and it was certainly not part of the furnishings of my flat: suddenly the accustomed environment seemed so alien, and yet, again, it felt reassuringly familiar. Oddly enough, I kept all these observations, reflections and feelings to myself; not a word of this unease did I mention to my friend as everything went on as normal and the conversation flowed without a break.

The changes to which the objects around me had been subjected were not limited to the furniture alone; the windows, doors, even the walls were aligned differently and suggested more massive masonry, indeed, more massive architecture altogether than is normal in a modern city building such as my own house. On the other hand, objects of daily use were unaffected by all these changes: the electric chandelier with its six bulbs cast its usual light on the strangely disrupted surroundings, and the cigar box, my cigarette case and the samovar with Russian tea – supplied by Lipotin at fantastically cheap prices – all mingled their usual aromas, which wafted across the room to us.

It was only now that I subjected my friend Gärtner to a conscious examination. He was sitting opposite me, snug in a similar armchair to the one I was in, a smile on his face and a cigar held between his fingers; he took advantage of a pause in the conversation – it seemed to be the first since we met at the station – to sip his tea. I quickly reviewed everything we had talked about and I suddenly had the sense that the conversation had been of deeper significance than I had thought. We had talked much of our youth, the things we had planned together, schemes that had never come to fruition, of vain hopes, missed opportunities, shelved projects. All at once the room was filled with such melancholy that I looked up and stared at my friend as if from a great distance, as if he were no longer my friend Gärtner. It seemed to me as if I had carried on the whole conversation with myself, taking both parts, as it were. To put an end to such speculation I quickly asked, distrustfully, with deliberately clear articulation:

"Tell me how you got on with your chemistry in Chile?"

With a twist of the neck, which was one of the characteristic movements of his that I recalled, he glanced over the rim of his cup at me, gave me a friendly look and said:

"What is it? Something seems to be bothering you?"

A shyness spread rapidly over me like a morning mist, but I broke through and dissipated it by telling him about the sense of dislocation that had been tormenting me for the last few minutes:

"Theodor. I cannot deny it: I feel there is something odd between us. It's true we haven't seen each other for a long time, and I do seem to recognise many things from the past – much in you seems unchanged – and yet – and yet – – forgive me, but are you really Theodor Gärtner? You – you're different from the person I remember; no, you're not the Theodor Gärtner I knew all those years ago, I – I can feel – I can see that clearly, but it doesn't seem to make you any less familiar to me, any less – how should I put it? – any less close, any less of a friend – "

Theodor Gärtner leant forward towards me, smiled and said:

"Look at me – closely, don't be shy! Perhaps you'll remember who I am."

I felt a choking sensation in my throat but mastered it, gave a rather forced laugh and said:

"You must promise not to laugh, but since you entered my apartment" – I looked round almost timidly – "I feel somewhat – disorientated. Normally this room looks, well, it looks – different. But that will mean nothing to you, of course; and to come straight out with it, you don't seem to be Theodor Gärtner, my old student friend – but then, of course, you're not any more, forgive me! – but you don't even seem to be the older Theodor Gärtner, Gärtner the chemist or, if you like, Professor Gärtner from Chile."

My friend interrupted me with a calm gesture:

"Well, you are right, my friend. Professor Gärtner from Chile is somewhere in the ocean – " here he made a vague, expansive gesture which, however, seemed to make sense to me. "He was drowned quite a while ago."

My heart seemed to stop for a moment: so it was true, I thought and I must have looked quite dumbfounded, for my friend suddenly laughed out loud and shook his head in apparent amusement:

"You needn't worry, my friend. I think you don't usually find ghosts enjoying a cigar and a glass of tea – an exceedingly good tea, by the way. But –" his face and his voice assumed their previous serious expression – "it is true that your friend Gärtner – – is dead."

"Then who are you?" I asked in a quiet voice, but calm now, for the explanation of my mysterious condition seemed like a welcome liberation. "I repeat: who are you?"

As if to emphasise his real, physical existence, the "other" took another cigar from the box, rolled it and sniffed it appreciatively like a connoisseur, cut off the end, lit a match, rotated the end of the cigar in the flame and drew in the smoke with such simple and obvious relish that even a man more timorous than myself would have relinquished all doubts as to my guest's *bona fides*. Then he stretched out in his armchair, crossed his legs and began:

"I said: Theodor Gärtner is dead. Now, you could take that for a not unusual, though rather highfalutin expression someone might use to say of themselves that, whatever the reason, they wanted to break with their past and become a new person. Assume for the moment that that is what I meant by it."

I interrupted him with such vehemence that I felt surprised at myself:

"No! That's not it! Your own inner being has not changed, God forbid! But it is one unknown to me; it is not that of Theodor Gärtner, the dedicated scientist, the sworn enemy of all miracles and mysteries, the man who would immediately start a tirade against fusty superstition and incurable stupidity as soon as anyone dared to start talking about the incalculable, or about the essence of nature being unknowable. But the man I see sitting before me is one whose eye is fixed unwaveringly on the very wellhead of life, and in everything you say I can hear that you love the mysteries. – That is not my Theodor Gärtner, not the one I knew – and yet you are a friend, a very old and close friend – only I do not know you by name."

"If that's the way you see it, I have no objection," my visitor answered calmly. His piercing gaze had an indescribable power, and slowly, tortuously the memory of a long forgotten past clawed its way back up from the depths. I could not say whether it came from last night's dream or whether it was the reawakening of an age-old chain of events that had lain dormant for a hundred years. Meanwhile Gärtner continued imperturbably:

"As you are making an effort to help me explain your doubts, I can put things more simply and briefly than might otherwise be the case – 'We are old friends!' That is correct. – But 'Dr. Theodor Gärtner', your fellow student and the companion of your trivial student pranks, has little to do with the matter. Therefore it is quite correct if we say: he is dead. You are quite correct in your assumption that I am someone else. – Who am I? Gärtner."

'You mean that is your profession?' I almost exclaimed, as it struck me that his name meant gardener, but I managed to suppress the silly question. The other continued, without heeding my involuntary movement:

"My work as a gardener has taught me how to handle roses, nurturing them, improving the strain. My special art is grafting. Your friend was a healthy stock; the one you see before you is the scion. The natural blossom of the stock has vanished. The child my mother bore has long since drowned in the sea of transmutation. The stock, the rootstock onto which I was grafted, was the offspring of another mother, of the mother of a former student of chemistry, Theodor Gärtner by name, the one you knew, whose unripe soul has passed through the grave."

A shiver went down my spine. His relaxed figure was as enigmatic as his speech. My lips automatically formed the question:

"And why are you here?"

"Because it is time," he answered, as if it were obvious. With a smile he added:

"I like to be there when I'm needed."

"And so you're not a chemist" – I wasn't concerned with whether it followed on from what he had just said – "any more; nor are you – –"

"I have always been one, even when your friend Theodor was turning up his nose like any ignoramus at the secrets of the royal art. I am, and have been for as long as I can remember – an al-chymist."

"How can that be, an alchemist?" I exclaimed, "You, who were always –?"

"I who was always –?"

Then I remembered that the old Theodor Gärtner I had known was dead.

The "other" continued:

"You should remember that in every age there have been both adepts and bunglers. You are thinking of the latter if you are thinking of the medieval quacks and charlatans, though it is from their pseudo-art that the

156

much-vaunted chemistry of today has developed, in which your friend Theodor took such childish pride. The quacks of the middle ages have become eminent professors of chemistry at the universities. We of the 'Golden Rose', however, have never been interested in dissecting matter, postponing death or succumbing to the hunger for gold, that accursed plaything of mankind. We have remained what we always have been: technicians in the laboratory of eternal life."

Again I felt an almost physically painful shock as a current of distant, elusive memory ran through me; but it would have been impossible to say why or to what end this memory was calling me. I suppressed a question and just nodded in agreement. My visitor saw it, and again the strange smile flitted across his face. I heard him say:

"And you? What has happened to you in all these years?" A rapid glance took in my desk: "I see you are a – writer. You ignore the advice of the Bible and cast your pearls before the reading public? You are rummaging about in mouldy old documents – you always enjoyed that – and intend to amuse the world with the peculiarities of some past century? I believe that the present world and the present age finds little meaning in the meaning of life."

He paused, and once again I caught a whiff of the drifts of melancholy that seemed to be settling over us. I had to pull myself almost physically out of the brown study by starting to talk about my work on the legacy of my cousin, John Roger. The more I related, the more my eagerness to confide increased, and it was a relief to find Gärtner listening to me calmly and attentively. As I went on I became convinced he would always be there with help if ever I should need it. For the moment, though, all I heard from him was an occasional "Really", until he suddenly looked up and abruptly asked:

"So – sometimes you feel that your function as a chronicler or editor gets mixed up with the burden of your own destiny that is threatening to become tangled up with the dead things of the past?"

Desperate to unburden my heart, I told him everything that I had felt and suffered in the weeks following the arrival of John Roger's legacy, beginning with the Baphomet dream and omitting nothing. "I wish I had never seen John Roger's papers!" – thus I finished my confession – "Then I would have kept my peace of mind; I would gladly have sacrificed my ambition as a writer for that, I assure you."

With a smile on his face, my visitor observed me through the clouds of cigar smoke. For a moment he seemed to be about to dissolve into the haze and disappear from view. The idea that he might in some way be about to leave me wrung my heart so painfully that my hands clutched at my chest. He seemed to notice it; the cloud of smoke dissipated and I heard his laugh as he said:

"Thank you for being so open. Do you want to get rid of me so quickly? Remember, I would hardly be sitting here with you if your cousin John Roger had kept his papers."

I exploded:

"So you know more about John Roger! You know how he died!"

"Calm down", was the answer. "He died as he had to."

"He died of John Dee's cursed legacy!"

"Not in the way you mean. There is no curse upon it."

"Why didn't he complete the work – this pointless, superfluous task that I have lumbered myself with?"

"Which you undertook voluntarily, my friend! 'Burn or preserve' – wasn't that what it said?"

Everything! The man in the armchair knew everything!

"I didn't burn it," I said.

"And you did well!" – So he had read my thoughts.

"And why did John Roger not burn it?" I asked, quietly.

"Presumably he was not the true executor of the will."

I felt feverishly obstinate:

"And why was he not?"

"He died."

A tremor ran through me. There was only one possible cause of my cousin's death: Black Isaïs!

Gärtner stubbed out his cigar in the ash-tray and twisted round towards my desk. Playfully he ran his hand over the papers that lay on it singly or in piles, leafed through some and pulled out one, as if by chance, that I had missed; it must have been concealed somewhere, perhaps stuck in the binding of one of the Dee notebooks. I leant forward in curiosity. "Do you know this? Not yet, apparently!" he said after he had glanced through the sheet, and handed it to me. I shook my head and read it; I recognised the sloping hand of my cousin:

It came as I have long suspected it would. I expected *it* from the very beginning, when I first started to look into the musty, mysterious papers of our ancestor, John Dee. It seems I am not the first to meet *it*. I, John Roger Gladhill, the bearer of the arms, am a link in the chain my ancestor forged. I am truly linked to these accursed things now that I have touched them. – – The legacy is not dead! – – Yesterday 'she' appeared here for the first time. She is very slender, very beautiful, and her clothes give off a delicate scent you can only just smell – the scent of a beast of prey. Since then I have been in such a state of nervous excitement that I cannot get her out of my mind. – Lady Sissy she calls herself, but I can't believe that is her real name. She claims to be Scottish. – She wants some mysterious weapon from me. A weapon that is supposed to have a connection with the arms of the Dees of Gladhill. – I assured her that I possessed no such weapon, but she just smiled. – Since then I have not had an hour's peace! I am obsessed with the urge to procure for Lady Sissy, or whatever she may be called, the weapon she so desires, cost what it may, my present or my future happiness. – – Oh, I think I know who Lady Sissy really is – – –!

159

John Roger Gladhill.

The sheet of paper slipped out of my hand and fluttered to the ground. – I looked at my visitor. He shrugged his shoulders.

"That was what sent my cousin John to his death!?" I asked.

"I believe the new task the 'Lady' set was too much for him," said the man whom I no longer dared to call Theodor Gärtner. A wild horde of dark thoughts rushed down upon me: Lady Sissy? Who was she?! Who else but Princess Shotokalungin! And she is: Who else but Black Isaïs!! – Bartlett Greene's Black Isaïs!! – The veil was suddenly rent apart and the hidden realm of the Powers of Darkness opened up, the realm to which John Dee had sold his soul; and after him the unknown author, who, in fear and trembling, made the annotations in John Dee's diary in which every word is a shriek of terror; and after him my cousin, John Roger; – and after him – myself, who have asked Lipotin to do all he can to help me fulfill the Princess' strange desire.

My friend opposite me slowly sat up in his chair. His face seemed brighter but his body less clear than before. As he spoke his voice lost its physicality, its tone of spatial presence; he whispered:

"Thou art the last Bearer of the Arms. The rays from the green mirror of things past are gathering on the crown of thy head. Burn or preserve! But do not squander! The alchymy of the soul ordains metamorphosis or death. Choose as thou wilt – – "

A thunderous crash, like rifle butts hammering against massive oaken doors, made me leap up with a start: I was alone in my study; before me stood Lipotin's present, the old English mirror-glass, greenish in its Florentine frame; otherwise there was not the slightest change in the familiar surroundings. The knock at my door was hesitant, not at all thunderous.

At my "Come in" the door opened and a young lady was standing rather shyly on the threshold. She introduced herself, "I am Frau Fromm."

In some confusion, I stood up. I liked Frau Fromm from the first. I shook her hand and looked absent-mindedly at my watch. It must have seemed rather impolite to Frau Fromm, who probably thought it had something to do with her late arival. She said in a quiet voice:

"I tried to get in touch with you at midday; I was unable to start before eight o'clock. I hope I have kept my word."

She had. My watch said seven fifty-two.

I had been home for less than ten minutes.

All this happened yesterday evening precisely as I have recorded it on these pages. It seems that I am being drawn ever deeper into the hidden chain linking my life with the fate of John Dee, my ancestor. And now the "Green Glass" he spoke about in his diary is in my hand.

And where did I get the green mirror from?

It came from Lipotin's junk shop; it was given to me as a "memento of his native land". From which native land? From the land of the Russian Czar, of Ivan the Terrible? A gift from the great-grandson – how many times removed? – of Mascee, the "Tutor to the Czar"!?

But who was Mascee?

Nothing easier than to coolly, calmly look for the answer in John Dee's notebooks: Mascee was the evil spirit behind the Ravenheads, the uprising of the mob; he it was who brought the messages and fatal gifts from the loathsome chief of the Ravenheads, from that dese-crator of graves and murdering fire-raiser, Bartlett Greene, the spawn of Isaïs, the destroyer, the eternal tempter and arch-enemy, the redbeard in the leather jerkin – who was sitting here at my desk only yesterday! So Bartlett Greene is present, is here; the enemy of John Dee and now my enemy! And he it was – through Lipotin – who smuggled the green mirror into my possession.

But I will beware of the orders that come from the mirror. The strange thing is that the first person to come out of the mirror was my friend Theodor Gärtner. And he came as a friend, to give warning, to help! Should I doubt him? Is something trying to confuse me?

Oh, how I am abandoned, alone on this mountainous ridge of consciousness, wherever I look down there are precipices – on both sides – precipices of madness which threaten to engulf me, should I make the slightest false step.

Once more I am urged by a longing to immerse myself in John Dee's papers, to gain from them a clearer insight, to wring from them confirmation of my own fate. This dangerous curiosity has grown, I can feel it, into an obsession, which I can no longer resist. It has become my destiny. I will not know peace until this destiny has fulfilled itself; the placid stream of my existence must mingle with the great river of my kindred that flowed underground, as it were, until it gushed forth at my feet and now bears me away – – –

I have made my arrangements accordingly.

For the next few days Frau Fromm has strict orders that I am not to be disturbed by any visitors. I am not expecting any friends; a recluse like myself has no friends. And the *other* visitors? Oh, how clearly can I sense them all waiting in the wings. I will deny them entry! Thank God, I already know what they want from me.

For that reason I also gave Frau Fromm particular orders that a Herr Lipotin, of such and such an appearance, is to be turned away. A lady, whatever her name – "Princess Shotokalungin" for example – is to be turned away.

It was odd, too: when I described the appearance and looks of the Princess to my new housekeeper, who is timid and strangely shy, she started to tremble noticeably and her pretty little nostrils twitched, as if she could already scent the undesirable visitor. She assured me with nervous emphasis that she would respect my wishes in every particular, that she would be most careful and take every step possible to ensure that no visitor should even get past the storm door.

She was so eager that I looked up and, thanking her briefly, for the first time looked more closely at my new companion. She is of middle height, with a delicate, girlish figure; and yet there is something in her eyes, in her being, that prevents me from describing her appearance as virginal or even as youthful. Her look is strangely old, veiled and distant. You feel as if it is constantly shying away from itself, or from the immediate environment, at which it is compelled to direct itself.

As I observed her, I was made uneasy by a vague sense of the vulnerability of my isolation such as I had felt in all its piercing sharpness for the first time yesterday evening; I was also reminded of how I was surrounded by strange beings and dark influences such as Bartlett Greene. As I thought of him I felt his terrible nearness and, like a worm in the fruit, a thought crawled its way into my mind: is this Frau Fromm another of these phantoms? Has a ghost hidden itself in this young woman and forced its way into my threatened existence in the guise of a housekeeper?

It may be that I looked at Frau Fromm, as she stood there in front of me, longer and with closer scrutiny than her reticent character could bear – she certainly blushed violently and once more started to tremble uncontrollably. And she gave me such an anxious look that I felt embarrassed when it occurred to me what she was probably thinking I had in mind. So I shook off all foolish thoughts and tried to erase the unfortunate impression as quickly as possible by scratching my head with calculated absent-mindedness, mumbling a few words about lack of time and need to be alone, and asking her once more to understand how important it was for me to be shielded from unwelcome distractions.

She looked past me, and said in an expressionless voice:

"Yes. That is why I have come."

I found the answer puzzling. Again I seemed to feel "links". I asked, more vehemently than I had intended:

"You had some purpose in taking this position? You know me?"

She shook her head gently:

"No, I know nothing about you. It is probably just chance that has brought me here. – – The only thing is, sometimes I dream…"

"You dreamed", I interrupted her, "that you took this temporary position? Such things do happen occasionally."

"No; that wasn't it."

"What then?"

"I have been ordered to help."

I gave a start, "How do you mean?"

She looked at me with a tormented expression on her face:

"You must forgive me. I'm talking nonsense. Sometimes I have to struggle with my imagination. But it is of no importance. I must get down to my work now. Please excuse me for taking up your time."

She turned quicky to leave the room. I caught her by the hand, perhaps a little too violently, for the pressure of my fingers around her wrist seemed to cause her some alarm. She gave a jerk, as if struck by an electric current, and then stood there, limp. In total submission, she left her hand in mine; her features underwent an odd transformation, her eyes became unfocused. I could not understand what was happening to her, but I found myself in the grip of a bizarre fancy: I have already experienced all this, right down to the last detail, so many – how many? – years ago. Without thinking what I was doing or saying, I gently forced her down into the chair by the desk. I kept hold of her hand and the words seemed to form on my lips of their own accord:

"There are times, Frau Fromm, when we all have to struggle with our imaginations. You say you want to help me. Let us help each other. You see, for the last few days I have been struggling with the idea that I am my own ancestor, an Englishman from the …"

She interrupted my with a soft cry. I looked up. She was staring at me.

164

"What is upsetting you?" I broke off. For the space of a few seconds her stare, which seemed to go right through me, was uncanny and glowed like a burning coal within.

Frau Fromm nodded absent-mindedly and replied:

"I was in England once. I was married to an old Englishman – –"

"Is that all?" – I had to smile and felt a sense of relief, though I could not have said why. At the same time I was surprised that such a young woman should already have two marriages behind her – "You were married to someone in England before you married Dr. Fromm?"

She shook her head.

"– – or Dr. Fromm himself was...? Forgive me for asking such a personal question, but I know nothing about your past life."

She gave a vigourously dismissive wave of her hand.

"Dr. Fromm was my husband for a very short time. It was a mistake. He died soon after we separated. He wasn't English and had never been to England."

"And your first husband?"

"I married Dr. Fromm when I was eighteen, straight from school. I have not been married again."

"But I don't understand. My dear Frau Fromm ..."

"I don't understand it, either," she said, with a tormented expression as she turned her face towards me, as if appealing for help. "It was on the day of my wedding to Dr. Fromm that I realised that – – that I belong to another"

"To an old Englishman, you said. Good. – Was he a childhood friend; someone you met as a young girl?"

She nodded her head vehemently then looked bewildered again.

"It's not like that at all. It's quite different."

She pulled herself together in the armchair – it obviously cost a great effort – withdrew her hand from my clasp, straightened up and spoke in a monotone, as if it were something she had learnt by heart; I have noted down the main points:

"I was an only child. My family was quite well-off. My father was a tenant farmer in Styria. Later he had some bad luck and we became poor. As a child I went on several short journeys, but never outside Austria. Before I married I had only once been to Vienna. That was the longest journey I had made. But as a child I often dreamed of a house in an area which I had never seen with my waking eye. And I knew: the house and the countryside are in England. How it was I was so sure, I cannot say. The obvious answer would be to put it all down to childish imagination, but several times I described the landscapes I dreamed of to a distant relative of ours who worked for a while on our farm; he was half English, had been brought up in England, and he said I must have been dreaming of the Scottish hills or of Richmond: my descriptions suited those two places precisely, except that the buildings were not at all as old-fashioned as I described them. Since then my dreams have had an odd confirmation, if you can call it that, from another side. Another dream I often had as a child was of an old, gloomy city; the image was so sharp and detailed that I could walk around in it and find my way easily to particular streets, squares and houses. And I always found what I was looking for so that it was hard to say it was only a dream. Our relative did not know this city and said he was sure it was not in England at all. It must be an old city on the continent. It lay on either side of a largish river and the two parts were connected by an old stone bridge which was guarded on both sides by dark fortified gates. Above the tightly-packed jumble of houses on one bank there rose a hill with a mighty castle towering over its tree-covered slopes.. One day I was told it was Prague, but many of the details, which I could describe precisely, had disappeared or been changed, although many of the things I knew corresponded to an old map. To this very day I have never been to Prague and I am afraid of the city. I never, never want to set foot in it! If my mind dwells on it for a long time, I am gripped by an uncontrollable dread and I can see a man the sight of whom, I do not know why, makes my blood freeze. He has no ears; they have been cut off and there are blood-red scars around the holes on either side of his head. He seems to me to be the evil demon of this terrible city. This city – I am sure of it – would make me unhappy and ruin my life."

Frau Fromm uttered the last words so vehemently that it shook me and I hastily interrupted her. My own agitation brought her back to herself; her expression relaxed and she passed her hand over her face, as if to wipe away the vision she had had. Then, visibly exhausted, she added, pausing at intervals:

"Even when I am awake I can transport myself to that old house in England, whenever I want. I can live in it, if I want, for hours or days; the longer, the clearer everything becomes there. I picture to myself – that is the right word, isn't it – I picture to myself that I am married to an old man. I can see him very clearly if I want to, only everything that I perceive is steeped in a greenish light. It is as if I am looking into an old green mirror – –"

Again I interrupted her with a violent gesture as I stretched out my hand towards Lipotin's mirror with the Florentine frame that was standing on the desk. Frau Fromm seemed not to notice it. She continued:

"Some time ago I learnt that he was in danger."

"Who is in danger?"

The distant expression settled on her face again; she looked almost as if she were unconscious. Fear spread across her features. "My husband," she stammered.

"You mean Dr. Fromm?" I said, deliberately trying to catch her out.

"No! Dr. Fromm is dead! I mean my real husband – – the head of our household in England..."

"Is he still living there?"

"No. He lived there a long, long time ago."

"When did he live there?"

"I don't know. It was a long time ago."

"Frau Fromm!"

She came to herself with a start:

"Was I talking nonsense?"

I couldn't answer; I just shook my head.

With an apology, she continued:

"My father used to say I was talking nonsense when I described my visions. He would have none of it. He called them 'sick'. Since then I have been afraid to speak of them – and you have heard it all on the very first day! You'll be thinking: 'This woman is ill and tried to keep it a secret! She got this job on false pretences,' and yet – and yet I feel I am in my right place here and that I am needed here!"

She jumped up in her agitation. I tried to calm her down, but in vain. It was only gradually that she accepted my assurance that I did not think she was ill and that I would definitely keep her here as long as my old housekeeper was away.

Then she seemed to quieten down. She smiled a grateful, embarrassed smile.

"You will see that I am quite up to the task I have taken on. May I get on with my work now?"

"One more thing, Frau Fromm: can you describe to me, roughly at least, what the old man in the house at Richmond looks like. And do you possibly know what his name is?"

She reflected. An expression of surprise appeared on her face.

"His name? No, I don't know that. It never occurred to me that he had to have a specific name. I just call him: 'He'. – And what he looks like? He looks ... like you, sir. – I must make amends to you!" – And with that she had slipped out of the door.

At the moment I have no desire to trouble my head with this new mystery of this Frau Fromm, who suddenly appears from nowhere. There is no doubt about it: she is subject to alternating states of consciousness; a doctor would see nothing unusual in the case – adolescent hysteria, he would call it, fixated dream images, drama-tised self-delusion, the experiences of a dissociated personality. In the latter case the dissociated personality had clearly been projected back into an earlier century. Nothing in all that is out of the ordinary.

But Richmond? And her dream husband's resemblance to me? – – Doctors are familar with such cases as well – what are doctors not familiar with!? Patients of this type tend to fixate on someone in the immediate vicinity they feel they can trust. – Someone she can trust? Am I someone she can trust? Of course I am. Did I not just say to her, "Let us help each other"? If only I knew what she meant when she said, "I must make amends to you". Is that the language of someone in a catatonic trance? – Well, time will tell whether I have acquired a servant who is not always quite right in the head, but I must say that something within me whispers a quite different message. I must not give in to it or I will be in danger of losing my grip on my mind – or on myself. I know only too well what I must do if my fate is to have meaning. The fate of most "normal" men is, if you look at it closely, as good as meaningless.

So back to work as quickly as possible!

On my desk in front of me is a thick bundle tied up in string which, obeying the instructions I received in a dream from – from the Baphomet, I fished up at random out of the drawer.

Perhaps it will provide the key to the new puzzle?

I open a volume stiffly bound in black leather; on the title page:

Private Diary.

On the next page, in John Dee's hand:

Log-book of my first voyage of discovery to the only true Greenland, to the everlasting throne and crown of England.

The 20th day of November in the year of Our Lord, 1582.

It is now plain that my misgivings were well founded, that beset me when I believed that Greenland, which I thought to subject to the temporal power of Queen Elizabeth, was to be found here on earth.

From the very first day of our collaboration, when in a vain delusion I threw in my lot with the Ravenheads, that villain and arch-deceiver, Bartlett Greene, has led me most treacherously astray and drawn me with his devilish wiles into the path of error. It is so with most men, that they take upon themselves a heavy burden here on earth because they do not see that our task is on the other side, and not here and now; they have not understood the curse of the Fall. They do not understand that our labour here is that we might be rewarded "over there". Bartlett Greene set me on the road to spiritual ruin when he whispered in my ear that I should seek the fruit of my ambition here on earth, so that I should not discover that the crown is "on the other side". My road was to be one of adversity, disappointment, sorrow and treachery that I might become grey before my time and tired of life.

Great was the danger for my soul's true destination, but as well as that he wanted to prevent the fulfilment of what was foreordained for our bloodline, namely that we it should be who would reach man's highest peak in his rise from the Fall. His counsel – that the path to this glory led through earthly power and majesty – was utterly wrong. Today I know for certain that it is ordained that I shall seek my Greenland, my Crownland, "on the other side", and that my whole life has had no other meaning: on the other side, where the undamaged crown of the mysteries and the "virgin queen" await their king.

For three days now an apparition has appeared to me, early in the morning but when I was wide awake, so that it has nothing of a dream or suchlike imaginings. I never knew before that there is something beyond waking or sleeping, dreaming or madness; a fifth way, a mystery: a clear vision vouchsafed of things that are beyond this world. And the apparition that came to me was quite different from those that Greene showed me in the polished coal in the Tower.

I saw a green hill and I knew it was Gladhill, the *glad hill* of our ancestral home that stands proudly in the arms of the Dee family. But there was no silver sword thrust into the top; instead, its gentle summit was crowned with a green tree, like the one in the left-hand field, and a living spring bubbled out of the ground at its foot. The sight was pleasing to my eye and I hurried from the dusty plain toward the hill to refresh myself from the old wellspring of our line. It was a miracle how I could see everything as real and yet symbolic at the same time.

As I made my way towards the hill I realised with piercing clarity that I was that tree myself and that I wanted to stretch up with its trunk – that is with my spinal cord – to heaven and spread all its twigs and branches, that were my branching nerves and veins become external and visible, in the free air. I felt the sap and the blood and the sensations and joy pulsating through the tree of veins and nerves before me and at the same time I was proudly aware of myself within it. The silver spring at my feet became my children and my children's children, a never-ending stream, returned from the future to celebrate an approaching, and yet already present, resurrection to Eternal Life. The features of each one were different and yet they all bore similarity to me; it seemed to me that it was I who had impressed upon them the stamp of our line, to preserve them for ever from Death and destruction. It filled me with a sense of reverent pride. – As I came closer to the tree I saw, framed by the highest branches as by a crown, a double face appear: the one as of a man, the other of a woman, and the two were grown together as one. And in the golden light above this double head there hovered a crown beneath a crystal of ineffable splendour.

Straightway I recognised in the woman's face my Lady Elizabeth and would have cried aloud for joy but that a sudden pain did stop me, for I saw and felt the man's head not as my own, but as that of a younger man; it was in every feature more carefree than the one I have borne on my neck since the days of my innocence. I would fain have been deceived by a regret for my lost youth that whispered to me that this scion of the tree was myself in days gone by, but I refused to let pity dim my eye and saw that it was not myself in the double head but one far off, one who rose out of the spring at my feet, one beyond my reach – Another! – –

And pain raged within me that it was not I but Another of my blood and seed, One from the latter days, who should inherit the crown and be conjoined indissolubly with my Elizabeth. And in my anger and fury I raised my arm against the tree – against myself – as if to fell it. But, from the marrow of my backbone, the tree spoke:

"Thou fool! Dost thou still not see thyself? What is time? What is metamorphosis? – After a hundred years and more, still I am: *I* after a hundred graves; *I* after a hundred resurrections! Wilt thou raise thy hand to the tree and art thyself but a branch thereof and no more than a drop in the spring at thy feet?!"

Shaken to the core, I raised my eyes to the top of tree and saw the double head move its lips and I heard a call as from a great height and distance that almost exhausted itself in its course to my ear:

"One that holds to his faith, lives in the end! – Cleave unto me and we shall be one! – Be alive to thyself and thou shalt be alive to me – to Baphomet!"

I sank to my knees at the foot of the tree and embraced its trunk most reverently; and I wept such that I could no longer see the vision through the veil of tears, and when my eyes were clear once more I perceived the faint glow of my chamber lamp as the first light of morning filtered through the chinks in

172

the shutters. I could still hear the voice from the tree, as if it came from within me:

"Wilt thou become immortal? – Dost thou know that the way of this metamorphosis leads through many trials of fire and water? Base matter must suffer much torment before it can be transmuted."
– – –

Three times now I have been shown the Image and the Meaning and the Way in these morning visions. The Way which will lead me to myself, after time and after the grave – whenever that may be, is a two-fold Way. One Way is uncertain, chancy, like a bread crumb cast upon the ground that the birds might eat up before I take that road. Nonetheless, I will essay it, for if it succeed it will be of mighty assistance in that future beyond time for me to remember myself – for what is immortality if not remembrance?

Therefore I choose the magic Way of the Script and set down in writing my fate and what has been revealed to me on the pages of this *diarium*, which I have hallowed and by certain means protected against the assaults of time and of evil spirits. Amen.

But Thou, thou Other, who shalt come after me and read this book at the end of the Days of the Tree: remember whence thou came and that thou arose from the silver spring that waters the tree and that the tree sends forth. And if thou shouldst hear the murmur of thy stream and feel the branches of the tree grow through thy flesh, then I, John Dee, Lord of the Manor of Gladhill, do beseech thee that thou look within thy soul and wake thyself from the grave of time and know: Thou art I! – – –

There is, however, another Way which I must follow for my sake, as I live here in the flesh and in the Castle of Mortlake: that is the Way of the alchymical transubstantiation of the body and of the soul, that both may achieve immortality in this present time.

And it is not only since this morning that I have known of this Way; I have been following it now for three years and I have reason to believe that the vision vouchsafed me on three mornings together is a result, the first fruits, so to speak, of my constant labour in this vineyard. It is two years ago that I came to understand the true nature of alchymy and at Christmas-tide in the year of our Lord 1579 I had a chymical *laboratorium* built here in Mortlake and equipped with all necessary devices – and I have bound to me a most capable assistant who came to see me unannounced on Christ's Birthday and who since then has served me honourably and showed himself above all expectation well versed and experienced in the mystical art. This same assistant, of whom I have grown right fond and call my friend, is one Master Gardner by name. He enjoys my trust, for he always looks after my interest and is ever ready with good counsel: this I wish to state and acknowledge here with due gratitude. For it saddens me that in recent days there have been increasing signs that his great knowledge and, especially, the trust I place in him, has made him stuffed up with pride and obstinacy so that he often contradicts me, gives me unasked-for warnings and unwelcome admonitions. I hope he will desist from this and show me the respect due to his lord and – well-disposed – master. Our quarrel touches not only on the proper methods in the practice of the art of alchymy; he also thinks it behoves him to oppose my conference with the good spirits from the other world beyond which I succeeded in establishing in remarkable fashion a short time ago. That it is impossible that in this matter I should be the prey of satanic demons, as he does suppose, or the plaything of the spirits of earth and air, is to be seen in the fact that every conjuration of the world beyond is begun and ended with a fervent prayer to God and to the Saviour of all creatures, Jesus Christ. The voices and spirits that manifest themselves appear so godfearing and all they do and say is done and said expressly in the name of the Holy

174

Trinity that I cannot and will not believe Gardner's warning that they are masked demons. Their counsels, namely how to prepare the philosopher's stone and the elixier of life, run quite contrary to those that he does profess to know, so that I think they wound his pride who thinks he knows all things. Such humours are not uncommon in human nature but I am not minded to bear his interference any longer, however well-meant it may be. I believe that my assistant is wrong when he avers that the only man who is secure against the wiles of the evil inhabitants of the world beyond is one who has undergone within himself all the occult ceremonies and processes of the spiritual rebirth, namely: the mystical baptism with water, blood and fire, the appearance of letters on the skin, the taste of salt on the tongue, hearing the sound of the cock-crow and other things, for example to hear a baby crying in the womb. What is to be understood by all this, he does not say; he maintains he is bound by a vow of silence.

As I was yet in two minds, thinking that perhaps after all I was being deceived by works of the devil, yesterday, when my assistant was absent, I conjured the spirits in the Name of God the Father, God the Son and God the Holy Ghost to appear and tell me whether they knew of a certain Bartlett Greene and whether he had been found worthy to be called their friend and companion. First I heard a strange whistling laughter in the air, which perplexed me, but straightway after the spirits appeared and repudiated such a suggestion with great uproar and all around me from the walls and floor curious metallic voices rang out, ordering me to to abjure any companionship with that selfsame minion of Black Isaïs, and later they told me in the presence of my old friends, Harry Price and Edmund Talbot, as a token of their omniscience, a secret known only to myself and that I had even kept hidden from my wife Jane. They spurned all suspicion against the inhabitants of the world beyond and told me that my relationship with Bartlett Greene could only be dissolved if I disposed of the coal scrying-glass that he had given me in the Tower. And in the Name of God they ordered me put this stone or coal crystal from me straightway and to consign it to the fire as a sign of my contrition.

This was a glorious triumph over the doubts of my assistant Gardner, who said not a word when I told him what the spirits had ordained; in my innermost heart I renounced him. As my chief desire was to break with everything which might remind me of Bartlett Greene, or even bind me to him, early this morning I took the coal out of its hiding place and burnt it before Gardner's eyes in a fierce fire in the alchymical furnace. I was no little astonished – Gardner showed no sign of surprise and observed the whole matter earnestly – to see the cool, smooth stone flare up in a green blaze without smoke and disappear, leaving no trace of ash or cinder.

Since then a day and a night have passed and in that night the head of Bartlett Greene appeared with a mocking grin; I presume he was grinning to conceal the fury he must have felt that I had consigned his coal scrying-glass to the flames. Then he disappeared in green smoke which distorted his features so that for a moment it seemed they had been transformed into those of a face I did not recognise – the face of a man, unknown to me, whose hair lay so close upon his cheeks that it almost seemed he had no ears. But that must have been my imagining. Thereupon I dreamed I saw the tree on Gladhill once more and heard its voice that said:

"Seek to further the healing process: matter must be mortified that the elixir of eternal life shall be extracted from it." That filled me with trepidation and a melancholy which continued long after I awoke, so that I felt a great urge to ask Gardner's counsel, whether he thought I was threatened with some misfortune; I felt it would be fickleness in me to turn to the man whom I had already repudiated in my heart but strangely my fear outweighed my pride. I went to our *laboratorium*. But instead of Gardner I found a polite but brief letter from him in which he bade me farewell "for a long, long time, if not for ever". – – –

I was no little surprised when, at about the hour of ten in the morning, my servant announced a visitor and an unknown man entered the room who, as I could see straightway, had had both ears cut off. The scars around the earholes told me that this mutilation must have taken place but a little while ago, perhaps for some crime against the laws of the land. As I knew that in these days all too often it is innocent people who are condemned to this punishment, I determined not to condemn him out of hand for it. I was strengthened in this by the fact that his features bore no similarity to those of the face I had dreamed of during the night. I presumed it must have been a prognostic dream for the following day. The stranger was taller than I, broader and of coarser features, which suggested no very noble parentage. His age was difficult to determine, for his almost chinless face with a receding forehead and impudent, beak-like nose was in part concealed by long hair and a full, somewhat unkempt beard. He seemed to be fairly young and I guessed he was in his late thirties. He later confided in me that he was not yet twenty-eight; that would make him younger than my wife, Jane Fromont. And yet at such an age this man claims to have travelled throughout these islands and undertaken many journeys to France and the Dutch provinces. His features bear witness to the truth of this: his expression is of a restless adventurer and one, to judge by his furrowed face, who has suffered cruelly under the plough of fate.

He came up close to me and said in a low voice that he had important matters to relate which would brook no interruption, for which reason I should lock the door from the inside. When this was done he took from a pocket concealed within his coat an old book of parchment leaves, bound in pigskin and with many strange characters and signs on its pages. He opened it and pointed to one especial passage. Before I could read the ancient, florid script, he abruptly asked me in a quivering voice and with a strange, flickering look in his piercing, mouse's eyes, whether I could explain to him what a 'projection' was?

From this I straightway saw that he had only a faint notion of the alchymical transmutation of metals. Thus I answered him that I did possess this knowledge, which was in truth a matter of mere chemistry, and explained to him the process of projection according to the rules of science. He listened intently and seemed content. As he then left the book in my hand, I soon realised I was holding a work of inestimable value, namely instructions how to make the philosopher's stone for the alchymical preparation of the body and the extraction of the elixier of immortality both here and beyond. I sat there, benumbed in mind, unable to bring a word out yet unable, either, to conceal my feelings; my face must have revealed a whole host of excited passions, for I saw that the stranger kept a sharp eye on me and that nothing of my ferment escaped him. Nor did I think to conceal anything from him; I closed the book with a snap and said, "Truly, a most excellent book. What do you purpose with it?" "To make the elixier and the stone, according to the directions therein", – as he answered he made a great effort to keep back the fear and greed which yet shone brightly in his eye. "For that, first of all someone must read the book who can understand it," I objected.

"Are you able to perform it – and will you give your word as a gentleman and swear an oath on Christ's Body and Blood?"

178

I answered that I was willing to try, but that was not to say my efforts would be crowned with success: there were many books containing such directions for the preparation of the red and white powders and yet all labour according to their receipts had been in vain.

At these words the face of my visitor was a battleground of passions that raged within his soul; distrust and triumph, darkest doubt and self-important pride pursued each other across his features with the speed of clouds on a wild night. Suddenly he tore open the shirt across his breast and took out a leathern pouch which he had kept concealed on his bare skin. He reached into it and held his hand out towards me – it held Mascee's two ivory spheres! I recognised them at once, for they bore the signs I had scratched upon them before I threw them out of the window at the time when Bishop Bonner's henchmen were searching for me to cast me into the Tower. This time I managed to conceal my thoughts and feelings better and I asked the stranger with apparent unconcern why he had produced the spheres in such mysterious fashion and what was special about them. At this he, without a word, opened the white sphere and showed me the fine grey powder it contained. I was astonished, for the colour and texture of the *materia* immediately called to mind the frequent descriptions I had read of the *materia transmutationis* of the alchymical adepts. A whirlwind of the wildest thoughts rushed through my mind: how was it that in that night of terror before my arrest I had not found the secret of these spheres, which were so easy to unscrew?! How was it possible that I had toyed with the spheres for hours, but instead of opening them had laboriously scratched signs on the hard ivory case and then, in a dark fit of revulsion, had thrown them out of the window? Had I then, thirty years ago, held the secret of life in my hand and, like a child that casts away a jewel as a worthless pebble, in my blindness discarded this divine gift and plunged into a sea of troubles and disappointment through my misunderstanding of the meaning of "Greenland"!

Whilst I, with my gaze fixed on the open hemisphere, remained sunk in such dark thoughts, which he presumably took for doubt and distrust, my guest carefully unscrewed the red ivory sphere and from the hollow cup shone the glow of the royal powder, the "Red Lion"! There was not for one second the possibility that I might be mistaken. I had too often read about such flaky purple granules in the best works of the old adepts to have been wrong about the nature of this material. I was almost overcome by the tangle of different thoughts that lay hold on me from all sides. I merely nodded dumbly when the stranger asked in a hoarse voice:

"And what is your opinion of this, Dr. Dee?"

I gathered all the strength of will I could muster and asked back:

"How did you come to be in possession of these two spheres?"

The stranger hesitated, then said irresolutely:

"First I would have your opinion on the book and the spheres."

I answered:

"I think that we must first test out their worth. If both live up to the promise of their appearance then it is a right royal possession."

My visitor mumbled something which sounded like an expression of satisfaction. then he said:

"I am glad that you are honest. I believe you are to be trusted. You are not one of those practitioners of the black arts who seek to defraud others of their lawful gain and profit. For that reason I have come to you, for you are a gentleman and a man of honour. If you will advise me and help me we will go equal shares."

I replied that he would do well to trust me and that it was my opinion that it was worth making a trial with the book and the substances in the two spheres. After we had discussed the terms of a contract to regulate our work together and vowed to trust each other, I asked him how he had come into possession of these things. In reply he recounted the following remarkable story:

Both book and spheres came from the grave of St. Dunstan, of that he was sure. When, thirty years ago now, the mob of the Ravenheads under their captain, a certain notorious Bartlett Greene, broke open the tomb, they found the body of the holy Bishop untouched by putrefaction, as if he had been buried that same day; the book, it was said, he held in his folded hands and the spheres were fixed to his mouth and forehead in some mysterious manner. The plundering heretics were sore disappointed to find no jewels about the corpse, as Greene had dreamed, and in their rage they had cast the body of the Bishop into the flames of the burning church. But the spheres and the book had been sold for a few pence to a Russian by the plunderers as they had no use for them.

"Aha! Mascee!" I thought to myself and questioned my visitor with mounting excitement:

"And you? How did they come into your possession?"

"Before myself, the last owner of these objects was an old man, formerly a secret agent for Bloody Bishop Bonner, who died in madness many years ago. He kept a bawdy-house in London" – which, the stranger added with a cynical laugh, he had often visited and slept at. "I had seen them there and immediately decided I must have them, for I had long known that St. Deniol had been a great adept with knowledge of alchymy. And it was just in time that I managed to procure them, for in the self-same night the secret agent was – – – that is, he died all of a sudden," the stranger swiftly corrected himself. "I learnt from a wench who resided in the bawdy-house that the old whoremaster had been charged by the Bloody Bishop to seek the spheres and the book, but that when he had discovered them he concealed his find and kept them for himself. For a time the spheres had mysteriously disappeared, but then just as mysteriously reappeared.

"Strange!" I thought to myself, for I remembered exactly how I had thrown the two ivory spheres out of the window before my arrest.

"And you bought them from the secret agent before his death?"

"N-no" – the stranger avoided my eye and looked to the side, but quickly recovered his composure and said, louder than need be, "he gave them to me."

I was sure the man was lying and I was beginning to rue the contract we had drawn up. Had he murdered the old bawd himself to get possession of the book and spheres? And I swithered and swayed, for the vision I had had in the night of a man without ears now seemed to be a warning. But I calmed my fears and told myself that my suspicion must be unfounded and that at the worst the stranger had stolen the two objects – and that from a dishonest finder. Moreover, the temptation to share possession of such rarities was so great that I could not bring myself to show my visitor the door, as a scholar and one of my station should properly have done. Rather I persuaded myself that Divine Providence had sent this man to me so that I should be blessed with the Stone of immortality. I further told myself that my own path in my youth had not always been straight and narrow and that I thus had no right to play the judge to this bold rascal. And so, after a short reflection, I resolved to accept my fate and welcomed the stranger, who told me his name was Edward Kelley, to my house and gave him my hand on our agreement to test the objects in his possession for their true value. He had been, I learnt, a lawyer's clerk in London, and had then become a travelling apothecary and quacksalver after he had had his ears

182

cut off by the public executioner for forging documents.

God grant that his arrival will bring blessing on my house!

I have taken him in despite the objections of my wife Jane, who from the very start has taken a strong dislike to this man with the cut off ears.

A few days later we made the first trial with the two powders in my *laboratorium* and were successful far beyond expectation: even with a very small projection we produced almost ten ounces of silver from twenty ounces of lead and from the same quantity of tin no less than ten ounces of pure gold. Kelley's mouse's eyes took on a feverish glitter and I was horrified to see how greed can transform a man. I told him that we would have to use the powder extremely sparingly, especially as there was only a little of the "Red Lion" left; Kelley would have preferred to turn everything into gold immediately.

I, however, vowed to myself by all things holy – and I told Kelley in no uncertain manner – that for my part I would not use even one grain of the valuable powders to enrich myself, but would endeavour to extract the secret of the preparation of the philosopher's stone from St. Dunstan's book; and when I knew how the red tincture was to be projected onto the incorruptible body of the resurrection I would use them for no other purpose. At this I presume Kelley secretly turned up his beak of a nose in disgust.

Inwardly I still could not rid myself of my unease that these treasures had yet been dishonestly acquired; and, moreover, I was tormented by the thought that there must perhaps be some curse laid on objects taken from the grave of such a great adept, especially as I could not entirely absolve myself from guilt on that account, as I was the originator – albeit distant – of the pillage by the Ravenheads. Thus I resolved at least to take an oath only to use the find for the most noble of purposes. Once the secret of the alchymical process is found, Kelley can leave me and go his way in peace, and can pour as much of the "Red Lion" as he wishes over base metals to turn them into endless gold which he can squander on whores in bawdy-houses. He may be as rich as King Midas – I shall not envy him for it, just as little as he will envy me, who strive for other goals with the priceless stone. Surely I will need but a tiny amount of the powder to distill from it the immortal essence, thus myself to live on until the day of the "chymical marriage" with my Queen, when I shall see the Baphomet within me realised and the Crown of Life above my head. May this "Lion" from this day forward lead me on to my Queen! – – –

What is remarkable is that I have daily come to regret more and more that my faithful assistant Gardner has left me, now that this vagrant Kelley is in my house and by me all the time and at every meal does slobber and belch like a pig. I would dearly love to ask honest Gardner what he thinks of this intruder and whether he might after all be an unknowing instrument of Bartlett Greene! Can it be that the loot from the desecrated grave of the Saint has returned to me like a bad penny? Was the one who first brought them not the uncanny Mascee, the accomplice of Bartlett Greene, that mysterious intermediary of fate?

But these misgivings slowly pass, like my long, dreary days. I see everything in a much calmer light: neither Mascee nor Kelley are emissaries of Greene, but both are blind instruments of a benevolent Providence and, despite the traps and pitfalls of the Evil One, will help me to my due salvation.

How otherwise could it have been possible for things that had belonged to a Saint to fall into the hands of a degenerate! Can ought ill reside in such objects? Can the Holy Bishop's curse be a threat from the world beyond to me, a humble and zealous student of the divine mysteries and a servant devoted to their fulfilment? No; I have atoned for the sins of my arrogant youth and my body bears the marks of my past foolishness. All is expiated, and today I am no longer an unworthy recipient of gifts from Beyond, as I was when the "Tutor to the Czar" offered me these mysteries for the first time and I toyed with them and marked them and threw them out of the window – so that thirty years later I should recognise them and receive them again with a more serious, truly prepared mind.

My trusty Gardner was certainly right to warn me not to turn to an alchymy that was devoted to the worldly transmutation of metals. To achieve that, beings from a dark, invisible world must be called down to meddle in ours – black magic, magic of the left hand Gardner would have said; that is my belief, too, but what has it to do with me? I do not take part in it and do not strive for gold, but for Life Eternal!

That spirits are involved, I will not deny: since the day Kelley entered my household there have been strange, unexplained signs of their presence: repeated knocking, a dry sound that dies away quickly, as if someone were stabbing a pair of compasses into wood, a crackling and rustling noise in walls and cupboards, in tables and other pieces of furniture; also the steps of invisible messengers coming and going, and sighing and breathless whispering that suddenly stops when one listens – and at the second hour of the night it is often accompanied by drawn out chords, as if the wind were blowing through taut strings. Often in the middle of the night I have raised my head and beseeched the invisible being in the name of God and the Holy Trinity to stand and speak and tell me why it had been aroused from the peace of the grave or sent to us from the world beyond, what its mission was and who had charged it to visit me, but until this day I have had no answer. Kelley is of the opinion that it is connected with St. Dunstan's book and spheres: the spirits, so he maintains, desire to preserve what is left of their mysteries; but he, so he boasts, will tear them from them. And he confessed that he had been plagued by such voices and noises since the very day he had procured the objects.

At this revelation I was mightily troubled, for again it made me think that the old secret agent and whoremaster, from whom Kelley had procured them, had perhaps after all been murdered for the possession of the book and spheres. And once more words spoken by my trusty Gardner came into my mind: it were, he said, a vain and dangerous enterprise to create the philosopher's stone by chymical means, if the arcane process of spiritual rebirth had not previously been completed, of which the Bible told, though in veiled words. First, he had warned, I should discover this process and undertake it, otherwise I would fall from one trap into another and from one sorrow into another, as if I were guided by a will-o'-the-wisp.

To calm my unease I called Kelley to me and asked him to swear on his soul's salvation that what he had told me was true: namely that it was a green angel and not a demon that had appeared and promised to disclose to us the secret of the preparation of the stone. And Kelley raised his hand and swore that it was true. The Angel, he said, had announced to him that the time was come when I was to be initiated and the Great *Arcanum* would be revealed to me.

Then Kelley told me what preparations were necessary that the Green Angel might be revealed to us in a physical body, according to the laws of the of the invisible world. As well as the two of us and, most important, my wife Jane, who was to sit close by Kelley's side, two of my friends should assemble at a given hour of a particular night during the waning of the moon, in a room that had a window giving onto the west.

Straightway I sent a messenger to two of my trusted friends, Talbot and Price, to beg them to come to me that the conjuration of the spirits might take place at the appointed hour acording to Kelley's instructions: the time ordained was the night of the Purification of the Blessed Virgin, the 21 November, at two o'clock.

The Conjuration of the Angel of the West Window

O the night of the Feast of the Purification of the Blessed Virgin! How deeply it is engraved on the memorial of my soul! Now all those hours of waiting, of feverish expectation are behind me, past and forgotten. A miracle, an unbelievable miracle has been vouchsafed me from the world beyond. I am dumbfounded with wonder and amazement at the might and power of the glorious, thrice blessed Angel. Deep within my heart I have made apology to Kelley that I ever thought ill of him and that I saw the mote in my brother's eye and not the beam in mine own. He is an instrument of providence, that I now know and I shudder at the thought of it.

The days that preceded the night were a torment to me. Every day I sent servants to London to enquire of the craftsmen that had contracted to make, according to Kelley's precise instructions, the table around which the five of us – Jane, Talbot, Price, myself and Kelley – were to sit when we conjured the Angel. It had to be made of pieces of costly sandalwood and laurel and greenheart and in the form of a five-pointed star. In the middle there was to be a large hole in the shape of a regular pentagon. Set in the edges were cabbalistic signs, seals and names in polished malachite and brown cairngorm. Now I am ashamed to the depths of my soul when I think of my miserable, mean-minded concern at the thought of the enormous sum of money this table would consume. Today I would tear out my eyes and use them as jewels to decorate the table if it were necessary.

And always the servants would return from London saying, tomorrow, the day after tomorrow. The table was never ready, there seemed to be a spell on it; for no reason this or that journeyman would suddenly fall ill and whilst working on it three had already died a sudden, inexplicable death, as if seized by the ghost of the plague.

I strode restlessly round the rooms of the castle, counting the minutes until the morning of the 21 November broke, dull and grey.

Price and Talbot were sleeping like winter marmots, a strange, heavy, dreamless slumber, as they later told me. Jane, too, had been nigh impossible to wake and she shivered with inner cold, as if taken by a fever in her sleep. My eyes alone were unresting; heat, unbearable heat coursed through my veins.

Days before, Kelley too had been seized with a mysterious unease; like some shy animal he avoided the sight of men; I saw him wander round the park in the twilight and start like a guilty thing surprised when steps approached. During the day he sat brooding on the stone benches, now here, now there, murmuring absent-mindedly to himself or shouting in an unknown language at the empty air, as if someone were standing there. When he awoke from this state it was but for minutes, and then he would ask breathlessly if all were prepared at last; and when I told him, despairing, that it was not, then he began to berate me with curses, which he would suddenly interrupt to return to his soliloquy ...

Finally, shortly after midday – I had not been able to force even one mouthful down, so wrought was I with the impatience and unrest of the long wait – I saw, on the brow of a distant hill, the carts and waggons of the London craftsmen approaching. In a few hours the parts – for it would have been impossible to bring it through the doors in one piece

– had been assembled in the room prepared for it in the castle tower. As Kelley had ordered, three of the windows – to the north south and east – had already been bricked up and only the high, arched west window, a good sixty feet above the ground, remained open. On my orders the walls of the circular chamber had been hung with the pictures of my ancestors, dark with age; chief among them was to have been a portrait of the legendary Hywel Dda, from the brush – and the imagination – of an unknown master, but we had had to remove it, as Kelley flew into a wild rage the moment he saw it.

In the niches of the walls stood my tall silver candelabra with sturdy wax candles in them in preparation for the solemn conjuration. Like an actor memorising his part, I had spent much time walking up and down in the park to commit to memory the enigmatic, incomprehensible formulae that were needed to call up the Angel. Kelley had given them to me one morning and told me they had been handed to him, scratched on a strip of parchment, by a disembodied hand lacking a thumb. My mind immediately saw the terrible Bartlett Greene as he bit off his thumb and spat it into Bishop Bonner's face in the Tower. The memory sent a cold shiver down my spine, but I shook it off: had I not burnt the outlaw's present, the polished coal skrying-glass, and thus broken all bonds between us ...?

After much toil, the words had finally seeped into my blood so that they would come automatically to my lips when I opened them to pronounce the conjuration.

The five of us sat in silence in the great hall as the bell in the spire of the parish church tolled the third quarter before two – excitement had so sharpened my ear that the noise was almost painful to it. Then we climbed up the tower. The five-pointed table that almost filled the chamber shone bright in the light of the candles as Kelley, tottering as if he were drunk,

189

lit them one after the other. Then we sat in order in the high-backed chairs. Two of the points of the pentagram were directed towards the west, where the clear moonlight and the ice-cold night air poured in through the open window. Jane and Kelley sat at these two points; I myself was sitting with my back to the east and my eye was drawn out into the wooded landscape, deep in shadow, through which the frosty paths and roads flowed like rivulets of spilt milk. On either side of me sat Price and Talbot in mute expectation. The candle flames flickered in the air, as if they too were restless. The moon, high in the sky, was hidden from view, but its bright light fell in dazzling cataracts on the white stones of the window-sill. The five-sided hole in the table gaped before me like a dark well-shaft. – –

We sat as still as the dead, though each one could surely hear his own heart thumping in his breast.

All at once Kelley seemed to fall into a deep sleep, for suddenly we could hear a snoring sound as he breathed. His face began to twitch, but that may only have been the light of the candles flickering over his features. I did not know whether to begin the conjuration or not, for I had expected to hear an order from Kelley. I tried to pronounce the formulae, but each time it was as if an invisible finger were laid upon my lips ... Is it all Kelley's imagination? I asked myself and was beginning to fall prey to doubt once more, when my mouth began to speak as if of its own accord and in a voice so deep and resonant that it seemed foreign to me, uttered the words of the evocation. – – –

An icy numbness filled the room. The candles were suddenly as still as death, their flames rigid and giving off no light: you could break them off from the candles, I thought, break them off like withered ears of corn ... The pictures of my ancestors on the walls had become black chasms, like the openings into dark dungeons, and the disappearance of the portraits made me feel as if I was cut off from those who were there to protect me.

In the deathly silence a child's voice rang out:

"My name is Madini; I am a little girl from a poor family. I am the second youngest of the children; at home my mother has a babe at her breast."

At the same time I saw hovering in the open air outside the window the figure of a pretty little girl of seven to nine years old; her long hair hung in ringlets over her forehead; her dress shimmered red and green and looked as if it were made from flakes of the jewel alexandrite, which appears green by day and at night blood red. Charming as the child looked at first sight, its appearance made a terrifying impression: it hovered outside the window, fluttering like taut, smooth silk, a shape without any physical depth, its features as if painted – a phantom in two dimensions. Is that the promised angel? I wondered, and a bitter disappointment fell upon me which the miracle of this inexplicable apparition could do nothing to lessen. Then Talbot leant over to me and whispered in a choking voice:

"It is my child; I am sure I recognise it. She died not long after birth. Do the dead continue to grow?"

There was so little pain and sorrow in my friend's voice that I felt sure he was as terrified as I was. Could it be an image, deep within him, that had been projected out into the air, that had somehow been released from his soul and taken visible form? – But I immediately abandoned the thought as the phantom was obscured by a pale green pillar of light which suddenly shot up like a geyser through the hole in the table and then moulded itself into a human shape which yet had nothing human about it. It congealed into an emerald form, as translucent as beryl, and as hard – a hardness which seemed to gather and concentrate at its centre more perceptibly than in any earthly material. Arms detached themselves from the stone, a head, a neck. – – And hands! Those

191

hands! There was something about them that I could not quite pin down. For a long time I could not take my eyes off them until I saw it: the thumb on the right hand pointed outwards, it was the left-hand thumb. I will not say that this terrified me – why should it? But this apparently trivial detail emphasised the otherness, the ahuman nature of the gigantic being rising up before me even more than its miraculous, inexplicably tangible emergence from the green pillar of light.

The face, its eyes without lashes and set wide apart, was fixed beyond description. There was something fearful, paralysing, deadening and yet shatteringly sublime in its gaze which froze me to the bone. I could not see Jane, she was blocked by the figure of the Angel, but Talbot and Price seemed corpses, so deathly white were their faces.

The lips of the Angel were red as rubies and formed into a strange smile, turned up at the corners, where they tapered to a delicate point. The child before had seemed unnatural in its flatness, this gigantic creature was stupefying in its corporeal presence, which surpassed all earthly measure: there was not the slightest shadow cast by its garments to give it emphasis or perspective. Yet in spite of – or perhaps because of – that, it made me feel that until that point I had in my whole life on earth seen nothing but flat surfaces, when compared with the sight of this being from another world.

Was I the one who asked, "Who are you?" Or was it Price? I cannot say. Without opening its lips, the Angel said, in a cold, piercing voice that sounded as if it were an echo from deep within my own breast:

"I am Il, the messenger of the West Gate."

Talbot wanted to ask a question, but all he could bring out was incoherent babbling. Price pulled himself up straight; he wanted to ask a question but all he could do was babble too! I gathered all my strength to raise my eyes to the Angel's countenance, but I had to let them drop; I sensed I would die if I insisted. My head bowed, I asked in a stuttering voice:

"Il, All-powerful Being, you know that which my soul longs for. Grant me the secret of the stone! I would give my heart, I would give my blood – so fervently do I desire the metamorphosis from a human animal into a King, into one that has risen from the dead both here and beyond. I would understand St. Dunstan's book and its secrets! Make me into the one that I ... was destined to be!"

Time passed – it seemed an eternity. Deep sleep threatened to overcome me but I fought it with all the strength of my longing. The room resounded with words, as if the floor and walls were joining in:

"It is good that thou hast sought in the West, in the Green Realm. I am well pleased. It is in my mind that I shall grant thee the Stone."

"When?" I screamed, almost consumed in wild, nameless joy.

"The day after tomorrow!" came the answer, syllable by syllable.

"The day after tomorrow!" My heart leapt up. "The day after tomorrow!"

"Dost thou know who thou art?" asked the Angel.

"I? – I ... am John Dee."

"You are? You are ... John Dee?!" the apparition repeated. The Angel said it in a piercing voice, even more piercing than before. I felt ... I dare not even think it: ... as if ... no, I will not let it pass my lips as long as I have power over them, nor will I let my quill write it down whilst I have the strength to control it.

"John Dee thou art, Lord of the Manor of Gladhill and Master of the Spear of Hywel Dda, oh, I know thee well!!" came a shrill, mocking voice from the window. I sensed it was the spectral child outside speaking.

"He who has the Spear is the Victor!" – the words echoed from the mouth of the Green Angel. "He who has the spear is called and chosen. The Watchers at the four Gates are all subject to him. But thou, follow ever thy brother Kelley. He is my instrument here on earth, he is appointed to lead thee over the abyss of pride. Him thou shouldst obey, whatever he demand. Inasmuch as the least of these my brethren demand it, grant it him, for I am he and thou grantest it unto me. Then I can be with thee, in thee and around thee until the end of time."

"That I solemnly swear to you, Blessed Angel!" I replied, struck to the very marrow and trembling in every limb. "I raise my hand and swear to you, even should I thereby perish!"

"Should ... perish!" came the echo from the walls.

There was a deathly hush in the chamber. I felt as if my oath were resounding through the depths of the cosmos. The candles flared up; the flames were horizontal as if in a blast of wind .

An icy cold that froze my fingers came from the Angel. With numbed lips I asked:

"Il, hallowed spirit, when shall I see you again? How can I see you when you are far from me?"

"Thou canst always see me in the coal-glass, but I cannot speak through it."

"I have burned the coal," I stammered, and I regretted that I had destroyed the skrying crystal in the presence of Gardner, my cursed assistant, for craven fear of Bartlett Greene.

"Shall I return it to you? John Dee ... heir to ... Hywel Dda?"

"Give it to me, mighty Il!" I beseeched him.

"Put thy hands together in prayer. To pray is to receive if ... a man ... has learnt to pray!"

"That I have," I rejoiced. I placed my hands together – an object swelled up between my palms, pushing them apart. When I opened them, there was the coal skrying-glass!

"Thou hast burnt it. Through that it lost its old life; now it has thy life in it, John Dee. It is reborn

194

and risen from the dead. Just like men, things live on too."

I stared at the thing, full of astonishment. How marvellous are the ways of the invisible world. Not even the devouring fire of earth can bring destruction! – – –

"I ... thank you ... Il ... I thank you!" I was about to stammer, but I was so moved that I could not speak. My voice was choked with tears. Then it burst out of me like a spring tide:

"And the stone? That too ...?!"

"The ... day ... after ... tomorrow", the whisper came as if from a great distance. The Angel had become a faint wisp and the child at the window seemed to my eye translucent, like milky glass. It hung in the air, lifeless as a scrap of silk. Then it sank back into the landscape, floated as greenish, shimmering mist to the ground and became a patch of meadow.

That was my first meeting with the Angel of the West Window.

After such favour, can fate hold any torment in store for me? Blest be the night of the feast of the Purification of the Virgin Mary.

We sat together for a long time and talked ecstatically of the wondrous occurrence. As if it were the greatest treasure in the world, I clutched Bartlett Greene's – no, no: the Angel's coal crystal as a constant reminder that I had been found worthy of a miracle. My heart was full to bursting when I remembered the Angel's promise: The day after tomorrow!

Kelley lay in a deep sleep until the dawn appeared in a sky flushed red, as if smeared with blood from wounded clouds. In silence, shuffling like a weary

195

old man, he went down the stairs without one glance at the rest of us.

How wrong is the common cry: Beware of him who bears the brand! I felt this as I watched the man with the ears cut off disappear down the stairs. "He is an instrument of providence and ... I took him, my brother, for ... a criminal. – – – I will practice humility", I resolved. Practice humility ... and be worthy of the stone! – –

One strange fact I learnt from Jane: I had assumed the Angel had stood with its back to her. To my surprise she told me that the face had been turned towards her the whole time, just as it had been turned towards me. She had heard what it had said, just as I had. Price spent his time trying to fathom how the miracle of the return of the coal had happened and what were the hidden laws behind it. He thought things were probably different than we, with our dull senses, supposed; perhaps they were not physical objects but visible manifestations of some unknown force. I did not listen to him! My heart was too full.

Talbot was silent. Perhaps he was thinking of his dead child.

Months, many months have passed and the records I have kept of the angelic conferences have gradually expanded to fill fat tomes. Despair comes over me when I look at them. Hopes, hopes – the consuming fire of expectation all those never-ending days! Still no certainty, still no fulfilment. It is the old torment renewed! The cup I have already tasted to the lees! Will it come to it that I must exclaim, My God, my God, why hast thou forsaken me?! So be it; but can I then hope to achieve the regenerate body? There has been no end to the promises of the Angel of the West Window – nor to the doubts that gnaw at me like the worm in the bud. At every conjuration, night after night during the period of the waning moon, sometimes with my friends, sometimes alone with Kelley and my wife Jane, the glittering promises are repeated, assuring me that untold wealth and above all knowledge and the secret of the Stone are ever more surely, ever more nearly mine. During the time of the waxing moon I count the hours and minutes until we start our seances again; the waiting wears on me and drains me of all energy. Time becomes a vampire, sucking the life force from my blood, and the maddening notion that awful, invisible beings are fattening themselves on it has me in its talons; I cry out in prayer to free myself from it, but in vain. I repeat my vow that I will never desire riches, and yet at the same time all my hope is fixed on Mammon, for daily my wealth melts away like ice in the sun. It is as if Fate would prove that I cannot keep my vow, as if it would force me, yes, force me to break it. Has almighty God given the Devil power to make me an oath-breaker? Or is the God whom we men believe in Himself a ... no I will put that thought from me, I will not let it take shape in words, I will not write it down: my scalp tingles!

And once more I conjure the spirits, time after time, in sitting after sitting, sparing no effort nor expense, forgetting the morrow: forgetting health, duties, reputation and wealth, I continue to invoke the insatiable Angel, my patron, my tireless benefactor, to plead with Him, to sacrifice hopes and heart's blood to Him. The book wherein I keep the record of these meetings becomes an oracle of mockery when I pore over it with burning eyes in sleepless nights, looking for errors I have made, seeking for conditions I can put the next time to give me the power to win the gifts of the fiery Green Angel, even if it cost the last drop of blood from a weary heart. I keep watch with feverish eyes and halting pulse, weary unto death, praying and searching until I begin to lose my faith in God. For days after such vigils I lack the strength and the will to examine the book of St.

Dunstan, and Kelley heaps reproaches on me, that I am delaying the enterprise and endangering its success.

Nights on end then are spent in prayer to my God until my knees ache and bleed, I do penance, I tear my garments in remorse, I make empty promises to renew my faith, to strengthen my soul and persevere in belief and trust in His heavenly messengers and His Green Angel. And yet all the while I know this: a man may expect nothing in the spiritual world unless he possess the unshakeable calm and grandeur of soul of an Elijah or a Daniel in the lion's den; how else shall he confront the temptation to feel God has forsaken him and there is naught but the gaping abyss before him? What justification have I to invoke the Other World and its shining messengers, miserable worm that I am? I, who am a prey to doubt and despair in spite of the most glorious revelations? I, who begin to feel hate instead of love for them, just because their promises remain unfulfilled? – Does not the Angel speak to me! Should I sink back into the company of the countless blind, unknowing human dwarves who do not even believe such things are possible, let alone have eyes to see their splendour? Has not the sight of the Angel been vouchsafed me a hundred times in his blazing majesty? In his unfathomable mercy did he not reveal to me at the very first meeting his perfect knowledge of all my sorrows, my heart's unquenchable hopes and my soul's most secret longings? – And did he not promise to satisfy them all? What more can I ask of the Eternal Being, fool and weakling that I am? Can I not see the signs everywhere around me that God's power and the mysteries of the hidden world beyond are about to be placed in my hands – if only these hands did not tremble like an old man's, enough to let the precious gift run through my fingers like sand. Is not sacrifice to the Lord, Christian communion and fervent prayer to the Giver of Life the be-all and end-all of our endeavours to keep the evil spirits

198

away from our sittings? And each time does not an unearthly light, yes: light, announce the fiery messenger? Are not the most secret things made manifest? Does not Kelley speak in tongues, as did the Apostles of the Lord on the Day of Pentecost? I have long established through careful, nay, cunning, trial that Edward Kelley knows scarcely any of the Latin he speaks when the spirit is upon him – not to mention Greek and Hebrew, or even Aramaic! All his speech concerns the noble mysteries of perfection, and often it seems as if the great masters of the ancient world were speaking through the unconscious Kelley – Plato, King Solomon, Aristotle himself, Socrates and Pythagoras.

Greedy for knowledge though I am, I must not let myself be eaten up with impatience, nor despair because the operations that are necessary, according to Kelley's instructions, to render the spirits visible and audible, are burning a deep hole in my purse. should I stint him when he brings costly ingredients from London at the command of the Green Angel which are necessary to test out the manufacture of the Stone, especially as the formulae in St. Dunstan's book become darker and more mysterious the farther we progress in our study of it? A further matter is that my house in Mortlake has become a hostelry for many of my former companions, who pour in from all sides because Kelley's boasting has spread the news of the success of our experiments. I no longer have the strength to put a stop to all this hustle and bustle; I let things take their course; my eyes are fixed on the Stone like a bird on a snake's. Soon I will not be able to provide for my wife and child, since every day Kelley indulges himself more and more in wine and feasting. I had to give way to him when he demanded that we should use more and more of the red powder to make gold, and in anguish I watch the precious substance daily diminishing. Now all my effort is concentrated on uncovering the secrets of

St. Dunstan's book with the help of the Green Angel's – dark, too dark – hints, before the "Red Lion" is completely used up.

In the meantime the rumours of necromancy, of nightly visitations and apparitions in my house, have spread far abroad and come to the ears of the court and Queen Elizabeth. Whilst all the marvels reap more mockery and scorn than scholarly interest from the Queen and her great nobles, the reaction of the superstitious rabble to my studies and their results is much more dangerous. The old suspicion that I am engaged in black magic and other satanic arts has been aroused once more and there is much muttering amongst the people. Old enemies scent new opportunities and seek to set in motion their old machinations against me – the much-honoured favourite of the Queen, now fallen into disgrace but still dangerous, the politician of uncertain influence but versed in the intrigues of the court. In short, all the old fears and jealousies of those I have humbled raise their hundred tongues against me and try to destroy me.

And whilst we here, behind closed doors, entreat heaven to lighten the darkness of our understanding, and search for the secret way that can raise men above themselves and free them from the curse of death and their animal nature, outside, beyond the walls of Mortlake Castle, the storms of hell are gathering and all are seeking to encompass my downfall.

Often, o my God, my heart is faint and my belief in my calling wavers. Can it then be true, the accusation that Gardner, the friend who left me in anger, once levelled against me when I contradicted him: that I wanted to grow a mighty oak before I had planted the acorn in the ground. If I knew where to find my friend, I would call him back and, like a child, lay my weary head on his lap … But for that it is too late.

Kelley's strength grows with my weakness. I have left the direction of all matters to him. My wife Jane endures it in silence; for months now she has looked on my distraught features with sorrow and pity. It is her courage alone that has kept me going. She is a delicate creature of no great bodily strength, and yet for my sake she does not flinch before the approach of our ruin. My salvation is her only concern. She will be a loyal companion on the hard and toilsome road. – – – I am often struck by the thought that as I become more tired, weak and weary, Kelley flourishes daily more and more not only in physical health, but also in his undeniable psychical powers – just as the Green Angel of the West Window and the spectral child that precedes it take on clearer, fuller form! I cannot get the words of John the Baptist from the Bible out of my mind: "He must increase, but I must decrease." Is this secret law of a spiritual world also valid for the dark beings of the Abyss? If it be so, then God have mercy on my soul! For Kelley is the one that does increase and I – – –. And the Green Angel would be – – – no! no! I will not even think it. –
– –

My nights are consumed with restless dreams; but the more my days are frittered away on vain hopes, the more splendid does the Green Angel appear when the moon is in the descendant: its raiment is ever more rich and glorious, covered in gold and jewels. So great is the glory of its appearance that were it to disappear and leave but a fragment of its cloak behind, we would be free from material cares for the rest of our lives.

Most recently its forehead has been decorated with gems of a fiery ruby red, like huge drops of blood, so that I seem to see the head of the Saviour torn by the crown of thorns in its otherworldly radiance. And drops of sweat, formed by the most brilliant diamonds, shine out from its forehead, just as they have stood on mine in many a sleepless night. – O

God, let me not blaspheme, but why does not one single drop of this immeasurably precious blood and sweat fall to the floor of my chamber.

I wait – – – wait – – – wait – – .

Time for me has become like a woman in labour who cannot give birth and who pleads for relief in an unending scream. My meat is hope, but it is a food which tears at my body; my drink is assurance, and I am parched. When shall I say: it is finished?! – – –

Now we spent all our time with the preparation of the tincture of gold and scarcely a sitting passes but that the Green Angel assures us that on the next day or at the next suitable conjunction of the stars it will reveal to us the secret of the Stone and the formula that will crown all our labours. And each time there is a new condition, a new preparation, one more last call on skill and wealth, one new sacrifice, one more plunge into the black abyss of hope and trust.

The wildest rumours are circulating amongst the local people at what is supposed to be going on in Mortlake, so that it seems best to let them – whether they wish us well or ill – know what is the purpose of my studies and experiments. Better, at least, than to allow calumny a free rein and suddenly find myself one day unexpectedly exposed to the fury, the enmity and blood-lust of the mob. It is for that reason that yesterday I gave way to the request from Lord Leicester, who still seems well-disposed toward me for old time's sake, and have invited him, together with several of the gentlemen of the court who are curious to see our marvels, to visit me at Mortlake.

And now Lord Leicester and his entourage, together with the Polish prince, Albert Lasky, are at the castle, filling every corner of house and yard with their noise, not to mention the costs of lodging and a well-supplied table. It has cost us another good pinch from St. Deniol's salt-cellar, but Kelley just laughed his mocking laugh and mumbled into his beard something about there being plenty of birds to pluck. I clenched my teeth in fury, for I knew what he was about. I have been spared nothing in my restless search for truth. How much filth, baseness, iniquity and evil has this travelling quack not brought into my life.

In my notebooks I have recorded what happened at the sittings the gentlemen from London organised at Mortlake. Both my house and my soul grow daily more confused. What is there for me to say of the recent change in the mystical exchanges between Kelley and the green spectral child? Their subject is no longer Immortality and "Greenland" and the Queen and the Crowning Glory of the person and all the celestial favours accorded the chosen ones; they no longer even talk of the preparation of the salt and the essence. With the worldly ambition and superficial chatter of the courtiers and the scheming little Polish chieftain, all meditation and self-examination have been turned into their opposites and the sittings echo with the questions of these people as to the prospects for all their little intrigues and personal aspirations, as if they were in the cave of the witch of Uxbridge, or listening to prophecies read from the dregs of their cups by fairground gypsies. But still Kelley is rapt in the same trance as when questions about the spiritual life were put to Aristotle, Plato and King Solomon – only now it is the flunkeys and bootlickers of the Royal Bedchamber that speak through his mouth. – – –

Loathsome, utterly loathsome! – And yet I do not even know what it is that disgusts me.

After every sitting I arise sucked dry, my legs can scarce carry me from the chamber; but Kelley, after each sitting, has an increase of robust strength, triumphant confidence and self-assurance. He is no longer the guest in my house, my pupil and assistant, it is I who am here on sufferance, the servant of his miraculous powers, the slave of his ever-growing appetites.

And that no jot of my shame shall go unrecorded: sometimes it is now Kelley who pays the household expenses from what he receives from my guests, in particular Prince Lasky, who seems to have fabulous wealth at his disposal, for the information he gives them in the name of the Green Angel. Now I and my family depend for our daily bread on the scraps from a charlatan's table! For I well know that Kelley does not refrain from deception and trickery at these sittings: he disguises his voice and pronounces what his foolish hearers in their insatiable pride want to hear and tells them things that flatter their boundless ambition. With insolent words and a cynical laugh he confessed as much to me and told me to pawn the blankets off the beds if I would rather feed my illustrious guests in that way. But there is another question that wounds me even deeper than the humiliation of being the accomplice of a cutpurse, so to speak: how can Providence suffer such fraud to be perpetrated in the presence – and the name! – of divine messengers such as the Green Angel and the spectral child at the west window?! For they do appear when it is taking place, in physical form, tangible and visible to all; I have seen it myself a dozen times. All this has overwhelmed me, as sudden as a desert storm, and I can see the gaping maw of fate ready at any moment to devour me. If Kelley is unmasked, then I fall with him, for I am linked to him – and who will believe I am innocent when even in my own eyes I am not? The invitations to go to the Queen in London become ever more pressing; the inflated reports of the Pole, Lasky, have aroused her curiosity and she will surely not let me keep from her the newly discovered marvel of the open door to the world beyond. If that should happen, then it is a matter of life or death. But I will never permit Kelley to practise his deceit on her! – Here thou must make thy stand, John Dee, here is the limit of thy errors and betrayal of the secret of the Baphomet! – –

Would that I had never written down my dreams! – How true is the wisdom of the old adepts: do not tell your dreams, even to paper, or they will become reality. Has he not become a reality, the man that I dreamed of with his ears cut off? Now he is revealed to me in all his filthy nakedness – my house guest and companion in fortune, Edward Kelley. And again and again I find myself thinking of Bartlett Greene and Mascee, both robbers of the dead and desecrators of graves and both instruments from beyond of the vengeance of St. Dunstan. I am the victim of a strange trick of fate that sent me the ivory spheres that they should be transformed into iron balls, chained to my ankles like those a criminal has to drag after him. – – –

Now the Pole, Lasky, with a fair note from the Queen, has sent for myself and Kelley to come to the court and conjure up the Green Angel in a solemn sitting – because the Polish princeling has had an attack of the gout and we are to conjure up the immortal spirit to find a remedy for his over-indulgence in port wine!

Oh, everything is taking the course I foresaw: doubt and confusion! Deprivation and want! Dishonour and destruction!

The order of the Queen makes refusal impossible and we must hasten to London. – – – Our reception at court was most welcoming, but at what cost to my soul!

Elizabeth insisted that we hold a sitting immediately; no visible apparitions came, but two spirits spoke through the mouth of Kelley, calling themselves Jubandalace and Galbah, and they promised the Pole that he would not only soon recover his health but would also become King of the Turks. Elizabeth could hardly repress a laugh, and I could see how she was tempted to start the old game of cat and mouse with me and what fiendish pleasure it gave her to see me teetering on the brink of shame and ridicule.

What is it that drives her to such acts? – How unfathomable are the ways of Providence! – Is this the fulfilment of the mystic, spiritual union that was pledged between us? – Is this the end of my road to Baphomet, who bears the crown and the eternal radiance of the crystal? – –

The only means by which I managed put a stop to this was by beseeching my old friend Leicester to use his influence to have the sessions in London stopped. Otherwise, I am sure, the spirits would have ended up promising Lasky the crown of this island and dominion over the whole world. Then I was fortunate to find a way to tear the Queen away from her devilish pleasure in my discomfiture. At a private audience I pleaded with her to curb her impatience to consult Kelley's spirits until I was sure of their nature. I represented to her that the world beyond might harbour diverse beings, including dissembling fiends who could take on the form of angels, so that Her Majesty's virgin reputation would be at the mercy of such mocking demons. At this the Queen thought long and then asked me if I thought my future invocations of the spirits would bring me more than my earlier plans for the conquest of Greenland?

I answered with a firm "Yes!" She fixed me with a seaching look as I continued, "Whatever way I choose to spend my life in, I am on a journey of discovery to the land of fulfilment, and shall continue it for as long as these eyes can see the sun. And wherever I strike land, I will raise the flag of my last love and take possession of my Green Land, just as Duke William of Normandy did when he swept across the sea and conquered England."

The Queen did not answer. I did not challenge her silence, but I could see her pride was provoked, and I could understand why she resorted to scorn to defend herself:

"Be that as it may, good Master Dee, it neverthe-less gives Us great satisfaction to hear that thy commerce with the world above has not been without its earthly rewards. We hear that these unworldly beings have revealed to thee the philosopher's stone and the secret of the preparation of the tincture for making gold."

I was no little astonished at this revelation, for I had kept my alchymical experiments hidden from everyone and could not understand how the Queen had come to hear of them. Nothing daunted, however, I answered frankly, for I suddenly saw the opportunity of solving all my difficulties. I told Her Majesty, therefore, that so far all my efforts to transmute metals had been vain and that my sole earthly reward had been the loss of my fortune.

At that Elizabeth seemed to respond as if her heart, usually so cold, had been touched by human feeling, and she asked me if I needed help from her privy purse.

I did not want to appear before her as a beggar, and so I answered with the last remnants of my pride that I would not abuse my Mistress' favour, but that I would remember her words should my need become greater. – – –

Now we have finally escaped the bustle of the city and are back in the peace and quiet of Mortlake where I can resume my alchymical experiments.

I did not have to wait long for further misfortune: during one of the experiments the whole *laboratorium* exploded. It was a miracle that I myself was unharmed, but there are wide cracks in the castle walls and it has so aroused the superstitious hate of the peasants that I hourly expect some kind of attack, for they have sent word that they will no longer suffer the Devil to remain in their midst. – My time here is almost over.

The Green Angel heaps promise upon promise, each one more definite, more confident than the other: all approaches its final fulfilment, it says. But we all know that help is too late; our ruin is imminent.

We had a final discussion of the situation with Kelley and came to the conclusion that we should not use any more of the red powder to make gold to pay for our needs, but should leave the country as quickly as possible and head for Bohemia where we could take up our work again under the protection of the Emperor Rudolf, himself a famous adept of the royal art, as were many of his noble friends; we had all the more prospect of success as we would be able to give the suspicious Habsburg a demonstration of the transmutation of metals before his very eyes, thanks to the remaining few grains in St. Deniol's ivory spheres. There in Prague we would have to make one final effort to discover from the book how to prepare the Stone, which would put an end to all our misery and open up the path to glory and fortune. There is no doubt at all that a successful alchymist enjoys much more favourable conditions in Prague than in England with its ungrateful Queen.

With my wife Jane I spent a long time weighing up the advantages and disadvantages of the step, for it was a wrench for me near to my sixtieth year to have to flee my native land once more; but the Green Angel had given the order to leave England for the Emperor Rudolf's court in such promising terms that I resolved to hesitate no longer. As if heaven itself wanted to give me a sign that I had made the right choice, yesterday I received a letter from Prince Lasky in Poland in which he invited me in the most flattering terms to stay with my wife, and Kelley as his guest on his estates for as long as it should please us. He would of course bear the cost of the journey, and beyond that he offered me a generous salary. My pleasure in the letter was short-lived: the very next morning there were notes threatening to set fire to the castle and murder us all nailed to the door. That is too much; I cannot endanger the lives of my loved ones. Should I call on the magistrates for help? There would be no point, they would leave me in the lurch.

I sense only too clearly that behind the peasants' uprising powerful enemies are concealed who wish me evil and seek my ruin. I must take the initiative myself! – – – No money has come from Lasky, and the situation has worsened, so that I have had to approach Elizabeth for help through Leicester's mediation. What more do I care! I have no pride left to lose. I will not be responsible for the murder of my wife and child! – – –

A messenger came from Elizabeth today and brought me forty gold nobles and a note wherein she answers my complaint that both our house and our lives are insufficiently protected: her power, she says, is no more than that of the appointed magistrates. Moreover she is surprised that the apparition, in whom I place so much trust, is not a better Guardian Angel than herself, a mere earthly ruler – – – and more such cold mockery.

Now therefore all has been settled and the arrangements have gone ahead in secret; we have kept our baggage to the minimum so that the journey may be done as cheaply as possible. Everything that I leave behind here in Mortlake, as well as the unknown future that lies ahead of us, I commit into the hands of the all-merciful power of heaven. – – –

Today, the 21 September, 1583, the day of departure has arrived. A carriage has been ordered so that we can leave the house quietly before sunrise and we hope to reach Gravesend before dark. – – –

Last night a mob of peasants and vagrants were rioting outside the castle walls and a burning torch was thrown into the closed courtyard, but my old servant stamped it out. During our flight we managed with great difficulty to evade another rabble of troublemakers in the early morning mist. – – –

O my God, it is as I have described it here in my diary: flight! Behind me lies everything that was mine and that linked our family name with England: Mortlake is abandoned to the attacks of the mob, perhaps will fall even before I have left the inhospitable shores of my native land. – – –

My eyes, dim with age, have seen the burning of Mortlake! Black clouds hang on the horizon over the place where the castle lies hidden behind the hills. Black clouds of billowing smoke – the inhabitation of demons puffed up with their own venom! – swirl in a witches' sabbath around the former abode of peace. The evil spirits of the past have descended like vultures – let them eat their fill. May they gorge themselves with the sacrifice and forget me in their orgy of desecration! – There is only one thing for which I deeply grieve: my beautiful library, my books which were so dear to my heart. The avenging demons will spare them just as little as the rabble in its ignorance. There were amongst those books many that were unique, the last of their kind on earth. A burnt offering of profound wisdom! True instruction going up in smoke! Dissolve back into the fire whence you came: noble words are wasted on beasts. Better to burn with an eternal flame and be borne up home to the source of the everlasting fire!

For a whole hour I have been sitting at my desk with the last page of John Dee's *Private Diary* in my hand. I have seen the castle in Mortlake burn as if I were standing there outside it myself. It was more alive than anything you see in your mind whilst reading.

Several times, on a sudden impulse, I have stretched my hand out to the drawer where the papers from my cousin's legacy are kept, but each time I do so my arm seems to go limp and I cannot bring myself to take out another document that might provide more details. More details? What on earth for? To stir up more clouds of mouldy dust? To dig up the past? When everything has taken on an immediacy so brilliant it is almost dazzling? It would be much better if I could make use of the intense peacefulness that cocoons me at this moment. Sitting here in my study, I feel as if I am cut off from the world and yet not alone – as if I were somewhere in empty space, outside human time. –

I am no longer in any doubt at all: John Dee, my ancestor, lives! He is present, he is here, here in this room, here by my chair, by me – perhaps within me! – I will put it down in plain, unambiguous words: it is probable that – that I am John Dee ... perhaps always have been ... have been from the very beginning, without knowing it! What do I care *how* that can be?! Is it not sufficient that I feel it with indescribable clarity and precision? There are, anyway, many theories and examples from all sorts of areas of modern science which back up, explain, categorise what I have experienced and give it a learned name-tag: there is schizophrenia, split personality, dual consciousness, not to mention various parapsychological phenomena. What is ridiculous is that it is the lunatic doctors who concentrate on such matters – and in their ignorance they label anything as mad which doesn't fit into their neat little pigeon-holes.

I have examined myself and declare that I am completely sound of mind. But enough of such protestations: I do not need them and the psychiatrists, those know-all moles of the human psyche, can go to hell, for all I care!

So: John Dee is not dead; he is a – let's call it a transcendental personality, which expresses and tries to realise itself through clear desires and goals. It may well be that this life force has been transmitted through the secret channels of the blood, but that is a minor matter. If we imagine the immortal part of John Dee as pulsing through these channels like an electric current through a wire, then I am at the end of the wire and the electrical impulse that is John Dee is building up within me with all his awareness of the world beyond. But that is of no interest! A thousand explanations are possible, but none can replace the terrible intensity of the experience. Mine is the mission; mine is the goal and the crown and Baphomet realised! If ... if I am worthy! If I am steadfast! If I am prepared. Eternal triumph or disaster – it all depends on me, the last of the line!

I can feel the promise burning down on my head – and the curse. I know what is necessary and I am ready. I have learnt much, John Dee, from the books you wrote to refresh your own memory, and I assure you, noble spirit of my blood, that the memory is still fresh! – Your goal is in good hands, John, and it is the decision of my own free will that you are me! – – –

Bartlett Greene could hardly wait for me to awake to myself! Not long ago he was here, standing behind my desk, in the belief that the mystical union between myself and his prey, John Dee, was already consummated. That was foolish, Bartlett Greene. You sought evil and worked for good, just as you devils of the left hand always do. You only speeded up my awakening, Bartlett Greene, you opened my eyes and sharpened them to the wiles of your ancient mistress from Scotland and to the abyss of the black cosmos. I welcome you, Lady of the Cat, always the same in your many guises! – Black Isaïs, Sissy, Princess Assja Shotokalungin. I know you. I have followed your way through timelessness from the moment you became a succubus feeding off my unfortunate ancestor until the day you sat here and demanded the spearhead of me. Behind her demand was a magic suggestion which I did not understand because it remained hidden from me. She cannot destroy the woman still sleeping within me, the royal "Elizabeth", because the magic future cannot be harmed as long as it has not become present, but she desires to take possession of the active male principle in me, and so to foil the coming "Chymical Marriage"! There will come a final reckoning between us!

Friend Lipotin offered his services before I could understand him. He called himself a descendant of the "Tutor to the Czar". He called himself, if only implicitly, Mascee. So be it; for the meantime I will believe him.

And what of my drowned friend Gärtner? I will ask the green glass, Lipotin's present here in front of me, and I know that Theodor Gärtner will step out from the mirror with a smile on his face, light himself a cigar, lean back comfortably in his chair and say, "Don't you know me any more, John, old friend? Me, your friend Gardner, your assistant? Who warned you? Who unfortunately warned you in vain? But we know each other now, don't we, and this time you will listen to my advice?!"

The only one missing is Edward Kelley, the charlatan with the cut off ears, the seducer, the medium: the man from John Dee's age who in our century has become a cancer that has multiplied a thousand times and grows and grows, even though it has no self any more. The medium! The bridge to the beyond and to Black Isaïs!

I am curious to see when this Kelley will bow his way into my life so that I can tear the mask of time from his face! – I am ready for anything, Kelley, whether you appear as a ghost in true spiritualist manner or as a vagrant prophet preaching in the street outside.

And that leaves: Elizabeth. – – –

I must admit that I am seized with a fit of trembling which makes it impossible for me to write down the thoughts beginning to surface in my mind. My brain is in turmoil. However hard I try, all my thoughts, all my ideas disappear into a swirl of mist when my mind turns to "Elizabeth". – –

That was the point I had reached in my reflections – reflections part confident, part despairing – when I was surprised by the sound of a violent altercation, which started out by the front door and grew louder as it approached my room.

Then I recognised the two competing voices: the brusque and imperious exclamations of Princess Shotokalungin, falling like whip-cracks, and the gentler but no less obstinate tones of my housekeeper, Frau Fromm, who was conscientiously obeying my orders.

I leapt up: the Princess in my apartment! The Princess who only recently had sent a message through Lipotin that she was expecting me to return her visit. 'Princess Shotokalungin'! – what am I saying? No: the demon of

213

the gruesome rite of 'Taghairm', the enemy from the very beginning, the 'Lady Sissy' of my cousin, John Roger, the woman of the waning moon; she is coming back onto the attack.

A wild joy surged through my veins, setting each nerve-end alight: welcome, welcome, you come to the ignominy of defeat, ghost-woman! – I am in the mood – I am ready! –

And with a few quick steps I was at the door; I pulled it open and called out, making the reproach in my voice as mild and friendly as possible:

"It's all right, Frau Fromm! You can let the lady enter. I've changed my mind. I'm quite happy to receive her. – Do come in!"

Frau Fromm shrank back as the Princess swished past her towards me, breathing deeply and audibly as she turned her irritation into a gently mocking greeting:

"I am quite astonished, my dear friend, to find you living in such strict retirement! But penitent or saint, I still think you can make an exception for a friend who has been longing to see you. Don't you agree?"

Frau Fromm was still leaning against the wall, glassy eyed and scarcely breathing – some inner chill sent repeated tremors through her body; I signalled to her that all was well and with a wave of the hand invited the Princess into my study. Just as I was closing the door behind me I saw Frau Fromm raise her hands towards me with a sudden movement. I nodded to her again, with a smile that said she was not to worry.

Then I was sitting opposite Princess Shotokalungin.

She bubbled with charming reproaches: I must have misunderstood her determination the last time we had met and avoided her for that reason and that would be why I had not kept my promise to visit her. It was difficult to get a word in. I brushed aside her flattery with a brusque but still just polite wave of the hand. For a moment silence reigned in the room.

"A stench of panther" – I told myself again. The Princess' perfume tickled my senses. I passed my hand across my forehead to calm the rising turmoil and began to speak:

"My dear Princess, your visit, let me repeat, is most welcome. I am not lying when I say that, had you not come, I would have done myself the honour of visiting you." – I deliberately took my time and paused to observe her. But all I saw was a coquettish Princess inclining her head to me in a dumb show of gratitude. I suddenly had the idea of trying to catch her off her guard, so I went on quickly:

"The reason is that I feel the need to tell you that I have come to understand what you want from me – that I understand your motives ..."

"But I am so glad about that!" exclaimed the Princess impulsively, "I am so extremely glad about that."

With a great effort I remained impassive; I ignored her interjection, turned a cool, clear eye on her seductive smile and said:

"I know you."

She nodded expectantly, eagerly, as if pleasantly surprised.

"You call yourself Princess Shotokalungin," I continued, "you have – or had, it is immaterial – a palace in Yekaterinodar."

Again an impatient nod.

"Have you not – or did you not once have – a castle in Scotland? Or somewhere in England?"

The Princess shook her head in bewilderment.

"What do you mean? My family has not the least connection with England."

I gave a cold smile.

"Are you quite sure of that, Lady – – Sissy?"

Now it was my turn to pounce like a panther, and I was trembling with anticipation as to the result. But my fair adversary had herself under better control than I had expected. Visibly amused, she laughed in my face and said:

"How amusing! Am I so like some Englishwoman of your acquaintance? People usually tell me – it may be to flatter me, of course – that my face is most distinctive, and of a pure Circassian shape. Are these the features of a Scot?"

"Perhaps, dear Princess, the flattery of my poor cousin, John Roger, took that form," – – actually I was going to address her as 'noble Lady of the Black Cats', but as I was about to say it I felt a strange resistance in my tongue and so left it unsaid – "but for my part I respectfully submit that your features are not so much Circassian as satanic. I hope you are not offended?"

The Princess almost toppled over backwards with amusement and her supple voice ran up and down the scales in laughter. Then she came to a halt, as if struck by a curious thought, and leant forward as she asked:

"But now I am eager to see where all these original compliments are leading, my friend."

"Compliments?"

"But of course. Quite an unusual selection of compliments. An English lady! A satanic physiognomy! I would never have thought myself worthy of such fascinating comparisons."

I tired of the verbal jousting. The tension within me snapped like an overtaut rope. I exploded:

"Enough, Princess, or however you wish to be addressed! Princess of Hell, certainly! I have told you that I know you, do you hear? That I *know* you! – Black Isaïs can change her dress and her name as she will, there is no mask that can deceive me – me, John Dee!" I leapt up: "You will not thwart the 'Chymical Marriage'!"

The Princess slowly stood up; I was leaning forward on the desk, looking her steadfastly in the eyes.

But things did not happen as I had expected.

My hypnotic gaze did not exorcise the demon, force it to retreat and disappear in a cloud of smoke – or whatever in the heat of the moment I imagined its effect would be. Nothing of the sort happened; rather, the Princess measured me with an immensely imperious and dismissive stare, scarcely bothering to conceal her scorn, and said after a pause:

"I am not fully conversant with the peculiar ways in which people here behave towards us Russian refugees; for that reason I am a little uncertain as to whether your bizarre words are not the result of some mental derangement. At home, where manners often seem somewhat rough, a gentleman does not receive a lady when he has had too much to drink."

It was like suddenly finding myself in a cold shower; I spluttered, unable to bring out a word. My face went bright red. Against my will the lifetime habit of politeness towards the opposite sex compelled me to stammer:

"I wish you could understand ..."

"Impertinences are always difficult to understand, sir."

On a mad impulse I leant forward and grasped her slim hand that was pressed vigorously against the edge of the desk. I pulled it towards me, sensing the sinewy tautness of a hand used to reins and riding crop, and, as if craving pardon, put it to my lips. It was supple and of a normal temperature, with a hint of the exciting, animal perfume that surrounds the Princess; but there was nothing ghostly or demonic about it. The Princess withdrew her hand and raised it in a half-serious threat.

"I can find a better use for this hand than as a vehicle for worthless flattery from a moody cavalier," she thundered; the gentle smack she gave me on the cheek was also of flesh and blood, even if the blood was blue.

I felt disappointed, empty, as if I had passed unresisted through the phantom of some imagined enemy, and was strangely lethargic after my vain attack on thin air. I became unsure of myself and completely confused. At the same time I could still feel the after-shock of an inexplicable emotion that was in some way connected with the contact between my lips and the back of the Princess' hand. A *frisson* composed of mysterious attraction and sudden fear. My skin crawled at the thought that I had offended a nature so much more delicate, more noble than mine. All at once I felt incredibly foolish, could no longer understand my earlier suspicion – it was an overreaction, almost deranged – could no longer understand myself. I must have cut such a sorry, comical figure in this sudden fit of bewilderment that the Princess gave a short, mocking laugh, which was not without a hint of pity, looked me up and down and said:

"*Touchée, mon ami*; I've been punished for my forwardness, I see, and now the scores are even I think the best thing would be to call it a day."

She made her intention clear with a quick movement in the direction of the door. – I awoke from my daze:

"No, Princess, I beseech you, do not go! Do not leave in anger! Allow me to correct your opinion of me, of my manners!"

"My dear friend, it's only a minor case of hurt pride," – she laughed as she continued towards the door – "it will pass. Goodbye!"

I could contain myself no longer.

"Grant me just a few seconds, Princess, to tell you how foolish I have been – not in my right mind – a complete idiot! But ... you realise, I'm sure, that I'm not a drunkard or a boor. – You don't know what I have been through these last few hours ... what I have been faced with ... what my brain has had to deal with ..."

"Just as I thought," answered the Princess, with genuine sympathy and not a hint of mockery. "It's quite true what everyone says about German poets; they fill their heads with otherworldly thoughts and incomprehensible fantasies! You ought to get out in the fresh air more, my dear; travel, it will take your mind off them."

"It has just been most painfully brought home to me how right you are, Princess," I answered, and I could hardly control my tongue any more. "There is a piece of writing which is threatening to get out of hand somewhat. I would consider myself fortunate if you would allow me to use my first break from it to pay a call on you – Lipotin suggested you would be happy to receive such a visit – and seek your forgiveness for my behaviour today."

The Princess, her hand on the door-knob, turned and gave me a long look; she seemed to hesitate for a moment then gave an amused sigh, which yet managed to sound like the yawn of a big cat, and said:

"If you insist, that's agreed, then. But I hope you realise you will be expected to make amends ..."

She gave me a mocking nod and in a moment had slipped out, forestalling any further attempt to hold her up. The door shut in my face and by the time I had gathered my wits, it was too late. A car horn sounded in the street outside.

I pulled up the window and watched the car disappear.

If nowadays the dreaded cat-demon of Bartlett Greene, or some Scottish she-devil, insists on paying her calls in a magnificent Lincoln limousine, I asked myself in self-mockery, how can one not fall for her satanic wiles?

Deep in thought, I closed the window and turned round to find Frau Fromm by the desk where only minutes before the Princess had been standing. In the first moment I felt a shock of horror, for I did not recognise her until I took a step towards her, so changed did both her posture and her expression seem. She stood there, silent and motionless, her features drawn but steadfastly observing my every move, fear in her eyes as she tried to read the expression on my face.

I quickly suppressed my surprise at her action, remembering my own contradictory orders and feeling instead a little ashamed – though I could not really say why – in the presence of this strangely agreeable young woman whose very presence seemed to purify the air. I rubbed my hand over my face: there was still a faint, provocative hint of the Princess' perfume, the scent of a wild beast, on my skin.

I tried to make a joke of it all to Frau Fromm:

"You're probably somewhat puzzled by my sudden change of mind, Frau Fromm. You mustn't mind; it's my work, you see," and I gestured towards my desk, a gesture which she followed with exaggerated precision.

"An idea that just came to me meant that, unexpectedly, the Lady's visit was welcome. I'm sure you understand?"

"Of course I understand."

"Well, then, you can see it was not mere caprice ..."

"The only thing I can see is that you are in great danger."

"But Frau Fromm!" I laughed – a somewhat forced laugh, embarrassed by the harsh tone of my house-keeper's voice. "However did you come you to such strange fancies?"

"It is not a fancy, sir. It is a matter of life and death for you."

Had Frau Fromm had one of her "visions"? Did she have second sight? I went up to her. Her eyes followed me closely and stood up to my gaze. That was not the expression of a woman in a half-trance. I tried to recapture my light tone:

"What on earth could make you think that, Frau Fromm? The lady – she is, by the way, a Princess Shotokalungin, a Russian refugee from the Caucasus and, I am sure, suffering the same deprivations as all those persecuted and driven out by the Bolsheviks – the lady need not trouble you; our relationship is not one which – which –"

"– which you are in control of, sir."

"How do you mean?"

"Because you don't know her!"

"Do you know the Princess?"

"I know her!"

"You ... know Princess Shotokalungin?! That is certainly very interesting."

"I – I don't know her personally."

"But – ?"

"I know her ... over there. – The place where it is green when I am there. – Not when the light is bright, as it usually is ..."

"I don't quite understand, Frau Fromm. What is green – over there?"

"I call it the green land. Sometimes I am there. It is as if it were under water and my breathing stops when I am

220

there. It is far below the surface, in the depths of the sea, and everything seems steeped in a greenish light."

The Green Land!!! I heard my own voice as if from very far away. The words overwhelmed me with the force of a tidal wave. I stood in a daze, just repeating, "The Green Land!" –

"Nothing good comes from it; I know that when I am there," continued Frau Fromm, without changing the almost indifferent, yet strangely harsh and threatening tone of her voice, which still contained a tremor of shyness and repressed fear.

I shook myself out of my daze and asked with observant concern, like a doctor:

"Tell me, what has this 'Green Land' that you keep on 'visiting' to do with Princess Shotokalungin?"

"She has another name there."

The tension was almost unbearable.

"What name?!"

Frau Fromm faltered, looked at me absentmindedly, hesitated:

"I ... I don't know."

"Think, think hard!" – I almost screamed.

I felt that she was under my control, but she just shook her head with a tortured expression. If I can establish rapport, I said to myself, the name must come. But Frau Fromm remained silent; for the first time her eyes slid away from mine. I saw that she was resisting but at the same time seeking spiritual comfort from me. I tried to calm my excitement and withdraw my influence from her – turn my will away from her so that she would come of her own accord. She made a jerky movement. And when she suddenly pulled herself together and slowly put out her foot, I had no idea what it meant. Then she started to walk and passed slowly in front of me, making a gesture as if she were searching, resisting, and it moved me deeply, tore at my heart, so that I was gripped by an irrational impulse to draw her to me, to comfort her, to cry with her, to kiss her like a long-lost lover – like my true and lawful wife. It took all my power of will that I did not do what I had already done in my imagination.

Frau Fromm walked round the chair, in which I usually sit when I am working, and proceeded towards the opposite end of the desk. Her movements were like those of an automaton, her eyes those of a corpse. When she opened her mouth, her voice sounded utterly foreign to me. I did not catch everything she said, only this:

"Are you back again? Go away, tormentor! You cannot deceive me! – I can sense you – I can see your snake's skin, black and silver – I am not afraid, I have my orders – I – I ..."

Frau Fromm had reached the left-hand end of the desk. Before I realised what she was doing, her hands suddenly leapt forward like a cat's paws and pounced on the Tula-ware box that Lipotin had given me from Baron Stroganoff and which I had so carefully placed along the line of the meridian.

"Now I have finally got my hands on you, you silver-black snake," hissed Frau Fromm, and her nervously trembling fingers felt their way along the inlay work of the box.

I wanted to leap up and tear it from her hands. I could not rid myself of the strange superstition that it would somehow disturb the cosmic order if the box was not left in the appointed alignment. This childish delusion took hold of me with a force akin to madness.

"Don't touch! Leave it where it is!" I imagined I was screaming, but all I could hear from my throat was a hoarse, stifled cry in which the words remained unarticulated.

The next moment Frau Fromm's restless fingers had gathered at one point on the smooth silver surface – it was like spiders coming together, like sentient beings suddenly attracted by the scent or sight of their prey and descending on the same spot. They clambered over each other, pushed and shoved, scrabbling at the same place with hungry movements until suddenly a spring gave a quiet click: the Tula box lay open in Frau Fromm's hands.

Immediately I was beside her. She had become quite calm and held the open box out toward me on the palm

222

of her outstretched hand in a gesture expressing disgust or horror at an ugly or dangerous beast. Her features bore a look of triumph and joy, and an inner radiance which I found difficult to interpret, but which affected me like the entreaty of a love too timid to declare itself.

Without a word I took the box out of her hand. At that she seemed to wake up and her face expressed bewilderment, anxiety. She knew how strictly I insisted that nothing on my desk should be touched, nothing moved from its place. Nervous, incomprehending and at the same time triumphant, she looked me full in the face, and I knew that one word of reproach in that moment would have driven her for ever from me and from my house.

The warm surge of mysterious affection which had flooded my innermost being stopped me from speaking the harsh word that was on the tip of my tongue. It was all the matter of a second.

Then I examined the Tula-ware box: on a neatly stitched cushion of green satin, faded and threadbare with age, lay John Dee's *Lapis sacer et praecipuus manifestationis*, that had been given to him in the last days at Mortlake by the Green Angel of the West Window: Bartlett Greene's polished coal which John Dee had burnt in the fire and then received back in such miraculous fashion from the world beyond.

After the very first glance there was no doubt at all for me: the gold stand John Dee had described so minutely, the precious setting of the gleaming black dodecahedron – it all corresponded: I held in front of me the gift of Bartlett Greene and the Green Angel.

I did not dare to let the lid of the box fall shut; my fate, which was in my hands, might have been closed to me, as it was to John Dee, all those years ago, when he threw the gift of the red and white spheres out of the window.

I have no time to lose, I said to myself, I am in the light and – I know, whilst my ancestor, John Dee, was feeling his way in the dark.

Carefully I lifted the marvellous crystal from its disintegrating cushion, meticulously checking the screws of the stand which held the smooth and gleaming piece of coal in place, and placed the miniature work of art in the middle of the desk. Then a mysterious movement began: the crystal started to tremble and oscillate about its axis; it appeared that at its poles it was not fixed, but could turn on the pins of the jewelled frame. As if searching, the coal gradually set itself in alignment with the meridian! Then it came to rest.

Frau Fromm and I watched the spectacle in silence. Then I took her hand in mine and said:

"I thank you, my friend and helper."

Pleasure flickered across her face. Suddenly she bent down and kissed my hand.

A bright light shot through me for a brief second. Without knowing what I did – without intending it – I said, "Jane!" and took the young woman in my arms, kissing her gently on the forehead. She bowed her head. A sob came from her breast and, as the tears gushed out, she stammered something I could not understand; then she looked at me in bewilderment – shame – horror and fled the room without saying another word.

The evidence, the proof is piling up. In the light surrounding me, why should I deliberately continue to grope around in the darkness of doubt. The past has become present! What is the present but the sum of the past in a moment of consciousness? And because the spirit can call upon this consciousness – this recall – at will, so the present is ever there in the stream of time and the flowing weave can become a broad tapestry spread out for me to contemplate; and I can point to the spot where a particular thread in the weft marks the start of a new design in the pattern. And I can follow the thread, knot by knot, forwards and backwards; it does not break off, it carries the design and the meaning in the design; it is the essence of the tapestry and has nothing to do with its temporal existence.

Here I stand, with my eyes opened, and I recognise myself at a nodal point: I am the reawakened John Dee, Lord of the Manor of Gladhill, who is to complete a design of fate – I am to join the ancient blood of Hywel Dda and Rhodri Mawr to the blood of Elizabeth, so that the design on the tapestry shall be completed! There is only one question left: what is the significance of the living threads drawn by other shuttles which are interwoven with mine? Do they belong to the plan of the tapestry or are they part of the infinite variety of the other patterns created by Brahma?

Frau Fromm – how foreign, how inappropriate the name now sounds to me! – is part of the weave. That it should have taken so long before I realised! She is Jane, John Dee's second wife – – – my wife! Fits of giddiness keep pulling me down into the abyss of the mystery of consciousness outside the bounds of time.

Ever since she was born into this world Jane has pursued a path closer than mine to the boundaries of the dream that is our life, always ready to wake from it. And I – I? – was it not only when John Roger failed that I was called?! Was John Roger also – John Dee? Is John Dee everywhere? Am I nothing more than a mask? A shell? A trumpet, which sounds as the breath passes through it, but which is blown by a mouth outside, beyond. But – no matter: I experience it as present reality, and that is what it is. I must cast off this shroud of thought! A clear eye and a firm hand! I shall not repeat your mistakes, John Dee. I shall not follow you in your defeat, John Roger. I shall not let myself be deceived by earthly beings, and even less by ones from the other world. I shall know who Princess Shotokalungin is before the sun has gone full circle in the sky.

I can tell a mere messenger from One who would seal my fate – can I not, friend Lipotin?

I spent a long time staring at the facets of the black crystal but, to my disappointment I must admit, there was not a hint of the smoke, mist, cloud – not to speak of images – which are reliably reported of magic mirrors and crystals. In my hand the coal remained a piece of coal, beautifully worked and polished, but a piece of coal, nonetheless.

The thought naturally occurred to me that perhaps Jane – I mean Frau Fromm – might have the power to draw the secret from the crystal. I have just called her. She is nowhere to be found. She has gone out, it seems. I must wait patiently until she returns. – – – –

Hardly had the echo of my shouts for Frau Fromm died away, than the telephone rang: – – Lipotin! Was I likely to be in? He had something interesting to show me. – Yes, I was staying in. – Good. With that he hung up. – –

I had not many minutes to admire the timing with which "fate" sent its next actor on stage, nor to wonder what Lipotin might have for me, before there he was on my doorstep and in my study – remarkably quickly, considering the distance from his shop to my flat.

No! – He had telephoned from nearby, he said; the idea had suddenly occurred to him, it was an impulse, pure chance that he happened to have on him the object he was sure would interest me.

I gave him a pained, doubting look, and said:

"Are you a ghost, or are you real? Be honest! You can tell me! You can't imagine how fond I am of ghosts; it'll only make our chat all the more cosy."

Lipotin was not at all put off by my rather odd joke, and there was a smile in the corners of his eyes as he replied:

"This time I am perfectly real, my friend. How else could I bring you such a ... find!?"

He dug into one of his many pockets and held out his hand towards me. In his fingers he held a small red ivory sphere.

I was thunderstruck – almost literally, as I felt a shock run through my nerves from the back of my head and down my spine to the tips of my toes.

"The sphere from St. Dunstan's grave!" I stammered.

Lipotin grinned his most cynical grin.

"You are dreaming, my friend. You seem to have a thing about red balls. Have you just had bad luck at billiards?"

With those words he put the red sphere back in his pocket and looked as if nothing had happened.

"Excuse me," I said, in some confusion, "certain things have been happening, certain ... give me the red ball, please, I am interested in it."

Lipotin seemed not to hear me; with an inquisitive look on his face, he had gone over to my desk and was now staring intently at the coal crystal in its gold setting.

"Where did you get that from?"

I pointed to the open Tula-ware box.

"From you!"

"Aha! Congratulations."

"What for?"

"So that was what was inside Stroganoff's last possession? Remarkable!"

"What is remarkable?" I insisted, waiting for an opportunity to pounce.

Screwing up his left eye, Lipotin said:

"Beautifully delicate workmanship! Bohemian. One is almost reminded of the celebrated goldsmith of the Emperor Rudolf, Jaroslav Hradlik from Prague."

Prague? Something within me responded to the name, but I said to Lipotin in irritation:

"Lipotin, you know very well that at this precise moment I am not at all interested in your expertise in the field of arts and crafts. This object is more important to me – –"

"Yes, yes. Just look at the excellent workmanship on the stand."

"Stop it, Lipotin!" I commanded angrily. "As you seem to know everything, tell me instead how to use this thing you have lumbered me with."

"What do you want to do with it?"

"I cannot see anything in it", I answered brusquely.

"Aha, so that's it!" said Lipotin in feigned surprise.

"There! I knew you understood what I mean." I crowed. I felt as if I had all the cards in my hand.

"Easy!" mumbled Lipotin, plucking the inevitable cigarette from his lip and casually tossing the glowing end into my wastepaper basket, something I found extremely irritating. "Easy! It's a magic crystal; a scrying glass, as they say in Scotland."

"Why Scotland?" I interrupted, like a judge conducting a trial.

"Well, it certainly comes from a place where they speak English," said Lipotin and pointed a languid fingernail at a finely engraved inscription, half-concealed by late Gothic tracery, running around the claws of the stand. I had missed it until now. It was in English, and ran:

"This ancient and noble stone, full of magical power, once belonged to the honoured master of all occult wisdom, the unfortunate John Dee, Lord of the Manor of Gladhill. In the year he was called to his Maker, 1607."

There – as if I needed it – was documentary evidence that John Dee's most valued possession, which he held higher than gold and all the riches of this world, had found its ordained way to me, his appointed heir and executor of his destiny. This discovery removed any last lingering doubts as to Lipotin's inner identity. I put my hand on his shoulder and said:

"Well, old messenger of the mysteries, won't you tell me what you have brought this time? What is the point of the red sphere? Are we going to transmute lead? Are we going to make gold?"

Lipotin turned his foxy face towards me and, in a calm, deliberative tone, gave his evasive answer:

"So you have already attempted to use the coal? And you couldn't see anything?"

He refused to listen to me. As so often, he obstinately went his own way. No matter; I am accustomed to it. You have to go along with it, otherwise you cannot get anything out of him. I replied coolly:

"No. I can't see anything in it, however I go about it."

"I'm not surprised." – Lipotin shrugged his shoulders.

"And how would you go about trying to see something in the crystal?"

"Me? I've no ambition to be a medium."

"A medium? Otherwise it's impossible, you think?"

"The simplest way would be to become a medium," Lipotin answered.

"And how does one become a medium?"

"Just ask Schrenck Notzing." A malicious smile played about his lips.

I ignored his mockery. "To tell you the truth, I, too, lack both the desire and the time to become a medium. But did you not just say that to be a medium is merely the simplest way. What would be less simple?"

"To give up the whole idea of crystal-gazing."

I had to change tack. "Your paradoxical mind has got it right again; I am unwilling to give up the whole idea. Certain circumstances lead me to believe that there are images fixed – that is the expression occultists would use, I presume – upon the faces of this coal, images of the past, let us say, which are not without their importance for me ..."

"Then you will have to take a risk!"

"What kind of risk?"

"Of being being deceived by – let's call it your own imagination. Using hallucination for the purposes of clairvoyance often becomes a kind of spiritual drug addiction. Unless ..."

"Unless ...?"

"You pass over."

"What do you mean."

"You leave your body behind."

"How?"

"With this!" Lipotin had the red sphere in his hand again, rolling it between his fingers.

"Give it to me! I have asked you for it once."

"Oh no, my dear sir, I cannot hand the sphere over to you. I have just remembered why it is impossible."

I was becoming annoyed: "What's all this nonsense again?"

Lipotin put on his serious face. "You must forgive me. There is one small detail I had forgotten. I see that I owe you an explanation. This sphere is hollow."

"I know."

"It contains a certain powder."

"I know."

"How on earth do you ..." – Lipotin feigned astonishment.

"Stop all this play-acting. I have already told you that I know precisely what booty Master Mascee took from St. Dunstan's grave! Now give it to me!"

Lipotin retreated a step.

"What is all this about St. Dunstan and Mascee? I can't understand a word of it. This sphere has nothing at all to do with the venerable Mascee. It was given to me as a present, many years ago. By a monk of the red-hooded order in the caverns of Ling Pa on the mountain of Dpal bar."

"Are you deliberately trying to annoy me, Lipotin."

"Not at all; I am completely serious. You don't think I would try to pull the wool over your eyes?! – It happened in the following way: several years before the outbreak of the Russo-Japanese War I was on a special mission for one of my patrons in northern China, on the border with Tibet; the purpose was to obtain some fabulously valuable Tibetan temple pictures: ancient Chinese silk paintings and the like. But to the point: first of all, it was essential I gain the friendship of my putative business partners before there could be any question of a deal; of, amongst others, the remarkable inhabitants of Dpal bar skyd. They are a sect that call themselves the 'Yang'. They have the most bizarre rituals; it is very difficult to find out anything about them. Even I, fairly well-informed as I am about magic in the Far East, did no more than scratch the surface. They have special initiations and one of the initiation rituals is the 'Magic of the Red Sphere'. Just once they allowed me to attend the ceremony – how I managed to attend, is irrelevant. The neophytes perform the rite of thurification with a powder that is kept in red ivory spheres. There is no point here is going into the details of *how* they do it, but the rite is led by the abbot and it enables the young monks, who have newly been admitted to the order, to achieve 'Yang Yin' or to experience the 'Marriage of the Perfect Circle'. What they mean by that is another thing I was never clear about, and it is something I prefer not to talk about. They claim that inhaling the red smoke enables them to 'step out' of their bodies and cross the threshold of death; there, through marriage with their female 'other half', which in their earthly existence almost always remains hidden, they acquire unimaginable magic powers such as personal immortality as the wheel of birth comes to a standstill; in short, they achieve a kind of divine status which is denied other mortals as long as they are ignorant of the secret of the blue and red spheres. Clearly there are ideas behind this superstition which appear in graphic form in the Korean coat of arms: the male and the female principles in an intimate embrace within the circle of immutability. – But, of course, you are more familiar with all that than I am."

There was dismissive irony in Lipotin's last sentence. He presumably has a fairly low opinion of my knowledge of Far Eastern mysticism, but he is wrong. At least I am well aware of the reverence in which the Yin-Yang symbol is held out there.

It is represented as a circle which a curving line makes into two parts, two pear shapes – the one red, the other blue – nestling against one another: the geometrical sign of the marriage of heaven and earth, of the male and the female principle.

I just nodded my head. Lipotin continued:

"The Yang sect believes that the secret meaning of the sign is the conservation of the magnetic force of the two principles instead of its waste through the separation of the sexes. The idea behind it is something like a hermaphroditic marriage ..."

Again it was like a bolt of lightning striking directly in front of me; so blinding was the brightness of its light I felt I must blaze up myself. – That I should wait so long for this illumination: Yin Yang – Baphomet! One and

231

the same! ... One and the same!! – "That is the way to the Queen!" a voice within me called so loud that it was as if I could hear it with my external ear. At the same time a marvellous calm settled over all my excited thoughts and senses.

Lipotin had observed me closely; obviously he could see the change within me, could see my shock and the smile of certainty that illuminated my features, for he smiled, too.

"I see you are acquainted with the old belief in the mystery of the hermaphrodite", he said, after a pause. "Well, in the Chinese monastery they told me that the contents of this red sphere induce the union with the female principle within us."

"Give it to me!" I shouted – I commanded.

Lipotin became solemn.

"I must repeat that there is one strange circumstance connected with the gift of this sphere which, for reasons that I cannot understand, only came back to me a few moments ago. The monk who gave it to me insisted that I should destroy it if I decided not to use it myself; on no account was I to hand it over to another person unless that person specifically demanded it."

"I demand it!" I quickly cried.

Lipotin did not bat an eyelid and continued:

"You know how we travellers treat the grotesque gifts of our half-savage hosts: on long journeys, such as I used to make, you collect all kind of things, so that you soon forget each individual item. You can hardly imagine how seldom I have felt any interest in the Yang monk's sphere. You drop it in your bag with all the other rubbishy curios and continue on your journey. For my part, anyway, I have never felt the slightest urge to let my 'Yin' nestle up to my 'Yang' or to ask my female principle if she would like to complete the circle with me." With a cynical grin on his face, Lipotin made a repulsive lascivious gesture, which I ignored. Impatiently I repeated:

"Can't you hear: I demand it! With all my strength and in all earnestness, I demand it, as God is my witness!" I

232

added, and was about to raise my hand to swear an oath when Lipotin interrupted me:

"If you insist on taking an oath on this, even if only as a joke, then you must take it after the manner of the Yang monks. Are you willing?" – – – When I agreed he made me put my left hand on the ground and say:

"I demand, and I accept the consequences that thou mayest be released from all karmic revenge." – – I smiled; it seemed a rather silly piece of play-acting, even though at the same time I could not repress a feeling of revulsion.

"That settles the matter!" said Lipotin in a satisfied tone. "You must forgive my being so finicky, but as a Russian I am part Asiatic myself and would not like to be disrespectful towards my Tibetan friends."

Without further ado he handed me the red sphere. After a brief search I soon found where the two halves were screwed together. – Was this not one of the spheres of John Dee and his apothecary Kelley? – The sphere opened up: in the hollow was a greyish-red powder, about enough to fill a walnut shell.

Lipotin was standing next to me. He gave me a sideways look and spoke in an undertone. His voice reached my ear as if from a great distance, in a strange, lifeless monotone:

"A stone bowl and a pure flame have to be prepared. Pour some spirit of alcohol into the bowl and light it. Empty the contents of the sphere over the flame. The powder must flare up. Wait until the spirit has burnt away and let the smoke from the powder rise. A Superior must be present so that the head of the neophyte ..."

I stopped listening to his whispering, took the onyx bowl I use as an ashtray and cleaned it out as carefully as possible given my haste, poured some spirit from the sealing-lamp, that I have on my desk, into the bowl, lit it, took the half of the red sphere with the powder and poured it onto the flame. Lipotin stood to one side; I ignored him. Soon the alcohol had burnt off. Slowly the

233

remains in the bowl began to glow and smoulder. A cloud of greenish-blue smoke formed and rose curling up from the onyx bowl.

"Thoughtless and foolish, indeed", I heard Lipotin say, and it sounded like a mocking cackle in my ears, "the old overhasty foolishness, wasting precious material without being sure that all the conditions which guarantee success are fulfilled. How do you know that one of the required Superiors is present to carry out the initiation? You are fortunate – undeservedly so – that one just happens to be present, that I just happen to be an initiated Dugpa monk of the Yang sect ..."

I could still see Lipotin, as from a great distance, and mysteriously changed, a figure in a violet cloak with a strangely formed, upright red collar, on his head a cone-shaped purple cap on which six pairs of glass eyes glittered; he approached me with a grin of satanic triumph distorting his mongoloid face. I wanted to call out "No!," but I had lost the power over my own voice. Lipotin – or the red-capped monk behind me, or the devil in person or whoever it was – grasped me from behind by the hair with irresistible force and forced my face down into the onyx bowl and the incense rising from the red powder. A bitter-sweet aroma rose through my nostrils, and I was in the grip of an indescribable trepidation, I was racked by death throes of such long-lasting, excruciating violence that I felt the mortal terror of whole generations flow through my soul in an unceasing, icy stream. Then my consciousness was obliterated.

I have retained almost nothing of what I experienced "on the other side". And I think I am justified in adding, "Thank God!" for the torn-off scraps of memory which swirl through my dreams like leaves in a storm are so steeped in horror that it seems a blessing not to be able to understand them in detail. All I have is a vague, dark memory of having seen and passed through worlds such as those Frau Fromm described when she spoke of the depths of the sea steeped in a dull greenish glow where she claims she met Black Isaïs. I, too, met something awful there. I was fleeing, terrified, from – – I think it was from black cats with gleaming eyes and gaping mouths shining white; my God, how can one describe half-forgotten dreams!

And as I was fleeing, numb with nameless terrors, one last, saving thought surfaced: "If only you could reach the tree! If only you could reach the Mother, the Mother of the ... of the red and blue circle – is that it? – you would be saved." I believe I saw the Baphomet in the distance, high above glassy mountains, beyond impassable swamps and painful hazards. I saw Elizabeth, the Mother, waving to me from the tree – – I cannot remember what the gesture signified, but at the sight of her my racing heart was gradually soothed and the numbness left me. I woke feeling I had spent hundreds of years in the green depths.

When I looked up, my head still whirling, Lipotin was sitting before me, his gaze fixed upon me, playing with the empty halves of the ivory sphere. I was in my study and everything around was as it had been before ... before ...

"Three minutes. That is sufficient", said Lipotin in a morose tone, his features haggard, as he put his watch back into his waistcoat pocket. I will never forget the puzzlingly disappointed expression on his face as he asked me:

"So the Devil didn't take you, after all. That indicates a sound constitution. – Congratulations, anyway. I think from now on you will be able to use this coal with a certain degree of success. It is charged, that I have been able to establish."

I bombarded him with questions about what had happened to me. It was clear I had been through one of the hallucinatory experiences that have always played such an important role in supposed magic practice. I had taken opium or hashish, I could tell by the mild headache

235

and the slight feeling of nausea the noxious fumes had left me with.

Lipotin answered in monosyllables and seemed unusually sullen. He left after gabbling a few ironic remarks:

"You have the address; go to Dpal bar skyd. Become adviser to the Dharma Rajah of Bhutan, you've got what it takes. You will be received with the proverbial open arms. The worst trial is behind you. My respects, – Master!"

Then he hastily grabbed his hat and hurried off. I heard a polite exchange in the hall: Lipotin had met my housekeeper as she arrived back. Then the outside door shut and a moment later Frau Fromm was standing in the doorway, looking most agitated: "I shouldn't have left you by yourself! I blame myself ..."

"But you have nothing to blame yourself for, dear Fr..." – The words died on my lips. I saw Frau Fromm recoil from me with a gasp of horror. "What is the matter, my dear?"

"The sign above you! The sign!" – she stammered hoarsely. – "Oh, now – everything – everything – is over for me."

I just managed to catch her in my arms. She clung to me.

I bent over her, shocked; at the same time there welled up within me a feeling of pity, of closeness, a dark sense of guilt and obligation. I was torn to and fro by a vortex of unclear but all the more violent emotions. Instead of checking to see how she was, I kissed her like a man – – like a man who has practised celibacy for centuries. And she, her eyes closed, semi-conscious, kissed me back with a violence, a wild abandon I would never have suspected in this quiet, shy woman.

Suspected? My God, what am I writing? Would I have suspected it of myself? It was not willed, not intentional, nor had we been ambushed by our own sensuality. It was – fate, guilt, compulsion and primaeval necessity! – –

We are now both of us clear that Jane Fromont and Johanna Fromm, that I and John Dee – well, how shall I put it? – that we are a motif in the tapestry of the ages, a motif that will be repeated until the design is complete: I am the "Englishman" that Johanna had "known" in her split consciousness since her adolescence.

And that ought to be the end of it, in all conscience; a dual life story can emerge from the strange depths of its parapsychological cavern and run a more normal course. – Deep within me I feel the same as Johanna. This miracle has so taken hold of me that I want no other wife than Johanna, the woman to whom fate has bound me over the centuries.

But Johanna – we have had a long discussion on the matter, just now, after she woke from her faint – Johanna stands by her initial exclamation: everything is over between us, indeed was pointless, lifeless, cursed from the very beginning. Her hope is lost and all the superhuman effort of her love and sacrifice wasted, for the "Other Woman" was stronger than she was. She could unsettle and hinder the "Other One" but never, never, never could she defeat and destroy Her.

She told me what it was that had so frightened her when she came into the room: she had seen a bright, sharply delineated light hovering over my head; a light in the form of a diamantine crystal about the size of a man's fist.

Johanna will not accept any explanation, however reasonable. She claims she knows it very well from her trances. She has been told, she says, that this sign indicates the end of her fate and the end of her hopes and nothing can persuade her to change her mind. She did not withdraw from my kisses, from my endearments; she assured me she was mine and would remain mine: "I am your wife of an older title than any other woman now living on earth can say of her wifely dignity." At that I freed her from my arms. The nobility of her purity, shining with love, forced me down at her feet, and I kissed those feet, kissed them as if they were an ancient, ever-young relic. I felt like a priest before the image of Isis in the temple.

And then Johanna resisted me, almost in desperation she resisted me and my adoration, throwing her arms around wildly, sobbing and crying again and again: hers, hers was the fault alone, and it was she who should struggle and plead for mercy, for forgiveness and atonement for her sin; she was called upon to make a sacrifice.

I could not get her to say any more.

I realised the nervous excitement was too much for Johanna to bear. I talked to her to calm her down and, in spite of her resistance, put her to bed myself.

She slipped into sleep with my kisses on her lips, my hand in hers. Now she can rest in a deep sleep.

What will she be like when she wakes up?

The First Vision

My pen can hardly keep pace with all the experiences and apparitions that threaten to overwhelm me. I use the quiet hours of the night to record all that has happened to me.

When I had put Johanna – or should I write: Jane? – to bed, I returned to my study and, as has become my habit, completed my notes by recording the incident with Lipotin.

Then I took up John Dee's *Lapis sacer et praecipuus manifestationis* and contemplated the stand and the inscription on it. Gradually my eye began to wander from the gold ornamentation to the oily surface of the coal itself. What then began to happen was similar – at least, so it seems to me in retrospect – to my experience when I looked into Lipotin's Florentine mirror and dreamed I was standing at the station waiting for my friend Gärtner.

However that may be, after some time staring at the shining black surface of the crystal, I found I could no longer take my eyes off it. I saw – or rather, I did not so much see as feel I was in the middle of a herd of milk-white horses galloping wildly over a surface of green-black waves. At first I thought – and I might add that my thoughts were clear and rational –: aha, Johanna's green sea! But after a short while I began to see the details more precisely and I realised that the riderless horses were rushing over night-dark woods and meadows like Woden's wild hunt. At the same time I knew that these were the souls of the millions upon millions of men who are asleep in their beds whilst their souls, without rider, without master, are driven by some dark instinct to seek their far-off, unknown home – they do not know where it lies, they only sense they have lost it and cannot find it again.

I myself was a rider on a snow-white steed that seemed more real, more *corporeal*, than the milk-white horses.

The frenzied, snorting mustangs – they were like crests of foam on a stormy sea – crossed some wooded hills that disappeared below us in long waves. In the distance was the narrow silver ribbon of a meandering river.

A wide landscape opens out like an amphitheatre embroidered with ranges of low hills. The furious gallopade is heading for the river. In the distance the mass of a city begins to rise. The bounding shapes of the horses around me seem to dissolve into grey clouds of mist. – – Then, all of a sudden, I am riding through the bright sunshine of an August morning, across a stone bridge with tall statues of saints and kings on the parapet. On the river bank I am approaching modest dwellings huddled together in an ancient jumble with a few magnificent palaces towering above them and, so to speak, shouldering them to one side; but even these proud edifices are humbled by the immense bulk of a tree-covered hill crowned with ramparts pierced by the outlines of towers, roofs, battlements and spires. A voice within me cries: "HradčanyCastle!".

I am in Prague, then!? – Who is in Prague? – Who am *I*? – What is going on all around me? I can see myself on horseback, scarcely attracting a second glance from the townsfolk and peasants who are likewise crossing the stone bridge over the Vltava, past the statue of Saint Nepomuk and on to the the *Malá Strana*, the 'small side' or lesser town. I know I have been commanded to appear before the Emperor Rudolf – Rudolf of Habsburg – in the Belvedere. Beside me, on a dapple-grey mare, rides my companion; in spite of the blue sky and scorching sun he is encased in a fur cloak of somewhat tarnished magnificence. The fur cloak is obviously the *pièce de résistance* of his wardrobe and he has donned it in order to make some kind of show before His Majesty. "A mountebank's finery," I think. It does not surprise me to find that I myself am wearing antiquated dress. How could it be otherwise! Is it not the Feast of St. Lawrence, the tenth day of August in the year of Our Lord, 1584. I have ridden back into the past, I tell myself, and find nothing odd about it.

The man with the mouse's eyes, the low forehead and receding chin is Edward Kelley, whom I had difficulty in restraining from taking rooms in the inn at the sign of the Last Lantern, where the immensely rich magnates and Archdukes stay when they come to court. He it is who keeps our common purse, and he is as full of himself as a fairground quack. Completely shameless and correspondingly successful, he constantly manages to fill our coffers where a gentleman would rather cut off his hand or lay down in a ditch to die. I know – I am John Dee, my own ancestor; how else could the events of the journey since my flight from Mortlake be so fresh in my mind: I see our tiny ship tossed by a storm in the Channel, relive my wife's mortal anguish as she clings to me and whimpers: "I will gladly die with you, John. Oh, how gladly will I die with you! Only do not let me drown alone, do not let me sink into the green depths whence there is no return!" – And then the miserable journey through Holland: lodgings and meals in the lowest taverns, in order to eke out our meagre funds; the torment of hunger and cold for my wife and child; a family of wretched vagabonds who would never have survived the rigours of the early winter of 1583 in the snow-covered north German plain without the sharp practices of our good apothecary.

We made our way through the bitter cold to Poland. In Warsaw Kelley managed to cure a Voivode of the dropsy in three days with a few grains of St. Deniol's white powder dissolved in a glass of sweet wine so that we could continue on our way to Prince Lasky with our purse bulging once more. There we were received with great honour and sumptuous hospitality. We spent a year, during which my companion filled his belly and prophesied in his spectral voice all the crowns of Europe to the vain Pole, so that I had to put an end to his deception and insisted we travel on to Prague. And so, after Kelley had squandered almost the whole of our – or, rather, his – ill-gotten gains, we set off from Krakow for Prague and the Emperor Rudolf, to whom I bore a letter of introduction from Queen Elizabeth. And now I am living in Prague with my wife, child and Kelley in the spacious house of His Majesty's learned personal physician, Doctor Tomas Hajek, in the centre of the Old Town.

Today, then, is the day, so important for me, of my first audience with the prince among adepts and the adept amongst kings, the mysterious, feared, hated and revered Emperor Rudolf. Beside me, Edward Kelley exudes self-confidence and sets his horse at a tripping canter, as if we were merely on our way to another banquet in Lasky's wooden castle. But my heart is heavy with foreboding, and I feel the dark nature of the Emperor hanging over me like the black cloud that is just passing across the gleaming facade of the castle above us. At the end of the bridge our horses' hooves echo as we ride through the gaping maw of a gloomy gatehouse. Behind us, closed off as if by a wall, lies the bright world of ordinary, cheerful folk. Steep joyless alleys climb up silently between houses cowering fearfully against the hillside. Black palaces bar the way, like gatekeepers of the ominous secrets that surround Hradčany Castle. But now the broad esplanade, that the Emperor's bold architect has blasted out of the hill and wrested from the narrow wooded gorge, opens up before us. Away on a distant hilltop the defiant towers of a monastery rise up. "Strahov!" a voice within me says – Strahov, that conceals, buried alive within its mute walls, many a man who was struck by a fateful bolt from the Emperor's eyes, and who yet can consider himself fortunate that he did not have to make the nocturnal journey down that other narrow alley to Dalibor's tower, when he could say farewell for ever to the light of the stars. The houses of the imperial servants are piled up on top of each other, like swallows' nests on a cliff, each one bracing itself on the one below: at all costs the Habsburgers want to have their German bodyguard close around them; they will not trust themselves to the teeming alien race down there across the Vltava. Hradčany Castle towers above the city, with bristling defences; every gateway echoes with the jingle of spurs, the clash of ever-ready weapons. We ride slowly up the hill; suspicious eyes follow us from the tiny windows above; three times already we have been unexpectedly stopped by guards who suddenly appear as from nowhere to ask us our business; the Emperor's letter granting us audience is checked again and again. Then we are out on the splendid approach, the city of Prague spread out below us. I look at the view around like a prisoner gazing out on the free world; up here everything seems to be in the tight grip of an invisible hand; up here the summit of the hill has become a prison! The city below seems to lie in a sea of silver dust. Above us the sun smoulders through a misty veil. All of a sudden silver streaks appear in the powdery blue of the sky: flocks of doves circle round in the still air, reflecting the light, and then disappear behind the spires of the Tyn Church. Not a sound … it is unreal. But I take the doves over Prague as a good omen. The bell of the high-vaulted cathedral of Saint Nicholas below strikes ten; from somewhere within the ramparts of the stronghold in front of us a sharp, imperative clock repeats the hour with a swift drum-roll: it is high time! The monarch, a fanatical collector of clocks, keeps to the precise second. Woe to anyone who appears late. Another fifteen minutes, I think, and I shall be standing before Rudolf.

We have reached the top and could set our steeds at a gallop were it not for the halberdiers that block our every step: there is no end to the checks and scrutiny. Finally the bridge over the deer moat thunders beneath our horses' hooves, and we are trotting across the quiet park of the hermit king.

Surrounded by ancient oaks, the green copper roof of the airy Belvedere rises before us like a huge upturned ship's hull. We jump down from our horses.

The first things to attract my eye are the stone reliefs on the balustrade of the loggia formed by delicate arches around the Belvedere: there is Samson wrestling with the lion and, opposite, Hercules overcoming the Nemean lion. They are the symbols that the Emperor chooses to guard the entrance to his ultimate refuge. It is well known that the lion is his favourite animal and that he has trained a huge African lion as a pet with which he likes to frighten even his intimates. – – All around it is deserted and silent. No-one to receive us!? A bell with a note like a crystal goblet sounds the quarter. Clocks even here!

At the last stroke a plain wooden door opens. Wordlessly, a grey-haired servant invites us to enter. Stable boys suddenly appear to take our horses. We are standing in the long, cool hall of the Belvedere Palace. The stench of camphor is choking – the whole room is piled high with glass cases full of strange, exotic specimens: life-size models of savages in bizarre poses going about their bizarre business; weapons; gigantic animals; all kinds of implements; Chinese flags, Indian totem poles; an abundance of curiosities from the Old and the New World. – At a sign from our guide we stop beside the immense nightmare figure of a shaggy woodwight with a satanically grinning skull. Kelley's bravura has withdrawn to the inmost recesses of his fur. He whispers some nonsense about evil spirits. – I have to smile at the mountebank who does not tremble at all before his own conscience, but cowers in fear at a stuffed gorilla.

But at that very same moment I feel my bowels gripped with a shock of fear as a black ghost floats soundlessly around the corner beyond the ape's case and a scrawny figure faces us: yellow hands pulling a shabby black gown tight around him and fidgeting under the folds with a weapon – the outline of a short dagger is clear to see; a pale birdlike head lit by yellow eagle's eyes: – the Emperor!

The thin, creased upper lip is drawn tight over the almost toothless gums but the heavy lower lip hangs slack and bluish over the firm chin. The beady predator's eye surveys us. He remains silent.

I kneel – just a second too late, it seems. Then, however, as we kneel before him, heads bowed, he waves his hand dismissively:

"Stuff and nonsense. Stand up, if you call yourself honest men. Otherwise go to the devil and do not waste any more of my time."

Such was the greeting of the Sublime Emperor.

I begin the speech that I had carefully composed long before. I have hardly mentioned the gracious intercession of my mighty Queen when the Emperor interrupts me impatiently:

"Let me see what you can do! My envoys bring me more than enough greetings from other rulers. You claim to possess the tincture?"

"More than that, Your Majesty."

"What, more?!" Rudolf hisses. "Insolence will get you nowhere with me!"

"It is humility, not presumption, that leads us to take refuge in the wisdom of a High Adept ..."

"I know a little. Enough to warn you not to try to deceive me."

"I seek only the truth, Your Majesty, not self-enrichment."

"The truth?!" – a malicious smile flickers across the old man's face – "I am not such a fool as Pilate to ask you,

'What is truth?' What I want to know is, have you the tincture?"

"Yes, Your Majesty."

"Out with it!"

Kelley pushes to the front. He carries the white sphere from St. Dunstan's grave in a leather bag hidden in the depths of his jerkin:

"If Your most gracious Majesty will only put us to the test!" – his obsequiousness is crude.

"Who is that? Your assistant, your medium, I presume?"

"My colleague and friend, Edward Kelley," I answer, sensing a spurt of irritation within.

"A quack by trade, I see", hisses the Emperor. The ancient, eagle eye, weary from having seen too much, scarcely acknowledges the apothecary. The latter grovels like a scolded urchin and is silent.

I try once more: "If Your Majesty would deign to hear me."

Almost against expectation Rudolf signals to an old servant, who brings a hard folding stool. The Emperor sits down and, with a curt nod, gives me permission to continue.

"Your Majesty wants to know about the tincture for making gold. We have the tincture; but we have – and we are striving for – more; I hope to God that we are worthy of it."

"What could be more than the philosopher's stone?" – the Emperor snaps his fingers.

"Wisdom, Your Majesty!"

"Are you canting priests?"

"We seek to be worthy to be counted with Your Majesty amongst the adepts."

"And what are you counting on?" The Emperor's tone is mocking.

"On the Angel who commands us."

"And what kind of Angel is that?"

"It is the Angel ... of the West Gate."

The Emperor's eye, that seems to see a world beyond ours, is hooded: "What does this Angel command you do?"

"The two-fold alchymy: the transmutation of mortal to immortal. The way of Elijah."

"Do you mean to ride up to heaven in a fiery chariot like the old Jew? There was one who tried it before. He broke his neck."

"The Angel teaches us no fairground tricks, Your Majesty. He teaches us how to preserve the body beyond the grave. I can supply the Imperial lodge of adepts with evidence and proof."

"Is that all you can do?" – the Emperor seems to be falling asleep. Kelley is becoming impatient.

"We can do more. The stone that we possess can transmute any metal – – –"

The Emperor's head shoots up: "Proof!"

Kelley pulls out his leather bag. "Your Lordship may command. I am ready."

"Thou seemest a reckless knave, but of a quicker wit than thy companion!"

I choke back the rising indignation. The Emperor Rudolf is no adept! He wants to see gold made! The vision of the Angel and its gifts, the secret of incorruptibility mean nothing to him, indeed, are a mockery to him. Does he follow the way of the left hand? – – Then the Emperor suddenly says:

"First of all let a man change base metal into gold, that I can hold in my hand, then let him talk to me of angels. A schemer is touched by neither God nor the devil."

I cannot say why, but his words cut me to the quick. With a swifter movement than would seem possible for such an aged, sickly figure, the Emperor sits up; the neck shoots forward, on it the eagle's head jerks from side to side, searching for prey; finally it nods at the wall.

Suddenly a concealed door opens before our eyes.

A few seconds later we are standing in the Emperor's tiny laboratory. It is well supplied with all

246

kinds of equipment. The crucible sits over a well-stoked fire. Everything is soon made ready. With a practised hand the Emperor himself carries out the assistant's tasks. With a gruff threat, he refuses any attempt to help. His suspicion is boundless. The meticulous precautions he takes would be the despair of any trickster. It is impossible to deceive the Emperor. Suddenly there is a faint clash of weapons. Behind the hidden door – I can sense it – lurks death. Rudolf deals summarily with any wandering mountebanks who dare to try and hoodwink him.

Kelley goes pale and looks at me for help. I can sense what is going through his mind: What if the powder fails now?! He is seized by the vagabond's fear …

Lead is bubbling in the crucible. Kelley unscrews the sphere, the Emperor keeping a suspicious eye on him. He touches the sphere; Kelley hesitates; the eagle's beak strikes:

"I am no thief, pill-pedlar! Give it to me."

Rudolf subjects the grey powder in the sphere to a long and searching examination. The mocking cast of his lips gradually relaxes; the bluish lower lip sags to his chin. The expression on the eagle's face becomes thoughtful. Kelley indicates the dosage. The Emperor carries out every instruction precisely and conscientiously, like a well-trained laboratory assistant: he makes it a fair test.

The lead is liquid. Now the Emperor adds the tincture and the projection has been made according to the rules: the metal begins to froth. The Emperor pours the "Mother" into the cold bath. With his own hand he lifts the lump up to the light: there is a gleam of pure silver.

The leafy garden shimmers in the afternoon heat as Kelley and I ride through, exhilarated, almost cocky. Kelley jingles the silver chain that the Emperor put around his neck this morning. The words of the Emperor were: "Silver for silver; gold for gold, Doctor Quack. The next time will come the test whether you made the powder and whether you can make it again. The crown – note this well – is only for the adept: chains indicate ... chains."

For the present we were dismissed from the Belvedere with this clear threat, but without seeing the armed guards.

From the window of Doctor Hajek's house on the Old Town Ring where I am quartered with my wife and child I have the most marvellous view of the broad market-place, flanked on the right by the bizarre, jagged towers of the Tyn Church and on the left by the magnificent Town Hall of the defiant burghers. Here there is always a stream of Imperial messengers coming and going. If they are dressed in linen and velvet it means that the Lord of Hradčany Castle needs money; to borrow at a high daily rate of interest. If they come fully armed, it means His Majesty has decided to collect the stipulated sum direct, willy nilly. Relationships between the Habsburgs and Bohemia have always centred on money.

A strange group approaches: a messenger in silk, but followed by a company of armed riders. What trouble do they bring the Burgomaster? – What? Why is the troop not trotting across the square to the broad gate of the Town Hall? – It's crossing the Ring, straight towards Doctor Hajek's house!

The Emperor's emissary, a Privy Councillor called Curtius is here. He demands that I hand over to the Emperor the "proofs": the Angel's gifts, my records of our seances, the book from St. Dunstan's grave! I refuse in no uncertain terms:

"His Majesty refused my offer of proof. First of all he demanded I demonstrate my skill at making gold. Now he wants me to give him the recipe for preparing the Stone. His Majesty will understand that I cannot accede to his request without securities and guarantees."

"The Emperor commands!" is the simple reply.

"I am sorry; but I must set conditions."

"It is an order. You risk His Majesty's displeasure." – The sound of weapons echoes up from the stone hallway of the house.

"May I remind you that I am a subject of Her Britannic Majesty! The Emperor has a letter from the Queen."

Curtius adopts a conciliatory tone. The swords and halberds outside are silent.

We haggle like tradesmen. When would I be prepared to hand them over?

"I repeat the request I have already made for a further audience with the Emperor; everything depends on that. I will only commit myself on the word of the Emperor in person."

Councillor Curtius threatens, bargains, pleads. His reputation is at stake. He has promised to deliver the chicken drawn and trussed. Instead of a chicken he faces a growling wolf.

It is good that that coward Kelley is not here.

The half silken, half iron-clad deputation disappears round the corner of the Town Hall, past the celebrated astronomical clock.

Kelley appears, strutting across the ring, like a heron trying to take off. He comes from the direction of the alleyways where the brothels are. He flutters up the stairs and rushes in:

"The Emperor has invited us?"

"The Emperor has sent us an invitation to stay in the Dalibor tower! Or to dine with his bears in the moat: the flesh of adepts is their favourite food."

Kelley pales.

"We are betrayed?"

"Not at all. The Emperor simply wants our ... documents."

Kelley kicks at a chair, like an ill-bred schoolboy.

"Never! I would rather swallow St. Dunstan's book, just as St. John the Apostle did on Patmos with the Book of Revelation."

"And what is the situation regarding deciphering the book, Kelley?"

"The Angel has promised me an explanation of the key for the day after tomorrow."

The day after tomorrow! ... O this eternal day after tomorrow! It sucks at my marrow and burns my brain.

I feel as if I am asleep.

And yet I am not asleep. I am walking through the old streets of the city of Prague, along the tree-lined rampart that leads to the Powder Gate. The trees are tinged with autumn. It is cool. It must be near the end of October. I pass through the gate into Celetná Street. I intend to cross the Old Town Ring and go down to the Old-New Synagogue and the Jewish Town Hall. I want – no: I have to visit the "High Rabbi" Löw, the miracle-worker. My generous host, Doctor Hajek, arranged our introduction a few days ago. We exchanged a few words about the mysteries ...

As I go on my way, one street follows another in a natural progression; and yet I feel under some kind of compulsion. I feel as if it is all a dream and yet it is certainly not a dream; it is just the same for Johanna Fromm who can walk round Prague – – if she wishes.

Johanna Fromm? Who is that? My housekeeper, of course! How can I ask! Johanna Fromm is my housekeeper. – – But – – I am John Dee!? John Dee, who is on his way to visit Rabbi Löw, the friend of Emperor Rudolf!

With that I am already in the Rabbi's low, bare chamber and talking to him. The only furniture is a seat of woven straw and a deal table. Fairly high in the wall there is a tiny alcove in which the Rabbi is sitting – or rather half standing, half leaning, like the mummies in the catacombs – staring fixedly at the geometrical diagram of the "cabbalistic tree" drawn in chalk on the wall opposite. He scarcely looked down as I entered.

The Rabbi is bowed, though it is unclear whether it is with hoary age or the effect of the massive weight of the low, smoke-blackened beams of his house. He seems to be of gigantic stature. The yellow skin of his head is criss-crossed by a maze of wrinkles. His face is like that of a bird of prey and reminds one of the Emperor's, only his head is much smaller, his profile more sharply hawk-like. The prophet's face seems scarcely larger than my fist, hidden in a tangle of hair – impossible to say where that of the head ends and the beard begins. Deep-set, merry eyes glitter below heavy, bushy brows. The abnormally tall, incredibly slim body of the Rabbi is clad in a neat, clean black silk caftan. His shoulders are hunched, his hands and feet in constant, expressive movement, as is the custom with Jews of the Levant.

We talk of the tribulations of ignorant men seeking the divine mysteries and of the purpose of earthly life.

"We must force Heaven's hand," I say and remind the Rabbi of Jacob wrestling with the angel.

The Rabbi replies:

"Your Honour is right. The hand of God can be forced through prayer."

"I am a Christian; I pray with my heart and with all the strength of my soul."

"And for what, your Honour?"

"For the Stone!"

The rabbi slowly rocks his head from side to side, like a melancholy Egyptian marsh heron.

"Prayer has to be learned."

"What do you mean, Rabbi?"

"Your Honour is praying for the Stone. That is right. The Stone is good. The main thing, however, is that your prayer strikes God's ear."

"How should it not?" I exclaim. "Do I pray without faith?"

"Faith?" the Rabbi rocks from side to side, "What use is faith to me without knowledge?"

"You are a Jew, Rabbi;" it slips out before I can stop it.

The Rabbi's eyes glitter:

"A Yid. Truly spoken, your Honour. – Why then do you ask a Jew about the … mysteries? Prayer, your Honour, is the same art the world over."

"Certainly you speak the truth there, Rabbi," I say, bowing to him, for I regret my cursed Christian pride.

The Rabbi laughs, but only with his eyes.

"The Goyim can shoot with the crossbow and the arquebus. An art it is, your shooting, a marvel it is how you aim and hit the mark. But can you pray as well? A marvel how seldom you aim … true and hit the mark!"

"But Rabbi! A prayer is not a ball from a rifle barrel!"

"And why not, your Honour? A prayer is an arrow at God's ear. If it strikes its target, then the prayer is heard. Every prayer is heard – must be heard, for prayer is irresistible … if it hits."

"And if it misses?"

"Then the prayer drops back down like a lost arrow, sometimes hits the wrong mark, falls on the ground like Onan's seed or … is caught by the 'Other One' and his servants. Then they answer the prayer … after their own fashion!"

"By which 'Other One'?" I ask, my heart filled with fear.

"By which 'Other One'?" repeats the Rabbi. "By Him who ever watches between Above and Below.

By the Angel Metraton, the Lord of a Thousand Faces ..."

I understand and tremble. What if my arrow fly not true?

The Rabbi's gaze is on the far distance. He continues:

"One should not pray for the Stone without knowing what it signifies."

"The Stone signifies the truth!"

"The truth –?" the Rabbi mocks just as the Emperor did. I imagine I will hear him continue, "I am not such a fool as Pilate ..." – But the high adept remains silent.

"What else can the Stone signify?" I press him, unsure in my heart.

"That cannot be learnt. It is something your Honour must feel, in your heart."

"I know that to find the Stone one must look within oneself, but ... it must then be prepared externally and is called the elixir."

"Beware, my son," whispers the Rabbi, with a sudden change of tone towards me that freezes me to the marrow. "Beware when you pray and plead for the Stone! Mark well the arrow and the target and the shot! Beware that you do not receive the false Stone from a false shot! The rewards of prayer can be terrible."

"Is it so difficult to pray aright?"

"Immensely difficult it is, your Honour. Your Honour is right. It is immensely difficult to strike God's ear."

"Who can teach me how to pray aright?"

"To pray aright ... the only man who can do that is one who was sacrificed at birth and made sacrifice ... a man who is not only circumcised but also knows that he is circumcised and knows the Name backwards and forwards."

Anger spurts up within me; the Rabbi's words tear open a hole and the old Jewish pride shines through. I cut him short:

"I will tell you, Rabbi: I am too old and too advanced in the teachings of the wise to have myself circumcised."

An incomprehensible smile lights up the depths of the adept's eyes.

"You do not want to let yourself be circumcised, your Honour! That is it! The wild apple tree does not want to let itself be pruned and what does it bear? Crab apples!"

I sense a hidden dimension beneath the Rabbi's words. I have a vague feeling I am being offered a key, I only need to grasp it. But at the moment my irritation at the Jew's proud speech has the upper hand. My reply is defiant:

"My prayer is not without direction. I may set the string askew, but an angel holds my bow and guides my arrow."

The Rabbi looks up sharply:

"An angel? What kind of an angel is it?"

I describe the Angel of the West Window. I make a great effort to enable him to visualise the Green Angel that advises us and that has promised to reveal the formula to us the day after tomorrow.

Suddenly the Rabbi's face dissolves into a wild laugh. Yes, a laugh; there is no better word for it and yet it is different from human laughter. It is like the agitated fluttering of the Egyptian ibis when it sees a poisonous snake nearby. Surrounded by the wild tangle of hair that dances up and down on the Rabbi's birdlike head the tiny yellow face contracts until it is a star formed of myriad lines radiating from a round black hole that is laughing, laughing, laughing; one long yellow tooth wobbles grotesquely in the black cavern ... mad! is the thought that comes to me. – "Mad!"

Restlessness, an uncontrollable restlessness drives me up the castle steps. – Up here in the German quarter I am well known as the alchemist from England who has the freedom of the castle. My steps are always watched, but up here I can go where I like; I need the quiet alleys and tree-lined paths; I need seclusion, I need to keep away from Kelley, the bloodsucker that has attached itself to my soul. – – I lose my way in the maze of alleyways: I find myself standing before one of the houses glued to the wall of the fortress and above a gothic entrance I see a stone carving of Jesus at the well with the woman of Samaria. And on the trough is written:

Deus est spiritus. – Deus est spiritus – God is spirit. Yes, He is spirit, not gold! – Kelley wants gold, the Emperor wants gold. I want ... do I want gold, too? My wife had held my little son Arthur out towards me, saying: "How shall I feed your child when the purse is empty?" And I saw that the jewelry that she used to wear about her neck was no longer there. Jane had sold her own possessions, piece by piece, to save us from the debtor's prison, from disgrace, from destruction.

Deus est spiritus. – I have prayed spiritually and corporeally. Have I shot my arrow into God's ear? Is the Rabbi right? Is the Rabbi always to be found sitting at the well of eternal life to comfort the drawer of water, the weary soul? Gold will not flow, a prayer for gold will not fly. – Without thinking, I ask a woman coming out of the gate:

"What is it called here?" – I want to know the name of the street.

The woman, who saw where my eye was fixed, replies:

"At the sign of the Golden Fountain, sir", and goes on her way.

I can see Emperor Rudolf in the Belvedere leaning against one of the tall glass cases in which an eskimo, wrapped up in furs and tied all round with leather belts to which rows of little bells are attached, is going about some business. The wax model with its slanting, oily glass eyes is holding, in hands that are far too small, a triangle and other, unknown implements. "A shaman," a voice behind him says.

Beside Rudolf appears a tall man in a black cassock. He bows awkwardly, visibly reluctant to adopt a suitably respectful attitude before the Emperor. A red skull-cap reveals the cardinal. I realise immediately who it is: towering above the Emperor and with the corners of his mouth drawn up in a fixed smile is the Papal Legate, Cardinal Malaspina. The Cardinal is speaking calmly, impressing something on His Majesty; his lips open and close with the precision of a scallop shell. Gradually I start to pick up what he is saying:

"And so Your Majesty cannot avoid the accusation of the unthinking plebs that You shower Your favours on magicians and grant such who are suspected – justly suspected indeed – of being in league with the devil freedom of abode, and more, in Your Majesty's most Catholic country."

The eagle profile jerks forward:

"Stuff and nonsense! The Englishman can make gold, and making gold is a most natural art. You priests cannot stop the march of the human spirit; the more it uncovers of the profane secrets of nature, the greater reverence it shows for the sacred mysteries of God ..."

" – and finally realises that all is grace," the Cardinal finishes the sentence. The Emperor's yellow eyes disappear completely behind the torpid leathern lids. There is the merest tremor of mockery perceptible on the heavy lower lip. The corners of the Cardinal's fastidious lips rise even higher in consciousness of superiority:

"Whatever we think about making gold, this English gentleman and his dubious companion has publicly declared that he is not interested in gold and silver but seeks the power of magic in this world and to overcome death in the next. The reports I have are most precise. In the name of our supreme Lord, Jesus Christ, and of His holy representative on earth, I accuse this John Dee and his assistant of meddling in satanic arts, of black and blasphemous magic practices, which are punished with the death of the body and of the soul. The secular arm cannot refuse its office. It would be to the detriment of Christendom. Your Majesty knows what is at stake."

Rudolf drums with his knuckles against the glass case and mutters:

"Must I deliver up all fools and heathens to the Vatican dungeons and the bonfires lit by the arrogance of priests? The Holy Father knows me and knows what a zealous son and defender of the faith I am; he should not try to force me to be the henchman of his henchmen, who follow my every move. Things might go so far that I would have to sign the death warrant of Rudolf of Habsburg, Holy Roman Emperor with my own hand – for black magic."

"Your Majesty determines the bounds in all secular matters. You are the judge and you are responsible before God for everything you think worthy of Rudolf of Habsburg ..."

"No insolence, priest!" hisses the Emperor.

Cardinal Malaspina sways back, like a snake before the talons of an eagle. His lips bear a pinched smile: "The servants of the Lord have learnt from their Master to accept mockery and taunts with the praise of God on their lips."

"And treachery in their hearts!" adds the Emperor.

The Cardinal makes a slow, deep bow:

"Wherever possible we betray the darkness to the light, weakness to majesty, the deceiver to the just condemnation. John Dee and all his entourage are the products of the worst excesses of heresy. He bears the stigma of blasphemy, of the desecration of holy graves and of consorting with proven associates of the Devil. It would grieve the Holy Father in Rome if he found himself compelled to anticipate the secular arm and – at what cost to Imperial authority? – to bring the previous trial of this John Dee *forma juris* out into the open."

The Emperor shoots a look of burning hatred at the Cardinal. He does not dare to lash out again with his beak. The eagle has lost the snake. With a hiss he draws his neck back into the darkness of his shoulders.

We are in the back room of our lodgings in Doctor Hajek's house; I have my arms round Kelley's neck and the tears are pouring down my cheeks:

"The Angel has saved us! The Angel be praised! The Angel has saved us!! –"

In his hands Kelley is holding the two halves of St. Deniol's spheres; they are both newly filled to the rim with the precious red and grey powder. The Green Angel brought it, last night in a seance that Kelley held alone with Jane, without informing me. And now I hold the new riches in my trembling hands; but much more important: the Green Angel has kept his word! He has not deceived me; He heard my prayer at the Golden Fountain! – My prayers did not fall to the ground. My prayers struck God's ear. They struck the heart of the Green Angel of the West Window! – O joy of certitude! – The way has not been in vain, it has not led me astray! In my hands I hold the testimony of the true covenant! –

Now the sufferings of the body are at an end. Now shall the sufferings of the soul and its longing be assuaged!

To my question as to the secret of the preparation of the Stone, Kelley replies that the Angel did not reveal it: the gift was sufficient for the present; trust and faith were justified. Another time the rest would be vouchsafed to us, according to our deserts. Watch and pray! God will grant to His own all that they ask for and all that they need.

Jane is beside us, pale and silent, the child in her arms.

I ask her how the glorious seance went. She looks at me, tired and distraught, and replies:

"I cannot say. I do not know. It was – dreadful …"
Astonished, I look across at Kelley: "What has happened to Jane?"

He hesitates. "The Angel appeared in unendurable fire."

"The Lord God in the burning bush!" is the thought that comes to me, and filled with the warmth of love, I embrace my courageous wife.

The days are a procession of vague images, misty memories between waking and sleeping: throngs and banquets, receptions with the grandees, with nobles decked in rich brocade, diplomats in silk and satin, scholars in dark velvet; riding through the narrow streets of Prague, Kelley always at the head, scattering coins from an ever-open purse amongst the cheering, jostling multitude. We are the talk of Prague, a scandal, a seven-day wonder. The wildest rumours are brought even to our own ears. People assume we are incredibly rich Englishmen who are amusing themselves bamboozling the court and burghers of Prague by pretending to be adepts and alchemists. And that is the most harmless and good-willed of all the stories that are spread about us.

At night, after the glittering feasts and banquets, there are long, exhausting arguments with Kelley. Kelley tumbles into his bed, heavy with wine and the rich Bohemian cooking. I grasp him by the collar, unable to bear the repeated scenes of waste and senseless dissipation any longer, I shake my drunken companion and scream at him:

"You sot! Scum! London guttersnipe! Wake up! Come to your senses! How long do you think this can go on? The grey powder is used up. The red is half finished!"

259

"The Green ... gr ... een Angel'll just have to come up with a second helping" – the reply is one long belch.

Arrogance, lust, prodigal squandering of unaccustomed wealth, puffed-up self-importance, tawdry ostentation: like gaseous bubbles in a marshy pool, these are the things that rise to the surface from the depths of Kelley's dark soul, released by the Angel's gold. The man with the cut-off ears is a tolerable companion in times of poverty, a master at making do, a virtuoso of survival; but now, abundantly wealthy for the second time, there is no holding him in his gross debauched frenzy of prodigality. –

God does not want riches to be spread about the earth, for it is the abode of swine.

Whether I want to or not, I feel a compulsion to visit the narrow alleys of the Jewish quarter down by the Vltava, where the Rabbi mocked my belief in the Angel with his wild, crazed laughter, and, with his one yellow stump of a tooth, laughed me out of his chamber and out of all reverence for my cherished belief.

I am standing outside one of the tower-like gatehouses of the dark ghetto. I am unsure which road to take when a voice whispers to me from the blackness of the archway: "Over here! This is the road that will take you to your goal." I follow the invisible guide.

In the dark entrance I am suddenly surrounded by a group of unknown men. Speaking in whispers, they shepherd me into a passageway, through an iron-studded door into a long, half-lit corridor where our feet send up clouds of dust from the rotten floorboards. The passage is lit from occasional apertures high up in the walls. Fear starts to crawl over my skin: I have fallen into a trap. – I stop: What do they want of me? The figures pushing me forward are masked and armed. One seems to be the leader. He lifts his mask. His face is that of an honest soldier.

He says, "By command of the Emperor."

I shrink back.

"Arrested? Why? I remind you I am under the protection of the Queen of England!"

The officer shakes his head and points to the end of the corridor:

"There is no question of arrest, sir. The Emperor wishes to see you and has His reasons for keeping your visit a secret. Follow us."

The corridor descends perceptibly. The last of the daylight disappears. The wooden planks under our feet give way to slimy, slippery mud. The walls beside me are rough-hewn, damp and give off a smell of decay. Suddenly we stop. My companions mutter amongst themselves. I start to prepare myself for a swift, cruel execution. I am beginning to suspect that we are in the underground passage which, popular rumour has it, runs from the Old Town, beneath the Vltava and up to the Castle. People whisper that when it was completed, all the workers who had dug it were drowned in the tunnel, so that they could not reveal the secret exits.

Then, suddenly, a torch flares up, several torches. In their light I can see that we are proceeding along a kind of mine gallery. From time to time massive beams support the arched roof that has been cut through the bare rock. From time to time there is a sound like a distant rumble of thunder somewhere above our heads. For a long, long time we make our way through the unbearably musty stench of the tunnel. Countless rats dart between our legs. Every step wakes strange crawling things from the rubble and cracks in the walls. Bats singe their fluttering wings on the smoky torches.

Finally the tunnel begins to rise again. In the distance a bluish light flickers. The torches are put out. When my eyes are adjusted to the darkness again I see that the men put them into iron rings let into the wall. Then I can feel wood under my feet again. The incline becomes steeper, sometimes there are steps. God knows where we are, where we will surface. But then the daylight reappears: "Halt!" Two men strain to lift an iron trapdoor. We climb out and find ourselves in a cramped, grubby kitchen: we emerge from the stove as from a well-shaft. It must be the dwelling of some menial, so tiny is the room and the door through which we go into a narrow hallway. Immediately I am pushed into another tiny chamber, which I enter alone. My escort disappears without a sound.

In front of me, in a huge winged armchair taking up half of the room is the Emperor, dressed just as he was when I saw him that first time in the Belvedere.

Beside him an open window full of gillyflowers is bathed in the warm gold of the afternoon sun. You might almost call it a cosy den. From the moment you enter it gives you a sense of comfort, pleasure and relaxation. Looking round, I almost have to laugh – it is the kind of room that ought to have a goldfinch singing in a cage – after my march through the gloomy, eerie tunnel under the Vltava where every stone seemed to whisper: Murder.

The Emperor greets me with a wordless nod and waves away my deep bow. He orders me to sit opposite him in an equally comfortable chair. I obey. The room is filled with silence. Outside the old trees rustle in the breeze. A glance out of the window only serves to increase my confusion: Where am I? That is no part of Prague that I know. Sheer cliffs rise up behind the treetops, that scarcely reach the window. We must be in a house in a gorge or mountain ravine? "The Stag Moat!" says an inner voice.

Slowly the Emperor sits up in his chair.

"I have had you brought here, Master Dee, because I have heard that you have had some success in making gold – unless you are the most cunning of tricksters, that is ..."

My silence says louder than words that I am above any insults from one who, by his position, is beyond any demand for satisfaction. The Emperor understands and nods his head.

"So: you can make gold. Good. I have long been seeking such as you; what are your conditions?"

I am silent; my eye does not leave the Emperor.

"Or: what do you want?"

"Your Majesty knows well that I, John Dee, Lord of the Manor of Gladhill, do not share the ambitions of mountebanks and alchymical charlatans, who look only to squander the gold the tincture brings them on dissipation. I came to seek counsel from an Imperial adept. – We seek the Stone of Transformation."

Rudolf puts his head on one side. Now he really does look like an old golden eagle, his head cocked and looking – half awe-inspiring, half unspeakably comic and yet melancholy at the same time – resignedly at the sky, from which he is separated by iron bars. "The Lord of the Skies in Captivity" – the thought comes to me involuntarily.

Finally the Emperor replies:

"Heresy, Sir! – The charm that will transform us is in the hands of God's Representative on earth; it is called: the Sacrament of Bread."

It seems half threat, half mockery.

"The genuine Stone, Your Majesty – at least this is my supposition – has one thing in common with the host: neither of them is of corporeal substance."

"Theology!" says Rudolf wearily.

"Alchymy!"

"Then the 'Stone' would have to be a magic *injectum* that transforms our blood," murmurs the Emperor, thoughtfully.

"And why not, Your Majesty? *Aurum potabile* is but a drink that mingles with our blood."

"You are a fool, Sir," the Emperor interrupts me brusquely. "Beware that the stone you seek so fervently does not turn into a millstone round your neck!"

Why is it, that at these words from the Emperor, Rabbi Löw's warnings about misdirected prayers suddenly flash in upon my mind? – – After a long pause, I answer:

"Wherefore whosoever shall eat this bread and drink this cup of the Lord, unworthily, shall be guilty of the body and blood of the Lord."

Emperor Rudolf shoots out his neck. I can almost hear the beak snap:

"My advice is good, Sir: do as I do and eat and drink nothing that has not been tried by someone else beforehand. The world is full of deceit and poison. Do I know what is in the cup the priest sets at my lips? Could not the body of Our Lord ... dispatch me to Heaven? It would not be the first time – –! Green angels and black shepherds – they are all of the same satanic brood! – – I warn you, Sir!"

A shiver runs down my spine. I remember what people have whispered in my ear here and there, even on my way to Prague. I recall Doctor Hajek's cautious hints: the Emperor is not always in his right mind, he is ... perhaps ... mad. –

A furtive, sideways glance momentarily meets mine.

"Once more, I warn you, Sir. If you want to transform yourself, transform yourself quickly, that is my advice. The Holy Office takes a keen interest in your ... transformation. It is doubtful, however, whether this interest is quite to your taste; nor whether I can protect you from the attentions of this charitable institution. You must realise: I am a lonely old man. My word does not count for much ..."

The eagle seems to be nodding off. What should I make of it? Rudolf, the Emperor, the most powerful man on earth, the monarch before whom princes, even princes of the Church, tremble, calls himself a weak old man. – – Is it a sham? Is it a trick?

His eyelids almost closed, the Emperor can still read my thoughts on my face. He clears his throat with a derisive cough:

"Become a king yourself, Sir. Your will find it brings nothing but travail. A man who has not found himself, a man who cannot grow a double head like the eagle of the House of Habsburg, should not grasp after crowns – whether they be crowns of this earth or spiritual crowns."

The Emperor slumps back into his chair like one who has long since exhausted his strength. My head is in a whirl. How does this odd, puzzling old man in the faded chair opposite come to know my innermost secrets? How can he guess ...? And I remember Queen Elizabeth sometimes saying things which could not possibly have come from her mind; things that sounded as if they came from another realm, from one beyond the reach of her conscious mind. – And now: Emperor Rudolf, too! – What is the mystery of those who sit on thrones? Are they shadows of greater beings who wear the crowns "on the other side"? – – –

The Emperor sits up again.

"Tell me about your elixir."

"If Your Majesty commands it I will hand it over."

"Good. Tomorrow at the same time," is the curt reply. "Tell no-one of our meeting today. It is to your own advantage."

I bow silently and then hesitate. Have I been dismissed? It seems so. The emperor has fallen asleep. I turn to the low door, open it – and shrink back: on the threshold there is a sandy-coloured monster which rises up with a fearsome yawn. A demon from the underworld? A second, more composed glance does not lessen my terror: it is a massive lion, its green cat's eyes fixed shortsightedly on me; its rough tongue rasps hungrily across its grinning lips.

As I retreat, step by step, the guardian of the threshold languidly moves its massive frame through the door. Now it raises its spine like a cat and now, so it seems, it is ready to pounce on me. I dare not make a sound. I am paralysed by mortal fear: that is no lion! The demonic face grinning out of a red mane ... the bared teeth – next will come a thunderous rumble of laughter; it is ... "The face of Bartlett Greene!" I want to shout, but my voice fails me ...

Then there is a click of the tongue from the direction of the Emperor, the yellow monster turns its head, pads obediently over to his chair and stretches out, purring; the impact of huge body makes the whole floor tremble. It is only a lion! An enormous specimen of a Barbary lion with a flaming red mane.

Outside the trees of the Stag Moat rustle.

The Emperor nods to me:

"See how fittingly you are guarded. The 'Red Lion' stands everywhere at the portal of the mysteries. Any novice will tell you that. Leave me now."

My ears are bombarded with noise. Raucous dance music. An enormous hall. – Oh, yes; it is the rout that Kelley and I are giving for the city of Prague in the great hall of the City Chambers. My senses are dizzy from the whirling dancers and the racket of the drunken mob. Kelley staggers towards me with a foaming tankard of Bohemian ale. The expression on his face is crude and vulgar; incredibly vulgar. The crooked lawyer's little rat face is no longer disguised by carefully combed hair. The scars of the cut-off ears glow a disgusting red.

"My brother", he slobbers drunkenly, "my br-br-brother, let me have the rest of the rep p-p-powder; it'sh t-time, I t-tell you; we're b-broke, brother!"

Shock and disgust strike me at the same time.

"What? You've already squandered all that the Angel gave us after months of praying till our knees bled?!"

"What do I care for your bloody kneesh, b-brother of mine?" blabbers the drunken lout. – "Let me have the red p-p-powder, do you hear, and we'll be out of this damned messh by m-morning!"

"And then?"

"Then? Count Ursinus Rosenberg, Lord High Constable and Imperial fool, has more money than he knows what to do with; I'll shoon find a use for it."

I see red as my fury boils over. I hit out blindly and the tankard falls to the ground, soiling my best coat with good Pilsener ale. Kelley lets out a foul oath. Tongues of hate shoot up from the debauchery all around. The band strikes up:

> Two groats and two lips
> Are all that I need.

"Show our claws, would we, my fine tom cat?!" screams the quack. "The p-powder I say."

"The powder is promised to the Emperor."

"The Emperor can ..."

"Silence, scum!"

"Who do the spheres and the book belong to, Sir Knight of the Light Fingers?"

"Who brought the spheres and the book to life?"

"Who orders the Angel: Fetch, boy! Yah!"

"Shut thy blasphemous mouth!"

"Sanctimonious hassock-warmer!"

"Out of my sight, blasphemer, or ..."

Two arms wrap themselves around me from behind, taking all the force from the dagger-thrust.

Jane is clinging to me, the tears streaming down her cheeks...

For a moment I am once more the man sitting at the desk, staring at the polished coal – but only for one, brief moment, and then I become my ancestor, John Dee, again, wandering aimlessly round the oldest, most dilapidated quarters of the medieval city, not knowing where my steps will take me. I feel an instinctive need to sink into the slime of the nameless, lawless, conscienceless masses, that fill their days with the satisfaction of base urges and are content with a full belly and sated lust.

What is the end of all striving? – Weariness ... disgust ... despair. – The dung of the nobles and the dung of the mob is the same excrement. – – The Emperor's digestive tract is no different from that of the serf who cleans out his cess-pit. What madness to look up to His Imperial Majesty in Hradčany Castle as if you were looking up to heaven! – And what does heaven send? Fog, rain, miles of dirty slush. For hours I have been trudging through heaven's excrement, the grubby, sticky flakes dropping from a leaden sky. – The end-product of heaven's digestive system – filth, filth, filth. I see that I have ended up in the ghetto, with the lowest of the low. The choking stench of a whole people crammed mercilessly into the compass of a few streets, a whole people conceiving, giving birth, growing, dying – piling corpse upon rotting corpse in its cemetery and the living on top of each other in its dark, towering houses, like herrings squashed in a barrel. – And they wait and watch and scrape their knees bloody and wait ... wait ... all the long centuries they wait ... for the angel. For the fulfilment of the prophecies ...

John Dee, what is thy waiting and praying, what is thy hope and faith in the promises of the Green

Angel compared with the waiting, believing, hoping, praying of these wretched Israelites?! And God, the God of Isaac and of Jacob, the God of Elijah and of Daniel, is He a lesser, a less faithful God than His Servant of the West Window?

I am struck by a burning desire to see Rabbi Löw and to ask him about the terrible mystery of waiting for God.

I know – somehow, I know – I am physically standing in the low chamber of the Cabbalist, Rabbi Löw. We have talked of Abraham's sacrifice, of the unavoidable sacrifice that God demands from those He would make his own blood-offspring. I have heard dark, mysterious words about a sacrificial knife that can only be seen by one whose eyes have been opened to the things of the other world which are invisible to mortal man: things that have more reality than the things of this earth and which can only be indicated through the symbols of letters and numbers. The enigmatic words from the toothless mouth of the old madman chill me to the marrow ... Mad? Mad like his friend up there in his castle, mad like the Emperor, Rudolf of Habsburg! The monarch and the Jew from the ghetto – brothers in the mysteries ... gods, both of them, under the ridiculous trappings of earthly appearance ... where is the difference?

At my request the Cabbalist has drawn my soul to his. I begged him to transport my soul, but he refused; it would collapse, he said, if he were to do that; it had to cling to his, which had been detached from the earthly body. – How those words made me think of the silver shoe of Bartlett Greene. – Then the Rabbi touched me on the collar-bone – just as the outlaw in the Tower did. And now I can see, can see with the calm, tearless, imperturbable eyes of the old Rabbi: my wife kneeling before Kelley in our chamber at the house on the Ring. She is resisting him, struggling to save my happiness, she thinks, to save the gold and the Angel. Kelley wants to break open the chest and take the book and the spheres, he has an iron bar because the keys are in my keeping. He wants to take his booty and flee from Prague like a thief in the night and leave us in wretched misery. Jane puts her body between him and the chest. She tries to reason with the knave, she pleads with him ... she does not know what she is inviting.

And I ... smile!

Kelley uses every kind of argument. Crude threats alternate with cunning ploys, cold calculation with feigned pity. He makes conditions. Jane agrees to everything. Ever more lustful glances play over the body of my wife. As she kneels before him the kerchief slips to reveal her bosom. Kelley checks her hand. He looks down at her. Desire burns in his cheeks.

And I ... smile.

Kelley raises Jane up. His hands grasp lasciviously, shamelessly. Jane protests, but weakly: her fears for my well-being sap all her strength.

And I ... smile.

Kelley finally agrees: everything that is to be done shall be done according to the orders of the Green Angel. He makes Jane swear that she – like him – will obey the commandment of the Green Angel to death and beyond, whatever He may command. That is, so he says, the only course of salvation. – Jane swears, fear draining the blood from her cheeks.

And I ... smile; but I can feel a tiny point of pain, as of a razor-sharp blade, cutting through the living artery. It is almost like the thrill of death ...

Then, as if I am hovering in the air, I see before me again the furrows of the Rabbi's ancient, tiny child's face. He says:

"Isaac, God's knife was set at thy throat, but the lamb that shall be offered up in thy stead is caught in the thornbush. If ever thou accept a sacrifice, be merciful as 'He' was; be merciful like the God of my fathers."

Darkness glides over me like a wave of moonless nights and I feel the memory of what I have seen with the eyes of the Rabbi's soul fade and disappear. It seems no more than a bad dream.

In front of me rise wooded hills. I am standing wearily on a rocky ledge, wrapped in my travelling cloak, shivering. A cold dawn is breaking. My guide for the night, some charcoal burner, some wood-lander, has abandoned me. I must climb up to where a patch of grey wall is visible through the leafless trees and swirling mists. Now the massive fortress becomes visible: a castle doubly ringed by battle-mented ramparts, a long, narrow hall and, jutting out above the sheer rock, the gatehouse; behind it is a low, squat tower with the Habsburg double eagle whirling above it as a huge weathercock. Even higher up, beyond a flower garden, is a huge, angular tower, six stories tall, with windows like the lights of a high, gothic church. A tower, half an impregn-able stronghold, half a cathedral containing holy relics: Karluv Tyn – Karlštejn Castle – the charcoal burner called it; the treasury of the Holy Roman Empire; venerable repository and feared custodian of the Imperial jewels.

I descend the narrow path down the cliff. Over there Emperor Rudolf is waiting for me. He sent for me at dead of night, unexpectedly, as secretive as ever, concealing his intentions and requiring com-pletely incomprehensible precautions to be taken. – An enigma of a man! Fear of treachery, suspicion of everyone, contempt for men and hatred of the world have robbed the old eagle of his finest feathers, of love and his natural nobility of charac-ter. – What an Emperor! – And what a strange adept!

– Is misanthropy the beginning of wisdom? Must the price of initiation be a constant fear of poisoners? These are the thoughts that occupy me as I approach the rocky gorge spanned by the vertiginous draw-bridge to Karlštejn.

A room gleaming with gold and precious stones: the Chapel of the Holy Rood in the 'Citadel'. Behind the altar, this I know, is the walled-up vault where the imperial insignia are hidden.

Before me is the Emperor, dressed, as ever, in his shabby black cloak; in these surroundings the con-trast between the rank and power of this man and his outward appearance appears crazier than ever.

I hand over to Rudolf the records I have kept of the "Actions", the seances we have had with the Green Angel since the first time in Mortlake. Each set of records is signed and witnessed by the partici-pants. The Emperor scans the signatures. The names of Leicester, Prince Lasky, King Stephen of Poland were the first to come to his notice.

He turned to me irritably:

"And what else? Be quick, Sir; the time and place are not such that I can long talk to you without other ears overhearing. The vipers pursue me, even to the resting place of my ancestors."

I take out the small quantity of the red powder I have been able to keep out of Kelley's grasp and hand it to the Emperor. His eyes light up. "Genuine!" the slack, old man's mouth groans; the bluish lower lip flops weakly onto his chin. The adept's sharp eye has recognised the great *Arcanum* he holds in his hands – perhaps for the first time in a life full of deceits and disappointments, insolent and stupid attempts by mountebanks to trick a determined and desperate seeker after truth.

"How do you prepare it?" – there is a tremor in the Emperor's voice.

"According to the instructions of the sacred book from the grave of St. Dunstan, as Your Majesty heard some time ago from Kelley."

"Give me the book!"

"The book, Your Majesty ..."

The Emperor's yellow neck extends, making him look more than ever like a lappet-faced vulture.

"The book! Where is it?"

"I cannot – for the moment – hand the book to Your Majesty, because I have not got it with me. It would not have been very safe in the pocket of an unaccompanied man on foot in the Bohemian Forest."

The Emperor hisses, "Where is the book?"

I recover my composure as I reflect on my reply.

"The book, Your Majesty – we ourselves are not always able to read it ..." the Emperor scents a trick – – how can I make the Angel's assistance sound credible? One thing is clear: I cannot, at least not yet ... Rudolf must only be allowed to see the book when ... when we have mastered the mysteries.

"Where is the book?" Rudolf spits out the question and again interrupts my hasty calculations. The eagle eyes glare an unmistakable threat. Have I ensnared myself!? I answer:

"Your Majesty, the book is in safe keeping, but the lock which guards St. Dunstan's precious gift can only be opened by Kelley and myself together: I have one key, he the other – both keys are necessary to open the iron chest. But if Kelley were here and the two keys at hand and the chest ... Your Majesty, what guarantee would ...

"Vagabond! Rogue! Gallows-meat!" The beak hacks at me.

I summon up all my dignity:

"Then I would ask Your Majesty to return the red powder. It is obviously nothing but worthless dust to Your Majesty, for how could vagabonds, rogues and *gallows-meat* come into possession of the thrice sacred secret of the *lapis transformationis*?"

Rudolf stops short, grunts. – I continue:

"Nor do I wish to enjoy the dishonourable security of knowing Your Majesty is protected by the inviolability of Your person from offering me satisfaction for the insult to my honour – the honour of an English gentleman ..."

My overbold words have the desired effect on the Emperor. His fingers clasp the box with the red powder even more tightly; he hesitates, then exclaims:

"Do I have to keep on telling you that I am no thief?! When will the book be in my hands?"

Play for time, is the one thought in my mind. Aloud, I say:

"When Your Majesty commanded my presence, Kelley was about to leave to attend to important affairs. When he returns I will persuade him to make St. Dunstan's book available to Your Majesty."

"And when will this Kelley be back?"

I pluck a day out of the air: "In a week's time, Your Majesty." (Now it is done.)

"Good. Ten days from today report to my Constable, Prince Rosenberg. I will make all the arrangements myself. But no more excuses!! You have already been excommunicated by the Church. Cardinal Malaspina has excellent eyes. Can you smell the bonfire, Doctor Dee? My power ends at the frontiers of Bohemia – and you will see those frontiers from the other side if I do not see St. Dunstan's book and receive instructions from you in its use by the agreed day. Is that understood? Good."

The chapel starts to spin. So this is the end? Within ten days I must learn to read St. Dunstan's book or we are lost, revealed as charlatans, expelled from the country, a prey to the servants of the Inquisition! – – Within ten days the Angel must come to our aid. Within ten days I must know the meaning of the cryptic lines of the parchment manuscript. Would that the pages had never been stolen from the

274

Bishop's tomb! Would that my eyes had never seen them! And who was it who despoiled St. Dunstan's grave. Was it not I who did it when I sent gold to the Ravenheads and encouraged them in their desperate deeds? Guilt will out, judgment comes in the end. Now come to my aid, thou who alone can help, Saviour of my honour, my life, my toil, O Angel of the Lord, thou miracle-worker of the West Window!

One smoky lamp gives off a dim light in the room. After days and nights of studying, waiting, pondering I can scarcely keep my eyes open: they are inflamed and burn, just as my soul burns – for peace ...

Kelley is back. I have told him of my desperate efforts to understand St. Dunstan's book. I have painted to him in clear colours the terrible fate that awaits us if we cannot satisfy the Emperor's demands.

Kelley is slouching half asleep in the armchair where I had spent hours torturing my brain. His face has a pinched look, occasionally I feel a tremor of fear as his eyes glint under the half-closed lids: what are the thoughts going through this man's mind, what plans is he hatching? And what should I do?

My limbs shake with feverish anxiety. My blood runs hot, then cold, and I can hardly stop my teeth from chattering. I say in a hoarse voice:

"Now you know what the situation is, my friend. In three days we must have the recipe for the preparation of the tincture, the secret of the powder from St. Dunstan's book, otherwise we will be regarded as common tricksters and treated accordingly. We will be handed over to the Inquisition and in a few days we will burn like ... like ..." – the words force themselves out between my lips – "like Bartlett Greene in the Tower."

"Give His Majesty the book, then." Kelley's languid reply is more infuriating than the most cutting mockery.

"I cannot give him the book if I cannot read it, nor even decipher it myself!" – At my exclamation Kelley raises his head a fraction. His eyes fix on me like the stare of a python waiting to pounce.

"If anyone can save us from this rat-trap that you have led us into, it is me – is that not so?"

I just nod silently.

"And what reward did you have in mind for … for the scum the great Doctor Dee picked up from the London gutter?"

"Edward!" I cry, "Edward, are we not blood brothers?! Have I not shared everything, everything with you like a true brother; more – have I not treated you as my own other half?"

"Not everything", mumbles Kelley.

A shiver runs over me.

"What do you want of me?"

"I? Want from … you, brother? Nothing, brother…"

"The reward, the reward! – What is the reward, your reward, Edward?"

Kelley leans forward in his chair: "The mysteries of the Angel are unfathomable. I, who am his mouthpiece, know the true awfulness of his power. I have learnt what fate awaits one who has sworn obedience and witholds it. I will not call up the Angel again …"

"Edward!" – it is a scream of terror that erupts from me.

"… I will not call up the Angel again, John, unless I am assured that his commands will be followed as ineluctably as day follows night. Will you, my brother John Dee, obey all future commands of the Green Angel of the West Window as I obey them?"

"Have I ever done otherwise!?" I object.

Kelley stretches his hand out to me.

"That is as may be. Swear obedience!"

My oath fills the chamber like drifts of smoke, like the whispering of countless demons, like the rustling of green – yes of green angel's wings.

It is the Lord High Constable, Prince Rosenberg, who is pacing up and down before me, shrugging his shoulders in a gesture of apology. – Then I suddenly realise where I am: the coloured half-light around us comes from the tall East window of a church. We are standing behind the high altar of the Cathedral of Saint Vitus in the castle.

Another strange meeting place, such as Emperor Rudolf and his emissaries like to choose to avoid the attentions – real or imagined – and passion for denunciation of the Cardinal Legate's army of spies. Here, in this majestic cathedral, the Emperor's confidant believes himself unobserved.

Finally he stops, right in front of me, trying to read my thoughts with his earnest gaze, the gaze of a good man with a tendency to somewhat naive enthusiasms. He says:

"Doctor Dee, I trust you completely. You do not have the look of someone trying to snatch a silver *Thaler* between the stocks and the gallows, like other rogues and vagabonds. It is a genuine zeal to penetrate the mysteries of God and nature that has brought you to Prague and Emperor Rudolf's castle – a place not without its dangers, mark you. I repeat: the service of the Emperor is no cushion of ease. Not even for his friends, Sir, as I can confide in you. And least of all for the friends of his great passion, for his fellow ... er ... initiates. – But to get to the point: what have you to tell me about the Emperor's business?"

My bow is a token of my genuine respect for the Constable.

"The Angel who commands us has unfortunately not yet found us worthy of an answer to our fervent prayers. He remains silent. But he will speak when the time is come. He will permit us to act."

I am astonished at myself, at how easily the lie trips off my tongue.

"So you want me to try to convince my sovereign that it depends on the permission of the ... of your so-called 'Angel' alone, whether you can give His Majesty the book of instructions from Saint Dunstan's tomb? – So be it. But what guarantee does the Emperor have that your 'Angel' will ever grant this permission? I must remind you once more, Doctor Dee: the Emperor will not be trifled with!"

"The Angel will allow it, Count, I am certain; I will vouch for it ..." – Gain time! Gain time, that is all that is left for me.

"Your word of honour as a gentleman?"

"My word of honour as an English gentleman!"

"I think I can do it, Sir. I will make every effort to persuade His Majesty to have patience with you. You must realise that I risk my own position in this as well, Sir. But you and your friend have promised to let me share in the revelations the book will bring. You give me your word on that, too?"

"My word, Count."

"We will see what can be done. – Hey! You there! –" The Constable swings round. Behind him, from the depths of one of the chapels that surround the chancel, a black figure emerges. A black cassock slips past, bowing as it goes. The Constable pales as he watches the figure recede.

"Vipers, wherever you go! When will they clear out that den of treachery? – The Cardinal will have more matter to report ..."

The night air is still trembling from the booming double strike of two o'clock from the Tyn Church. The house of Doctor Hajek, the Emperor's personal physician, resounds angrily with the echoes of the brazen monster up in the bell-tower.

We stand together before the heavy trapdoor and Kelley turns the key; his face is empty of expression, as it always is when the Angel is about to appear.

Pine torches in our hands, we clamber down an iron ladder that seems to stretch endlessly into a dreadful, yawning abyss. Kelley ahead; above me my wife, Jane. The ladder is attached to the wall with pins as thick as a man's arm; there is no masonry in the shaft we are descending, it is a stone cavern, perhaps formed by a rushing whirlpool in primaeval days? Doctor Hajek's house is built above it. The air is dry, not dank and heavy as is usual in grottos. It is as dead and as arid as the desert air and soon our mouths are parched, in spite of the dreadful cold, which intensifies with every step. From the depths to the vaulted roof the cavern is filled with the suffocating smell of the dried herbs and exotic drugs which the physician stores down here, and I am tormented by a dry cough. The walls are dull black stone, worked to a hard smoothness. I have only a vague idea of where we are, the silent darkness seems to swallow up all sound as well as the meagre light of our torches. I feel as if I am descending into the boundless space of the cosmos itself. The cellar floor must be a good thirty feet above us before my foot touches the ground. I sink to the ankles in a soft, black layer of ash that swirls up at every step.

The objects around us loom up out of the thick darkness like pale spectres – a broad table, barrels, sacks of herbs. Something hanging in the air bumps against my forehead – an earthenware lamp; it is dangling from an iron chain which disappears up into the blackness. Kelley lights it; its sparse gleam scarcely reaches down to our waists.

In front of me I gradually discern a grey stone wall about six foot square: we go up to it and see that it encloses a yawning shaft. "Saint Patrick's Purgatory" is the thought that comes to my mind. Doctor Hajek has told me of this shaft and of the stories that are told about it. Its depths have never been plumbed; it is known throughout Bohemia, and people say that it leads straight down to the middle of the earth where there is a circular, sea-green lake with an island on which Gaia, the mother of darkness lives.

279

Torches which have been dropped down have always gone out after a few fathoms, smothered by the poisonous gases of the darkness.

My foot stumbles on a stone the size of my fist; I pick it up and drop it into the gaping hole. We bend over the parapet and listen – and listen and listen, there is not the slightest noise to tell us the stone has reached the bottom. It has disappeared soundlessly into the depths, as if it has dissolved into thin air.

Suddenly Jane bends so far forward that I grab her by the arm and pull her back.

"What are you doing?" I cry; the air is so incredibly dry that all that comes out is a hoarse croak. Jane does not answer. Her face is distorted.

I sit beside her on a crate at the worm-eaten table and hold her hand, which is as cold as death from the icy air around.

Kelley, with the restlessness which we have learnt to interpret as announcing the advent of the Angel, has climbed up onto a pile of sacks and is sitting there, legs crossed, the pointed beard on his chin jutting out, his head thrown back and his eyes turned inward so that only the whites are visible, gleaming like milky glass. He is so high up that the light from the oil-lamp, the flame of which is stock still, like a ghost-light, illuminates his features from below, and the shadow of his nose is like an upside-down black triangle on his forehead, or a jagged hole deep in his skull.

As has been our practice since the days of Mortlake, I am waiting for his breathing to become deeper, so that I can begin the conjuration.

My eyes are fixed on the darkness before me; an inner voice tells me that there will be an apparition above the wall around the shaft. I am waiting for a green shimmer of light, but it seems as if the darkness there is getting deeper, thicker. Yes, there is no doubt, it is deepening, thickening; it is coagulating into a mass of incredible, inconceivable blackness compared to which total blindness would seem light. In contrast to it the darkness in the room around suddenly seems grey. And the black mass begins to take on the contours of a female form which then starts to tremble and hover over the abyss of the shaft like flickering smoke. I cannot say: I see it. With my physical eye I cannot see it. I see it with an inner organ which I cannot call my "eye". It becomes clearer and clearer to my perception, ever more sharply defined, in spite of the fact that not the tiniest ray from the lamp falls on it; I see it more sharply than I have ever seen any earthly object. It is a female figure, obscene and yet with a savage, exotic, disconcerting beauty; its head is that of a gigantic cat: it is no living being, but carved, probably an Egyptian idol, a statue of the goddess Sechmet. I feel paralysis creeping over my limbs, for my brain screams: that is Bartlett Greene's Black Isaïs! But the feeling of terror runs off me like water from a duck's back, so complete is the hold the consuming beauty of the statue has on me. I feel the desire to rush up to the demon and throw myself headlong into the bottomless pit at her feet, crazed with ... with ... I have no name for the self-destructive urge which grips me in its talons. Then there is a faint tremor of pale green light somewhere in the cavern; I cannot find the source, the dull glow is all around. – – The figure of the Cat Goddess has disappeared.

Kelley's breathing has become audible: slow and relaxed. The moment has come to pronounce the conjuration, which was given to me by the spirits so long ago. The words are from an unknown, barbaric language but I know them as well as the Lord's Prayer. O God, they have been etched on my heart for many years now.

I am about to say them out loud but I am filled with a nameless fear, Does it come from Jane? Her hand is trembling, no, her whole body is quivering. I pull myself together: I must do it! Did Kelley not say this morning that tonight at the second hour the Angel would have a great commandment for us and would … reveal the ultimate mystery, so greatly yearned for, so hotly prayed for through so many years? I open my mouth to pronounce the first word of the conjuration when I see the figure of Rabbi Löw rise up, as if a great distance away; his hand is raised and in it he holds the sacrificial knife. And then – for the fragment of a second – the figure of the Cat Goddess reappears over the shaft; in her left hand she is holding a small Egyptian mirror and in her right an object in onyx that looks like the tip of a lance or a dagger held upwards. Immediately both figures are swallowed up in a dazzling green radiance which comes from Kelley and falls on me. Blinded, I shut my eyes. It is as if I am closing them for good, never to see the light of the sun again, but I do not fear death, I feel I am already dead: calmly, all passion spent, I say the words of the conjuration out loud.

When I look up, Kelley has … disappeared! There is still somebody sitting up there on the pile of sacks, and the crossed legs are Kelley's – I can clearly recognise his tramp's hobnailed boots in the green light – but his body, chest and head have been transformed. Incomprehensibly, mysteriously transformed: it is the Angel, the Green Angel crouching cross-legged up there just like … just like a seated devil portrayed in ancient Persian images. The Angel is much smaller than I have ever seen it but the features, the threatening, awful and sublime features, are the same. The body becomes radiant and transparent, like an immense emerald, and the slanting eyes gleam like living moonstones; the narrow, delicate lips are turned up at the corners in a beautiful, enigmatic, fixed smile.

The hand in mine is lifeless as a corpse's; is Jane dead? – Just as dead or alive as I am, I think. I can feel she is waiting, waiting as I am for some fearful command.

282

What will the command be? I ask myself. No, I do not ask, for within me there is knowledge of what it will be, but the "knowledge" does not surface in my conscious mind. – – – I ... smile.

Words are issuing from the mouth of the Green Angel ... Do I hear them? Do I understand them? ... It must be so, for my heart stands still: the sacrificial knife that I saw at the Rabbi's house tears at my breast, at my entrails, at my heart, cutting through sinew, skin and brain. In my ear I can hear a loud voice, as of a torturer, counting slowly, cruelly slowly, from one to seventy-two. – – – Have I lain for centuries, rigid with death, only to wake to the dreadful words of the Angel? I do not know. All I know is: I am holding an ice-cold hand in mine and praying, wordlessly, that Jane is indeed dead! – Within me the words of the Green Angel burn like fire:

"As ye have all sworn allegiance I will now reveal to you the mystery of all mysteries. But first ye must take off all that is human, that ye might become as gods. John Dee, faithful servant, thee I command: Thou shalt lead thy wife Jane and my servant, Edward Kelley, to the bridal couch, that he may enjoy her as an earthly husband enjoyeth his earthly wife and that they too may become one in the night: for ye are blood brothers, forged in the fire with thy wife Jane into a triple union which shall continue for ever in the Realm of the Green Empire! Rejoice, John Dee, and be glad!" –

Again and again the terrible knife twists and turns in my body and soul, and bottled up inside me a voice screams a prayer, a desperate prayer to be released from life and consciousness.

I wake with a start, my whole body a prey to shooting pains: I am sitting hunched up in my desk chair, my numb fingers still clutching John Dee's polished coal. The sacrificial knife has cut me, too! Cut me into seventy-two pieces! – And the inconceivable pain, the waves of pain, like razor sharp bands of light pulsating through boundless space, through boundless time, strike me too, pass through me … from galaxy to galaxy, for aeons of light years – or so it seems to me.

Heaven only knows whether the pains in my limbs come from the awkward position I found myself sitting in when I woke from the trance, or whether it was the fault of the drugs Lipotin got me to inhale. Whatever the reason, I feel wretched as I stumble up out of my chair. My head is still ringing with the echo of the strange events that – half spectator, half active participant – I experienced in my abstraction, or whatever the name is for that absorption into the strange coal crystal, for that entrance to the past through the darkly gleaming portals of the *lapis praecipuus manfestationis*.

I need time to find my way back into the present. My muscles are still burning with the sharp pains. There is no doubt in my mind that everything that I experienced in my "dream" – what a ridiculous word! – that everything that I experienced in my magic transportation into the past was actually experienced then by me when I … was John Dee in flesh and blood and mind and soul.

But I have no time for reflection now, although such thoughts pursue me, even into my restless sleep. For today it is enough to note the main insights these moments have brought:

Who we are remains a mystery to mankind. We are only aware of ourselves, we can only experience ourselves in the particular "package" that faces us in the mirror and which we call our person. How reassuring it is for us to see the parcel labelled: "From: the parents; To: the grave, parcel post from 'address unknown' to 'address unknown'", with varying customs declarations: "registered, value xx" or "samples – of no value" according to our vanity.

In short: what do we parcels know of the contents of the packages? It seems to me that the content can be transformed by the energy source which determines its fluidity. There are quite different beings whose radiance can be glimpsed through our dull clay. ... Princess Shotokalungin, for example? Certainly, she is not what I took her for in my overwrought state; she is, certainly, no ghost! She is just as certainly a woman of flesh and blood, as I am a man of flesh and blood. But Black Isaïs transmits her rays from the other side through the medium of this woman and transforms her into what she was from the very beginning of her being. Each mortal has his god, his demon; and in him, in the words of the Apostle Paul, we live and move and have our being. And within me is John Dee; what difference does it make who John Dee is? Who I am? – There is One who has seen the Baphomet and is to attain the double face or perish.

I suddenly remembered Jane – – that is, Johanna Fromm. The game that fate is playing with us includes names. But this is all according to the law: our names are entered in the Book of Life.

I found Jane – as I will call her from now on, instead of Johanna – awake once more. She was sitting up in bed and smiling strangely to herself and so self-absorbed that she did not even notice I had entered.

She looked beautiful against the pillows; my heart leapt up at the sight, and miraculous was the combination of present affection and age-old union, like the strains of two melodies intertwining. It was almost a shock to recognise how similar this Johanna Fromm is to the Jane I have just left in the Prague of Emperor Rudolf.

I sat with her on the edge of the bed and kissed her. Confirmed bachelor that I am, there is no other thought in my mind than that I am her husband, bound in destiny to my wife Johanna.

And Jane took my presence as a matter of course; she lay there, relaxed in the security of a familiar relationship.

But not the relationship I wanted. Her gentle hand pushed away my more intimate advances. Her expression remained friendly but at the same time had a strange seriousness which separated her feelings from mine. I bombarded her with questions, then more carefully, more cautiously sought the key to her soul, to the torture chambers of her passions. In vain.

"Jane," I cried, "I too am dazed by the miracle of this ... this reunion" – a shiver ran down my spine – "but now you must wake up to the living present. Take me as it was predetermined you should find me! Let us live! Forget! – And ... remember."

"I remember." A gentle smile plays about her lips.

"Then forget!"

"That too, my love. I ... am .... forgetting –"

Fear tightens my throat, as if a dying soul were gradually slipping away from me:

"Johanna! – Jane!! How strange are the ways of destiny that bring us together again!" She slowly shakes her head: "Not the ways of destiny – the way of sacrifice, my dearest."

My scalp prickles at the thought. Did Jane's soul accompany my spirit on its journey into the past? I stammer:

"That is the deception of the Green Angel!"

"Oh no, my love, that is the wisdom of the High Rabbi." And she smiles so deeply into my eyes that tears, streams of tears dim my sight.

I do not know how long I rested on the gentle rise and fall of her breast until the tears dried up and my taut nerves relaxed, drinking from her deep repose, like a child at its mother's breast ...

Finally I understood the words she whispered as her hand kept stroking my head:

"It is not easy to tear oneself up, my darling! Roots bleed; it hurts. But it is only the mortal part. On the other side everything is different. At least, my love, that is what I believe. I loved you too much ... once – when is immaterial, love knows nothing of time. Love is also destiny, is that not so? – And yes, I did betray you ... I did betray you then. O God! ..." Her body shook with short, painful spasms, but she ignored them and bravely continued:

"...it must have been my destiny. For it was not my will, not that. As we might say today, it was like the switch on the points: such a small thing, so inconspicuous, and yet it can shift the power of an express train onto another line and send it hurtling off into the distance, to send it home. See, my love, my betrayal of you – of John Dee – was such a switch: and your destiny went rushing along a path to the right, mine to the left. How should the two lines, once they had separated, reunite? Your way was leading you to the – 'Other' woman, mine to ..."

"My way was leading me to the 'Other' woman!?" I raged; I laughed, I was indignant; I was the victor! – "Johanna, how can you think that of me! My jealous little Jane! You think the Princess could be of any danger to you?!"

Jane started up from the pillows and stared at me blankly.

"Princess? What Princess do you mean? – Oh, yes. the Russian woman. I had forgotten that she ... that she is still living." – Then her face took on a thoughtful, almost rapt expression and she said aloud to herself:

"My God! I hadn't thought of her!" – and she grasped both my arms with such horrified violence that I was fixed motionless in the vice of her fear. I could not understand what she was talking about and what she was afraid of. I looked at her questioningly.

"Why this great fear, Johanna, my foolish, little darling?"

"We still have that to face!" she whispered to herself. "Oh, now I know what must happen."

"You know nothing of the sort!" I chaffed her and felt my laugh echo in the silence. She said:

"My love, your road to the Queen is not clear yet. I … will clear it for you."

I felt a vague fear – of what, I could not say – pass through me like a long flare of lightning. I wanted to speak, but could not. Silent, I looked at Jane. She was smiling sadly down at me. All at once I had a dark sense of what she meant and felt paralysis creep over me.

I have left Jane alone, at her request.

Now I am back at my desk, trying to write down an account of what has passed:

Was it jealousy? A feminine pre-emptive strike against a sensed – or just imagined – danger? One possible explanation is that Jane's express determination to relinquish her claim on me in favour of a phantom, a romantic illusion is a determination with a secret reservation. Where is the "Other" woman, this "Queen", then? Who will bring the vision of the Baphomet to me, down from the world of dreams into this year of grace? It may all represent a mission, a spiritual goal, symbolise a deeper awareness of life which I am at present not yet able fully to comprehend but, however that may be and however I may look up to it, what has it to do with the immediate physical beauty of the woman I love? For I am in love with Jane, in love with her, that is certain, that is the positive gain from the strange twist of fate that deposited John Roger's legacy on my desk, like flotsam from a shipwreck.

Either Jane will make me forget the road to the "Queen" or, with her goodness, her special spiritual abilities she will clear the way to the other side. Where does that leave Princess Shotokalungin? Whenever I indulge in irony, enjoy a sense of male superiority, Johanna's earnest face always appears to prick the bubble of my arrogance: her intense gaze seems fixed on a goal that I cannot even sense. I feel that this woman has a definite plan, that she knows something that I do not know – as if she were the mother and I not much more than ... her child.

There is much I have to catch up on. I will have to compress it, for my life has started to move at such a pace that the hours spent at my desk seem wasted time.

The day before yesterday, my writing was interrupted by a kiss from Jane, the kiss of the dearest woman, who had crept up, unheard, behind me.

She chatted like any sensible wife, returning after a long absence to take charge of the household and asking the sensible questions. I teased her a little about it and she laughed, relaxed and secure. I kept having to restrain myself from reaching out to her and her maternal embrace. Suddenly, without apparent reason, her clear, open face took on again that same strange earnestness I had noticed before; she said calmly:

"My love, you must visit the Princess; it is necessary."

"What, Jane?" I cried in astonishment. "You want to send me to that woman?"

"Of whom I am so jealous, aren't I, dearest?" Her mouth smiled, but her eyes retained their pensive earnestness.

I did not understand. I refused to make such a visit. Whatever for? And for whose sake?

Jane – I only call her Jane now, and every time I say the name I take a deep breath and seem to draw strength from the cool well of the past – Jane refused to give in. She dreamed up all sorts of reasons, absurd reasons: I owed the Princess a visit; but she – Jane – was also keen for me to keep up relations with the Princess, indeed, keener than she could express in words. Finally she accused me of cowardice. That did it. A coward!? Never! If there is some old account of John Dee's or of John Roger's, to be settled then it shall be settled, right down to the last ha'penny. I jumped up and told Jane of my determination and she fell down at my feet, wringing her hands and – crying.

On my way to Princess Shotokalungin's I thought about the strange way Jane kept changing. When, under the influence of things from the past, she feels herself to be Jane Fromont, John Dee's wife, her whole being becomes subservient, deferential, a little tearful. When, however, it is Frau Johanna Fromm who speaks she exudes decisiveness, an inexplicable strength, a maternal firmness and kindness which masters me.

Occupied with such thoughts, I had reached the villa where Princess Shotokalungin lived on the edge of the hills outside town before I realised it. As I pressed the electric bell at the gate I felt a slight sense of apprehension, although a quick glance at the front garden and the house should have assured me that I would scarcely meet with anything out of the ordinary here. The villa was of a common type, built some thirty years ago, since when it would have been in the hands of several speculative landlords. The Princess, so I had heard, had only rented it because it was always available: an ordinary house set in an ordinary little suburban garden on the edge of the city.

The automatic lock clicked open. I entered the garden. There was already someone waiting to receive me under the frosted glass roof of the little porch. It must have been the refracted light, falling from above through the milky glass that gave the servant's hands and face such a ghastly blue colour – I said to myself to calm my shock at the sight of the man in the dark Circassian costume. His face had an unmistakably Mongolian cast; the eyes were scarcely to be seen beneath the lowered lids. To my question as to whether the Princess was available he said nothing, just gave a jerky nod, inclined his upper body, crossing his arms over his chest in the Oriental manner – all as if he were a puppet with someone above him pulling the strings.

Then the livid, corpse-like gatekeeper disappeared behind me, and I entered the dimly-lit hall where I was received by two further figures, who silently appeared, took my coat and hat and, like well-oiled, functional automata, sent me on my way like a parcel. "A parcel" – I felt as if I were the incarnation of the image I had recently used in my log book as a symbol of man's life on earth.

Meanwhile one of the two Kurdish demons had flung open the double door and, with a peculiar movement of the hand, invited me to proceed.

"Is that really a human being?" – it seemed a mad question to ask oneself, but as I walked past the bloodless, clay-complexioned figure I caught a whiff of the grave – a zombie?! I rejected the crazy notion immediately; of course it's quite natural that the Princess, coming from the East herself, should have old Mongolian retainers, perfectly trained ... 'automata'. I must be careful not to put a romantic gloss on everything, not to let my imagination see dangers where there are none.

Whilst these thoughts occupied me I was ushered with deep bows through several rooms of such ordinariness that I can remember nothing about them. Then, suddenly, I found myself alone in a room furnished in the oriental style; walls and floor were covered with costly oriental rugs, low cushions were strewn everywhere and at every step the foot sank into rich furs: the whole effect was more like the tent of a nomad prince than a German suburban villa, but that was not what gave the room its particular atmosphere.

Was it the tarnished weapons that bristled from every fold of the wall-hangings? You could see straight away that they were not mere decorations brought in by some interior designer: they were visibly flecked with blood and still gave off a faint bitter odour of their cruel use, weapons still quivering with the sound of dark betrayal, merciless butchery and senseless slaughter.

Or was it the contrasting functionality of a huge bookcase which took up one whole wall and was full of old volumes bound in leather or vellum? On the top shelf stood a few bronze heads, black with the patina of age: half barbaric gods, from whose obsidian black faces eyes of onyx and moonstone stared down at you with a demonic glitter.

Or was it …?

In one corner, behind me, as if it were guarding the door I had just come in through was a kind of altar in black marble overlaid with matt gold laquer. Above it was the statue of a naked goddess in black syenite, not much over three feet tall: as far as I could tell it appeard to be Thracian work, possibly with some Egyptian influence, representing the lion-headed goddess Sechmet, or Isis. The feline face with its evil smile was remarkably alive; the excellently done female body was realistic to an obscene degree. As an attribute the Cat Goddess held in her left hand an Egyptian mirror; the fingers of her right hand were curled round empty space – clearly they had originally held some second attribute, now lost.

Closer inspection of this strangely beautiful and, for its semi-barbaric Thracian origin, artistically outstanding object was made impossible by the arrival of the Princess, who suddenly appeared, as silently as one of her Kurdish zombies, from behind one or other of the Persian wall-hangings.

"Our connoisseur of art indulging his critical faculties again?" her voice purred in my ear.

I swung round.

Assja Shotokalungin certainly knows how to dress! She was wearing a short dress in the latest fashion, but I have no idea what kind of material could produce this effect of darkly glinting bronze; it was too dull for silk, for linen too metallic. No matter; she looked like the Cat Goddess in front of us, clad in a translucent metal skin, which suggested with every movement of her body the voluptuous curves of the stone goddess brought to sensuous life.

"A favourite piece of my late father's," she purred. "The crowning point of many of his studies – and of mine. I was my father's pupil."

I trotted out the usual banalities in praise of the stone goddess, of its owner's scholarly researches, of the strange fascination the statue seemed to exert, all the time aware of the Princess' smiling face before me – and of something else: of some indistinct feeling, some vague, half-remembered torment which I kept trying to force into the clear light of consciousness as I was speaking. It kept flitting past my eyes like a waft of grey smoke, shadowy, impalpable ... One thing I felt sure of: this need to remember was in some way connected with that statue; absent-mindedly my glance kept settling on it, trying to suck the mystery from it. What words I mumbled to the ever-smiling Princess I can no longer remember.

Whatever I said, she took me in her usual charming fashion by the arm, chaffing me gently about the eternity it had taken me to return her visit. No trace of any barbed hidden reference to the unfortunate scene between us. She seemed to have forgotten it, or never to have taken it seriously, never to have taken it for anything other than teasing banter. She waved away all my attempts to apologise for my behaviour with an elegant hand:

"Anyway, now you are here at last; my severest critic and now my guest. I am not going to let you leave until I have made sure you have had the opportunity to form a clear picture of all my modest abilities. I presume you have brought the object I asked you for. Or have you?" – she laughed as if she had made a joke.

Monomania! was the thought that went through my mind. So she is mad, after all. Why else should she go on about that damned spearhead? – "Spearhead!?" A sudden insight twisted my head round and I stared at the empty fingers of the black statue, curled round nothing! The Cat Goddess!

She is the mistress of the symbol that is so persistently demanded of me! – My head was whirling with guesses, with confused attempts to connect known fact and vague suspicion, with intuitions that suddenly slipped from my grasp: "What did the statue originally have in its hand? You know; of course you know – and I must know, you must tell me ..."

"But of course I know", was the laughing reply. "Is it really so important? It will be a pleasure to put my modest archaeological knowledge at your service. If you will allow me, then, I will give you a short private lecture. Just like a professor ... a German professor!" – the Princess' laugh was a sparkling arpeggio; at the same time she clapped her hands in the oriental manner, almost inaudibly. Immediately a Mongol servant appeared in the doorway, silent as a robot. A wave of the hand, and the yellow spectre disappeared, as if swallowed up by the warm half-light of the hanging carpets.

That strange, glowing half-light. It was only at this point that I noticed that the tented room had no window, no obvious source of illumination. I had no time to find out where the soft light came from that bathed the room in a golden, evening glow. It crossed my mind that there might be a blue, daylight lamp such as photographers use concealed somewhere, that was somehow mixed with the light of weaker red and yellow bulbs to create the impression of warm evening twilight. And I noticed a gradual but constant change in the lighting as the red tone gave way to a deeper, greenish glow; I almost felt that it was adjusting to the mood that was slowly developing between the Princess and myself. – – I presume that this was all the product of my imagination.

The servant, in dark livery with baggy trousers over faultless, high-shafted patent leather boots, reappeared without a sound. He was carrying a silver tray on which were silver bowls with black inlay work; "Persian", I noticed. They were filled with various sweetmeats.

The next moment the Mongol had vanished again; the bowls had been placed between myself and the Princess on a low stool and politeness compelled me to take a piece of the confectionary.

I have not a particularly sweet tooth; I would have preferred a cigarette, if the charming hostess routine was absolutely necessary. So it was with a certain reluctance that I picked up a lump of the sticky oriental stuff and chewed on it as the Princess started:

"So you really want a lecture, my friend? Shall I start with the Thracian goddess Isaïs. You see, along those parts of the Black Sea she is called Isaïs, not Isis. – You find that surprising?"

"Isaïs!" the name had slipped out, or, rather, I think I shouted the word; I had jumped up and was staring at the Princess. But she placed a gentle hand on my thigh and drew me back into my chair.

"It's nothing more than a vulgar Greek variant of the name Isis and has nothing to do with the revelations of scholarly research, as you seem to think. The Goddess has had to put up with various changes of name as her cult went from temple to temple, from congregation to congregation. The black Isaïs that you can see there, for example – " the Princess pointed to the statue. I just nodded. All I could manage was a murmured, "Excellent". The Princess probably assumed I was referring to her explanation, though all I had in mind was the sweet I had just finished; one of the ingredients was bitter almonds, which made it more acceptable to the male palate than the usual tasteless cotton wool. Without the Princess having to ask me I took a second piece from the bowl in front of me and popped it in my mouth.

Meanwhile the Princess was continuing:

"However, Black Isaïs has a different ... let us say a different significance as a cult figure than the Isis of the Egyptians. As is well known, in the Mediterranean area Isis became Venus, the mother goddess, the patroness of fertility, of childbearing. Our Thracian Isaïs, on the other hand, appears to the faithful ..." The bright flash of memory that came at this point so blinded me that I could scarcely find the words to exclaim:

"She appeared to me in the cellar vault of Doctor Hajek in Prague when I conjured up the Green Angel with Kelley and Jane! She it was who hovered over the measureless depths of the well-shaft, a prophetic image of my sufferings to come, a bitter portent of how I would come to cherish my hatred of Kelley, my hatred of all that was dear to me!"

The Princess bent forward: "How interesting! So the goddess of black love really appeared to you once? Well, then, you will find what I have to tell you about Black Isaïs all the more easy to understand. Above all, the fact that she rules in the realm of anti-Eros, whose power and extent no-one suspects who has not himself been initiated into the mysteries of hate."

My hand reached greedily for the silver bowl; I felt an uncontrollable craving for this bitter-sweet confection gradually assert its hold over me. And then – did it only seem so to me or did it actually happen? – all at once the light in the room was a strange green. I felt as if I were suddenly deep under water, at the bottom of the sea or an underground lake, in the ancient wreck of a ship or on an island on the sea-bed. And at the same time I knew: this woman opposite me was Black Isaïs. *How* Black Isaïs managed to appear through the very tangible flesh and blood of a Circassian Princess I do not know, but I knew that facing me was John Dee's enemy, the arch-enemy of our sex and the destroyer of the road that leads us beyond humanity. And an ice-cold jet of hatred spurted up my spine to the back of my head. I thought of Jane and looked at the Princess; disgust welled up within me.

The Princess must have had some sense of what was going on inside me, for she looked me straight in the eye and said in a half-whisper:

"I think you are a model pupil, my friend; you are quick to understand; it is a pleasure to instruct you."

"Yes, I understand and I would like to leave," I said coldly.

"What a shame. Just when I could reveal so much to you, my dear friend."

"Everything has been revealed. It is enough. I ... hate you!"

The Princess leapt up.

"At last! Thus speaks a man! Now victory will be complete!"

I found speech almost impossible because of an incomprehensible excitement which I could scarcely control. I heard my own voice as if from outside and it was hoarse with hate:

"My victory is to have seen through you in spite of everything. Look over there" – I pointed to the stone goddess – "that is you. That is your true face. That is your beauty and its whole secret. And the mirror and the spearhead that is missing are the symbols of your primitive power: vanity and lust; the age-old, wearisome game with cupid's poison darts!"

As I spat this out, and more along the same lines, the Princess, listening attentively and giving cool nods of agreement, stepped over to the statue of the Cat Goddess and, with swift, supple grace, took up the same attitude as the stone image, as if to invite close comparison. Smiling, she purred:

"You are not the first man to flatter me by saying there is a certain similarity between me and this venerable work of art – –"

I dropped all considerations of politeness:

"It is true! The similarity is true, right down to the most intimate details of this feline body, my dear Princess!"

A mocking laugh, a twist, a snake-like ripple and the Princess stood naked beside the statue. Her dress seemed to foam about her feet, like the waves at the feet of Aphrodite.

"Well, my pupil, were you right? Does this confirm your supposition. Can I flatter myself that I match up to your expectations – perhaps I should say your hopes? See: I take the mirror in this left hand" – with a swift movement she picked up an oval object that must have lain on top of the altar and for a brief moment she held up towards me an antique bronze mirror overlaid with verdigris – "the mirror – your interpretation of its significance was quite superficial, by the way – the mirror in the hand of the Goddess is not at all a sign of feminine vanity. It is a symbol of the error that lies at the base of every desire for *reproduction* and – if you can understand this – of the rightness of all human *multiplication*, be it in the physical or the spiritual sphere. And now, as you can see, all that is lacking for the similarity with the image of the deity to be completed is the spearhead in this right hand. The spear I have so often asked you for. You would be very far from the mark if you imagine it is the attribute of your little bourgeois cherub, Eros. It is an insult to accuse me of such a lack of taste. You will, I hope, learn today from your own personal experience, what the invisible spear is." With complete assurance she stepped out of the circle of her dress on the floor. Her marvellously smooth body, light bronze in colour and of a virginal suppleness, which seemed never to have suffered a lover's caress, was indeed a more beautiful work of art than the stone Isaïs. A wild fragrance, it seemed to me, rose from the dress on the floor, a perfume I knew well and which was beginning to numb my already overwrought senses. I needed no further proof that here I was faced with the struggle to prove my strength, to test the genuineness of my calling and to settle my fate for good or ill.

Leaning back against the dark edges of the bookshelves, the Princess stood there with inimitable, unselfconscious animal grace, and her beautiful, velvety voice told me of the ancient cult of the Thracian Isaïs that had developed amongst a secret sect of the priests of Mithras.

"Jane! Jane!" I cried inwardly as I tried to close my ears to the dark melodious voice continuing its explanation in even, rational tones. The image of Jane seemed to hover in a greenish nimbus; it nodded to me with a melancholy smile; it became fuzzy and indistinct in a current of green water. – She is back "on the other side", as I am now, on the green sea-bed, I thought. But my eyes lost the vision and were once more the captive of Assja Shotokalungin's perfect physical presence and the clear and measured flow of her speech.

She was talking of the mysteries of the esoteric Thracian cult dedicated to Black Isaïs which compelled its priests, in a frenzy of spiritual perversion, to dress in women's clothes, to approach the Goddess with the left, female, side of their bodies alone, and to sacrifice their sense of maleness to her. There were even some degenerate weaklings who, in the drugged delirium of the rite, actually made a physical sacrifice of their maleness. This barred them from any further initiation, any further progress in the priestly hierarchy; these mutilated neophytes were destined to remain in the forecourts of the temple and some, later sensing the higher truth from which they were forever barred, were horrified to realise the consequence of their wild rashness and committed suicide. On the "other side" their ghosts formed an eternal retinue serving the Lady.

"Jane! Jane!" again I tried to pray inwardly for help, for I could feel my inner resistance crumbling, as if an upward spurt of flame were burning the post supporting a vine heavy with grapes.

My appeal was in vain. I could sense that Jane was far from me, immeasurably far; perhaps she lay in a deep sleep, helpless herself, in a trance, cut off from any earthly communication with me.

Then I became furiously angry with myself. "Weakling! Coward! Already a eunuch? Preparing for the same end as a Thracian neophyte? Pull yourself together! Rely on your own strength, on your own self-control. Self-control is what is at stake in this satanic struggle! Control over your own will is what they want to take from you! It is no use praying to the Mother – or to her incarnation in any woman – to be saved you must exercise your own will, otherwise you will be wearing the woman's clothes, you will be a priest of the Cat Goddess, whole or not."

Assja Shotokalungin was calmly continuing her dissertation:

"I hope I have managed to make it clear to you that in the Thracian cult of Isaïs candidates for the priesthood found their self-control put to the test mercilessly. For the key idea behind the religion is that the salvation of the world and the destruction of the demiurge comes not from the abandonment and betrayal of self in the procreative, erotic urge but solely from the hatred of the sexes for each other, which is the real mystery of sex. The arcane wisdom of the cult of Isaïs teaches that the attraction which the vulgar feel for their opposite sexual pole and which they dignify with the false designation of 'love' is the odious means by which the demiurge ensures the continued existence of the common herd. 'Love' is base, mean; for 'love' robs both man and woman of the sacred principle of the individual self and thrusts both into the impotence of a union from which the only awakening is a rebirth in the lower world whence they came and ever will come. Love is mean; hatred alone is noble!" – The eyes of the Princess were fixed on me with a fiery glow which ignited my heart like an electric spark detonating dynamite.

Hatred! My heart burnt white-hot with hate for Assja Shotokalungin. She stood there naked before me, taut as a giant cat about to pounce, an enigmatic smile playing about her lips, apparently listening for something.

With an effort I contained the tumult within my chest and regained control of my tongue, although I could only whisper: "Hatred! That is the truth, woman! Would I could say how I hate you!"

"Hate!" she whispered sensuously. "Hate! Beautiful! At last you are on the right road, my friend. Hate me! Aah, I can feel it flowing, but only tepidly ..." – a maddeningly disdainful smile flitted across her face.

"Come to me!" I tried to shout but my throat would scarcely obey.

The smooth, voluptuous fur of the cat-woman before me twitched lasciviously:

"What are you going to do to me, my friend?"

"Strangle you! I am going to strangle you, murderer, demon, hellcat!" my breath came in gasps, my breast and neck were constricted, as if by iron rings; I felt that if I did not destroy the creature in front of me immediately annihilation would be my lot.

"You are beginning to take pleasure in me, my friend; I can feel it," she breathed huskily.

I prepared to leap at her but I found it was impossible; my feet were rooted to the floor. So: play for time, calm down, gather strength. With a supple movement the Princess took a step towards me.

"Not yet, my friend."

"Why not?" screamed a voice from within me, a voice that was scarcely audible, so hoarse was it with senseless anger and – desire.

"You do not yet hate me enough, my friend," purred the Princess.

At this the paroxysm of disgust and hate suddenly turned into a miserable, creeping fear, and just as suddenly my throat cleared and I cried:

"What do you want of me, Isaïs?"

The naked woman answered calmly, lowering her voice in gentle persuasion:

"To erase your name from the Book of Life, my friend!"

A new outburst of scorn and self-confidence once more swept away the fear; this feeling of assurance neutralised for the moment the cold onset of paralysis. With a mocking laugh I said:

"Me?! I will destroy you, you ... *thing* from the blood of butchered cats! I will not rest; I will stick to your trail, follow the scent that you leave behind you. Panther, you have already been wounded; wherever you run, my hate will pursue you, man-eater, until I put a bullet through your heart."

The Princess nodded, her thirsty gaze fixed on mine.

Consciousness slipped from me for a brief eternity. – – –

When, with an indescribable effort of will, I managed to tear myself from this state of lethargic paralysis, the Princess was no longer standing naked between the altar and the bookcase; rather she was lying, fully clothed, on the divan and was just directing a languid gesture of confirmation in the direction of the door.

Instinctively I turned round.

There in the doorway, dressed in the Princess' livery, pale as a corpse and silent, like all the servants here, lids almost closed over expressionless eyes stood – my cousin, John Roger!

The horror crackled over my head like St. Elmo's fire. I heard a half-stifled cry from my own mouth, steadied my stumbling feet and turned my staring eyes to the door once more – my overwrought nerves must have played a trick on me: the servant, who was still there, was indeed tall and blond. A European, at any rate, a German servant amongst all the Asian riff-raff but, apart from a vague similarity it was, after all … not … my cousin, John Roger.

And then I saw something else. At first, because I was still recovering from the shock at the sight of the servant, I merely registered the fact that the black statue of the Thracian Isaïs was now holding in the curled fingers of its right hand the end of a spear. –

I took a couple of steps towards the altar and saw that the broken-off fragment of the shaft as well as the spearhead itself was made of black syenite – just as was the statue itself. Stone had merged with stone, it was all hewn from one block of stone, as if the attribute had never left the Goddess' hand. It was only after I had made sure that I was not mistaken that I remembered – and the force of it was like a hammer-blow to the head – that earlier the clutching hand of the statue had been empty! How did the spearhead come to be in the stone fist?!

But there was no time for further reflection on the matter.

The servant's announcement to which the Princess had given a gesture of acceptance concerned a visitor who was waiting outside. I heard Assja's soft voice:

"What has made you so silent, my friend? For minutes now you have just been staring into space and not paying the least attention to my learned account of the Thracian cult. I flatter myself that I

303

am as interesting a speaker as any German professor
– and you fall asleep in the middle of my lecture?!
Where are your manners, my friend?"

"I ... Did I ...?"

"Yes indeed! You fell fast asleep, my friend. I will
try" – the Princess' peals of laughter cascaded over
me again – "I will try to salvage a little of my
shattered pride by assuming your interest in the finer
details of Thracian art and culture was merely
feigned. Of course in that case all my scholarly
efforts were in vain ..."

"I don't know what to say, Princess," I stammered, "I am confused ... please forgive me ... but I
can't have just imagined it ... the statue of the lion-
headed Isis over there, for example ..." – beads of
sweat were dripping from my forehead. I had to
mop my brow with my handkerchief.

"Of course! It's much too warm in here," the
Princess cried in her vivacious manner. "Forgive me,
my dear, I'm just too fond of the heat. – In that case
I'm sure you will be happy to go to another room to
meet the visitor who has just been announced?"

I suppressed my startled question in order not to
admit too openly that I had slept, but the Princess
seemed to understand it all the same.

"It is Lipotin who is waiting in the other room. I
hope you are not angry with me for not sending him
away; he is a mutual acquaintance?"

Lipotin! Only now did I feel I had fully recovered
my senses, my spiritual strength. I cannot find a
better way of putting it than to say that I felt I had
risen from the bottom of ... where was the greenish
light that had filled the room a moment ago? –
Behind where the Princess was reclining a heavy
khilim rug had been half drawn back; she leapt up
and opened a concealed window. Motes of golden
dust danced in the warm afternoon sunshine.

As far as I could, I forced myself to ignore the
storm of doubts, questions and self-accusation the

events of the afternoon had raised and accompanied the Princess into the next room, where Lipotin was waiting. He came to meet us and greeted us warmly.

"I am eternally sorry, Madam", he began, "to find I have disturbed you the first time you have received a visitor whom I know you have long expected in vain. But I am sure that anyone who has once seen these venerable rooms will not miss any opportunity to repeat the visit. My congratulations, sir!" Still suspicious, I tried – without success – to spot any glance or gesture of collusion between the two. In the clear light of this ordinary drawing room the Princess was quite the lady of the house greeting an old friend. Even her strikingly well-cut dress seemed to me, elegant as it was, no longer as unusual as before; I saw now that it was made from silk brocade – rare, it is true, but not supernatural.

With a swift smile the Princess took up Lipotin's words:

"On the contrary, Lipotin, I am afraid our mutual friend has formed a most unfavourable impression of his hostess. Just imagine: I insisted on giving him a lecture – he fell asleep, of course!"

The conversation sparkled with laughter and teasing banter on all sides. The Princess insisted she had forgotten one of the first principles of female hospitality: she had forgotten – yes, really, forgotten – to have the coffee sent in! And all because she could not resist the opportunity to parade her own learning, which was, after all, only second-hand, in front of a connoisseur such as her guest. One should always remember to provide one's audience – one's victims – with a stimulant before lecturing at them. Amidst all the badinage I felt a blush spread over my face as I remembered the fantasies I had indulged in during the minutes when the lady of the house thought I was asleep!

To make matters worse, at that moment Lipotin gave me a sideways glance which seemed to say that his antiquarian's instinct permitted him to read my thoughts with a fair degree of clarity. This only served to increase my embarrassment, but fortunately the Princess did not seem to notice and interpreted my blush as the after-effects of drowsiness.

Suppressing a mischievous grin, Lipotin helped me out of the awkward situation by asking the Princess whether it was the inspection of her unique weapon collection which had so exhausted me; given the multitude of amazing treasures it contained, he could well understand how I felt. The Princess denied this with mock desperation and laughed, what on earth could Lipotin be thinking, she had not had time to get round to it and, anyway, she hardly dared ...

That was my cue to restore my somewhat damaged reputation, and I begged her, with Lipotin's support, to be allowed to see what I had heard described as a fabulous collection. Jokingly I offered to allow her to put my attentiveness to the severest test: I would follow the most abstruse exposition of the most recondite facts in a field where my own knowledge was superficial in the extreme ...

The Princess acceded to my request and so, laughing and joking, we went back through the inner rooms to one, obviously in another wing of the villa, which stretched out before us like a gallery.

Between the glass cases the walls shone dully with the metallic gleam of countless suits of armour. Like the empty husks of insect-men they stood in a long row, as if vainly waiting for a shouted order that would bring them back to life. Around them and above them were burgonets and tilting helms, chain mail overlaid with gold and silver thread, damascened breastplates, artfully riveted scale armour – most, as a quick glance told me, of Eastern European or Oriental origin. It was the fullest armoury I had ever seen, full, above all, of richly ornamented weapons encrusted with gold and jewels from a Merovingian *skramasax* to Saracen shields and daggers of the best Arabian, Sassanid and Thracian swordsmith's work. The overall impression was strange, fantastic; in spite of its ordered rigidity, it somehow seemed alive, threatening, as if the weapons gleaming from the walls were beings in suspended animation. But even stranger and more fantastic to me was the sight of the owner in her fashionable dress passing elegantly amongst all these instruments of murder, commenting knowledgeably on this or that piece. A lady, a fickle woman – the passionate custodian of a chamber full of instruments of torture and death! However, I had little time to indulge in these thoughts. The Princess sustained a fluent stream of conversation about her late father's passion for collecting and her own. She kept on pointing out priceless rarities, though, of course, I can remember only a few. What I do remember is that the collection did not seem to be organised according to the usual principles. The eccentric old Prince had obviously been particularly keen to acquire weapons whose value lay in their origin or in some story connected with them. He must have become fascinated by historical, not to say legendary, curiosities: there was Roland's shield and Charlemagne's battleaxe; on a cushion of purple velvet lay the lance of the Centurion Longinus from Golgotha; there was the magic dagger of the Emperor Sun Chiang Sen with which he drew the line which no Western Mongol dared to cross and along which later emperors built the Great Wall – to their own glory, as it was unnecessary given the existence of the magic boundary. Glittering cruelly, there lay Abu Bakr's damascene blade, with which he had beheaded the seven hundred Jews of Kurayza without pausing once to draw breath in the course of his bloody work. Thus the Princess showed me a seemingly endless hoard of the weapons of the greatest heroes of three continents or of such as were associated with blood, horror or the most fantastic stories.

Again I soon began to tire. I felt stifled by the ghostly aura of these mute and yet so expressive objects. Lipotin must have noticed, for he turned to the Princess with an ironic smile:

"After the grand tour round this veritable Aladdin's Cave of marvels, perhaps, Princess, you would like to acquaint our long-suffering friend with the gap which is your secret sorrow, the central point – the vanishing point, if you like – of the whole, magnificent collection? I think he has earned the right."

I had no idea what Lipotin was talking about, and even less about what he and the Princess then whispered and muttered to each other in a hurried exchange in Russian. When they had finished, she turned to me with a smile:

"You must excuse us! Lipotin is pressing me to tell you about the spear ... the spear I assumed was in your possession – you remember? I think it's time I gave you an explanation, isn't it? Of course it is! I hope that when I have told you about what Lipotin calls the 'secret sorrow of the Shotokalungins' you will perhaps ... you will, after all ... "

Once more my throat tightened at the thought: they were going to start their little game about the mysterious spearhead again; and that might bring back all the rather dubious events of this afternoon. I pulled myself together and said, in as expressionless a tone as possible, that I would be happy to hear her explanation.

The Princess led me over to one of the high, glass cabinets and pointed to an empty case lined with velvet and just long enough to take a twelve-inch dagger. She purred:

"You will have noticed that every item in the collection has a card in Russian next to it – my father took care of that – which records its origin and story. You don't speak Russian, so all I need to say is that each card contains the so-called legend of the individual piece. Weapons have often had more interesting lives than the most interesting people, especially as they live longer and have a greater wealth of experiences. It was above all the stories associated with these weapons that fascinated my father, and I must admit that I have inherited this ... this lust for knowledge about these things – if 'things' is the right word for them. And here, you will see, is an empty space. The item it is reserved for was ..."

"Aha!" – I almost startled myself at the speed with which I guessed – "it was stolen."

"N-no." The Princess hesitated. "N-no, not from me; in fact, not stolen at all, in the precise sense of the word. Let us say: lost in some inexplicable way. I prefer not to talk about it: for my father it was the most valuable piece, irreplaceable: and it still is for me. It has been missing since I can remember; I used to dream about the empty velvet even when I was a little girl. Although I bombarded him with questions, my father never told me how the spearhead came to be lost. Every time I asked he would go around with a sad face for days on end." The Princess broke off abruptly and, half absent-mindedly, murmured something to herself in Russian in which I thought I caught the word Isaïs; then she continued out loud: "Just once, shortly before our flight into exile from the Crimea and only a few weeks before his death, he said to me: it will be your task to recover the lost jewel, my child, if all my efforts here on earth are not to have been in vain; I sacrificed more for it than should be expected from any mortal man. You, my child, are wedded to the spearhead dagger, it will be with you on your bridal day.

You can imagine the impression these words of my father's made on me, my friend. Lipotin, who was in his confidence, will tell you how deeply moving was his dying remark about his lifelong efforts to regain possession of the missing spearhead."

Lipotin nodded in agreement. It seemed to me he did not find the memory a pleasant one.

The Princess meanwhile had taken out a tiny bluish steel key and opened the cabinet. She took out the flecked yellowed card and began to read it out to me:

"No. 793b: spearhead of an unidentified alloy (manganese ore with meteoric iron and gold?). At a later period reworked as a dagger blade. Hilt: late Carolingian, probably Spanish/Moorish work, not later than mid-10th century. Thickly encrusted with oriental alexandrites, chrysolites, beryls and three Persian sapphires. Acquired by Piotr Shotokalungin – this was my grandfather – as a gift from Catherine the Great. Originally part of a set of Western European curios, which Tsar Ivan the Terrible is said to have been sent by the great English Queen, Elizabeth. The following traditions are associated with it:

In ancient times this precious blade adorned the irrestible spear of the old hero and Prince of Wales – Hywel, known as 'Dda' which means 'the Good'. Hywel Dda is said to have obtained the weapon with the magic aid of the White Elves, who are the servants of a brotherhood named 'The Gardeners' which guides the fortunes of mankind. Prince Hywel once did these White Elves, who are considered a mighty spirit tribe in Wales, a great favour, for which the King of the Elves instructed him how to make a weapon by grinding a special stone to powder and then mixing it with some drops of his own blood, all the time repeating certain secret magic formulae; from this mixture was forged a spearhead the colour of bloodstone, tougher than any metal, harder than the hardest diamond, which would

310

render its owner invincible, invulnerable for all time and worthy of the highest kingship. And not only that, but protected against the wasting death that comes from woman. Down the centuries the knowledge remained alive in the family of Hywel Dda, the spear was carefully guarded, hope nourished and the rise of the descendants of the great Rhodri to the highest honours repeatedly seemed about to come to pass. But the spearhead was most shamefully lost by one of the line of Hywel Dda – now calling themselves Dee – who, mindless of the elves' promise, fell into evil ways and sought a path to an earthly crown in a wanton bed. And he lost the dagger and his strength and the elves' gift, and a curse fell upon the spear, a curse which will never be broken, unless perhaps the last in the hapless line of Hywel Dda can recover the spear and the old hope. For not until Hywel Dda's spear is washed clean of the blood that once stained it can Hywel Dda be freed from the curse that ends in darkness and destruction."

Here Lipotin interrupted the Princess and said quickly, turning to me: "Moreover, there is a prophecy according to which if a Russian should come into possession of the spearhead, Russia will rule the world in days to come; if it should come into possession of an Englishman, then England will conquer the Russian Empire. But that," he said with an air of studied indifference "leads us to politics, and who is interested in matters of such little consequence?"

The Princess ignored his interruption; she put the faded note back in its place. She looked at me with a tired, absent-minded expression; she seemed to be gently grinding her teeth. She continued:

"Well, my friend, perhaps now you can understand my keenness to follow up any clue that promises to bring back the spear of Hywel Dda, as the legend of my ancestors calls it; for what can excite and satisfy a collector's enthusiasm more than to have carefully locked up in his cabinet an object which would mean life, fortune and eternal bliss for someone in the world outside, if he could only get his hands on that thing that – – I have and I hold!''

At first I could hardly conceal from the others the storm of contending ideas and feelings that all this set off within me; but I was also immediately aware that it was essential to do so. The last mists hiding the fate of my ancertor, John Dee, of my cousin, John Roger, and of myself, were blown away. A wild joy, a wild impatience, a haphazard – and therefore dangerous – bubbling up of all my thoughts, ideas and plans threatened to run away with my tongue, and it was only with the greatest difficulty that I managed to preserve the mask of the polite visitor pretending to a lively interest in the fairy-tales of a past, superstitious age.

At the same time I was shocked by the expression of devilish malice on the Princess' face when she spoke of the sadistic pleasure of the collector who experiences an almost sensual lust in keeping shut away in futile sterility an object which, if it were allowed to fulfil its purpose in the world, could play a decisive role in someone's destiny, save their life or their soul. I found it loathsome that it was precisely the knowledge that such opportunities were being denied that added the real spice to the pleasure of collecting that the Princess had cynically revealed as her own: to find one's highest pleasure in emasculating the virile power of fate, in killing the fruit in the womb of providence, in rendering infertile the fecund force of magic in the world!

It seemed as if Assja Shotokalungin sensed the mistake she had made. She broke off, relocked the case with a moody jangle of keys and murmured a few meaningless phrases as she hustled us out of the gallery. Already turning away, she hardly seemed to be listening to Lipotin's half-serious objection:

"But what will our friend think of me, Princess? He will think that, because I hinted to you that I had discovered a legal heir to the estate of the highly respectable descendants of Hywel Dda, I planned to rob him of a family heirloom that I presumed had come to him like a pigeon home to roost. But I am completely innocent of anything of the kind, my dear lady, even though the Shotokalungin family has employed me for forty years now to seek and recover the lost centre-piece of the family collection, wherever it be, whatever the cost. My forefathers were performing similar services for my lady's ancestors, as far back as the days of Ivan the Terrible, but that is irrelevant as far as my personal respect for your ladyship is concerned. – But I can see that you are a little tired from showing us round the collection, Princess, and here am I chattering on like this. I will come to the point: my instinct for antiques has never yet let me down. When, after all these years, I saw again the empty case that used to contain the dagger I had such a definite presentiment that we would come across the blade in the near future that I almost interrupted you." – He turned to me: "It is one of my little quirks, you see, a superstition of my profession, one of the mysteries of heredity down an almost endless chain of forebears – they all spent their time searching for relics, antiques, traces of old curses and old blessings – that enables me to sense like a truffle-hound when a discovery is near, whether the nearness is one of time or of space. The question is, do I approach the things I seek, or do they come to me, drawn by my desire, or whatever you may call it? The cause is immaterial: I can sense, scent when I will find them. And, dear Princess, I *scent* – may Mascee, the Tsar's tutor, flay me alive if I am wrong – I scent the dagger, the spearhead of your ancestors ... of the ancestors of both of you, if you will permit me to say so ... I can smell ... can scent it nearby ..."

Lipotin's chattering, which, I must admit, had a cynical and rather crude suggestiveness that I found mortifying, accompanied us out of the long gallery and back into the room where we had been before; and there I had the distinct impression that the Princess wanted us to leave.

That corresponded to my wishes entirely; after I had thanked her I was about to add that it was high time for me to go, when the Princess, in a much more lively tone than was to be expected after our rapid exit from the gallery, suddenly asked our forgiveness for her temperamental behaviour. She, too, she said, had felt surprisingly weary; her sleepiness was obviously a punishment for the way she had teased me. She supposed it came from the stale air and smell of camphor that was inevitable in such rooms. However, she rejected the usual suggestion that she should have a lie down almost angrily and cried:

"What I need is fresh air! I'm sure you feel the same, don't you? How is your headache? If I only knew where to suggest we go – my car is at our disposal ..."

Lipotin interrupted her, clapping his hands like a schoolboy on a treat:

"If you have the Lincoln why don't we all go up to see the geysers?"

"Geysers? What geysers? Here? We're not in Iceland, you know," I asked in surprise. Lipotin laughed:

"Haven't you heard that some hot springs have suddenly erupted, out near the lower slopes of the mountains a few days ago. In the ruins of Elsbeth-stein Castle. The locals spend all their time crossing themselves, it's supposed to fulfil some old prophecy, though exactly what it says, I don't know. What is remarkable is that these hot springs bubble up right in the middle of the inner court of Elsbethstein, where a former mistress of the castle, the so-called English Elsbeth, is supposed to have drunk of the water of life. Anyway, it's good publicity for the health spa they'll soon be setting up there."

Lipotin's casual anecdote set off within me a tangle of indistinct echoes; I was going to ask him about this "English Elsbeth" since I, who was born here, had never heard of any such legend connected with Elsbethstein Castle, but everything went too quickly and, anyway, I was still suffering from a distinct tiredness, my brain was still sluggish as you might expect when recovering from a faint – I was tempted to write: narcosis. The quick-fire chatter went over my head and I only caught up with the conversation when the Princess asked me directly whether I would like to spend the rest of the afternoon on an outing in her car to Elsbethstein – it would, she said, be the best thing for a muzzy head.

The only thing that made me hesitate was the thought of Jane; I had promised to be back by now. The image of Jane suddenly dominated my mind, and it seemed the moment had come when I ought to express publicly for the first time what was only the logical consequence of my recent experiences and new attitudes. I did not spend time thinking about it, indeed, I almost blurted out:

"Your invitation to take a trip out into the countryside is, as you might say, just what the doctor ordered, it would restore my shattered nerves somewhat. However, I will have to refuse your kind invitation unless – I hope you will not mind my asking – unless my ... fiancée can accompany us; she expects me back any moment now."

I gave the Princess and Lipotin no opportunity to express their mild surprise, but rushed on:

"You both know my fiancée already, it is Frau Fromm, the lady who ..."

"Ah, your housekeeper?" cried Lipotin, genuinely taken by surprise.

"Yes, my housekeeper," I said with a certain relief, covertly watching the Princess. Assja Shotokalungin shook my hand and gave the gently mocking laugh of an old comrade as she said:

315

"I'm so pleased for you, my friend. So it is only a comma and certainly nothing like a full stop?!"

I could not understand this odd remark; I assumed it was some kind of joke and answered with a laugh. Immediately I felt the laugh was false and a cowardly betrayal of Jane, but again the rapid train of events swept on without me and the Princess continued:

"There is no greater privilege than to share in the happiness of a happy couple for a few hours. Thank you for your suggestion, my friend. It looks like being a charming afternoon."

From then on everything seemed to take place at heightened speed. In a second we were outside the garden gate climbing into the purring limousine. With a shock, I recognised the chauffeur at the wheel: it was John Roger! – No, of course not John Roger. It was the one of the Princess' servants who stood out amongst the orientals because of his height and European features. Naturally the Princess would not want some wild Mongol as a chauffeur.

In a flash we were parked outside my house. Jane seemed to have been expecting us. To my secret astonishment she showed no sign of surprise or hesitation when I told her who was below and that we all planned an outing together along the farther bank of the river. She was excited by the idea and got dressed and ready in an astonishingly short time.

Thus began the memorable trip to Elsbethstein.

Even the meeting between the two women as Jane got into the car went differently from how I would have imagined it. The Princess, as ever, was bright and charming with a hint of mockery in her voice; but Jane was in no way awkward and embarrassed, as I might have feared, not at all overwhelmed by suddenly finding herself in this rather strange situation. Quite the contrary. She greeted the Princess with polite reserve, but with a strange, joyful sparkle in her eye. Her thanks to the owner of the car sounded almost like the calm acceptance of a challenge.

The first thing that struck me when we were all sitting in the wide and luxurious limousine was a certain nervous note in the Princess' laugh which I had never heard before. As she pulled a shawl around her shoulders it almost seemed as if she felt a slight chill.

But my attention was immediately drawn to the chauffeur and the speed he drove at as soon as the suburbs were behind us. It scarcely seemed to be driving, more a kind of gliding, smooth and silent and completely free of the jolting that I would have expected from a country road full of potholes. A glance showed that the needle of the speedometer was on ninety miles an hour and still rising. The Princess did not seem to notice; certainly she said nothing to the chauffeur who sat motionless at the wheel, as if lifeless. I looked at Jane; she was coolly watching the landscape go by out of the window. Her hand lay, relaxed and still, in mine; clearly she was not in the least surprised by the mad speed we were travelling at.

Soon the needle was on ninety-five and creeping up towards a hundred. Then I too was overtaken by a complete indifference to the outward sense impressions of the journey: the sharp crack with which the leaves of roadside trees whipped past, the fleeting glimpses of a dizzying procession of pedestrians, carts and other vehicles which we overtook with a wail of the horn.

I gradually sank into a silent reverie, thinking back over the events of the past few hours. Next to me the Princess's proud profile stared at the landscape rushing wildly past. She sat there like a bronze idol; her face had the expression of a panther poised over its unsuspecting prey: supple, smooth coated and ..

naked. – I pressed my eyes shut, trying to wipe away the film blurring my vision: in vain; I still saw the naked advocate of the sensuous esoteric cult of Isaïs, preaching the erotic pleasures of hatred, of unfathomable, white-hot hatred. Once more I felt the urge to coil my fingers round the throat of this demonic cat-woman and abandon myself to an orgy of hate and fury. A glow of fear crept though my veins and I prayed fervently to ... Jane; as if she were not sitting there hand in hand with me in the speeding car, but were far distant, like a goddess high above the stars, like a mother, inaccessible in heaven.

At that moment a shock gripped my whole body with a jolt of terror: a cart towing tree-trunks in front of us! Two cars approaching from either direction and we racing towards them at a hundred miles an hour! No time to brake! The road too narrow! A steep drop on either side!

The driver! He's still sitting at the wheel, totally unmoved. Has he gone mad? He's accelerating up to a hundred and ten! Overtake on the left? Impossible! The road is blocked by the three vehicles. So he's going to edge out to the – right! My mind screams: He's mad! He'll have us over the side! Another second and we'll be spiked on the tree-trunks over-hanging the back of the cart, better to crash down the precipice! There! The right-hand side of the car is hovering over the yawning abyss with the foaming torrent raging between the rocks below! –

There was scarcely a yard of road left outside the forestry truck as we overtook with only the left-hand wheels on the road: our furious speed kept the car up and saved us from falling.

A quick glance back: the tangle of cars is far behind us, hardly visible any more in the cloud of white dust. "John Roger" is still sitting at the wheel, unmoved, as if it were all child's play. "Only the devil could drive like that," I think, "or a living corpse." And once more we are purring along past swishing three-foot thick sycamore trees.

Lipotin laughed:

"A pretty brisk drive, what? If good old gravity hadn't been taking forty winks, then …"

Slowly, with the stinging of pins and needles, the blood returned to my numbed limbs. I must have been grimacing as I replied:

"A little too brisk for ordinary flesh and blood like mine."

Once more I fell prey to deep suspicion of my companions, even though it was clear to the eye that this trip through familiar countryside was all too real. In spite of all that I told myself, this suspicion included Jane as well. Were these really living human beings that I was sharing the car with? Could they be dead? Spectres from a world that has long since ceased to exist? – –

The Princess turned to me with a mocking expression:

"You are afraid?"

I chose my words carefully. It had not escaped me that since the beginning of the journey Assja Shot-okalungin had shot a number of concerned glances in the direction of Jane, who was sitting next to her. That was something new in her. I was tempted to probe a little, so I answered with a similar smile:

"Not that I am aware of. Unless it is catching amongst friends. I couldn't help noticing that you seem uneasy about something yourself."

The Princess twitched perceptibly. We thundered underneath a bridge, making any answer impossible. Instead of the Princess, Lipotin shouted into the wind:

"I wouldn't have thought the lady and gentleman would be arguing about who is more afraid instead of enjoying the healthy, refreshing air! Anyway: no need for fear when you travel with me. In our family an excessively undramatic manner of coming into the world and leaving it is hereditary."

After a short while Jane said quietly:

"How can anyone be afraid who is following his own way? Only someone who resists his fate will feel fear."

The Princess remained silent. Her face was smiling, but I, and I alone, could see it darken for a split second with the flickering shadow of some inner storm. Then she tapped the chauffeur on the shoulder:

"Why are we going so sluggishly, Roger?"

I felt a slight shock: the chauffeur was called Roger!? An eerie coincidence!

The man at the wheel nodded and the whole car started to sing. The speedometer leapt up to a hundred and twenty and swung wildly to and fro before sticking at some outrageous speed. I looked at Jane: if I die, let it be in her arms.

How we managed to reach the top of the steep and incredibly bumpy track to the ruin of Elsbethstein will always remain a mystery to me. The only explanation I can think of is that we flew up. The tremendous power and solid construction of the limousine made the miracle possible. It was certainly the first car that had ever been seen up there.

We were quickly surrounded by workmen – dripping figures emerging like beings of the underworld from the drifting clouds of hot steam; they leant on their spades and mattocks, marvelling at our arrival, before a fizzing backcloth of spurting geysers. We wandered silently round the pleasantly wooded ruins and I was struck by the sense of design in the arrangement of the bushes, as if some gardener had created the delightful vistas through the trees down into the depths of the valley. The half overgrown flowerbeds beside the massive, crumbling walls formed a strange, romantic contrast. It was like walking through an enchanted garden where moss-covered statues without arms or heads suddenly popped up, as if placed there by some fairy to frighten or tease the visitors. Then there was a fissure in the rock, and, glistening in the depths, the foaming current.

Someone asked:

"Who can it be who keeps this ravishing disorder in such beautiful order?"

No-one knew.

"Didn't you tell us about a legend connected with Elsbethstein, Lipotin? Something about a lady of the castle called Elsbeth, who drank of the water of life here?"

"Someone or other told me something of the kind, yes", said Lipotin dismissively; "I couldn't remember the whole story any more. It just came to me this afternoon; I intended it more as a joke."

"We could ask one of the workmen in the courtyard", remarked the Princess, casually.

"It's an idea."

We made our way slowly back to the inner courtyard.

Lipotin took out his ivory cigarette case and offered it to one of the workmen.

"Who does the ruin actually belong to?"

"Nobody."

"But it must belong to somebody!"

"Nobody. Ask the old gardener in there!" muttered one of the group and continued to clean his spade with a wooden splint as carefully as if it had been a surgical instrument. The others laughed and exchanged knowing looks.

One young lad looked longingly at the cigarette case, and when Lipotin held it out to him he became talkative.

"He's not quite right in the head, the old man. He pretends he's the castle steward, but nobody takes him seriously, he's just not quite right in the head. I think he's a gardener or something like that, at least he's always digging up the ground. He's not from hereabouts. And ancient. My grandfather knew him. Nobody knows where he came from. Ask him yourself." The young workman suddenly dried up; the mattocks thumped into the earth again, once more the spades heaved clods of earth out of the ditch. Not another word could be got out of the workers.

We set off for the keep, Lipotin in the lead. A door of rotten wood held together with rusty wrought iron bands guarded the entrance. When we pushed it open it screeched like some animal startled out of a deep sleep. A decrepit old oak staircase, that had clearly once been richly decorated with carvings, led up into a blackness barred with slanting strips of light falling from above.

Lipotin squeezed through an arched entrance, whose massive wooden door was half off its hinges, into a kind of kitchen. We followed.

I started:

There in the skeleton of an armchair – there were still strips of leather hanging down – lay the corpse of a white-haired old man. On the broken stove was a cracked earthenware pot with a little pool of milk in the bottom. Next to it was a mouldy crust of bread.

Suddenly the old man, whom I had assumed was dead, opened his eyes and stared at us.

At first I thought my eyes must be deceiving me: the old man was dressed in rags which had buttons with a coat of arms on them and a few gold threads so that they looked like a livery from a former century; together with his yellow face as dried as a mummy's this all suggested we were in the presence of a corpse, long since forgotten and decayed.

Lipotin was undaunted: "May we go up the tower, steward, to look at the view from the top?"

The answer he received – after politely repeating his request – was strange enough:

"There is no need today. Everything has been taken care of already."

As he spoke the old man kept shaking his head, though it was not clear whether this was from old age or to emphasise his refusal.

"What has been taken care of?" Lipotin shouted in his ear.

"Going up and keeping a lookout. She will not be coming today now."

We assumed the old man was expecting someone. In the dim recesses of his consciousness he probably thought we had come to help him keep an eye open for his visitor. Probably someone who brought him his frugal meals.

The Princess took out her purse and hastily handed a gold coin to Lipotin:

"Give that to the poor devil. He's obviously weak in the head. Let's go."

Suddenly the old man opened his eyes wide and looked at us one after the other; but not in the face, rather he looked over our heads. "It's all right", he murmured, "it's all right. Go on up. Perhaps my Lady is coming after all."

"Which lady?" – Lipotin handed the old man the Princess' gift but he rejected the money with a hasty gesture:

"The garden has been taken care of; there is no need for a reward. The Lady will be content. If only she did not stay away for so long. When winter comes I cannot water the flowers any more. I have been waiting for ... for ..."

"Well, how long have you been waiting, old man?"

"Old man? – But I'm not old. No, no I'm not old. Waiting keeps you young. I'm young, as you can see."

The words sounded funny but we did not feel like laughing.

"And how long have you been here, my good fellow?" Lipotin persisted.

"How ... long ... have I been here? How should I know that?" the old man shook his head.

"Think! You must have come up here for the first time once? Or were you born up here?"

"No, no I came up here. That is right. I came up here, thank God! And when? You can't count time."

"Can you not remember where you were before?"

"Before? But I wasn't anywhere before."

"But my good fellow! Where were you born, if not up here?"

"Born? I wasn't born; I was drowned."

The more meaningless the mad old man's answers seemed to become, the more uncanny they seemed to me and my curiosity began to torment me to uncover the perhaps trivial secret of this shipwrecked mariner on the shores of life. The workman's words: "He's always digging up the ground", came back to me. Was it some treasure that the old man kept searching for in the ruins and was it that that had driven him mad?

Jane and Lipotin seemed to be in the grip of the same curiosity. Only the Princess was standing to one side in a proud indifference which I had not noticed in her before; in vain she kept trying to get us to leave.

Lipotin, who not unnaturally could make no sense of the old man's last reply, raised his eyebrows at us and was trying to think up some cunning, probing question, when abruptly the old man started to talk, hastily, almost as if driven by some machinery like an automaton. Some cogwheel must have been released, setting in motion a memory which whirred on of its own accord:

"Yes, yes; then I surfaced out of the green water. Yes, yes; rose straight up to the surface. And I walked, walked, walked until I heard of the Queen at Elsbethstein. Yes, I came here, thank God. I am a gardener, yes, yes. And I dug … until … thank God. And now I keep the garden tidy for the Queen, as I have been told. So that she will be glad when she comes, you understand? That is not difficult to understand, is it? Nobody should be surprised at that, should they?"

At these words an inexplicable tremor ran through me. I grasped Jane's hand as if a squeeze from it could help protect or support me. Lipotin's cynical features twisted themselves – or so it seemed to me, at least – into a fanatical expression of blind sadistic lust. He pressed the old man:

"And won't you tell us who your lady is. Perhaps we can give you news of her."

The old man shook his head violently, but his straggly-haired skull wobbled uncontrollably in all directions so that it was impossible to tell whether he intended to express agreement or disagreement. His hoarse croaking could have just as well been a denial as an outburst of mad laughter.

"My Lady? Who knows my Lady? You, I should think, Sir" – he turned to me and then to Jane – "you know her; and you, young lady, I am sure you know her very well, your face tells me that. Yes, your face tells me that. You ... you ..."

He wandered off into incomprehensible mutterings whilst his gaze bored into Jane's eyes with the expression of one who is desperately trying to bring some memory back to mind.

Involuntarily she took a swift step towards the mad old gardener, or whatever he was, and immediately his trembling hand grasped at her dress, catching the coat hanging loosely round her shoulders. He clutched it fervently, and such a beatific expression came over his features that it seemed for a moment as if his brain had cleared. But the moment of clarity went as quickly as it had come and the expression of indescribable emptiness returned to his face.

I could see by the look on Jane's face that she too was making every effort to awaken some memory that was sleeping in the inner depths, but with no greater success. I assume that she asked her question just to fill the embarrassing silence, so uncertain did her voice sound:

"Whom do you mean by your Lady, my friend? You are wrong if you think I know her. And I am sure this is the first time I have ever seen you, either."

The old man kept shaking his head as he stammered:

"No, no, no; what are you saying! I'm not wrong. No, no, I know better – and you, young lady, you know ...," he spoke swiftly and with a mysterious urgency and his gaze was directed into the empty air, as if that was where he saw Jane's face, instead of right in front of him, "... you know: Queen Elsbeth rode out hunting for a husband when all thought she was dead. Queen Elsbeth drank of the water of life! I am waiting for her here ... they told me I have been waiting since ... I saw her ride off out of the West, where the water is green, to find her bridegroom. One day she will rise from the earth when the waters flow. She will rise from the green waters, just as I did, just as you have, young lady ... yes, yes, just as we all have .... You know as well as I do: she is the enemy of the lady there! Yes, yes, I have heard all about it! We gardeners come across all sorts of things, hee, hee! when we are digging. Oh yes, I know, the enemy wants to obstruct Queen Elsbeth's wedding. And that's why I have to wait so long until I pick the bride's posy. But that doesn't matter. I can wait. I'm still young. And you are young too, young lady, and you know our enemy. Oh yes you do or I'm very much mistaken. No, no, I don't make mistakes, not I, young lady."

The sad encounter with the mad old gardener of Elsbethstein was beginning to become embarrassing. It was true that the old man's confused ramblings did seem to make a kind of sense – at least to my prejudiced ears – that somehow fitted in with the mysterious and fantastic events I had been through. But what does one not see or hear as a secret revelation of the voice of nature when the heart is full and wants to hear?! The most likely explanation

326

was that the old madman was weaving experiences of his own, which had engraved themselves on his mind, with the popular legends about Elsbethstein into a crazy, half real, half imaginary garland.

Suddenly, from one of the dark corners of the hearth, the old man took up an object which reflected the dying rays of the sun in a fiery glitter and held it out to Jane. Lipotin's head shot forward like a vulture's. A hot current coursed through my veins too:

In his claw-like fingers the old man held a dagger with a long handle. A noble example of the sword-smith's art with a short, broad and obviously still dangerously sharp blade, it was of a metal unknown to me and a strange bluish-white in colour; the general shape was that of a spearhead. The haft seemed to be inset with Persian chrysolites, but I could not see them very clearly, for the old man was waving the dagger about in the air and the light in the tower kitchen was growing dim.

The Princess, as if by instinct – until that moment she could not have seen the dagger – turned round to face us. Until then she had stood apart, prodding the crumbling brickwork with her umbrella in bored irritation. In a most unladylike manner she pushed us aside and grabbed at the weapon, her collector's lust brushing aside all considerations of politeness.

Like lightning the old madman withdrew his arm back to his chest.

A strange sound came from the Princess' mouth. The only thing I can compare it to is the hissing of a cat facing up to battle. It all passed so quickly that a second later it seemed unreal. Then I heard the old man bleat:

"No, no; not for you, old ... old woman! There, take it young lady. The dagger is for you. I have been keeping it long enough for you. I knew that you would come."

The Princess did not register the insult which the phrase "old woman" must have contained, especially as she could scarcely be much older than Jane. Perhaps she just ignored it. She stretched out her hand again and offered fabulous and ever increasing sums for the blade. I found the collector's blind passion to possess the desired object highly amusing. I did not doubt for one second that the old pauper, mad as he was, would accept the offer, especially as such a sum must have been wealth beyond his wildest dreams. But the unexpected happened. What caused it I could not tell. Was it some other, weird spirit that had taken control of a soul that had lost its senses anyway, or did the old madman no longer have any idea of the meaning of riches? Whatever it was, he raised his eyes to the Princess and a horrible expression of insane hatred flickered across his features. Then he screamed at her, his shrill voice cracking:

"Not to you, old ... woman! Not to you, not for all your filthy lucre! Not for all the filthy lucre in the world. There, take it young lady! Quick! The old enemy is here! See her hissing and spitting, see her mouth gape. Grab it quickly! There ... there ... there ... take the dagger! Keep it safe. If the enemy should get it, then that is the end of my Lady, that is the end of the wedding, that is the end of me, poor unworldly gardener that I am. I have kept it until today. I have never betrayed my Lady. I have never told where I had it from. Go now, all of you, go now!"

Jane, as if hypnotised by the strange words, had taken hold of the dagger and with a quick twist of the wrist concealed it in her clothes, out of the reach of the Princess' hawk-like swoop. My eye caught the dull, flinty gleam of the spear-shaped blade. Like a flash the thought went through my head: the blood-stone of Hywel Dda! The dagger of John Dee! – But there was no time to say it out loud. I looked at the Princess; she had herself under control again. Not a flicker betrayed what must have been going on inside her. I sensed the wild passions raging within, like tigers trying to tear down the bars of their cage.

Lipotin's behaviour during the whole sequence of events had been bizarre. At first merely curious, at the sight of the dagger he seemed to go mad. "You're making a mistake," he had screamed at the old gardener, "a stupid mistake not to give it to the Princess. It's not a dagger at all, it's …" The old man did not even glance at him.

Jane herself behaved in a way I did not understand either. I assumed she would fall into one of her trances, but no sign of it appeared in her eyes. Rather she gave the Princess the sweetest of smiles, even held out her hand to her and said:

"This trivial matter will bring us all the closer together, will it not, Assja Shotokalungin?"

What a way to talk to the Princess! What did Jane think she was doing? To my even greater astonishment, however, the normally so proud Russian aristocrat answered Jane's rather sudden familiarity with a charming smile, threw her arms around her and kissed her. A sudden voice shouted inside me: Jane, keep hold of the dagger! I hoped she would sense what was in my mind, but, to my horror, she said to the Princess, "I will, of course, let you have the dagger when a suitably … festive occasion presents itself."

Not another word could be got out of the old man in his skeleton chair. He just went on chewing his crust of bread with his toothless gums as if he were completely alone. He seemed to have forgotten our presence. A disconcerting old fool.

It was not a talkative group that left the tower by the last light of the setting sun, whose rays were refracted into all the colours of the rainbow by the billowing steam-clouds from the geysers.

On the dark wooden stairs I gripped Jane's hand and whispered to her:

"Are you really going to give the dagger to the Princess?"

She replied hesitantly; there was something I found alien in her voice:

"Why not, dearest? If she is so desperate for it?"

As we were preparing to drive down from the ruins I turned round for one last look; framed in the gate as in a massive proscenium arch I saw a spectacle I shall never forget: lit by the fiery red of the setting sun and surrounded by crumbling piles of masonry, the flowerbeds of Elsbethstein were a blaze of wild glory. A sudden gust of wind swept the clouds of mist from the geysers across the overgrown park and it seemed to me to that it coalesced into the majestic figure of a woman dressed in flowing silvery robes striding towards the tower. The Lady of the castle? The legendary Queen Elsbeth, suggested to my receptive senses by the mad steward of the tower, the "gardener"?

Then I was back in the car, dazed by the breakneck drive down to the valley. No-one spoke.

Suddenly I heard the Princess say:

"Frau Fromm, what would you say to a repeat of our outing to that fairytale castle in the near future?"

Jane gave a smile of agreement and replied:

"There is nothing that would give me more pleasure than to accept such an invitation."

I was quietly pleased that the two women got on so well together, especially when I saw the Princess take Jane's hand and press it warmly. This mutual friendship seemed to remove a burden of dark forebodings that had weighed upon me, though I could not say why. Reassured, I looked up out of the window of the noiseless, gliding Lincoln at the radiant evening sky.

High up in the turquoise vault of the sky gleamed the thin sickle of the waning moon.

The Second Vision

The moment we were back in my apartment I asked

330

Jane to let me have a closer look at the mad old gardener's strange gift.

I subjected the dagger to a thorough examination. I immediately saw that the blade and the handle had not originally belonged together. The blade had obviously been a spearhead which had snapped off at the socket. There was something strange about the metal, which I had not come across before. It looked oily – not at all like steel– with a dull gleam, almost like flint. And then the jewel-encrusted haft! There could be no doubt about it: the copper alloyed with a small amount of tin showed all the signs of south-west Carolingian or early Moorish work. Beryls, chrysolites and there, an interlacing ornament, difficult to decipher – some dragon-like being? Three rings around it, two empty, the stones removed. In the third a sapphire; above the dragons' heads a crowning gem. Spontaneously the image of a shining rock crystal appeared before my mind's eye.

I said to myself: this dagger fits the description in the Princess' glass case like no other. No wonder she was so excited when she saw it.

The whole time Jane was behind me, looking over my shoulder.

"What do you find so interesting about that old paper knife, dear?"

"Paper knife?" At first I could not understand what she was talking about; then I had to laugh at female ignorance that could see a thousand-year-old blade as a letter opener.

"You're laughing at me, love. Why?"

"Darling, you're a little off target; that isn't a paper knife, it's a Moorish dagger."

Jane shook her head.

"You don't believe me, Jane?"

"Why shouldn't I? It just looked like a paper knife to me."

"How did you come upon such an idea?"

"It was the other way round; the idea just came to me."

"What came to you?"

"That it is a paper knife. I knew that straightaway."

I looked at Jane; she was staring at the dagger. I had a sudden thought:

"Have you seen the dagger, the ... paper knife before?"

"How could I have seen it before if it was only this afternoon that ... but, wait a moment, you're quite right: now I look at the thing ... the longer I ... the longer I look at it ... the more I'm sure that I have seen it before." More she would not say.

I was too full of excitement to risk an experiment with Jane. I would not have known how to go about it anyway. There were so many thoughts and ideas crowding into my mind that, in order to be alone, I pretended I had some important writing to do to get Jane to go about her housework. I covered her face with kisses as she left the room.

Hardly was the door shut behind her than I rushed to my desk and started rummaging through John Dee's papers and the pile of my own excerpts to find where my ancestor might have mentioned the dagger that was an heirloom in the family. I found nothing. Eventually my hand fell on the green notebook; I opened it at random and read:

And in that night of darkest temptation I lost the thing that was most dear to me: my talisman, the dagger – the spearhead of my ancestor Hywel Dda. I lost it in the park meadow during the conjuration; and I seem to remember that I held it in my hand, according to the instructions of Bartlett Greene, as the spectre approached and I stretched out my hand to it. – But after that, no more! – Thus it was that I rewarded Black Isaïs for anything that I afterward received of Black Isaïs. – – And it seems to me too high a price for her deceits.

I pondered long: what did "too high a price" mean? –
There were no more clues in the documents. Suddenly I had an idea; my hand snatched up the polished
coal scrying glass.

But it was just the same as the first time I tried to
read in its darkly shining surfaces. The coal in my
hand remained a lump of coal.

Then I remembered Lipotin and his incense. I leapt
up and soon found the red sphere, but it was empty,
completely empty and useless.

At the same moment I noticed the onyx bowl in
which we had heated the incense. Had Jane, with the
instinctive action of a housewife, cleaned it out? No,
there was still a dark brown crust left by the magic
drug. From that moment on there was no more calm
reflection; it was as if I were acting under compulsion. I grasped the lamp and poured some spirit from
it into the bowl. As it flared up the thought passed
through my mind: Perhaps what I am doing is not so
stupid – perhaps there is a little left ...

The flame soon died down. There was a tiny
glowing ember amongst the ashes. A thin column of
smoke rose up.

Quickly I leant over the bowl and breathed deeply.
The smoke tasted even more acrid than before as I
felt it spread down to my chest. Disgusting! Unbearable! Will it be possible for me on my own, without
outside help, to cross the threshold of suffocation
and reach the other side? Should I call Jane? Ask her to
hold my head fast over the bowl, unwavering as I
suffocate? The red-capped "Lipotin" did it with a
grip of iron, but Jane?! Calling on all my reserves of
strength and determination, I clenched my teeth
against the upsurge of nausea ... "Do or Die!" – the
watchword of my ancestors suddenly came back to
me, the motto of the Dees!

Then the terrible shudders of the death throes.
Scraps of thought course through my veins: it is like
drowning in shallow water. – Do or die! – Suicide in a

wash-basin ... only hysterical women can manage that, I once heard it said. Well done, hysterical women, then! I am only a man and it seemed damned difficult to me. Damned difficult ... aah! Help! Save me! ... There he is ... a long way off ... the red-capped monk, gigantic ... the Master of Initiation ... he doesn't look at all like Lipotin ... he is raising his hand, his left hand ... he is going behind me ... all at once I plunge down into the realm of the dead.

When I staggered to my feet, the back of my head ringing with pain, the poison seeming to penetrate every fibre of my body, all that was left in the stinking bowl was ashes. I had to collect my scattered wits before I remembered what the purpose of it all was: I grabbed the coal scrying glass and stared at its polished surface. A feeling of calm came over me: for the second time, and all on my own, I had passed through the portals of death.

Then I saw myself sitting in a car going back-wards, the boot first then the bonnet and the radiator, racing in ghostly silence along the river. On either side of me sat Jane and Assja Shotokalungin. Both were looking straight ahead; not an eyelid, not a muscle in their faces moved.

The ruins of Elsbethstein flew by. "The fountain of life," I said to myself. Clouds of fine white steam rose from the courtyard. On top of the high tower stood the mad old gardener, waving at us. He waved his arm violently in a north-westerly direction and then pointed at himself, as if to say: First of all over there and then ... back to me.

"Damn," whispered a voice inside me, "the old man doesn't know I have returned to my true self, Doctor John Dee." But if that's the case, it occurred to me, how is it that Princess Assja Shotokalungin is sitting here beside me? I glanced at her. Next to me was – the dark bronze idol of the Thracian cult of Isaïs, holding the mirror and the spear and bending towards me, naked – naked and in an attitude that set

334

all my senses on fire. My reason desperately tried to reassert its control: once more the Cat Goddess is trying to ensnare me in the tentacles of lust. Must I succumb, whether I want to or not? Am I no longer master of my own body? What is it that compels my mind's eye to keep on seeing the Princess as she never appeared to me in the flesh. I refuse! I refuse! I refuse to share the fate of my cousin, John Roger.

The youthful goddess with the firm, glistening skin threw me an indescribable glance. It combined the unapproachable majesty of a goddess with the seductive accessibility of a woman: a slight, sensual tautening of the breasts, a voluptuous stretching of the limbs, profound contempt in her enigmatic expression, ruin glinting from the slits of her eyes, the stench of panther ...

The limousine has long since acquired a sharp-edged keel and dived down through a froth of green waves. We speed along through the green water, impossible to say how deep below us, how high above us it stretches, impossible to tell which way is up, which down.

Now there is nothing left of the green waters except a small circular lake which I am looking back at with great concentration. Like a tunnel entrance it gradually reduces in size amidst the deepest darkness.

Then I have the feeling of rising to the surface; of rising to the surface of a deep well-shaft surrounded by a parapet of white stone with immeasurable depths yawning below me. Above the edge of the well-shaft drifts the nebulous form of the bronze Thracian Isaïs. With a malevolent smile she points downwards with the broken-off spearhead. She holds the mirror aloft as she appears to sink. It is as if the tiny, circular green lake is gleaming at the bottom of the well.

Is it the Goddess herself who drew me here? Here? Where am I?

I have not fully formulated the question when a shock cuts through me. There, right in front of me in the semi-darkness – – Jane, my wife! I can see her troubled gaze. She is wearing a dress from the time of Queen Elizabeth and I know that she is the wife of John Dee – the John Dee who I am myself. It is the awesome well in the cellar of my host, Doctor Hajek, in Prague and she is about to throw herself into it. It is the night following the command of the Green Angel and I, with breaking heart but obedient to my oath, have had to hand over my wife Jane, my only love, to Edward Kelley, my blood brother, that he should enjoy – o what torment! – the same conjugal rights. It has broken her spirit.

No time to think about that. I jump up to pull Jane back, my old man's knee gives way, I slip, scream, see the insane, dead look in the eyes of my beloved, my violated wife – and the blood freezes in my veins as I witness the terrible fall; the farewell of my despairing wife is something that can never be purged from my soul.

My mind is numb, as if my brain were dead. One thought penetrates to semi-consciousness: my heart is cut up into seventy-two pieces. The well-shaft, the awesome well-shaft! Paralysed, I sense rather than see the circular gleam of the mirror of Isaïs …

With all sensation gone from my legs, I climb the ladder out of the cellar. Every rung groans: "alone … alone … alone … alone …" A head appears through the opening of the trapdoor: a distorted face, the face of a criminal at the gallows, the face of Kelley, the man with the cut-off ears.

My first thought is: he will take hold of me and push me down; he will throw me down the shaft to join Jane.

I do not care, indeed, I long for it. –

He does not move. He lets me finish my pre-cipitous climb, lets me crawl out of the void onto firm ground. Step by step he backs away from me, as if from a ghost. The lust for revenge, which the miserable coward is so frightened of, has died within me.

He stammers something about coming to save her about women being over-excitable ...

In a toneless voice I say: "She is dead. She has gone down into the abyss to prepare the way for me. On the third day she will rise again to ascend into heaven and sit at the right hand of God, whence she will come to judge the murderers in this life and the next ..." then I hear the insane blasphemies my lips are repeating and am silent.

God will not – I think, but it's a lame excuse – hold a soul in such distress responsible for these blasphemies. Would that I were already resting on ...

Kelley heaves a sigh of relief. Becomes bolder. Slides up to me cautiously and offers me his slimy condolences:

"Brother, her sacrifice – and yours – has not been in vain. The holy Green Angel ..."

I look across to Kelley, my eyes burning; the first pain I feel in my numb body is in my eyes. "The Angel!" I exclaim and a wild surge of hope fills me: has the promised Stone been granted? Then ... perhaps ... with God all things are possible ... miracles have occurred ... the daughter of Jairus rose from the dead. The Stone of Transformation can work miracles in the hand of one who uses it with the true faith! Jane?! Is she less than the daughter of Jairus? Aloud I cry: "Has the Angel brought the Stone?"

Kelley is all eagerness:

"No, no, not the Stone, not yet ..."

"The key to the book?"

"N-no, that neither. But red powder: gold, fresh gold. And he has promised more, much more ..."

A cry tears its way out of my tormented heart:

"Did I sell my wife for gold, thou cur?! Slug! Cheapjack!"

Kelley jumps back. I see my clenched fists drop limply to my sides. Nothing will obey me any more. I want my hands to murder, but they are paralysed. I

337

cannot find the command that will compel them to obey. A laugh, bitter as gall, rattles my throat:

"No need to fear, thou of the cut-off ears; I will not kill my instrument ... I intend to question the Green Angel face to face."

Kelley hastens to reassure me:

"Oh my brother, that is right; the holy Green Angel can do anything. If he so desires he can bring our ... no, no, I mean: your wife back from the dead."

My body becomes an animal poised to pounce; I leap forward instinctively, without thinking. My hands grasp Kelley by the throat:

"Bring the Green Angel to me, villain! Bring him to face me and I will spare your life!"

Kelley sinks to his knees.

The picture dissolves into a kaleidoscope of blurred images rushing through my brain; every time I think I can grasp one, it dissolves into mist. Then the screen clears to reveal Kelley in costly garments trimmed with rich furs strutting proudly about the state apartments of Rosenberg's Palace. He calls himself God's ambassador who is chosen to bring the secret of the threefold transformation of mankind: not to the common mass, but to the chosen few. And from now on the divine mystery is to have an indestructible earthly temple; and Rudolf, the Holy Roman Emperor, and those of his paladins that are worthy will be the guardians of the new grail.

In a secret, secluded chamber of the Palace, Rosenberg leads Kelley by the hand towards the Emperor, who is awaiting the prophet in an ominously over-excited state.

I have been compelled to join in the solemn procession: Rudolf has commanded just the two of us and Rosenberg into his presence. Rosenberg falls to his knees before the Emperor and washes his hands with tears of joy.

"Your Majesty, the Angel has revealed himself to us; truly, he has revealed himself," he sobs.

The Emperor can scarcely conceal his excitement. He clears his throat:

"If that is so, Rosenberg, then we will all bow down and worship him, for we have spent our whole lives waiting for the Lord." – Then, darkly threatening, he turns to us:

"You are three, as were once the Wise Men who brought news of the birth of man's salvation – and gifts: the one on his knees has brought me the news – may it bring him blessing: you other two wise men – where are the gifts you bring?"

Kelley rushes forward and merely sketches a bow:

"Here; this is the gift the Angel sends to His Majesty, Emperor Rudolf."

He hands over to Rudolf a golden casket containing twice the amount of the red powder as we possessed when we first arrived in Prague.

Disappointment etches itself on the Emperor's face; he accepts the casket reluctantly:

"That is a great gift. But it is not the truth I have so long yearned for. Any fool can make gold with it." He turns his burning eyes on me. I am the 'Wise Man' from whom he expects the true, redeeming gift. I tremble with cold as I kneel down, for my hands and my heart are empty. But Kelley raises his voice once more, and his cocky self-assurance is remarkable:

"We have been commanded to hand over for Your Majesty's inspection the scrying glass that the Angel granted from the storehouse of his grace to his servant, Doctor John Dee, on the night of his first calling. For all mysteries have their orders and ranks of initiation."

I do not know where it came from, but suddenly the scrying glass, the polished coal of Bartlett Greene with its gold stand, is in my hand. Without a word, I present it to the Emperor. He reaches out for it with a hasty hand, examines it; his lower lip droops:

"What use is this?"

Kelley kneels and fixes his eyes on a spot between the Emperor's eyes.

Rudolf, receiving no answer, turns with a frown of irritation back to the glistening surfaces of the black crystal. Kelley's eyes seem to bore into the Emperor's forehead. In his effort, the sweat drips unnoticed from his brow.

The Emperor sits as if spellbound, holding the glass in both hands. His pupils dilate, like a man in a trance. Suddenly: astonishment, a flutter of pity, anger, horror, trembling expectation, relief, triumph, proud exultation, a tired nod of the eagle's head and then – – a tear!

A tear in the eye of Emperor Rudolf!

All these emotions follow each other in quick succession across the Emperor's face. The tension amongst us is unbearable. Finally Rudolf says:

"I thank you, messengers of the world above. It is, indeed, a precious gift and one that gives satisfaction to a man whose head has been consecrated with the holy oil. For not every head that bears a crown in this world will bear it in the next. We will redouble Our endeavours." The Emperor bows his proud head. I cannot control the sob that rises in my throat to see His Majesty humble himself before the seducer with the cut-off ears.

The people are crowding outside the Church of the Maltese Order in the narrow square in Prague known as the Square of the Grand Prior. The whole of the Malá Strana seems to be on its feet. Everywhere there is a glint of weapons and in the open windows of the palaces the costumes of the nobles watching the approaching spectacle glitter with jewels.

A stately procession leaves the Church of the Maltese Order.

Kelley, now a Bohemian Baron, has just been dubbed Paladin of the Holy Roman Empire by order of the Emperor at the altar of the ancient church.

The procession sets off, led by three heralds in yellow and black, two with long trumpets at their lips, the third bearing the Emperor's parchment. At every street corner there are fanfares and a reading of the Emperor's patent for the new baron, "Sir" Edward Kelley from England.

From the balconies and decorated oriel windows of the nobles' palaces, curious faces look down, pale faces with proud, impenetrable expressions or moved by a flicker of scorn as they acknowledge the latest malicious jibe.

I watch the hubbub from a window of the Nostitz palace. My soul is enveloped in dark thoughts like thick November mists. In vain are all the compliments of Count Nostitz, who has invited me along with Doctor Hajek, about the true pride I have shown in my ancient line of nobility by refusing all such flummery titles, however exalted the hand that grants them. It is all one to me. My wife Jane has gone from me, lost in the green abyss ...

A new strange picture takes over: Rabbi Löw is standing in his favourite posture, his long body leaning against the wall with his fingers spread out behind him, in the tiny room in the Street of the Alchemists. Before him Emperor Rudolf is slumped in a chair; sleeping like a pet cat at his feet is the Barbary lion. The Rabbi and the Cat-King are the best of friends. I am sitting at the little window; outside the trees have almost lost their leaves. Looking down through the bare branches I can see two gigantic black bears peering up, their shaggy heads raised, noses aquiver above red, gaping jaws.

Rabbi Löw rocks back and forth against the wall; then, with a jerky movement, he pulls his hand out from behind his back. He grasps the coal scrying glass that the Emperor holds out to him and looks long and hard at the polished surface. Then he throws his head back so far that his bony Adam's apple is visible beneath his white beard; his mouth is open in what seems to be a soundless laugh:

341

"In a mirror a man sees nothing but himself. He who wants to see will see what he wants in the coal, for the life that was once within it has long since burnt out."

The Emperor starts up:

"Do you mean the glass is a trick, my friend? I myself saw ..."

The old Jew does not move from the wall. He looks up at the ceiling and shakes his head:

"Is Rudolf a trick? Rudolf has been polished into majesty like a stone, polished hard so that he can reflect the history of the Holy Roman Empire. But neither the majesty nor the stone has any heart."

My soul is cut to the quick. I look at the High Rabbi and feel the sacrificial knife at my throat ...

Need has been banished from Doctor Hajek's hospitable house. Gold pours in from all sides. For the favour of being allowed to attend one of Kelley's seances Rosenberg sends gift after gift, each one more magnificent, more costly than the last. The old count is prepared to sacrifice not only his goods but his whole life to the revelations of the new temple, to the "Lodge of the West Window".

He has been allowed to accompany us down into Doctor Hajek's cellar. –

The seance begins in the gloomy cellar. All is just as it was the previous time. Only Jane is missing. I feel as if I am suffocating, so tightly does expectation constrict my throat. Now the Angel must answer for the woman I sacrificed to it.

Rosenberg is trembling all over; he keeps on mumbling prayers to himself.

Kelley is in his seat. He falls into a trance.

Now he has gone. In his place a green glow announces the arrival of the Angel. Rosenberg prostrates himslf in awe before the vision. I can hear his choking sobs: "I have been found worthy ... I have b–been f–found ... worthy ..."

342

The sobs become a whimper. The Count lies in the dust, babbling like an old man in second childhood.

The Angel turns its icy eye on me. I want to speak, but my throat is dry. The sight is too much for me. I make a supreme effort; I pull all my strength together – once – and again – and again – – in vain! The stony stare paralyses me, paralyses me completely.

From an immense distance the Angel speaks to me:

"Thy presence is not welcome to me, John Dee. It is not wise to kick against the pricks, not God-fearing to set thy face against the trials. How shall the holy work of salvation be performed if the apprentice cannot free his heart of unholiness? The key and the Stone are won by obedience alone! Disobedience brings waiting, banishment. Attend my will in Mortlake, John Dee!"

The signs of the zodiac in the sky? What can they signify? A turning wheel? Ah, I understand: years and years and years that slip by: time, time. Then desolate, burnt-out ruins all around.

I am walking through blackened walls, with rotten tapestries flapping in the wind. My foot stumbles over long-lost thresholds without me, the former carefree lord of the castle, being able to tell into which room they have led me. And I cannot say that I walk; I shuffle, dragging tired, tired feet.

I clamber up a half-burnt wooden staircase. Splinters and rusty nails tear at my threadbare coat. I enter a musty room – the laboratory where once I made gold! The floor is made of worn-out bricks packed together, ends uppermost. In one corner is a stove on which sits a bowl my dogs used to drink out of; there is a little pool of milk at the bottom and a crust of dry bread next to it. The room is protected from the open sky by a sloping roof of bare planks; the cold autumn wind whimpers through the gaps. This is Mortlake Castle which burned behind me when I left for Prague and Emperor Rudolf five years ago.

The old laboratory is the best-preserved room within the walls. With my own hands I have made it into a rough and ready shelter that I share with the owls and bats.

I see myself: completely neglected, a tangle of snow-white hair, a tangled silver beard sprouting from my nostrils and ears.

A ruin of a house and a ruin of a man.

No crown of England, no throne of Greenland – no Queen at my side and no crystal shining over my head. My one happiness is to know that my son, Arthur, is safe with relatives of my dead wife, far away in Scotland. – I have been obedient to the Angel of the West Window, obedient to his command and obedient to his sentence – – – of banishment?

I am freezing, even though my friend Price has brought blankets to wrap me in. It is the cold of old age within me. And always deep within my decaying body there is a burrowing pain, something gnawing at my vitals.

Price bends over me, listening at my back with his doctor's trained ear. He murmurs:

"Healthy. Sweet breath. Bodily fluids well balanced. A heart of iron."

I giggle:

"Yes. A heart of iron."

And Queen Elizabeth is long since dead! The charming, courageous, cutting, seductive, regal, destructive, gracious, ungracious Elizabeth is dead ... dead ... long since dead. She left no message for me, sent me no message where I should seek her. No sign that she sees me. I sit in my chair at the brick stove under the deal roof, listening to the crump of the mass of snow as it slips to the ground and cocooning myself in the past.

Price appears at the ladder, old Talbot Price, my doctor and my last friend. I talk to him about Queen Elizabeth. Only of Elizabeth ...

344

After a lot of hesitation he tells me a strange story. He was called to her sick-bed as she lay dying. She insisted on having the Windsor country doctor about her; in the past he had given her much good advice. He was alone at her bedside one night. She was feverish, her mind wandering. She talked of her departure for another land. For a land across the sea where her bridegroom lived, the bridegroom who had been waiting for her all her life: "There, where stands the castle with the fountain and the water of eternal life!" There she would go and there she would live in the sweet-scented garden and wait for her bridegroom. The waiting would never seem too long. There neither age nor death could harm her. For there was the fountain with the water of life; she would drink of it, the water would keep her young – young as she had never been since the days of King Edward. And there she would be queen in the gardens of the blest until the gardener gave the sign to the Bridegroom to come and take her from the enchanted castle of patient love ... – such was Talbot Price's story.

Again the desolate room. I am alone. Price is not with me any more; is it days or weeks since he was here?

I sit facing the stove and poke the dead ashes with trembling hand. Twinkling sunbeams slant through the gaps between the planks of my roof. Has the snow gone? It is all one to me.

Kelley suddenly comes to mind. The only thing I know of him is that he met a gruesome end in Prague – or was that only a rumour? It is all one to me.

What was that? A noise on the rotten staircase? I turn my head slowly: laboriously, panting at every step, someone is clawing his way up the stairs. What is it that makes me think of the cavernous cellar with the iron ladder in Doctor Hajek's house in Prague? It was just the way that I climbed from the depths, feeling with my feet for every rung, my knees trembling because Jane ... And at the top, above the void – Kelley.

There! There: Edward Kelley, as large as life; his head gradually appears at the stairhead, then his chest, his legs; he sways as he stands leaning against the doorpost – no, he isn't standing; I look more closely: he is hovering, perhaps a hand's breadth, above the floor. He couldn't stand if he wanted to, both his legs are broken, broken several times at the thigh and shin. Here and there the bones poke out through the mud-covered trousers of finest cloth like bloody skewers.

He is still richly clad, the man with the cut-off ears. But his face is ravaged and his courtier's garments are in tatters. – The man is dead. Blank eyes stare at me, blue lips move soundlessly. My heart beats calmly. The deep calm of my senses is undisturbed. I watch Kelley ... Then:

Images, like coloured scraps of wind-tossed mist. They gradually come into focus: a forest, the Bohemian forest. Above the tree-tops a tower with the Habsburg double eagle as a black weather-cock on the roof: Karlštejn. High in the donjon tower which is built against the smooth-ribbed rock face a cell window has been forced open. A human body is clinging to the precipitous rock like a tiny black spider, scraping and fingering its way down, its life hanging from a thin thread ... slowly, slowly it descends the weak rope attached to the mullion ... pity the poor insect trying to get down there! Now it is swinging free in the air, for the wall curves gently inwards; the man who built these cells thought of every possibility; there is no escape, poor human spider on your thin thread. The man spins round in the air as he tries to climb back up. Then: a flurry in the window frame, the curling drop of the rope, a scarcely perceptible impact. The pale visitor on my threshold gives a spectral groan, as if he has to go through the moment of falling again and again, of falling into the green depths from Karlštejn, the fortress of a capricious emperor.I see how Kelley, the ghost on my threshold, keeps trying in vain to speak to me. His tongue has gone, decayed in the earth. He raises his hands beseechingly. I feel that he wants to warn me. What of? What is there left for me to fear?! Kelley's efforts are futile. His eyelids begin to tremble and close. The phantom loses all appearance of life and slowly pales into the empty air.

It is summer in my ruined castle in Mortlake. Impossible to say how many years have passed since my return from exile. Yes, from exile! For the exile *in* Mortlake to which the Green Angel condemned me – I am beginning to smile to myself at the dark orders of the Angel – exile here is really a homecoming! Here is the maternal ground – oh, had I never left it – from which my worn-out body draws healing and strength. Strength which may yet help me to find the way to myself. Here my foot treads in the footprints of my Queen; here the evening breezes over Mortlake are scented with the breath of the high hopes of youth. Here is the tomb of my ruined life, but here too is the place of my resurrection, however long it may be in coming. I sit day after day at my cold hearth and wait. There is nothing left to do, for Elizabeth has reached "Greenland" and nothing now can take her from me, no pressing affairs of state, no wild chase after the illusions of vanity.

Another noise on the stairs! A royal messenger stands before me. After he has looked round in some surprise, he gives an extremely stiff bow:

"Is this Mortlake Castle?"

"It is, my friend."

"And I am speaking to Doctor Dee, Lord of the Manor of Gladhill."

"You are, my friend."

It is grotesque how pained the courier manages to look. The fool can only recognise an English gentleman if he is dressed in silk and satins. Clothes do not make the gentleman, nor rags the beggar.

The messenger hastily hands over the sealed packet, bows stiffly with all the grace of a puppet without joints and scurries back down the rickety stairs that lead to my "audience chamber".

In my hands is a packet sealed with the arms of Count Rosenberg, Lord High Constable of Prague. When I open it the miserable belongings of the late, unlamented Kelley roll to the floor; there is also a smaller bundle with the Emperor's seal.

The black and yellow ribbon is well tied; tear at it as I might, it refuses to undo. Have I no knife on me? Instinctively my hand goes to my left side; where is my paper knife? The place where I used to carry the dagger, the heirloom of the Dee family, is empty. – Now I remember that the ghostly phantom of Elizabeth took it out of my hand, that night when I conjured her up in the park of Mortlake, according to the directions of Bartlett Greene. Since that night I have always worn an exact copy I had made, to use for opening letters. "I always used to carry the paper knife with me," I recall, "instead of the dagger I lost. I must have lost the copy, too. It is no great loss."

Finally I manage to loosen the ribbon with the help of a rusty old nail, which does just as well as the spearhead of Hywel Dda: out onto the floor rolls the coal scrying glass which the Emperor has sent back without greeting or explanation.

A dreary succession of memories drags slowly past; the bailiffs have auctioned off every last square yard of land around the ruin. Once more snow is drifting in through the gaps and holes. Between the stone flags the floor is covered with withered, frozen bracken, clover, bindweed and thistles.

The visits of my last friend, Talbot Price, are becoming less and less frequent. A dishevelled, grumpy old man himself, he sits at the hearth with me for hours on end without saying a word, his chin on his stout stick, his head quivering to and fro. Whenever he comes I have to go through the whole rigmarole of conjuring up the spirits: long prayers which Price, who is getting old and somewhat childish, lays great store by, complicated and meaningless ceremonies ... And Price keeps dropping off to sleep and I nod off too, now and again; – and when we wake up we have both forgotten what we were doing, or it is already evening and dark and cold. Then Price gets to his doddery feet and mutters:

"Till the next time, John, the next time."

Price, whom I was expecting, has not come; instead there is a terrible storm brewing up. Although it is still early evening it is almost completely dark in the room. Lightning flickers. Its yellow glare brings fantastic shadows to life in the hearth. Mortlake is enveloped in rattling thunderclaps and never ending sheets of lightning. Bitter wrath warms my heart: let it strike me down! What more could I desire?! I pray for a bolt of lightning.

I pray – and suddenly realise that I am praying to "Il", to the Green Angel of the West Window.

At that, a blaze of anger flares up within me, brighter than any lightning. My eye is suddenly clear: since that fearful seance in Doctor Hajek's cellar in Prague the Green Angel has not appeared again and none of his promises have been fulfilled – except the miracle of my unbelievable, superhuman patience. Now, in the coruscating brilliance of a lightning flash, I seem to see the stone face of the Angel grinning out at me from the sooty darkness of the old hearth.

349

I leap to my feet. I half remember old, long forgotten incantations, which Bartlett Greene taught me before he set off for Bishop Bonner's bonfire, formulae to be used in the hour of great danger when help is sought from the powers of the world beyond to whom sacrifice has been made; formulae which can also bring death.

Have I made sacrifice? Have I not made sacrifices enough in my life?! And automatically the long forgotten conjurations come to my lips complete, and fall like hammer blows. My soul still does not understand their meaning, but they arrive "on the other side;" syllables and words are heard by invisible ears, I sense it clearly; those on the other side obey, for the dead are drawn by dead words. Between the gnarled and pitted slabs of the rough hearth a pale face gradually takes shape – the face of Edward Kelley!

I am filled with wild, triumphant exultation: so now I have you in my power, my old comrade? I'm afraid I must disturb your restless sleep in the land of the shades, my dear ghost. I am truly sorry, but I am compelled to call upon your services, brother of my heart ... How long did I keep up this bitter, futile address to the dead charlatan? Sluggish hours seemed to drag by.

Finally I pull myself together and command Kelley by our mingled blood. At that I see the phantom move for the first time – the figure is racked by a long, icy shudder – as I command him by virtue of our commingled blood to call up the Green Angel immediately.

Terrified, Kelley makes pleading gestures: in vain. Desperately he writhes to escape the spell: in vain. Mutely he implores me to wait for a more favourable moment: in vain. With the suppressed fury of a torturer equally impelled by a determination to wring a confession from his victim as by a bloody, sadistic frenzy, I bind Bartlett Greene's incantations tighter and tighter round Kelley's spectral body. Slowly his cruelly tormented face dissolves into the stone figure of the great Green Angel.

It is as if the Angel is eating the defenceless Kelley alive.

Then the Angel is alone in the shadows of the fireplace.

Again I feel the paralysing look. Again my heart begins to pound, driving the blood to the extremities as a shield against the intense cold that creeps in from outside. But to my surprise the cold the Angel exhales seems to have no effect on an old man's leathery skin. I realise the cold is already deep within me.

And I hear a musical voice, with which I am long familiar, like the voice of a cheerful, unfeeling child:

"What is thy will?"

"I know you keep your word."

"Dost thou think I care aught for words?"

"Here on earth men believe it is God's command that a word given is a faith pledged; that must hold on the other side, or else heaven and hell would tumble into chaos."

"Take me at my word, then."

"I shall take you at your word."

Outside the storm continues unabated but to my ears the deafening crackle of lightning striking round the castle and the continuous waves of thunder are muted background music to the sharp, clear utterings of the Angel:

"I have always sought what is best for thee, my son."

"Then give me the key and the Stone!"

"St. Dunstan's book is lost. What use is the key?"

"Yes: Kelley – your instrument – lost it. If the key is no use to me any more, you must know what I am in need of."

"That I do know, my son. But how can a thing be found that has been lost for ever?"

"With the help of Him Who knows."

"That is not within my power. We are all subject to the Book of Fate."

"And what is written in the Book of Fate?"

"That I do not know. The Book of Fate is sealed."

"Then open the Book!"

"If thou wishest it; give me thy knife to loosen the seal."

Realisation, understanding and despair strike me like lightning bolts. I collapse to my knees at the hearth, as if it were an altar with the Blessed Sacrament on it. I beseech the stone guest. Futile! – Yet wait. He is smiling. A gentle, kindly smile lights up his pale green, jade face:

"Where is the spearhead of Hywel Dda?"

"Lost ..."

"And still thou takest me at my word?"

Futile rebellion flares up within me once more; I cry out in impotent fury:

"Yes, I still take you at your word!"

"What is thy courage? What is thy right?"

"The courage of the martyred soul. The right of the sacrificial lamb."

"What dost thou want of me?"

"The fulfilment of the promises made through the years."

"Thou demandest the – Stone?"

"I demand the Stone!"

"In three days thou shalt have it. Use the time to prepare thyself to set off on a new journey. The time of trial is over. Thou art called."

I am alone in the darkness. The glow of the sheets of lightning reveals the yawning emptiness of the grate.

Day breaks. Wearily, wearily I drag myself round the blackened ruins to gather together whatever left-overs of the former wealth of the Dees are still to be found. My back – every limb – aches whenever I have to bend down, as if red-hot knives were being jabbed into my muscles. I pack my rags and tatters into a bundle, ready for the journey.

Talbot Price suddenly appears. Without a word he watches me. Then:

"Where to?"

"I don't know. Prague, perhaps."

"Did He come? To you? Has He commanded it?"

"Yes, He was here. He h – has com – manded it." – I feel myself slowly fall into a swoon.

The neighing of horses. The rattling of a carriage rolling up. A strange coachman comes into the kitchen and looks at me questioningly. This is not the neighbour who promised to take me to Gravesend. For one third of all that I possess. I have never seen the man before.

It matters not! I try to stand up. I cannot. It will be difficult to make my way to Prague on foot. I gesture to the man, trying to make myself understood:

"Tomorrow ... perhaps tomorrow, my good man ..."

I cannot set out on a journey. I can hardly raise myself from the bed of straw they have laid me on. The pain in my back is ... much ... too great.

Good that a doctor, Talbot Price, is here. He bends down over me and whispers:

"Courage, John old boy, it'll soon be over. Human frailty, old boy, natural human frailty. It's the gall-bladder, it's the kidneys. That damned stone's the trouble, the stone, old friend. It's the stone that is causing you such pain."

"The Stone!?" I gasp, collapsing back onto the straw.

"Yes, John, the stone. Lots of people suffer from the stone and we doctors can do nothing to relieve it as long as we are not allowed to cut into the flesh."

The excruciating pain sets piercing rays of light flashing before my inner eye:

"O wise Jew of Prague, o Rabbi Löw!" the cry seems to be squeezed out of me like the cold sweat from my chest. So that is the "Stone"?! A cheap trick. I feel all hell is mocking me: "The Angel brought you the stone of death and not the Stone of Life. Long ago. Did you not know?"

I seem to hear the Rabbi calling to me from a long way away in time:

"Beware when you pray for the Stone. Beware that your prayer-arrow is not caught by the Other One!"

"Is there anything else I can do for you?" I hear Price ask me.

Alone, wrapped up in rags and mangy furs, I am sitting in my old armchair. At the fireside. Now I remember: I asked Price to set my chair so that I face East – so that I can receive my next visitor, whoever that shall be, looking in the opposite direction from the one I spent my whole life facing: with my back to the green West.

The visitor I am waiting for is death ...

Price has promised to come in the evening to see how I am; he will make death easier.

I am waiting. Price has not come.

I have been waiting like this for hours, impotent against the tormenting pain and hoping Price will appear to release me. The night passes; Price, my last friend, has failed me.

All promises, whether from mortal men or immortal beings, have left me stranded, alone.

Nowhere is there help. That I have learnt. Nowhere is there pity. God is in His heaven and sound asleep in a soft bed, like my doctor. None of them suffers the torment of the stone cut with seven times seventy razor-sharp edges in his side. Why is not Hell here to savour my suffering? Lost! Betrayed! Abandoned!

My mind is benumbed by pain; my hand gropes over the surface of the hearthstone; it stumbles on something cold: a scalpel. Price left it here so that he could bleed me. Blessed chance! May you be rewarded for it, Talbot Price! This little blade is worth more to me at this moment than the blunt Spearhead of Hywel Dda. It will make me free ... free at last!

I lean my head back, making the skin on my neck taut, raise the knife to my throat ... the first rays of the morning sun strike the blade red, as if it were already dripping with my sluggish life-blood. At that moment, above the scalpel, I see a broad face grinning at me from the empty air of the half-lit room: the wall-eyed face of Bartlett Greene. He nods expectantly: "Cut! Cut! Cut your throat open. That will help. That will unite you with Jane, your wife, that other suicide. That will bring you down to us. That is as it should be."

Greene is right; I want to join Jane. –

How friendly the blade looks, twinkling in the sunshine!

What!? Pressure on my shoulder from behind! – NO! I will not turn round; I will not look to the west. There is heat in the pressure, as if from a human hand, it fills me with a warm glow.

I do not need to turn round: before me stands Gardner, my old, long forgotten assistant, Gardner, who left me after a quarrel. Why should he suddenly appear here in the castle ... and at the very moment when I am about to turn my back on Mortlake and the whole deceiving – and deceived – world?

He is strangely apparelled, my worthy assistant. He wears a white linen gown with a gold rose embroidered over the left breast. It twinkles in the morning sun. And his face has stayed young, so young! Not at all as if twenty-five years had passed since we last saw each other.

With a friendly smile, the eternally young Gardner comes up to me:

"You are alone, John Dee? Where are your friends?"

All my woe melts into a stream of tears. I can only manage a dry croak, faint with pain and weariness:

"They have abandoned me."

"You are right, John Dee, not to put your trust in mortal men. Everything mortal is double-tongued; it brings the doubter to despair."

"But the immortal powers have also betrayed me!"

"You are right, John Dee; men should not trust the immortal powers, either; they feed on the prayers and sacrifices of mankind and hunger after them like ravenous wolves."

"But I no longer know where God is."

"That comes to all who seek Him."

"And who have lost their way?"

"It is not you who will find the way; the way will find you. We have all lost the way at one time or another; for our task is not to make our way, but to find the jewel."

"You find me here, lost and alone; how should I not faint with thirst, astray in the wilderness?"

"Are you alone?"

"No, you are with me!"

"I am ..." – Gardner's figure becomes shadowy, disappears.

"So you, too, are nothing but deceit?!" – the words rattle in my throat.

From a great distance the cry is hardly audible to my ear:

"Who is it that calls me a deceiver?"

"I do!"

"Who is this I?"

"I am."

"Who is it that would compel me to return?"

"I do."

Once more Gardner is visible before me. He smiles at me:

"Now you have called on the One who never abandons you when you have gone astray: the Unfathomable Self. Ponder the formless being you see with your physical eye; ponder the being of primal form you see with the eye of conscience."

"Who am I?" something groans inside me.

"Your name is recorded, though you be nameless. You have lost your sign, son of Rhodri. That is why you are alone!"

"My sign?"

"This!" – from his cloak Gardner takes the paper-knife, the lost dagger, the jewel of the Dees, Hywel Dda's spear.

"There it is." My assistant is mocking me, his cold smile cuts me to the heart.

"There it is, John Dee: once the most noble weapon of your ancestors, then the jealously guarded fetish of your line, then a common paper-knife for the degenerate heir, and finally a tool for black magic, frivolously employed, frivolously lost. – Idolatry! Do you understand me? A noble talisman from ancient times has sunk to an ignoble use through you, John Dee!"

Hatred, hatred glowing as hot as a lava flow erupts from me: "Give me the dagger, deceiver!"

My former assistant does not move an inch as my hand grasps at the dagger.

"Out with the dagger, thief! Thief! The last deceiver, my last enemy on earth, my ... mortal enemy."

The words stick in my throat; I gasp for breath. I can feel my nerves tear like frayed strings. Yet my mind is clear: this is the end.

My trembling body collapses.

A gentle laugh wakes me from my faint:

"Thank God, John Dee, that now you distrust all your friends – even me. At last you have found yourself. At last I can see that you put your trust in yourself alone, that you have the strength to follow your own course."

I sink back. I feel myself defeated in some strange way. My breathing is shallow; I murmur:

"Give me back what once was ours, my friend."

"Take it!" says Gardner and holds the dagger out to me. Hastily I grasp at it like – like a dying man the sacrament. My hand closes on empty air. Gardner is still before me. The dagger in his hand shines in the morning light with a glow as real as the dull gleam of my own bloodless hand trembling before me in a ray of sun ... but I cannot grasp the dagger. Softly Gardner says:

"You see: your dagger is not of this world!"

"When ... where ... can I take hold of it?"

"On the other side, if you seek it there. On the other side, if you do not forget it there."

"Help me, my friend, not ... to ... for ... get."

Something within me screams: I do not want to die with my ancestor, John Dee! With a violent jerk I pull myself back and the next moment my study appears around me; I am once more the one I was when I looked into the coal scrying glass. But I will not put it away yet. I want to learn what happened to John Dee afterwards.

And straightaway I am back in the ruinous chamber in Mortlake Castle. But this time I am only an invisible witness to the events there, not John Dee himself any more.

And I see my ancestor, or the larva that for eighty-four years bore his name: Doctor John Dee, Lord of the Manor of Gladhill, upright in his armchair at the brick hearth, his blank gaze turned to the East, as one who has centuries of time for waiting. I see the dawn break once more over the rotten planks of the makeshift roof of this once noble seat. I see the first rays of the morning sun flit over the face which does not really look dead, but seems to be listening for something, leant back in the chair with the breeze playing in his silver locks. It seems to me that I can sense an alertness, that I can see hope, can see life in the blank gaze of the old man; and I am sure I hear a sigh of release from the sunken breast. – Who could say I was deceiving myself?

All at once there are four figures standing in the wretched hovel. I sensed rather than saw them emerge through the walls, each from a different point of the compass. They are tall, almost too tall for human beings, there is something unearthly about them. It may be that it is their garments that give them a ghostly look: they are dressed in long, blue-black habits with broad cowls across neck and shoulders. Their faces are hooded. They resemble medieval gravediggers, masked, hidden from view, just as the first stages of bodily corruption are.

They carry a strangely shaped coffin in the form of a cross. It is made of some matt, polished metal; lead or zinc it seems to me.

They lift the dead man out of the chair and lay the corpse out on the ground. They stretch out his arms to make a cross.

Gardner is standing at the dead man's head.

He is wearing his white linen gown. The golden rose on his breast shines. In his outstretched hand he holds the dagger of the Dees with the spearhead of Hywel Dda, gleaming in the sunlight. Slowly Gardner bends down over the dead man and lays it in John Dee's open hand. For a moment I seem to see the yellowed fingers tremble and curl around the haft.

Then, all of a sudden, the gigantic figure of Bartlett Greene shoots out of the ground, broad teeth grinning out of a flaming beard.

With a grunt of satisfaction the ghostly captain of the Ravenheads contemplates the corpse of his former cell-mate.

An appraising look, a butcher assessing the value of a carcase.

Every time Greene's milky-white wall-eye passes over the dead man's head, he blinks as if dazzled by an irritating light. He ignores the white-gowned adept. Soundlessly – like the speech in dreams – he talks to the dead John Dee – and I feel I am being addressed as well.

"All the waiting over at last, is it, old soldier? You must have waited and hoped the soul out of your body, old fool. Are you all set for your journey to Greenland? Come on, then."

The dead man does not move. Bartlett Greene kicks roughly with his silver shoe – the flaky crust seems to have become thicker – at the corpse's legs, which are stretched out straight along the ground. A puzzled look comes over his face.

"No cause to crawl away and hide in the decrepit hovel of this pile of flesh, my dear Sir. Come on, speak up! Where are you?"

"Here I am!" answers Gardner's voice.

Bartlett Greene gives a start. He pulls himself up sharply to his full, massive height. He is like a watchful bulldog who hears a suspicious noise and looks up, growling:

"Who speaks?"

"I do!" comes the answer from the other side of the body.

"That is not my brother Dee," snarls Greene. "You did not ask for this doorman to guard your threshold, brother Dee, not you, I know; send him away."

"What do you want of one you cannot see?"

"I want nothing to do with invisible folk! Go thy way and let us go ours."

"Very well. Go then!"

"Up you get!" roars Bartlett Greene, shaking the corpse, "up you get in the name of the Lady, to whom we are bound, comrade. Get up, accursed coward! It is no use pretending to be dead when you really are dead, my lovely. The night is over. The dream is ended. It is time for your journey; quick march!" With long, gorilla's arms the giant bends over the body and tries to lift it from the floor. It does not move. Panting, he bellows at the empty air:

"Leave go, hobgoblin! That is cheating."

Gardner does not move a muscle, motionless by the corpse's head:

"Take him. I will not stop you."

Like one of the beasts of the Apocalypse Greene falls upon the dead man; he cannot lift him.

"The devil take you, man, why are you so heavy? Heavier than damned lead. You must have managed to pile up a greater weight of sin than I would have expected of you! – Right then, up we come!"

But the corpse seems to be rooted in the ground.

"Weighted down with sin, you are, John Dee!" groans the redbeard.

"Weighted down with the rewards of suffering!" comes an echo from the other side of the dead man.

Greene's face is a greenish hue and distorted with rage:

"Invisible deceiver! Nightmare! Goblin! Get off and I will pick him up with one hand."

"It is not I that you must blame," comes the reply, "not I; you have made him so heavy and now you are surprised?"

In Greene's pale wall-eye there appears a venomous gleam of triumph:

"Then stay where you are till you rot, craven scum! – You'll come for your cheese soon enough, my little mouse; we have your cheese safe and sound, as you know. Come and get the spear of Hywel Dda, come for your dagger, your paper-knife, your little toy, John Dee!"

"He has the spear!"

"Where?" – – Only now does the butcher seem to see the dagger in the dead man's right hand. He swoops on it like a hawk.

The dead man's fingers move perceptibly. They curl round the handle and grip it tight.

The furious snarls of a bulldog with its teeth in its victim come from Greene's throat. The adept in white turns his upper body towards the sun; a ray is refracted in the golden threads of the rose; radiance spreads over the ghostly figure of Bartlett Greene. Waves of light wash him away.

The hooded men return. They lift up the body and lay it gently in the cross-shaped coffin. Gardner signals to them with his hand and leads them out to the glory of the warm sun. His figure dissolves into crystalline light, the pallbearers follow him and the silent procession floats out through the East wall of the hovel.

A garden. Masonry gleaming between high cypresses and shady oak trees. Is it the park of Mortlake Castle? It could be, for there are mournful burnt-out ruins amongst the glowing beds planted with all kinds of flowering shrubs and luminous sunflowers; but Mortlake never had such forbidding towers and ramparts as can be seen everywhere here through the foliage; and beyond the crumbling fortifications a vista opens out onto a deep blue valley with the line of a winding river etched into its floor. One flowerbed is a jumble of plants and soil where a grave has been dug; the cross-shaped coffin is being lowered into it.

Whilst the dark pallbearers fill the grave with earth the adept in the white gown moves from place to place, bending down at some mysterious task. He seems to be tending plants and shrubs like a gardener; he prunes, he ties, weeds and waters, steadily, calmly, as if he has long since forgotten the burial.

A mound rises over the grave. The blue-black pallbearers have gone. Gardner, the strange alchymist's assistant, has tied a strong, young rose stock to a newly cut, slender stake. The roses glow blood red amongst the wealth of leaves.

I am tormented by a question which is forcing its way to my lips. But before they can form the words, the adept looks over his shoulder at me: it is Theodor Gärtner, my friend who drowned in the Pacific.

The coal dropped from my hand; my head throbbed. I felt convinced that I would never again see anything in the black glass. I had been through some kind of metamorphosis, of that I had no doubt, although I could not say precisely what it was. "I have become heir to John Dee in all that he was or did" might be the best way of putting it. We have become fused; he is no more and I am here in his stead. He is I and I am he for ever.

I threw open a window; the stale reek from the onyx bowl was unbearable. It stank of decay.

Hardly had I filled my lungs with fresh air and removed the bowl and its disgusting smell than Lipotin arrived.

As he entered he sniffed the air as unobtrusively as possible but said nothing. He greeted me rather loudly and effusively; his normal calm and languid air became nervous, fidgety. He kept laughing without reason and said "Yes, yes" and made a whole ceremony of sitting down. He crossed his legs in a rather exaggerated fashion, hurriedly lit a cigarette and started abruptly:

"I represent a client, of course."

"The client being ... ?" I asked with excessive politeness.

He bowed: "The Princess, of course."

Without doing so deliberately, I stuck to the tone of exaggerated dignity in which our conversation had begun and which made it sound like the negotiations of two stage diplomats.

"Yes, my benefactress, Princess Shotokalungin."

"And?"

"I have been commissioned to purchase from you – if possible – this ... this ... poignard, shall we call it.

363

May I?" His long, slender fingers took up the dagger which lay on the table and he pretended to examine it thoroughly, screwing up his eye like a caricature connoisseur:

"Actually it's not difficult to run this piece down. Look at the crude workmanship. A mish-mash!"

"I must admit that I, too, have the impression that it's value as an antique is not all that great."

Lipotin interrupted me with an anxious gesture. He was afraid of an overhasty decision. He stretched out in his chair and made an effort to get back to the lighter tone:

"As I said, I have come round to talk you into selling the dagger. Why shouldn't I be open about it? It's not the kind of thing you collect. But the Princess does. And she thinks ... of course I don't share her view at all ... but she thinks ... "

"... it is the piece missing from her father's collection." I kept to my aloof tone as I completed Lipotin's sentence.

"Yes! That's it! ... Right first time!" Lipotin leapt up from his chair and put on a show of pleased astonishment at my astuteness.

"I concur with the opinion of the Princess," I remarked.

Lipotin leant back in satisfaction.

"You do? Then that's all right." His expression suggested he assumed the bargain had been struck.

In the same calm tone I said:

"And that is precisely why the dagger is of great value to me."

"I quite understand," interrupted Lipotin in his alacrity to agree with me. "We must make the most of our opportunities; my sentiments entirely."

I ignored the insulting suggestion:

"I have no wish to be involved in any kind of deal."

Lipotin squirmed about in his chair:

"Of course not! And I am not here to make you an offer. Hmm ... It would be very tactless of me to try

364

and pry into your thoughts. Of course. But the Princess has taken a fancy to it and when a beautiful woman takes a fancy to something, ... I would have thought it was a sacrifice worth making, I would have thought ... to put it in a nutshell, I have been empowered to ... please do not misunderstand me; the Princess is not offering money! She leaves it to you to decide yourself. You know how charming and how ... liberal the Princess is, and what a high opinion she has of you. An act of generosity – the gift of this curio – would evoke an even more generous response on the part of the Princess."

Never before had I found Lipotin so halting and at the same time so wordy. His eyes probed my face for any sign of a reaction so that he could adjust to the new situation. I could not suppress a brief smile at the pains he was going to:

"Unfortunately the charming Princess is wasting her time making me such attractive offers; the dagger does not belong to me."

"Does not ... belong ...?" Lipotin's astonishment was amusing to see.

"It was given to my fiancée."

"Oh ... so that's it."

"That is the situation."

The Russian cautiously tried a new tack:

"Gifts, I find, often have a tendency to be ... given. I have the impression that this gift is already – or could at any moment be – in your hand."

I had had enough; I said brusquely:

"You are correct. The dagger is mine. And it will stay mine; it is very valuable."

"Is that so? And why?" there was an undertone of mockery in Lipotin's voice.

"There is much about this dagger which makes it exceptionally valuable to me."

"But my dear sir, do you know anything about the dagger?"

"Its value is not visible to the naked eye, but if one looks into the coal scrying glass ..."

Lipotin was so startled and went so deathly pale that there would have been no point in his trying to conceal his consternation. He was clearly aware of this himself, for he suddenly changed his tone and attitude:

"How on earth ...? But you cannot look into the glass. You need the red powder. Unfortunately my supply has run out."

"No need, my friend", I interjected. "Fortunately there was a pinch left over." And I pointed at the ash-tray.

"And you ...? Without assistance ...? Impossible!" Lipotin had sprung up from his armchair and was staring at me dumbfounded. The surprise and fear were so patent that I was tempted to reveal all:

"Yes: I have inhaled the incense! Without the assistance of the red-cap monk – and without any help of yours!"

"Anyone who dares to do that – and is still alive to tell the tale – has overcome death."

"Perhaps. But it does mean that I know of the nature, origin and value of the dagger – and of its future; or at least I have a strong intuition as to what it will be. Let us say that I am just as superstitious as the Princess or as you."

Lipotin slowly sat down beside me. He was completely calm, but his whole being seemed changed. He took the half-smoked cigarette from his mouth and stubbed it out in the onyx bowl, which was back on duty as an ash-tray. Then he ceremoniously lit a fresh one, as if to indicate that what was past, was past, and that a new round had begun. For a long time he sucked on the cigarette and puffed out the fragrant Russian smoke. I did not interrupt his enjoyment; I was determined to wait and see what would come. When he realised this he lowered his lids and started:

"True, true. Well, that changes the whole situation. You know about the dagger. You intend to keep the dagger. You have won the first round."

"You are not telling me anything new", I said, completely relaxed. "Anyone who, like myself, has come to understand the nature of time and to see things in it not from outside but from within, anyone who has progressed beyond dreams to fate, beyond fate to where reality appears in its pure forms, will find the right names at the right moment of the conjuration and the demons will obey."

"O..b..ey?" Lipotin drew out the word. "May I give you a piece of advice? The most dangerous demons are the ones that you call up yourself. Take that from someone who knows of old – of very old – these shadow worlds that cling to relics of past days. But the truth is, sir, that you have been called, for you have made yourself master over death; that much I can see. I can also see, to my astonishment, that you have resisted a number of challenges; but that does not mean that you have been chosen, by any means. The worst enemy of the victor is arrogance."

"Thank you for your honest opinion, Lipotin. I must admit that I assumed you were with the enemy."

Lipotin raised his heavy eyelids in his usual languid manner:

"I, my dear sir, am on no side at all, for I am only a ... Mascee: I support whoever is the stronger."

The expression on the desiccated features of the old antiques dealer was an indescribable mixture of sceptical irony and profound sorrow, yes, even disgust.

"And you think I am ... ?" I crowed.

"For the moment I think you are the stronger. And that is why I am ready to serve you."

I did not respond but just stared into space.

With a swift movement he sat up:

"So you want to thwart Princess Shotokalungin? But, my dear Sir, that is impossible. It is true that she is a woman possessed; but are not you a man possessed? If you don't know that yourself, then the worse it is for you. And she comes from Colchis; most likely one of her ancestors was called Medea."

"Or: Isaïs," I added in a matter-of-fact voice.

"Isaïs is her spiritual mother." Lipotin's swift response was just as factual in tone. "You must learn to distinguish clearly if you want to master her."

"Do not worry; I shall master her."

"Do not overestimate your strength. Since the world began woman has always proved the stronger."

"And where is that written?"

"If it were not so, the world would not endure."

"What do I care about the world! Am I not Lord of the Spear?"

"Anyone who withholds the Spear spurns half the world. Half of the world, dear sir, but the problem is that half is always the whole world, grasped half-heartedly."

"What do you know of my heart?!"

"Much; much indeed. — Did you not see the Thracian Isaïs?"

My cheeks burnt under Lipotin's mocking glance. I had no defence against his biting scorn. I knew for certain that the Russian could read my thoughts. Had he not read what was in my mind at the Princess' house and on the drive to Elsbethstein? I blushed like a schoolboy.

"There we are!" said Lipotin in his best bedside manner. I looked away in shame.

"No-one has ever avoided it, my friend", Lipotin continued in a murmur, "and no-one is ever likely to. Only mysteries should be veiled. Woman is all-pervading, profane reality; naked she burns in our blood, and when we do battle with her our best tactic is to strip her naked, in the mind or in fact. Otherwise no hero has ever defeated Dame World.

I tried to wriggle off the hook: "You know much, Lipotin."

"Much indeed. Much, much," he replied like a robot nodding off to sleep.

I could feel anxiety beginning to claw at my throat and felt the need to hear the sound of my own voice:

"You imagine I spurn the Princess, Lipotin. That is not true. I do not spurn her; I want to know her. To know her – do you understand? If necessary in the straightforward physical sense it is used in the Bible. I want to settle with her once and for all."

"My dear sir!" Lipotin gripped his cigarette in his teeth as he croaked; his eyelids popped open like those of an old parrot. "You underestimate the power of women. And when it appears in the form of a Circassian princess ... I – I would rather not be in your shoes!" With an expression worthy of Chidher, the eternal Wanderer, wiping the scum of the earth from his lips, Lipotin removed a few strands of tobacco from his mouth. Abruptly he went on: "And even if you could kill her, that would only transfer the battle to another field – and to one that would be much more dangerous for you, since there your view would be even more restricted than here and you could very easily find yourself on a slippery slope. Woe to you if you slip on the 'other side'."

"Lipotin!" – I shouted; I was almost beside myself with impatience, sensing that my nerves were about to give way. "Lipotin, if you really are ready to help me: what is the true way to victory?"

"There is only one way."

Again I noticed that Lipotin's voice had the monotonous tone that had already struck me several times. Did I really control him? Was he really the instrument of my commands? Was he a medium compelled to obey me like ... like? Jane, too, had once shut her eyes and answered me in the same way when this unaccountable power within me began to ask its questions. I pulled myself together and concentrated my gaze on a point between the old Russian's eyebrows:

"How do I find the Way? How?"

Pale, leaning back in his chair, Lipotin answered:

"The Way is prepared by ... a woman. Only a woman can overcome our Lady Isaïs."

"A woman?" The disappointment deflated me.

"A woman that has the virtue of ... the dagger."

His words were so delphic that I went numb. Distraught, eyes flickering to and fro, mumbling incomprehensibly to himself like a senile old man, features haggard, Lipotin began the struggle to regain consciousness. He had regained control of himself remarkably quickly when the doorbell rang and a second later Jane appeared in the doorway with a gigantic figure towering behind her – my cousin, John Roger! ... I mean, of course, the Princess' chauffeur. I was puzzled to see that Jane was dressed ready to go out. She came in and made way for the tall chauffeur. The Princess had sent him to collect us all for the second trip to Elsbethstein that we had arranged. The car was at the door. The Princess was sitting below, waiting.

Jane expressed her thanks. She was ready; one could not reject the Princess' charming offer and the weather was so beautiful. What objection could I have raised?

The uncanny chauffeur had sent a chill through my veins; vague, dark forebodings weighed on my chest. Without quite knowing why, I took Jane by the hand. Enunciating slowly, with difficulty, I said:

"If ... you do not ... genuinely want to go, Jane ..."

She interrupted with a firm squeeze of the hand and a remarkably radiant look on her face:

"I genuinely do want to go."

It sounded like some secret accord; about what I had no idea.

Briskly, Jane walked over to the desk and picked up the dagger. Without a word, she put it in her handbag. I watched her in silence. Finally I forced myself to ask the question:

"The dagger, Jane? What are you going to do with the dagger?"

"Give it to the Princess. I've made up my mind."

"To the ... Princess?"

Jane gave her childlike laugh: "I think we have kept our charming hostess waiting long enough."

Lipotin stood, silent, behind his chair. With a tired air, he looked from one to the other of us, undecided, now and then gently shaking his head, as if sunk in mute astonishment.

Not much was said. We collected our hats and coats and put them on with a feeling of dismay which numbed both body and soul.

We went down; the tall chauffeur darted on ahead, silent and supple.

The Princess waved to us from the back of the car. It was a strangely wooden gesture.

We climbed in.

My skin prickled and every cell in my body seemed to whisper: Don't go! Don't go!

Paralysed in heart and voice, we settled down in the car, like marionettes obedient to the strings, for our pleasure trip to Elsbethstein.

That journey to Elsbethstein has etched itself for ever on my soul: steep vineyards sweep down to a river which has scoured out tight curves in the valley; we careered wildly round them. In between, spread out like smooth cloth, shone the soft green of the meadows waving through the dust and glittering light. Villages flashed past, fluttering in our wake. Thoughts and fears were torn apart, blown away like autumn leaves dancing in the gale; the soul cried inaudible warnings; the senses, too weary for amazement, merely registered a blur of images.

The limousine raced up the slope towards the crumbling buttresses of Elsbethstein, skidded round in a screaming curve, which threatened to land us all in the river below, and screeched to a halt before the gate of the outer wall; its flanks seemed to heave with the effort.

We got out and entered the inner courtyard in twos. I led the way with Lipotin and the women followed slowly, trailing farther and farther behind. I turned back and saw Jane in animated conversation with the Princess whose characteristic peal of laughter rang out. I felt reassured to see them chatting happily together with no signs of any dispute.

There is little left to see of the steaming springs; they have been led into stone basins with ugly wooden huts above them. Sleepy workmen were pottering about the courtyard. We inspected everything, but there was a voice deep within me saying that all this keen interest was only a thin pretext for the quite different things which had brought us here and which we were all waiting for with concealed trepidation. As if by tacit agreement, we all began to make our way to the keep whose massive door, as at our last visit, was ajar. In my mind I was already hurrying on up the steep, dark, rotting stairs to the feeble-minded old gardener's kitchen. And I knew why I wanted to visit him: I wanted to ask the strange old man ... Suddenly Lipotin stopped and grabbed my arm:

"Look, over there! We are spared a visit to the kitchen. Here comes our Ugolino from his tower. The lord of the dagger has seen us already."

At the same moment we heard a faint cry from the Princess. We turned round. With a half laugh and a wave of the hand she called to us:

"Not the old madman, not now." She turned away with Jane. We automatically followed the two ladies and caught them up. Jane had a serious look on her face; the Princess laughed and said:

"I don't want to see him again. I find people who are not right in the head rather creepy. And he won't give me any of his dilapidated ... kitchen utensils, will he?" It was meant as a joke, but I felt there was an undertone of injured pride or jealousy of Jane.

The old gardener was standing there by the door of the keep and seemed to be watching us in the distance. He raised his hand, as if he were waving to us. The Princess saw it and pulled her coat tighter around her, as if she felt a shiver of cold. An odd gesture on this warm, late summer's day.

"Why have we come back to this creepy old ruin? The very stones are hostile," I heard her murmur to herself.

"But you were in favour of it yourself," I replied innocently. "It would be a good opportunity to ask him where he got the dagger."

The Princess' reply was curt:

"What do I care for the ramblings of an old fool! – – Jane, my dear, I suggest we leave these gentlemen to satisfy their curiosity whilst we find a more comfortable spot from which to admire the pictur-esque charms of this spooky ruin." She took Jane by the arm and set off with her towards the gate of the courtyard.

"You want to leave already?" I asked in astonish-ment and Lipotin also looked rather bewildered.

The Princess nods; Jane turns to me with a strange smile:

"That's what we've arranged. We are going to ta-ke a round trip together. Now, as you know, a round trip ends where it started. We'll see ..." The wind blew away her final words.

Lipotin and I were so nonplussed that we just stood there. By the time we had come back to our senses the women were too far away to hear our objections. We hurried after them, but the Princess was already in the car and Jane about to get in. I was gripped by an inexplicable fear and called to her:

"Jane, where are you going? He waved to us. We must go and talk to him." Somehow the words came to my lips, any words just to stop Jane.

Jane seemed to hesitate a second; she turned her face towards me and said something that I could not hear: for some reason the chauffeur revved up the car and the engine roared like some primeval monster in its death throes; the hellish racket drowned out every word. Then the car shot forward so abruptly that Jane was jolted back into the seat; the Princess pulled the door shut. I screamed over the roar of the engine:

"Jane! Don't go! What are you ..." – it was a wild cry from the depths of my heart. But the car plunged down the track with a screech of tyres; the last thing I saw was the figure of the chauffeur leaning back from the wheel as the machine-gun fire of the exhaust faded; in the distance it looked like a glider sweeping down the precipitous slope.

I turned to Lipotin with a questioning look. He was staring after the car, eyebrows raised. His yellow face seemed fixed, like a faded mask from some past century stuck between the leather cap and coat of a twentieth-century motorist.

In mute accord we turned back to the castle courtyard. In the middle we were accosted by the old man with the wild eye.

"Show you the garden," he whispered, his gaze above our heads, as if he were not looking at us. "Old garden. Beautiful garden. Big. Tend it – lots of work ..." his lips continued to move, but nothing comprehensible emerged.

He led the way and we followed automatically, in silence.

The tour took us through gaps in the masonry and between ramparts, with an occasional stop at flowerbeds or groups of trees. The old man rambled on, telling us when he planted the trees or laid out the beautifully tended beds that suddenly appeared in the middle of rubble and crumbling masonry where glossy lizards were basking in the sun. Without batting an eyelid, he told us he planted some centuries-old yews as tiny seedlings one hard winter; he brought them from "the other side" – he waved his hand vaguely at the distant horizon – for the grave.

I gave a start: "What grave?"

He shook his head and I had to repeat the question often before he understood. He gestured to us. We went up to the dull red trunks: in the middle of the massive yew trees was a small mound, such as you might find in an old park with a moss-grown column or temple on top. There was nothing of the kind on this mound, but it was covered with rose bushes afire with deep red blooms. Behind it was the grey gleam of the outer wall, and a gap in the stonework gave a broad vista to the valley and the silver river.

I had seen the view before; but where?

It is a not uncommon experience. The scene around me suddenly seemed to become familiar; I had seen all this before: the trees, the roses, the gap in the wall, the view of the silver river. It was as if I were returning to where I belonged. At first I thought it was a memory of the images on a coat of arms; then I felt it was the place I saw in John Dee's glass as the ruin of Mortlake Castle. Perhaps that wasn't Mortlake at all, I said to myself, perhaps it was this castle that in my vision I took for the home of my ancestors?

The old gardener parted some of the rose bushes and pointed out a hollow covered in moss and ferns. He gave a foolish grin and muttered:

"The grave. Yes, yes, the grave. Down there rests the quiet face with open eyes and outstretched arms. I took the dagger from his hand. Only the dagger, Sir! You must believe me! Only the dagger. – You see, I knew that I had to give it to the beautiful woman, to the kind young woman who is keeping a look-out with me for the Lady."

I had to hold on to one of the yew trees. I tried to call out to Lipotin, but my tongue would not obey. All I could do was stammer:

"The dagger? – Here? – A grave?"

Suddenly the old man understood me perfectly. He nodded encouragingly and a smile lit up his haggard features. Following a sudden thought, I asked him:

"Tell us, old man: to whom does the castle belong?"

The old man hesitated: "Elsbethstein? Who it belongs to?" He sank back into his old listlessness; his lips moved, but no sound came from them. With a confused nodding of the head, he motioned us to follow him.

A few steps took us to a small gate in the wall concealed behind elderberry bushes and overhung with wild roses. Above the arch of the gate I could see evidence of some crude carving. The ancient gardener pointed at it eagerly. With a half decayed stick I pushed aside the tangle of branches and flowers and saw a moss-covered coat of arms carved above the lintel. It was clearly sixteenth century work and showed a sloping cross; from one of the arms a rose branch grew with three flowers: one in bud, the second half opened, the third in full bloom with one petal about to fall.

For a long time I mused over the mysterious symbols on the coat of arms. The weathered stone, the grey-green tufts of moss, the aura of melancholy which pervaded the carving of the rose with the blooms in three stages of flowering: it all entrapped me in a state between memory and premonition, so that I did not notice that my companions had left me by myself. A dream vision gradually focused in my mind: the burial of my ancestor, John Dee in the magic garden of the adept, Gardner. More and more the outlines of the vision from the past merged with my present surroundings.

As I stood there, full of strange doubts and rubbing my eyes and forehead to clear them of the enchantment, I was startled by an unexpected appearance in the darkness of the entrance: it was Jane, of that there could be no doubt. But her approach was noiseless, hovering and – what could it mean? – she was dripping wet, her light summer dress clung to her body. The expression on her face was fixed and serious, almost frightening, so penetrating was the mute warning her features radiated.

A dead woman projecting her image by telekinesis? – Then I heard the words that seemed to come from her mouth:

"Finished. – Free. – Help yourself! – Be strong!"

"Jane!" I called. For a moment I was overtaken by dizziness and when my senses cleared it was no longer Jane before me but a majestic woman of otherworldly appearance, a crown on her head; her piercing gaze seemed to come from distant centuries and pass through me and go on to some future time of my fulfilment.

"So it is you, Queen and Lady of the Garden …;" more I could not say.

I stood facing the miraculous woman, eye to eye, indissolubly bound – and a maelstrom of thoughts, insights and furious decisions ricocheted off my external being into a spiritual world, sparking off a turmoil of devastation and upheaval. Then my physical ear caught the sound of Lipotin and the mad gardener returning; my eyes saw the old man start, raise his hands and sink to his knees. His face radiant, he knelt close to where I stood and crying and laughing and sobbing he looked up at the queenly figure and stammered:

"Praise and thanks be, Lady, that you have come. My weary head and my long years of service I lay at your feet. See if I have served you faithfully."

The vision of womanhood gently inclined her head to the old man. He fell to his face and was silent.

Once more the regal apparition turned to me and I seemed to hear a voice, like a bell ringing from a distant tower:

"Greetings: – Longed for – Chosen – Not yet tested!" and as the echo died away I seemed to hear

Jane's earthly voice return, repeating her anxious warning: " – help yourself. – Be strong."

Suddenly the vision paled as a noise of uproar came from the courtyard beyond the wall.

I looked up to see Lipotin staring incomprehendingly at myself and the prostrate gardener in turns. A few brief words told me he had seen nothing of the vision. He was merely puzzled by the old man's strange behaviour.

But before he had time to bend down to him, men rushed towards us from the castle courtyard, shouting. I hurried to meet them. Words battered at my ear like breakers in a storm and a second later my eyes saw: in a shallow spot in the middle of the river – below where the road follows a sharp bend high above a rocky precipice – picked out by the white lines of foam from the current, was the wreck of the Princess' car.

Slowly the pandemonium around me resolved into words: "All three dead! It seemed to take off into the air, right into the air. The chauffeur must have been out of his mind, or blinded by the devil!" – – "Jane! Jane!" It was my own cry that woke me! I turned to call Lipotin, but he was kneeling next to the gardener who was still lying motionless on the grass. He raised the old man's head and looked at me with empty, soulless eyes. The old man's body slipped from his hands onto its side. The old man was dead.

Lipotin continued to stare at me as if in a trance. I was incapable of speech. I just pointed over the parapet down to the river. He stared down into the valley for a long time, then passed his hand lightly over his forehead: "So: sunk into the green depths once more. Steep banks! I am weary ... Did you hear? They are calling me."

A flotilla of little boats brought the bodies from the shallow rapids. Only the two women; the chauffeur had been carried away downstream. "Corpses that those waters bear away are never found," someone said, "they are swept away without coming to the surface until they reach the far-off sea." I shivered at the thought of seeing the face of my cousin, John Roger, staring up at me from the waters, deathly pale and bloated.

And then the dreadful question: was it an accident? ... And this? What could this mean? Jane's dagger was lodged deep in the Princess' breast, piercing her heart.

She must have impaled herself on the spearhead by accident when the car crashed – at least that was what I told myself. I felt almost like a corpse myself as I stood for a long time before the dead women: Jane seemed to be sleeping with an expression of peace and contentment on her face. Her quiet, budding beauty seemed to blossom on the withered stem and dried my tears and turned my lamentation into prayer: "Holy guardian angel of my life, intercede for me that I may bear it all ..."

The Princess' brow was furrowed. Her lips, closed tight in pain, secmed to repress a cry. It was almost as if she were still alive and about to wake up at any moment. Tiny shadows from the leaves dancing in the breeze flitted across her eyelids. – Or did she suddenly open them and close them again quickly when she saw I might notice. No, no: she is dead! The dagger has pierced her heart!! Then, as the hours passed, the tension in her features relaxed and her face was distorted by a repulsive, cat-like trait.

Since the funeral of the two women I have not seen Lipotin. But I await a visit from him hourly; as we parted at the cemetery gate he said:

"Now it begins in earnest! Now we will see who will be Lord of the Dagger. Put your trust in yourself alone, if you can. – But I will, of course, remain your obedient servant, and when the time is ripe I will come to ask if you have need of me. By the way, the red Dugpa monks have sent me the black spot ... That means ..."

"Oh, yes?" I asked, preoccupied; my whole being was filled with mourning for Jane. "Well?"

"That means ..." Lipotin did not complete the sentence but just drew his hand across his throat.

By the time I had taken in his gesture and asked him what the meaning of it all was, he had disappeared in the crush of people getting on and off a tram.

I often go over in my mind all that he said and did; and still I ask myself: was it real? Or did I just imagine it? These events have a different place in my memory from those that I went through at the same time ...

How long is it now since I buried Jane side by side with Assja Shotokalungin? How can I know? I have not counted the days, nor the weeks, nor the months; – or is it years that have passed since then? The dust lies inches deep on all the papers and objects around me; the windows are clouded over with dirt and that is all to the good: I have no desire to know whether I am in the town of my birth, or whether I have become John Dee in Mortlake, caught like a fly in time's web. Sometimes I have the strange idea that I died long ago and am lying in my grave alongside the two women without being aware of it. How can I prove to myself that this is not the case? There is a mirror on the wall and from its dull glass a face stares out at me that could be me, a face with a long beard and tangled hair, but perhaps the dead can see themselves in the mirror and imagine they are still living? For all we know, they may think of the living as dead!? – No, I have no proof that I really am still alive. If, with a great effort, I force my mind back to the time when I stood at the grave of the two women, then I seem to remember that I came straight back here to my house and dismissed all my servants and wrote to my old housekeeper, who was still on holiday, that she should not return and I made arrangements with my bank to pay her a pension. – Maybe it is all a dream; maybe I am dead and my house is empty.

One thing is certain: all my clocks have stopped, one at half past nine, another at twelve o'clock, and others at times I have not even bothered to note. And spider's webs are everywhere, everywhere. The spiders have come in their thousands; where can they all have come from in such a short time, say a hundred years? Or is it only one year in the life of men outside? What do I care? What is it to me?

What have I lived on in all this time? The question seems worth pursuing. Perhaps if I could answer it I would know whether I am dead or not! I think back and, like a memory of a dream, I see myself slipping through the quiet streets of the town at night, eating in ale-houses and low taverns and running into friends and acquaintances who spoke to me. Whether I replied and what I replied, I could not say. I think I walked past them without a word so as not to reawaken my sense of loss at Jane's death. – Yes, that must be it: I have slipped unnoticed into the realm of death, into a lonely realm. But what do I care whether I am alive or dead?

I wonder whether Lipotin is dead? – There I go again. It makes no difference whether one is alive or dead.

One thing I am sure of: since the burial Lipotin has not come to me, in any shape or form. Otherwise the picture I have of him would not be the last one in my memory: he disappeared in a crowd outside the cemetery after he had said something about the Tibetan Dugpas which I have forgotten. He drew his hand across his throat. Or was that at Elsbethstein? –

381

– What do I care? Perhaps he has gone back to the East and turned back into John Dee's Mascee, the Tutor to the Czar. Since then I have departed this world, so to speak. I do not know which is farther, Asia or the land of dreams where I have taken refuge. Perhaps I have only half woken up and my study looks to me as if the world outside my window had dreamed away a hundred years.

All at once I am gripped by a feeling of unease: I see my house as a nut, eaten away on the inside and covered in dusty mould, in which I sleep on like a mindless grub that has missed its transformation into a moth. What has caused this unease? A sudden memory torments me: was that not the shrill sound of a bell? In the house? No, not in the house! Who would ring the bell of a deserted house? It must have been a ringing in my ears. I have read somewhere that hearing is the first sense to waken when a person in suspended animation returns to life. And then I remember – and admit it openly to myself – I have been waiting, waiting, waiting, for how long I do not know, for the return of my dead Jane. In the nights and days I crawled around the house from room to room, praying on my knees to heaven for a sign from her, praying and praying until I lost all sense of the passage of time.

There is no object that used to belong to my beloved Jane that I have not made into a fetish, that I have not prayed to, pleaded with to help me compel Jane to come down to me, to call her back from the grave, to send her to me to save me from the pain of loss that hangs above my neck like an executioner's axe. But it was all in vain; I have not seen nor even felt the presence of Jane, I who have been her lawful wedded husband for three hundred years.

Jane has not come ... but Assja Shotokalungin has! Now that I have awoken from my lethargy – as it now seems to me – and forgetfulness, I know: Assja Shotokalungin is here, has always been here ...

At first she came through the door and I knew straightaway that there was no point in locking the door. How should a simple door-key keep out one whom the grave cannot hold?

Now that I think back to my feelings when she first came I cannot hide the fact that her visit was welcome to me. I will confess my guilt – o thou eternal face that hath watched me night and day since these dreams began, thou double face with the crystal above, shining so that my eyes hurt whenever I dare to return thy glance, I will confess this guilt before thee and before myself. My one excuse is that I thought Assja was Jane's messenger from the kingdom of the dead. I was a fool to believe she would bring me tidings of love, tidings for the soul …

Assja visits me daily. Now that memory has returned I have to acknowledge that fact. She no longer comes through the door; she simply appears.

Usually she sits on the chair at my desk and – my God, how pointless it is to try to conceal the truth from myself – she always comes in the same dress of black and silver; it has a flowing, wavy design – the Chinese symbol of eternity – which is the same as the decoration on the Russian Tula-ware box.

My eyes are attracted towards the dress of the dead Princess, all the time, and my lustful gaze seems to wear it away so that it has gradually become older and more and more transparent. It sits more and more loosely on her body, the weave becoming sketchier, gradually falling to pieces, until now the Princess – or rather the Thracian Goddess Isaïs – is gleaming in all her naked beauty on the chair before me.

All the time I have concentrated my gaze on the decay of her dress. At least that is what I tell myself. Perhaps I wished it away! Or am I not deceiving myself after all? It could be so, for I know that not a word of passion has been spoken.

Have we talked to each other at all? No! What could I have said in the face of this slow uncovering of the Princess?!

And I call on thee, thou awful, double-faced guardian of my dreams, Baphomet, be thou my witness before God: did impure desire fill my thoughts or was it not rather a time of amazement, of hate-filled curiosity, and of the will to do battle? Have I ceased to call upon Jane, my saint, for aid against the emissary of Black Isaïs, the companion of Bartlett Greene, the destroyer of John Roger and of my own blood-line?

But the more fervently I called upon Jane, the more swiftly, the more surely did Assja come, triumphant, glowing in the beauty of her golden-brown flesh. She came – – she still comes ...

Did Lipotin not prophesy this? Prophesy that the struggle was only just beginning ?

I am prepared; I am armed. But I do not know when the battle began. It began imperceptibly at a time that I have now forgotten. I do not know the manner of the struggle nor how it is to be won. The first attack that I must make fills me with apprehension, for I am afraid of stabbing the empty air and losing my balance. I am filled with dread at the thought of the days spent sitting opposite each other in silence, locked in a psychokinetic struggle..

I am filled with dread. I sense that at any moment the Princess can materialise again.

Again the jangle of a bell. I listen; no, it is not a ringing in my ear as I imagined. It is the front door bell, an ordinary front door bell – and yet I still feel dread seeping through my veins. But the ringing drags me from my chair; I press the buzzer to let the door open, hurry to the window and look down: in the street two silly boys dash away when they realise they have been seen.

Nothing – and yet the dread does not loosen its grip on me.

384

The front door is open, I remind myself and feel uneasy at the thought that I am open to the world, that any foolish, prying busybody can walk straight into my carefully guarded life and secrets. I am about to go down and shut the door for good when I hear footsteps on the stairs, familiar footsteps, swift, smooth and elastic.

Lipotin appears!

He greets me with an ironic twinkle beneath the heavy drooping eyelids.

We exchange a casual greeting, as if we had last seen each other the previous day. He stands on the threshold of my study, sniffing at the air like a fox who finds strange tracks outside the entrance to his den.

I say nothing; I for my part am examining him.

He seems changed, though it is difficult to say exactly in what way. It is almost as if he were not himself, but his own double: there is something insubstantial, shadowy and strangely monotonous about all his utterances. Are we perhaps both dead? is the odd thought that comes to me. Who knows exactly what the social conventions amongst the dead are!? Round his neck is a red scarf that I have never seen him wearing before.

He turns his head towards me and whispers in a hoarse voice:

"It is approaching. This is almost like John Dee's kitchen."

My blood runs cold at this unearthly voice; it has the discordant whistling of someone with cancer articulating laboriously through a tube in his throat. Lipotin repeats with mocking self–satisfaction:

"It is approaching."

I ignore it. Don't understand it. I am spellbound by horror and without thinking, without realising what I am saying before I hear my own words outside me, I gasp:

"Lipotin, you are a ghost."

385

He looks up sharply; his eyes glitter with a greenish light. He wheezes:

"My dear Sir, as far as I can see, you are the ghost. I still belong to the same level of reality that pertains to my being. What is understood by "ghost" is usually some person – or part of a person! – returning from the dead. Every living person is a being who by the act of birth has returned to the earth, *ergo* every living person is a ghost. Is that not so? Nothing essential happens through death, only through birth and that is the whole trouble. – But shouldn't we be speaking of something more important than life and death?"

"Is there something wrong with your throat, Lipotin? Since when have you had it?"

"Oh, that? Er, that means ... " – a terrible coughing intervenes, then he continues, exhausted: "That means nothing, or very little. You will recall my friends in Tibet? Well then, you will remember what I told you about them," and again he makes the same unmistakable gesture with his hand across his throat as he did outside the cemetery gate.

The red scarf!

"Who cut your throat?" I stutter.

"Who other than the red butcher? A ruthless fellow, he is. Tried to kill me on orders from his paymasters, but in his frenzy his tiny brain forgot that I have never had blood in my veins. He sought recognition for his act, but in vain. He scotched the snake instead of killing it ... " the rest of his speech is veiled by the dry whistling of his breath in the tube. "You must excuse the leaky organ-pipes," he says, when he has got his breath back, and gives me a polite bow.

There is nothing I can say. On top of it all I can sense the pale face of the Princess listening outside the grimy window and I have to strain my nerves to fight off the icy cold creeping over me from behind. Quickly I invite Lipotin to sit down in the chair where the Princess usually sits in the rather foolish hope that Assja will not enter if she sees her chair occupied. I feel I could not stand the presence of two ghosts at once. My one comfort is the thought that I myself must still be alive, otherwise I would not be so clear in my mind that these two are not. But Lipotin seems to be able to read my mind, for he says:

"Can you not see, Sir, that neither of us is far enough advanced to be sure whether we are dead or not? No-one in our situation can know that. There is nothing to prove it. The fact that everything around us appears the same as before: is that proof? It might be an illusion. How can you be sure that the world you knew previously was not just as much a figment of your imagination? Are you really absolutely sure that we did not die in the accident at Elsbethstein as well and that you just imagined your fiancée's funeral? That could be the case, could it not? What do we know of the cause of our imaginings? Perhaps imagination is the cause and mankind the effect! No, no, all that about 'life after death' is rather different from what we are told by people who know nothing but, when you contradict them, claim they know 'best'. Lipotin lights another cigarette and I squint over at him to see whether smoke comes out of the red scarf ... Then he goes on in his croaky voice:

"Actually you should be grateful to me. It was in your service, after all, that I got this little scratch. Or did I only imagine that you made use of the drug from the Tibetan monks. As a member of the order I should have stopped that happening. Well, we have both ended up with wounds that heal damned slowly! Yours is not in the throat, but in the nerve centre which controls your sleep: the valve will not close properly, that's why you don't know whether you're dead or not. Don't worry, it's not just a physical defect, it's also an escape route to freedom."

I have also lit a cigarette; inhaling the smoke helps me control the feverish dread inside ... I hear myself ask:

"Tell me honestly, Lipotin, am I a ghost or not?"

He puts his head to one side; the heavy lids almost close; then he sits up with a sudden jerk and says:

"The only ones who are not ghosts are those who have eternal life. Do you have eternal life? No, what you have is the same as all men: infinite life, and that is something quite different. – But I think it better if you stop asking me about things which you cannot understand until you possess them yourself. You can only understand something that you already have. Asking questions never did anyone any good! What you really want to know is how to deal with phantoms!" As he speaks he gives a quick glance at the window and waves his arm in a circular movement. It creates a draught, and the dust swirls up from the papers on my desk, releasing a musty, ancient odour that sets off images in my mind of crows flapping up from carrion or of great grey owls in ivy-clad towers.

"Yes, it is true, Lipotin," I admit. "It's no use trying to hide it from you – I do deal with ghosts ... That is, I see – here, in the chair you're sitting in – a figure ... it appears every day ... I see the Princess! She comes to me whenever she wants. She haunts me with her eyes, her body, her whole being! She will trap me in her web; – as the thousands of spiders catch the flies here. Help me, Lipotin! Help me, help me not to ..."

Like a dam breaking, the words just burst out of me, unprepared and unexpected; I am so overcome that I slide to my knees beside the chair the old Russian is sitting in and stare at him through a veil of tears as if he were some powerful, mysterious magician.

He slowly raises his left eyebrow and inhales so deeply that I can hear the whistling in the tube again.

He wheezes softly as great clouds of smoke mask his features:

"But, my dear Sir, I am entirely at your service; of course," – an uneasy glance flickers in my direction – "you still have the dagger, don't you?"

Quickly I take the Tula-ware box from my desk and press the hidden catch.

"Aha, aha!" murmurs Lipotin with a grin, "excellent; I can see you are doing your best to keep Hywel Dda's legacy safe and sound. But there is one piece of advice I would give you: choose a different hiding place for the family jewels. Have you not noticed that this little box has a certain ... let us not say relationship, let us say similarity with the earthly dress of our distinguished Princess? It is not a good idea to combine symbols; the forces that stand behind them can easily start to mingle."

A storm of half-understood insights rages round my soul. I snatch the dagger from the box, as if that would break the spell that has kept me bound for days, weeks – or years? But Lipotin raises his eyebrows in an expression that drains the courage from me: I cannot bring myself to stab him – or even his phantom.

"Our magic is still in its infancy." – Lipotin laughs at me, starts whistling again – "We cling to externals, although we also neglect them, like a novice mountaineer with all the latest equipment but forgetting to keep an eye on the weather. And the goal has moved on; it is no longer conquering the peak – that is left to self-tormenting ascetics – but transcending the world and humanity." I decide to reveal all my secrets and sorrows:

"You will help me, Lipotin, I am sure of that. To put you in the picture: I have called upon Jane with all the power of my soul. But she does not come. The Princess comes instead of her."

"In magic what comes is what is closest to us. And what is closest is what resides within us. That is why the Princess has come."

"But I do not want her to come!"

"That makes no difference. She senses the erotic force in you and in your call."

"But, for God's sake, I hate her!"

"That is what she feeds on."

"I curse her; may she rot in the lowest depths of hell where she belongs! I abhor her, I would strangle her, murder her if I could, if I only knew how."

"Such fire is like a declaration of love to her – and she is not entirely wrong."

"You think I might love the Princess, Lipotin?"

"You hate her already. That creates a high degree of magnetism or attraction – scientists are agreed on that."

"Jane!" I cry out.

"A dangerous appeal" warns Lipotin. "The Princess will intercept it. Do you not realise that what you call 'Jane' is the vital erotic energy within you? A fine suit of armour you have there! Nothing but gun cotton: it might keep you warm but it's highly explosive; it might go up in flames at any moment."

The world goes out of focus; I am near to fainting. I grasp Lipotin's hand.

"Help me, old friend! You must help me!"

Lipotin flashes a glance at the dagger lying on the table between us and grudgingly agrees:

"I think I have no choice."

There is a gnawing distrust at the back of my mind, and I place my hand firmly on the weapon in front of me. I draw it nearer to me and never let it out of my sight. Lipotin appears not to take any notice at all and lights a fresh cigarette. His wheezing voice comes through a cloud of smoke:

"Do you know anything at all about Tibetan sexual magic?"

"A little."

"Then you will perhaps have heard of an oriental practice called 'Vajroli Tantra' which makes it possible to transform sexual energy into a magic force."

"Vajroli Tantra!" I murmur the words to myself. I vaguely remember having read in a rather bizarre book about something of the kind. I do not know precisely what it is, but an inner feeling tells me it must be something foully perverse, something contrary to all healthy, normal human sentiments. There must be good reason why it is a secret kept by all who know of it on pain of death.

"Some kind of exorcism rite?" I ask absent-mindedly.

Lipotin shakes his head slowly:

"Exorcise sex!? What would that leave of man? Not even the external form of a saint. Elemental forces cannot be destroyed. That is why there is no point in trying to drive out the Princess."

"Lipotin – sometimes I think it isn't the Princess at all but ..."

The ghostly antiquarian gives a whinnying laugh:

"You think she is the Thracian goddess Isaïs? Not bad! Not bad, my friend. Not so far off the mark."

"It is really all the same to me whether she is Isaïs or Bartlett Greene's Black Mother called up by the blood of his Scottish cats! Once she appeared to one of her victims as Lady Sissy."

"Whatever guise she appears in, the being that appears to you in this chair, currently occupied by my humble self, is more than a ghost, more than a living woman, more even than a goddess neglected for thousands of years: she is the power of blood in man, and whoever would defeat her must be beyond the power of blood."

Instinctively I raise my hand to my neck; I can feel the artery hammering feverishly, as if demanding entrance to deliver its message – perhaps from some alien force exulting in its power over me? All the while I stare at Lipotin's crimson scarf. Lipotin gives me a friendly and understanding nod.

"Are you beyond the power of blood?"

Lipotin seems to deflate; he suddenly becomes grey, old, frail; he croaks feebly:

"Being beyond the power of blood is almost the same as never having been subject to it. You tell me: where is the difference between being beyond life and never having lived? There is none, is there? Is there?"

It sounds like a cry from the depths, like an appeal from a scarcely concealed desperation, like naked fear, whose cold tentacles I could feel stretching out towards me. But before I could relate this unexpected question to his normal behaviour, the glimpse of Lipotin's bared soul – for want of a better word – was over; he smoothed down his hair, sat up straight and once more smiled his enigmatic smile from above his red scarf. He leant across to me and said, stressing every word:

"Take it from me, young man: the realm of Isaïs and of Assja Shotokalungin is the realm of the blood from which there is no escaping, neither here, nor on the other side, neither for the good Doctor Dee, nor for John Roger, Esquire, nor for you. You have to accept that."

"Where can I find salvation?" I cry, leaping to my feet.

"Vajroli Tantra," comes the answer from a cloud of smoke. It strikes me that he always conceals his face in that manner when he speaks those words.

"What is Vajroli Tantra?" I ask curtly.

"The gnostics called it 'making the Jordan flow backwards'. You can easily guess what that refers to. But it not only refers to the physical action, which is pretty obscene. You must discover the mystery behind it yourself; if I were to try to explain it, you would be left with an empty shell. The physical rite without the inner mystery is like dabbling in red magic: it just creates a fire you cannot extinguish. Mankind has little idea of these forces; they ramble on about black magic and white magic. But the inner mystery ..." suddenly, in the middle of the sentence, Lipotin's explanation becomes a droning sing-song, like the monotonous prayers of a Tibetan monk. It sounds as if it is not Lipotin, but some distant, invisible being speaking from the red scarf:

"What is bound shall be loosed; what is divided shall be joined through love; love shall be overcome through hate; hate through knowledge; knowledge through oblivion: that is the stone of the diamantine void."

The words swirl past me; I cannot grasp them, cannot hold them. For a brief moment I feel the Baphomet above me, listening. I bow my head and try to listen with him, but my ears remain deaf.

When I look up again – despondent – Lipotin has disappeared from my room.

Was he really ever there?

More "time" has passed, time that I have not measured. I have wound up all my clocks, and I can hear them busily ticking away, but as I did not set them, each one shows a different time – which seems appropriate to my strange state. I sleep whenever sleep overcomes me, in some chair in some room or other, it does not matter which. Light I take for day and dark for night, whether it be the blackness of real night or merely the overcast sky and the grimy windowpanes which awake the countless pale shadows in my rooms to spectral life.

I know that writing down my recent conversation with the phantom by the name of "Lipotin" is no proof that I am alive or, as men put it, have died, but I have done it, and will continue to do so. Perhaps I only imagine the ink and the paper and the letters and in reality I am etching it onto my memory. But where, basically, is the difference?

The idea of "reality" is unfathomable, but more unfathomable still is the "I". When I try to describe the state "I" was in before Lipotin entered, announced by two cheeky schoolboys ringing my bell, the only word that seems appropriate is: unconscious. And yet there is a voice within me saying that I was not unconscious, but that I was in some other state of being that I can no longer recall. If it had been eternal life, how could I have returned from eternity to the infinity of life? that would have been impossible: eternity is separate from infinity and no-one can fly back and forth across the abyss dividing them. Perhaps Jane partakes of eternal life and that is why she cannot hear my cries for help. My cry goes up into infinity and instead of Jane comes Assja Shotokalungin.

In what state of being did I spend all that "time"? I become more and more certain that someone who has progressed far beyond human life instructed me in an occult science, for which human tongues have no words, in secrets and mysteries which will be made plain to me one day. Oh that I had a trusty adviser, as my ancestor John Dee, whose being and essence I have inherited, had in his assistant Gardner!

Lipotin has not come back, nor do I miss him. What he had to bring, he has brought; a strange messenger of the unknown, faithful and faithless at the same time.

I have spent a long time pondering his advice and I think that I have some inkling of the deeper significance of "Vajroli Tantra", but how can I put it into practice? I will make every effort to get to the bottom of it, but I keep coming up against Lipotin's words, that it is impossible to escape from the realm of sexuality.

I will keep a record of my doings from day to day, but will not date them. What point would there be in a dead man insisting on the right date? What do I care about the calendar people submit to in the world outside. I have come to haunt my own house.

I feel an immense weariness and, at the same time, curiosity. Are they harbingers of Assja Shotokalungin?

The night that has just passed was the first that I have spent with a clear mind.

No, it was not coincidence that I was overcome with such profound tiredness. But from my tiredness emerged the iron resolve to risk the first sortie. As one combats poison with a counterpoison or antidote, so I determined to combat the sleep that was creeping over me; I called up the "counterpoison": not Jane but Princess Shotokalungin.

But she did not appear as I had expected. She did not obey me. She was lurking behind the curtain of my senses, I could feel her hidden presence.

Ultimately it was for the best: this waiting for the enemy enabled me to concentrate my forces all the more against her and with each heartbeat I felt the hatred inside me grow, sharpening my "dragon's eye". Or, at least, that was what I thought!

In that night I learnt a terrible lesson and I thank fate that I learnt it in time: hate which grows beyond its object is weakened.

It was hate alone that kept me awake during that night. Just as a double dose of a drug will stimulate a flagging body, so the increase of hate kept my senses alive. But the point came when I no longer had the strength to redouble my hatred once more, and my hate began to trickle away like sand through the fingers. And my wakefulness slackened as the mists of mental exhaustion closed in and I fell into an an indescribable weariness where abstinence and lust are indistinguishable. Did Assja come to me? I did not see her!

During the last hour before daybreak I rushed wildy about the apartment. None of the arcane secrets of self-control seemed reliable enough. Wretched and humiliated, my heart racing with fear, I concentrated purely on physical movement to ward off the attacks of sleep, which was constantly trying to slip its mask over my face and to which I must not succumb before daybreak. In a desperate frenzy I ran here and there and back again, in order not to lose control over my body.

And I made it; I managed to save myself from falling defenceless into the net of my enemy.

As the first rays of the morning sun seeped pale yellow through the dusty windowpanes I collapsed in the middle of my frenetic exercise, to awake on the sofa late in the afternoon, my body still fatigued and my over-confident soul drained of all energy. I realised one can be defeated by one's own excessive resistance.

I have three days to learn the lesson of this night; how I came by this knowledge I do not know, but an inner feeling tells me it is true.

The task once begun must be carried out to the bitter end: that was Lipotin's instruction.

Lipotin! I spend hours thinking about him and his purposes. Was it as a friend that he gave me his eager advice and pointed me in the direction of the Tantra???

When was it that I wrote that last sentence that ends in three question marks? Where I am now there is no place for time. Men on the sun-lit planet called earth might say: it was three, four days ago. It could just as well be three or four years.

Time has no meaning for me any more, just as writing has no meaning for me. This record, which preserved the past and focused it on its goal in the eternal present of *Baphomet*, has fulfilled its task. Bathed in the clarity which the end has brought, I now conclude with an account of my final errors on earth:

On the third evening after my inglorious night watch, I was once more "prepared".

Oh, how cunning I thought I was this time not to wait for the enemy in my "highly explosive armour of hatred"! With arrogant self-confidence I relied on my own will power, toughened by the exercise of Vajroli Yoga and the insights I had gained into the veiled mystery at the heart of this method. I could not yet bring everything into the clear light of consciousness, but I felt that instinct and feeling had grasped the key elements. I was concentrating on thinking of Princess Assja Shotokalungin with equanimity, even with a certain benevolence. I did not peremptorily command her; I invited her, as if to a negotiating table.

She did not come.

I kept my watch. As before, I tried to feel the lurking presence of the temptress behind the curtain of my senses. She was not there. A gentle silence lay over all three worlds.

I remained patient, for impatience, I knew, would quickly lead to hate and that was a battlefield where I could not match her.

Nothing happened. And yet I knew that this night would be decisive.

About the second hour after midnight strange thoughts and images appeared in my mind. As if my soul had become a limpid pool, I saw reflected in it Assja Shotokalungin's terrible fate; I saw her, too, as a victim and my heart was seized with pity as the scenes succeeded each other: the cheerful hostess, full of bantering good humour, the pampered child of a princely house transformed into a morbidly sensitive young woman by a nerve-shattering flight from the clutches of the Bolshevik Cheka into the insecurity of exile. One among many, to be sure, but what a change in fortune and what fearful experiences! And in spite of it all, a brave woman who loved life; but one who also had a dark side to her character – a legacy of the Shotokalungin blood – leaving her vulnerable to demonic influences which led to her gruesome early death. She had long since atoned for any family guilt which had been passed down to her. At worst, I told myself, she was merely a medium, a victim of that fate which we men are quick to call "guilt". A great and noble plan pulses through my veins: I will redeem her through the power of my own newly strengthened will! that must be the aim of the mysterious Vajroli Mudra: I will draw her into myself so that she will be purged of all hatred. I will not hate her, neither will I love her: with my own release I will release a suffering soul.

That was the last thought to go through my mind, for immediately after I found Assja Shotokalungin lying by me: looking up at me from the pillows of my bed was the happy, seventeen-year-old, virginal Princess from the Palace at Yekaterinodar. And the innocent child threw her arms around me, her saviour – her saviour from herself, from the Assja within her who had dedicated herself as a priestess to the evil Thracian goddess, Isaïs.

How strange that she does not seem to know that she herself is the other Assja as well. Seeking help from her other self, she abandoned herself completely to me ...

Then just as suddenly the succubus disappeared. My body felt drained and wretched, as if I had participated in unimaginable dionysian orgies which could well have lasted a year as one night. But I forgot my physical state as I was engulfed in melodies from an Aeolian harp; they accompanied words which ran through my blood like some sweet poison. Then, like a childhood song, my veins tingled to a verse which I could no longer get out of my mind:

> From out of the waning moon
> From the silver black of the night
> Look down on me,
> Look down on me
> Lady, bless me with Thy dark light
> Come to me, Lady, o come to me soon ...

The lines were still tripping from my untiring lips when Lipotin appeared at the foot of my bed. He stretched his red-scarfed neck like a thirsty stork, and waited and nodded and smiled.

Then he started to speak, softly; the words in the tube sounded like lead shot dribbling onto a sheet of glass and there was an audible hiss of air from under the scarf:

"Hmm, well, my friend, well well – we were the weaker after all?! I am sorry, sir, I am truly sorry; but I can only serve the strong. You know that is one of my little peculiarities. I regret I must return to the opposing side. All I can do is to inform you of that fact. You will appreciate what that token of loyalty means. I see that according to popular wisdom you are 'lost', but nevertheless I congratulate you on your ... hmm ... performance. And now I must say farewell; business calls, I think. The rumour in the coffee house is that some rich foreigner from Chile has bought Elsbethstein. Perhaps there are other old daggers buried there? They say the new owner is someone called Doctor Theodor Gärtner; personally I have never heard the name. And now, dear sir" – he waved – "fare thee ill."

I was incapable of standing up, I was incapable even of answering. He paused in the doorway and I read, rather than heard, the words from his lips: "The Dugpas send their greetings"; then he gave a ceremonial bow and as he disappeared I saw a glint of mocking, satanic exultation in his eyes.

That was the last I saw of Lipotin.

"Theodor Gärtner!" – Those were the first words in my mind when I surfaced from unconsciousness. Theodor Gärtner? But he drowned in the Pacific! Or am I mad and Lipotin named a completely different name? Weak and dizzy, I collapsed back onto my bed several times before I finally managed, with a supreme effort, to get to my feet. I was convinced that I had lost the contest and was damned beyond

399

redemption, destined for some unknown fate – unknown and therefore all the more gruesome to my imagination. For a brief moment I saw the death mask of my cousin, John Roger, hovering over me.

Oh, how easily, how ridiculously easily Black Isaïs had overcome me with her satanic cunning!

There is no need for me to describe the depths of humiliation I felt, the mortification of pride in my manly strength and, worst of all, the consciousness of my own boundless stupidity.

Should I call upon Jane? I felt my own heart pleading to do so, but I mastered myself and remained silent. She might hear me after all, and I felt I should not disturb her in the realm of eternal life. I might wake her from a dream of eternal union with me, my cry for help might drag her from her sphere far down into the misery of finite being, down into the force field of the earth where love is nothing and hate everything.

I sank back onto my bed and lay there motionless, waiting for night. The sun shone into my room for a long time, and more brightly than usual, so that I thought: would I were Joshua and could make it stand still. – –

Again around the second hour of darkness Assja lay with me and everything was as it had been the night before – I even deceived myself that I was her saviour.

My senses belong completely to the succubus. In the desperate battle of my soul and my reason with the seductress of my drugged senses I tasted all the pain and torment that hermits and anchorites submit to, right to the bitter end when either the vessel is shattered, or God himself breaks open the prison. At the very last moment God broke open my prison. I will tell briefly how that happened, but first I went through hell.

Assja Shotokalungin came in all shapes and forms – even by day – with all the seduction of her untamed soul and with all the ravishing power of a majestic nakedness which grew ever more radiant and unearthly.

Assja Shotokalungin was everywhere. After wearisome trials I found the words of exorcism which banished her from my presence and she left me with the sad expression of a misunderstood lover, no reproach, only a mute plea for forgiveness in her eyes. It took me an immense effort of will to harden my heart and ignore the pleading look.

But soon after that she manifested herself in every object in the house which had a reflecting surface: in the varnished wood of the wardrobes, in a glass of water, in a polished brass knife, in the dull, opalescent windowpanes, in a gleaming decanter, in the cut–glass chandelier and in the glaze of the tiles round the stove. My torment increased a hundredfold, for Assja seemed to have withdrawn to another level and yet to be so close the heat of her presence scorched my senses. I had tried to banish her by an exertion of will, but now my will seemed to have turned upon me and I longed for her. I was torn by the tug of contradictory desires: I wanted to be rid of her and I longed for her touch.

Until that point I had kept Lipotin's green Florentine mirror covered with a cloth and turned to the wall, for fear of seeing Assja step out of it towards me, as Theodor Gärtner once had. Now, overcome with burning, sensual desire, I tore off the cloth and looked into the glass:

She stood there as clear as life, thrusting her naked breasts towards me and at the same time pleading for mercy with the sweet expression of the Holy Virgin. In horror I thought this must be the end.

In one, last, desperate effort I raised my fist and hit out in wild fury at the mirror, smashing the glass into a thousand splinters.

But with each tiny splinter her image ripped through the flesh into my veins, burning in my blood like stinging nettles; and looking up at me from each gleaming fragment on the floor: Assja, Assja, the naked, devouring succubus, Assja, Assja, Assja. Then, like a swimmer from the sea, she rose from the images, and came towards me, a whole army of smiling sirens, enveloping me in the warm scent of her hundred naked bodies.

The air all around me was permeated with the smell of her skin and it was the sweetest, most intoxicating odour I can ever remember inhaling, more intense even than the odours of a warm spring night. – Every child knows how smells can benumb the senses and transport one into contented dreams.

And then Assja-Isaïs began to envelop me in her aura, in her astral body. All the while she gazed at me with the bright, innocent eyes of a reptile that kills because it is the law of the species. She injected the essence of her being under my skin and grew around me, grew through me. What defence had I? How could I resist?

Once more I was bewitched by the melody that wound in and out of my ear:

> From out of the waning moon,
> From the silver black of the night,
> Look down on me – – –

I felt it was a dirge for me … then a sudden thought pulled me back from the edge of the grave that initiates call the threshold to the "eighth world" and which means complete annihilation – I remembered that I still had the ancestral dagger, the spearhead of Hywel Dda.

Can a thought on its own create fire? There is fire sleeping all around mankind, hidden, invisible but everywhere. A magic word, perhaps, and in an instant it ignites and consumes the whole world.

As if it was the mere thought of the dagger that called up the fire, a huge flame spurted up from the floor in front of me, sizzling like an explosion of

402

powder, so that the whole room was bathed in a flickering glow. I plunged through the middle of it; I must go through the fire, even if I am burnt alive, I must find the dagger and hold it!

I cannot remember how I came through the wall of fire, but come through I did and found myself in my study. I opened the silver box and snatched up the dagger. I clutched the handle just as John Dee did when he was in the coffin, and when Bartlett Greene appeared towering over me and tried to wrest it from me, I repulsed him with one blow in the wall-eye which sent him tumbling back. I raced down the stairs in a shower of sparks and a suffocating blanket of smoke and threw the whole weight of my body at the door so that it gave way with a thunderous crash ...

I felt a waft of cool, fresh night air. My hair and beard were singed, my clothes still smouldering.

Where? Where can I turn?

Behind me I heard the crash of beams collapsing, consumed by the unquenchable supernatural fire. – Away, away from here! I kept the dagger clutched tight in my hand, it was worth more than anything in this world or the next. Suddenly, in front of me, stopping my wild rush, there appeared a vision – the gentle, majestic lady I had seen in the overgrown park at Elsbethstein. I was filled with rejoicing:

It is Elizabeth! The Queen of my blood and John Dee's Elizabeth, Elizabeth who has patiently awaited this hour! – I sank to my knees before her, oblivious of the fire of the Dugpas that was stretching out its fingers towards me ... Then, as if the blade in my hand had transmitted its sharp clarity to my brain, I saw through the apparition: it was a disguise, a subterfuge, an image stolen by the dark deceivers and projected to drag me down to perdition ...

I close my eyes and dashed through the phantom. I ran as if all the demons of the wild hunt were on my tail and suddenly – my running had direction:

Elsbethstein was the goal that lit up my whole being – away to Elsbethstein! I was drawn, held, protected by invisible hands; the blood pounding in my temples blinded me, but wings sprouted on stumbling feet as my headlong rush finally took me to the highest tower of the castle.

Behind me – a bloody sky as if the whole city was burning with the fires of hell.

Thus too did Mortlake burn as John Dee, my restless ancestor, left behind him his past life with its honours and dignities, its errors and enmities: that was the thought that came to my mind.

But I possessed one thing that he had lost: the dagger! Hail to thee, John Dee, that thou shouldst rise again to live on in me.

The Castle of Elsbethstein

"Have you the dagger?"

"Yes."

"Good."

Theodor Gärtner holds out both hands to me. I grasp them as a drowning man grasps at a rescuing hand. And immediately I feel a current of warmth and goodness flowing from him through me. And the fear that had wrapped itself tight round me like a mummy's bandages begins to loosen its grip.

I see a faint smile on my friend's face:

"Well, and have you defeated Black Isaïs?" The question is put in a matter-of-fact way and without any threatening undertone and still it resounds in my ear like the last trump. I bow my head:

"No."

"Then she will enter our Kingdom, for she always appears where she has a debt to collect."

Fear begins to pull its bands tight around me again:

"I have tried all that can be expected of a man – and more!"

"I know how you have tried."

404

"My strength is all gone!"

"And did you really imagine that the black arts could bring about the transformation?"

"Vajroli Tantra?!" I cry, staring at Theodor Gärtner.

"A farewell gift from the Dugpas, intended to destroy you. If you knew what strength is needed to practise Vajroli Tantra without being utterly destroyed! Only Orientals are capable of that. It is sufficient that you have twice inhaled their poisonous fumes and survived. You did that of your own strength and that is why you are worthy of help."

"Help me!"

Theodor Gärtner turns and beckons me to follow him.

It is only now that my senses wake to the scene around me. We are in a chamber in a tower. In the corner is a massive fireplace and in front of it the large stove usual in alchymical laboratories. All round the room are shelves on which, in neat order, stand the tools and vessels of that high art.

Is it John Dee's laboratory? Slowly understanding dawns upon me: I am "on the other side", in the realm of first causes. This chamber is so like the earthly one and at the same time unlike it – in the same way as the face of the child resembles the old man's. Fearfully I ask:

"Tell me true, my friend – am I dead?"

Theodor Gärtner hesitates a moment, gives a sly smile and an ambiguous answer:

"On the contrary! Now you are really alive!" He is about to pass out of the room and motions me to accompany him.

He holds the door open, and as I go past him I have the same experience as before when the room seemed both familiar and new: I feel as if I have seen his face – long, long before this life. But the scene outside prevents me from musing on this impression. We cross the castle courtyard. There is no sign

405

of decay, no sign at all of the ruin I knew. Nor, however carefully I look, can I find any signs of hot springs and the stone well-head over them. In my surprise I cannot restrain a questioning glance at my guide. He smiles, nods and explains:

"Elsbethstein is one of earth's ancient stigmata, a place where the springs of earthly fate well up. But the springs that you saw were only a sign that we have returned to take possession once more of what has always been ours by right. The hot springs, which men wanted to tame to serve their greed, have already dried up. All this around us is invisible to men; they have eyes – and cannot see."

I look about me in astonishment. The walls of the great hall, formerly open to the sky, are covered with a high hipped roof; towers and look-outs are crowned with fine slates. And it does not look at all new or restored; it is all covered with the patina of gentle ageing.

"Your place will be here if ... if we stay together." Theodor Gärtner gives a brief wave of the hand and turns away. In spite of his unconcerned manner a dark cloud of fear settles on my breast.

Then my friend leads me to the old garden between the keep and the outer ring of walls.

In the far distance I can see a sunlit river and broad, fruitful fields and meadows spread out between gentle slopes, as quiet and peaceful as if it had never known change. But within me the garden and the distant view stirs up uneasy memories of primordial elemental forces behind the visible world. I have a keen, almost painful sense of having seen them before. I stop abruptly and clutch Theodor Gärtner by the hand:

"But this is Mortlake Castle, as I saw it in the coal scrying glass! And yet ... it is not the same; it is a shimmering image contained within Elsbethstein, within the ruin above the river of which you are Lord. – And you are not just Theodor Gärtner, you are also ..."

With a happy laugh he puts his hand to my lips and leads me back into the tower.

Then I am alone. For how long? I cannot say. When I look back to this period of solitary peace I feel as if, in some way I cannot comprehend, I had taken root in my native soil after an absence of centuries.

As I look back I have no sense of the passage of time. Later I do distinguish night and day, for I remember the sun once shining down on the magic circle of our conversation, and once it was dark and scented candles cast huge shadows onto high, strangely shifting walls. – –

It was probably the third time that evening fell on Elsbethstein when Theodor Gärtner interrupted our quiet conversation. Casually, as if it were some trifling matter, he remarks:

"Now it is time for you to hold yourself ready."

I start. A vague fear rises from the pit of my stomach.

"You mean … that is …?" I stammer.

"Three such days would have been enough for Samson to let his hair grow again! Look within yourself. Your strength is renewed!" Theodor Gärtner's open and completely unworried look immediately transmits a marvellous calm to my nerves. Without understanding what I am doing, I follow his instructions and close my eyes for meditation. Scarcely have I done so than my inner eye sees the Baphomet above me, and the white cold light of the crystal blinds me.

From that point on I am calm and ready to accept my fate, whether it lead me to victory or cast me down before the eyes of the steadfast.

Quietly I ask:

"What must I do?"

"Do? – Do what you must."

"How can I?"

"In the realm where your destiny is decided you do not ask to know. You must act without knowing."

"Act without knowing what I must do? That ..."

"That is the most difficult part." Theodor Gärtner stands up, shakes me by the hand and says, as if his mind is on other things:

"The moon is above the horizon. – Take the dagger that you have won back. Go down into the park. There you will meet with one who would drive you away from Elsbethstein. If you step through the outer ring of walls you will never find your way back to Elsbethstein and we will never see each other again. – But I hope it will not end in that way. Go now. That is all I have to say to you." He turns from me and does not look back as he strides off into the darkness and disappears behind the flickering candles. I think I hear a door close in the distance. Then it is deathly quiet around me; I can hear my heart beating wildly.

The moon has just risen above the castle roof, opposite the great window.

I am in the garden, clutching the dagger tight in my hand, although I do not know what use I am to put it to. I gaze at the stars. They hover in the still air with a clear light, not flickering at all, and I can physically sense this imperturbable calm of the cosmos settling on me. My mind is empty, relaxed – unquestioning.

"Magic is to act without knowing." The significance of these words of my friend flows through me and brings an immense calm.

How long I stood there I do not know; the meadow seemed spellbound by the moonlight. In the distance – or nearby, it is difficult to tell in the emerald half-light – is the dense, black mass of a group of huge trees.

Suddenly a wavering glow approaches from the trees.

It is like a thin mist rendered translucent by the fluctuating moonlight. My eyes fix on the apparition. It is a figure stepping lightly through the bushes, now pausing a moment, now moving more rapidly – it is the same figure I once glimpsed far off through the shimmering midday heat haze: regal, mysterious, majestic – it is the long awaited Mistress of Elsbethstein, the enigmatic Queen Elizabeth.

And as if drawn by my burning desire, the apparition approaches; all remembrance of the purpose of my presence here in the nocturnal meadow has been erased from my mind in an instant. Inwardly rejoicing, and with a heart-splitting intensity which I am only half conscious of, I hurry towards her, then hesitate for fear the fair apparition might withdraw at my approach, evaporate into the air, turn out to be a hallucination.

But she does not disappear.

She hesitates when I hesitate, hurries on when I hurry, and at last she stands before me in all her majesty – the Mother, John Dee's goddess, destined for me from beyond the bonds of blood. Her smile promises the fulfilment of primordial longings.

She spreads out her arms and smiles and beckons me to follow; her slim, silvery hand lightly touches the dagger in mine and my fingers slacken their grip to give her the gift that is her due.

But at that moment another radiance than that of the moon flashes in the sky above me. Instinctively I know the Baphomet is there and the crown jewel. It does not blind me, but bathes everything in a cool, clear, sharp light. A smile flits across the features of the mysterious Lady close in front of my face, but I sense the secret struggle between this smile, promising unknown delight for aeons to come, and the icy radiance of the crystal above me. At that fleeting shadow of an exultant smile my spirit checks in its headlong flight for an infinitesimal, angel's wing-beat of time – and I awake from my trance and see that my vision has thrown off the shackles of space and that I can see both before and behind, like the double-faced Baphomet. I see before me Dame

World with her tempting smile and the mask stolen from the Holy Lady – and I see her from behind, ripped open from the nape of her neck to the soles of her feet, her whole body teeming with vipers, toads, worms and loathesome vermin. And whilst from the front her whole figure breathes the sweet fragrance and majesty of the Goddess, from the side she keeps turned away from me comes the stench of rotting flesh, filling the soul with nameless horror at the ultimate mystery of decay. –

My fingers grip the dagger more tightly and my eye is bright and my heart of good cheer. My words to the ghost are gentle and friendly:

"Go, Isaïs, I dismiss you from this place. You will not deceive one of Hywel Dda's line a second time with the form of our chosen mistress. Give up and be satisfied that once in the park of Mortlake Castle you prevailed. That error has been expiated."

And while I am still speaking a sudden gust of wind moans through the grass and the moon disappears behind leaden clouds. At about knee level a grimacing face is blown hither and thither across the meadow, baring its teeth and glowering at me in raging fury; by the red beard streaming in the wind I recognise John Dee's comrade and first tempter, Bartlett Greene.

A wild dance begins: with lightning speed Black Isaïs changes form, each one more seductive than the other, more naked, more shameless in her desperation – and with each transformation she loses more of her potency as she descends to the pitiful wheedling of a common whore.

Then the meadow is at peace and the air around me still and above me the clear light of the stars. And I look and see that I am less than one step from the little gate in the wall and the path that leads steeply down and away from Elsbethstein.

And only then do I realise how close I was to that boundary which, according to Theodor Gärtner's words, eternally separates Elsbethstein from the world of Black Isaïs. For although I imagined I was standing still, the demon had drawn me to her and it was only at the last moment that I was held back and saved by the grace of the Baphomet. Thanks be to him that I have been found worthy! – –

I see Theodor Gärtner once again – or is it my assistant Gardner? They seem to have become one man who calls me brother.

I hear him speak, and although many of his words are drowned in the upsurge of exultation within me, yet I can understand all that he says and commands. With an inner eye I see the golden chain of the creatures of light stretching out in front of me, and one link is opened to join with me, the new link. And I know: this is no symbolic rite reflecting a higher reality, such as those performed as "mysteries" by men in the shadow realm of earth; this is living, creative, life-giving action in another world. – "You will be called, chosen, accepted, John Dee!" – the song of joy pulsates with the steady rhythm of my blood.

"Spread out your arms, o upright man!"

I spread my arms wide.

Immediately hands appear from the right and from the left which grasp mine and I am filled with contentment as the circuit is closed. At the same time I feel deep within me the reason for this contentment: anyone who is part of the chain is invulnerable; any blow that is struck at him, any affliction that is visited upon him strikes countless others in the chain at the same time. And so all the power in the blow, all the weight of the affliction, all poison, physical and spiritual, is warded off with a thousandfold strength ... Whilst I am still exulting in the joy of eternal belonging, eternal union, a voice rings out in the hall saying:

"Lay aside your pilgrim's garments."

I happily obey. The clothes I wore on my pilgrimage are still scorched from the fire in my earthly house; they peel away from me. – A brief moment of surprise and reflection: that is how it should be at journey's end, no matter where the journey led. The clothes of Princess Shotokalungin also peeled away ...

At that moment I am struck a gentle blow on the forehead, as if from a light hammer. It does not hurt, indeed, it is a pleasant sensation, for suddenly rays of light spring from the back of my head, endless rays of light that fill the sky with stars ... and to look up into this sea of stars is bliss.

Consciousness returns, hesitantly, against its will almost.

I am wrapped in white vestments; a beam of light strikes my face from below; I look down and see that my habit, too, bears a glittering golden rose on the breast.

My friend Gärtner is by me and all around in the high, spectral hall is a soft humming, as of swarms of bees.

Radiant white figures surround me, approaching from afar. The humming becomes clearer, more rhythmical, more vibrant. A dark melody breaks into words:

Men of the Rose are we,
Chosen of old.
Darkness repelled have we;
Light shineth gold.

Forged is the Spear for thee,
Bright is its blade;
Danger it wards from thee,
Comes to thine aid.

Joined in the Ring, now we
Open the Chain;
Forge the new link, then we

Close it again.

Hail to the victor who
Set himself free.
We raise our anthem, to
Worship with thee.

How many friends are with you! I think to myself;
and in the night of fear you did not know where to
look for aid!

For the first time I feel the desire to share my
feelings, a desire that weaves itself into the delicate
veil of melancholy that once more surrounds me and
whose origins I cannot fathom.

But, as I sink into these tentative reflections,
Gärtner takes me by the hand and leads me back, by
paths I do not remember, to the garden and the low
gate into the courtyard. Then my old friend stops
and points to the flowerbeds that give off a warm
scent:

"I am Gärtner; I am Gardner. That is my profession, although you saw in me the chemist, the
alchymist. This is only one rose of many that I have
lifted from the rubble and planted in the open beds."

We step through the gate in the wall and stop in
front of the tower.

My friend continues:

"You were always versed in the art of making
gold" – a smile crosses his features, indulgent and at
the same time with a gentle hint of mocking
reproach that makes me cast my eyes down — "and
so we have chosen for you a task that will allow you
to do what your heart has longed for from the very
beginning."

We climb the tower. It is the tower of Elsbethstein
and yet it is not. Slowly my spirit accustoms itself to
the interplay of symbols and higher meaning in this
realm where I now belong, in my new home.

We climb the broad and darkly gleaming porphyry
steps of the spiral staircase to the familiar alchymist's

laboratory. I am strangely moved to find all this splendour where once stood the narrow old decaying wooden ladder. The laboratory is an immense vault; the glittering stars follow their courses round the dark blue walls; the roof is the night sky itself and far below on the earth the forges of labour glow.

The hearth glows with creative fire. The whole world seems to be reflected in it. Showering sparks hiss, darkness flares into light, colour pales, clouds of smoke thicken and disperse: terrible forces of destruction, chained and imprisoned in iron vats, seethe and bubble infernally – the wisdom invested in the retorts and furnaces holds them captive.

"This is your workplace; create the gold you have longed for – but the gold of the sunlight. He who increases the light is one of the noblest of our brotherhood."

I am instructed. The wisdom spreads around me like the radiance of the sun. Its glory destroys all my puny earthly knowledge. One last question still buzzes round my mind like a tiny will-o'-the-wisp:

"Tell me, my friend, before the questions cease for good: who was ... who is the Angel of the West Window?"

"An echo, that is all. It was right when it said it was immortal; it was immortal because it had never lived; if it had never lived, it could never know death. All knowledge and power, all good and evil that came from it, came from you. It was the sum of all questions, wisdom and magic that was hidden within you, but that you did not know you possessed. Each of you contributed to that sum and each of you marvelled at the "Angel" as at some divine revelation. It was the Angel of the West Window because the West is the green realm of the dead past. There are many such "Angels" in the realm of growth and the realm of decay. It would be better for mankind if no such angels crossed into the world, but there are paths of hope that lead astray. Behind your Angel of

414

the West Window was Bartlett Greene. Now he has ceased to be since your questioning has ceased." – Gärtner turns back to the forge – "The ancients said: everything is a *vinculum*, a link in the chain. One of our brotherhood had called this "everything" an image. – These vats only seem to boil. These tools hammer away – but nothing happens. This globe here: merely a *vinculum*. When your ignorance is complete, then you will know how to release the gold this apparatus contains. Then you can touch one spot on the earth with your finger and streams of forgiveness will spread through that spot from the warmth of your finger; and whirlwinds of destruction, like spiritual volcanoes, will descend on that place from the cold of your purifying hand. So guard your fire well! Remember: men will impute all your deeds to their God and call up angels from the West. Many a one who was not called, but still trod the path, found himself thus translated into the dead form of an "Angel".

"And – that – is – my – task?!" I stammer, trembling at the burden of responsibility.

Calmly the adept replies:

"That is the greatness of mankind in every rebirth: Not to know any more, but to act. God has never broken his word nor diminished it one iota."

"How should I weave fate without mastery of the art or knowledge of the pattern?!" – that is the last outburst of despair from the cowardice that sits deep in every human breast.

Gärtner says no more, leads me down the porphyry steps and accompanies me to the little gate in the wall. He points to the garden, then disappears ...

In the midday glare my eye rests on a sundial fixed to the white wall and a fountain tirelessly splashing in restful melody. The sunlight strikes the rusty pointer, a dead lump of iron fixed to the wall, to create the shadow; and the shadow makes: – time.

A shadow can make time! And the time-shadow is accompanied by the fountain's self-important pit-ter-patter. The splash of water is activity in the time of the shadow – links all around, links in all things; even time and space are links within which images move.

Deep in thought and immersed in landscapes of the creative spirit, I turn away and wander through the flowerbeds towards the yew-tree arbour that shades the deserted grave. Again the sun's magic wand seems to give the surrounding garden a strange depth. Again I see in the distance a shimmer as of some shining garment. Fear and lust are far removed as I watch the radiance take shape, float forward, pause, then slowly move towards me, like a mirror image following me – and yet this is no mirror image! Gliding towards me is a creature of light that is beyond the shadows of reflected images.

I stride forward; approaching me with firm tread, no longer imprisoned in the golden cage of myth, is the Queen. Her eye is clear, joyful, steadfast, calmly fixed on mine. I draw near to Elizabeth, two comets about to converge after thousands – millions – of years in different orbits. How weak are such thoughts, for they speak the language of images, of time-shadows and splashing fountains!

I feel the heat of the first contact with the other orbit and, finally, Elizabeth stands before me. Close. So close that eye seems to touch eye; so close now, that Elizabeth has become invisible to my physical eye and invisible to the head of the Baphomet hovering above. Every nerve and fibre and feeling and thought tells me that the two orbits have crossed and the two comets united. No more shall I seek, no more shall I find – the Queen is within me, I am within the Queen: child, husband and father from the very beginning. A chorus of blessed thoughts rejoices inside me: Woman no more! Man no more!

And yet: there is one tiny, distant spot in the sunlit landscape of my soul darkened by a small cloud of sorrow – Jane! Should I call for her? May I call for her?! I can call her, that I do know, for I feel an awful strength growing within me since Elizabeth united with me. And already I see a sweet, pale face appear from the shadow of my grief – Jane!

Immediately Gärtner is by me with a cool reproach:

"Have you not had enough of torment from the Angel of the West Window? – No "angel" can harm you any more, but do not disturb the balance of nature."

"Does Jane … know where I am? … Can she see me?"

"You, my brother, have crossed the threshold of initiation with your gaze still turned back towards the world, for you have been chosen to succour mankind, as have all of us in the chain. You will be able to see the earth until the end of time, for through you flows the energy from the realm of eternal life. But what this eternal life is, we of 'the brotherhood of the chain' can never learn, for we stand with our backs to the radiant, unfathomable abyss of procreation. But Jane crossed the threshold of eternal light looking forward. Can she see us? Who knows?"

"Is she happy … there?"

"There?! – We have no words adequate for the non-place that we refer to by the misnomer 'realm of eternal life'. – And 'happy'?" – Gärtner smiled at me. "Did you seriously expect an answer?"

I blushed for shame.

"The poor children of Adam, wandering through the ring of endless life out there, cannot see even us, and we are but a pale reflection of eternal life. How then should we see, or even sense, the eternal realm of the unknown, unknowable godhead? We are close to it and yet immeasurably far away, as a solid body is to the dimension, or a line to an insubstantial mathematical point. Jane has taken the woman's road

417

of sacrifice. It leads to where we cannot follow, nor want to follow, for we are all alchymists in the sense that we remain here in order to perform transmutation. But on the woman's road she has escaped both being and non-being; for your sake she cast off everything that she was. Had it not been for her, you would not be here!"

"Men will not ... be able ... to see me any more?" I ask in astonishment.

Gärtner laughs: "Do you want to know what they think of you?"

Not even the tiniest wavelet of curiosity disturbs the blessed sands of Elsbethstein. But when my friend smiles and nods at me with almost childlike exuberance, a little spurt of interest in the errors of the world flickers in the back of my mind.

"Well?"

Theodor Gärtner bends down and picks up a lump of rotting clay from the edge of the path: "There! Read it!"

"Read it?" In a second the damp yellow clay in his hand has become – a scrap of newspaper. A meaningless phantom of an object from an immeasurably distant sphere. This materialisation from the ghost world of men strikes me as sad, poignant, ridiculous beyond words.

Gärtner has already returned to his rose beds and is pruning and binding the shoots.

I read:

The Metropolitan News.

Haunted House in 19th District

Our readers will doubtless recall the great conflagration last spring when a substantial house at number 12 Elisabethstrasse burnt down to the ground. It was noticed at the time that for some unexplained reason the fire proved impossible to extinguish. A local expert in geology put forward the theory that the flames were of volcanic origin; at the same time a similar subterranean eruption was observed at Elsbethstein. A Scottish labourer working with the gang that cleared away the rubble said that such phenomena were not uncommon in his country; in Ireland and Scotland they were called St. Patrick's Purgatory. The fire resisted the noble efforts of the City Fire Brigade and continued for several days; brick and stone burnt like tinder and were reduced to lumps of something resembling pumice stone. Even today it has not been established whether the owner perished with the house; a representative of the Tax Department claims to have knocked at the door countless times in the weeks preceding the accident in an attempt to collect long overdue taxes. Children playing in the street, on the other hand, say they once saw his face looking out of the window. The tragic conclusion is that the owner, engrossed in his – it must be said, rather dilettante – literary work was surprised by the outbreak of fire and burnt to death. This theory is supported by the fact that, as our investigations have revealed, the house was insured for an enormous sum and up to the present time no-one has appeared to claim it. It must be added, though, that in recent months the owner had shown increasing signs of mental instability.

These strange events have once more given rise to absurd superstitions amongst the more credulous sections of the population. Ghostly figures are claimed to have been observed hovering over the site of the fire; these supposedly only appear when the moon is on the wane. But it is not only schoolboys – who should be in bed at that time – who make these claims, they are also supported by many local citizens who ought to know better. The obvious explanations of a prankster returning slightly the worse for wear from a carnival celebration, or of some natural phenomenon connected with volcanic activity, are rejected out of hand. We receive frequent reports of a slender female ghost (perhaps the vice squad should investigate?!), wandering round the site as if searching for something. A local resident – a lay-preacher and Conservative councillor who has several times pursued the lady to remonstrate with her for disturbing a respectable neighbourhood by appearing at night in such provocative attire – maintains that every time she vanishes a naked woman appears on the same spot a few seconds later and tries to seduce him. Other ghost-hunters tell of a fearsome apparition, a man with a shaggy red beard in an old-fashioned leather jerkin who digs up the blackened ground, cursing and swearing. Then – people will see what they want to see – he kneels before the naked female shaking his head miserably, as if he feared some punishment. Did it not all take place in the dark, we would be tempted to ascribe it to the activities of some pornographic film-maker. Finally, an old lady was recently accosted by an elderly gentleman with a red scarf who said, with a leer, that he was very interested in antiques. Another feature that popular rumour associates with the supernatural phenomena is the countless black cats that appear on the site of the burnt-down house when the moon is shining. A more likely explanation is the new cat licence the city has introduced; the economic difficulties we are going through mean that many hard-up citizens have been forced to turn their pets out onto the streets.

It was recently announced that two eminent scientists in the field of mass hysteria, Professor Rosenburg and Doctor Goliath Wellenbusch, are planning to visit the district to conduct a research project into the widespread hallucinations. It is to be hoped they will finally lay the ghost of the victim of the conflagration. Baron Müller was a well-known local eccentric; many remember how he used to call himself *Lord of the Manor of Gladhill* – may his ashes rest in peace.

Stop Press: An announcement has just been made by Police Headquarters of a find which miraculously survived the fire at the house in the Elisabethstrasse: inside a silver casket, which had melted to a shapeless lump, was a perfectly preserved miniature portrait on ivory. It is of Dr. John Dee, who played an important role in the political life of England at the time of Queen Elizabeth. The late Baron Müller claimed to have been a descendent of Dr. Dee. Those who knew the Baron will not be able to deny a distinct family resemblance in the portrait which gives some support to his claim.

Engraved by W.N. Marshall from a Picture in the Ashmolean Museum, Oxford

DR JOHN DEE.

Born in London 1527. Died at Mortlake Surrey 1608